Last Stand

R. H. Sheldon

booth
&bohn
press

Last Stand

R. H. Sheldon

ISBN-13: 978-0-9910741-1-2
Library of Congress Control Number: 2015911617

Cover photo by R. H. Sheldon

Booth & Bohn Press
Seattle, USA

To the family and friends and all the Parkers in my life who've already headed to the next juke joint.

Keep the music playing and your hearts ignited. We'll be harmonizing again as soon as I hit last call.

Heaps of Gratitude

To Allison and Jim for their multiple reads and invaluable feedback and endless encouragements.

To Jean for time and again sharing her expertise and talent about book design and electronic publishing and all the quirky, crazy, creepy intricacies that go with them.

To all of you and many others, I am forever grateful.

Part I

If I should ever die, God forbid, let this be my epitaph:
The only proof he needed for the existence of God was music.

—Kurt Vonnegut

Parker: An Introduction

T he Boy Wonder. That's what they used to call him. Eighteen years old with a hit single that shot up Billboard faster than a speeding bullet. Twenty-six solid-gold weeks in the top ten. Thirteen at number one.

Even Elvis couldn't compete. "Hound Dog" lasted only eleven measly weeks. Same with "Don't Be Cruel."

Parker knocked the King's ever-growing ass out of the water.

Parker assumes it was his own successes that contributed to Presley's ailments and pharmacological mishaps and eventual heartbreaking demise. Parker could be wrong, of course. He's been wrong about so many things.

Yet such speculation brings comfort in his declining years, especially when focused on someone else's misery. All Parker has to show for his own meteoric rise to fame is a maple-framed, gold-plated, 45-RPM record boasting his name, Parker Davis, and the name of his 1969 solid gold hit, "Last Stand."

The record still hangs here in his parents' house, a memorial to his once-great self, between the front door and the staircase, amid the cracked plaster and peeling yellow-beige paint.

Parker sent his mother the record in the early '90s, right after Whitney soared to the top with her hit single "I Will Always Love You."

When Parker first heard the song, he dismissed it as sentimental claptrap, convinced it would be forgotten by the time Michael

Jackson took center stage at Super Bowl XXVII. But Whitney climbed to unparalleled heights, claiming the number one spot for fourteen record-shattering weeks.

Parker toasted the end of his reign with a fifth of Jack Daniel's and an ounce of cocaine, some of LA's finest.

He remembers little about that night except sitting on the curb outside the Studio City bar where he'd just been eighty-sixed, shortly after Whitney's song played for the fourth time. It was there, in the wee hours of the morning, while nursing a cracked tooth and bloody lip and sucking up the last of his blow, that a life-altering revelation descended upon him much like an Elvis second coming.

Amid the metaphorical smoke and thunder and flashes of light, Parker finally accepted what he had refused to believe all the years leading up to that crystalized moment. The music industry never was and never would be anything but a money-grubbing, corporate-controlled, blood-sucking enterprise feeding on a country chock-full of sniveling, fickle, dim-witted, tone-deaf fans. And those who would call themselves musicians were nothing but a bunch of petty and pretentious hacks whose interest in being celebrities and superstar entertainers far outweighed any loyalty to the music itself.

The next afternoon, he mailed his solid-gold record to his mother.

One day, Parker will take down the soured memento, just to prove his point. Why he waits, he has no idea. The record represents nothing but forty years of cigarettes and alcohol and drugs and all the madness that pours out of a life that starts out big and ends up a withering oasis with nothing to show but ankles that swell and lungs that wheeze and a heart that flutters and flips and flickers with each gasp of his sixty-year-old body.

Yet the record remains, still hanging right where he had found it, nothing changed, not the hallway or staircase or walls or anything. Even the small rug, one of those oval braided rag types, dulled by age, worn by footsteps, lying here, just like it did the day his mother died.

That was four years ago, when she fell down the steps and came to a rest on the rug, amid a pile of dirty clothes and a scattered collection of twenty-year-old *Life* magazines.

R. H. Sheldon

The laundry basket had tumbled into the living room, near the ballerina lamp and the tweed armchair, where his father had died nine years earlier.

When Parker discovered her sprawled out at the bottom of the stairs, he had little doubt about her condition, given the position of her neck and the stark hollow look in those cloudy eyes. The strange part was her lips, turned up in a slight grin, almost a sense of anticipation.

The coroner placed her death four hours earlier, about the time he had stepped out of the taxi and into a bar down on Broadway, several blocks from where she lived, where he lives now.

What strikes him most about that day was not so much finding her dead like that, but discovering she had hung his gold-plated record in the front hallway. She was never one given to sentimentality, to break out of her stoic forbearance, and she cared little for his music or way of life. Perhaps she had felt some sense of pride in her son after all, saw in him a glimmer of redemptive light. Sure, she knew he was a fuck-up, but maybe not so complete a fuck-up as he was led to believe.

After she died, he inherited the house, a dilapidated wood-framed pseudo-Victorian complete with mid-century furniture, the big-breasted ballerina lamp, and a spinet piano that had not been tuned since his mother's subscription of *Life* ran out. The house also came with Parker's gold-plated record, hanging on the wall like a setting sun.

Parker

P arker thinks about his mother, his record, his life every time he stands at the bottom of the steps, although that's not why he stops here now. His hesitancy is not so much about memories as about trying to remember. What did he want from upstairs? Blood pressure pills? Acid reflux medicine? Maybe his nitro. But why that? His chest feels fine at the moment, as good as it's going to get at this point, and he's not planning anything risky—except climbing the stairs. So why go after something he might need only if he would need it if he went up after it?

Whatever he was after, it must have been pretty damned important to have dragged him from that old tweed chair and half-smoked joint and practically fresh bottle of Jack Daniel's. He only hopes he recalls what it was after he gets to the top.

He clutches the banister, wincing from the arthritis in his fingers, as he always does when he grabs the railing, though he never seems to remember from one trip to the next. He eases his grip and places his right foot on the first step. His ankles grow more swollen and stiff and decidedly weaker with each passing day.

He's about to ease upward when voices drift in through the front door. He twists around. Pain shoots through his neck. For some goddamn reason Myron has left the door half-opened. Cold air pushes through the corroded screen, along with the voices, like insects circling in the hot summer sun. Only it's not summer. It's

November. And it's not sunny. It's cold and dank and dark and filled with Northwest gray.

He lets go the banister and slips to the side of the hallway, up close to his solid-gold hit and behind the inside door. The voices grow louder. He peeks around the door's edge and through the screen.

Two women walk toward his front porch, mother and daughter, judging by their ages and thick-boned frames and round meaty faces, the older one, forty-five, maybe close to fifty, with a bulging nose and big horse teeth and thick salt-and-pepper hair that looks like it got caught in a jet engine. One of those weird headsets hangs off her right ear, like a cancerous growth, giving her head a deformed, lopsided look. She wears khaki pants and an ugly off-white sweatshirt with extra large letters that read *I'm all or nothing*.

The daughter might be in her early twenties, perhaps late teens, with an unnaturally white face and unnaturally black hair and unnaturally gray lips. Her own headset dangles from her ears. A thin black wire disappears into her coat pocket, a coat also black, long, open at the front.

She reminds Parker of an old porn video that takes place in a convent.

The two women draw nearer. They each wear a serious going-to-church look. The younger one carries a satchel that pulls her slightly to one side. If they weren't dressed so casually, he'd suspect them of being Jehovah's Witnesses.

Even so, he's willing to bet they're trying to sell something, and chances are it's something to do with religion. The last thing he needs is a couple of crusaders preaching and proselytizing and parading their pretentious airs on his front porch.

He flattens himself against the wall. The record frame digs into the kink in his neck and in an odd, somewhat miraculous way loosens the muscles. He lets out a breath.

They climb the front stairs one step after the other, like soldiers, solid, strong, full of defiance, walking the walk of the righteous, the proud, the few. Their steps rattle the porch and shake the wall on which he leans. One of them pounds on the wooden screen door.

He waits. Listens. Glimpses them through the slit of a window in the front door.

"Go away."

"Is Parker Davis there?" A husky voice, mature. Must be the mother.

"Who wants to know?"

"I received a phone call, asking for help. Someone called my office and insisted I come over right away. Are you okay?"

"I didn't call anyone."

"I didn't say you did. But the call...he gave me your name and address."

"Must have been a joke. Now leave me alone."

"It didn't sound like a joke. It sounded like you were in trouble."

The other voice says, "Forget it, Mom. He doesn't need us."

The mother says, "Mr. Parker. It might seem like a joke to you, but someone was very concerned."

"Mom."

Parker sticks his head out from behind the door. "I don't want your help. Do you hear me? Now go away."

The daughter pulls at her mother's sleeve. Her young breasts jiggle like two fat marshmallows.

"Mr. Davis. I'm Reverend Olympia Culpepper from the Lighthouse Sanctification Church. Perhaps if you would let me in, we could talk about this."

"Not interested." He tries to close the door, but it stops three inches short. For a moment, he thinks he sees his mother lying on the floor.

"Mr. Davis."

"Mom."

"Go away."

"We're here to help."

"Mother."

"Mr. Davis, please."

They want Mr. Davis? Okay, he'll give them Mr. Davis. All of him.

He peels off his bathrobe and drops it to the floor. He pulls the door open all the way. He points an accusing finger at them. He shouts, "Minions of the devil!"

They stare through the screen, first with looks of disbelief, then looks of despair, and finally looks of terror. The daughter flies off the porch and lets out a piercing screech, like an atheist caught in the eye of Armageddon. The mother leaps down after her.

Parker throws open the screen door and hobbles onto the porch. "Neighborhood alert! Minions of the devil! Minions of the devil! Neighborhood alert!"

The young one catches her satchel on the front gate and lets go, leaving it hang like a flap of skin. The mother tries to unsnag it, fails, takes off after her daughter, but she stops at the curb, turns toward Parker, steps in his direction, only slightly, her eyes all flame. Parker wonders whether he's taken on the wrong woman. Another Amazon.

The daughter screams for her mother to hurry. The reverend turns, races down the street. She meets up with her daughter at the corner, next to the giant apartment building, a post-modern Bastille. They glance toward him, then disappear around the corner onto Tenth.

Parker reaches the gate and stops. He rubs his chest, grabbing the fence for support, most of it rusted, missing links, missing large chunks altogether. A string of crows sits on the power line that stretches from his house to the pole near the curb. The birds stare without moving, without the courtesy of a squawk.

He looks up and down the street, across the park toward the newer buildings on Eleventh. Change everywhere. An urban makeover of monstrous proportions.

His house stands as one of the last holdouts in a neighborhood lost to the painfully hip and trendy and gentrifying forces sweeping through Seattle, a neighborhood no longer a neighborhood, a neighborhood defined not by its people or history, but by a geologic upheaval called Capitol Hill. And on it stands his worn and tired wooden home, one of the few to survive the onslaught of development that would turn an entire landscape into nothing but multi-purpose high-rises with all the style of a Fondeaux music video.

Not that Parker cares what antics that no-talent hack whips up, any more than he cares what gets developed—indifference defining his attitude about most things—but all the towering tombstones pitted one against the other leave him feeling squeezed out, obsolete, flanked by opposing forces that push and poke and prod until he's nothing but a shadow of his former rock-star self.

Parker unsnags the minister's bag and pulls out a brochure. On the cover, a white lighthouse floats mystically against a stormy sea of blues and greens, at the bottom, in swirling print, *The*

Lighthouse Sanctification Church, and beneath that, in small plain letters, *We're all or nothing.*

He lets the brochure flutter to the ground.

Parker is about to toss the bag over the fence and into the street, but stops when he hears rustling behind him. He turns. Myron sits beneath the dead maple tree next to the house, his back slumped against the trunk, a regular faun, holding that fucking feline on his lap. All Myron needs are the goat horns, though with that forest of black frizzy hair, they might already be there.

Parker turns back toward the street, pretending he doesn't see Myron and pretending too that Myron doesn't see him pretending not to see Myron. Parker should have known Myron would be there. Myron is always somewhere, watching, waiting, lurking in the quiet shadows.

Better to ignore Myron. Better for Parker to spend his time with Jack and his savory elixir. But first, get rid of the bag. Once again, he's about to launch it over the fence when his detestable dyke neighbor, Stephanie-the-Hun Schmidt, shouts his name and waves her arms and storms across her yard.

Parker concluded years ago that everything that happens in life has to do with timing—good luck, bad luck, opportunity, no opportunity at all. Genius, he believes, is defined not in visionary acumen but in the ability to be in the right place at the right time in order to take full advantage of the accumulated knowledge of those who come before you. The fates, those little darlings, either put you in the most opportune situations or, as is more often the case, leave you hanging.

When Parker sees his neighbor storming across her dyked-out yard—with its manure-mulched garden and rainbow-waving wind chimes and plethora of near-naked goddess statues—he considers first that she's the last person he wants to see, now or any other time. Second, that unlike most straight men, he's never fantasized about lesbian sex, as a voyeur or a participant, especially with a gray-haired, shriveled-up old hag like Stephanie. Third, that perhaps running out into his yard wearing nothing but his father's bedroom slippers had not been his smartest move.

"Parker Davis, what the hell you doing standing out here naked?" Her thick, bellicose voice sounds like a tweaked-out foghorn, leaving him to conclude that his theories on timing had again been borne out by a mean and vindictive universe.

R. H. Sheldon

She stops at the edge of her yard, near the bramble of blackberry. A white-picket fence surrounds her lot, reminding him of those little cemeteries out in the prairie, where there's nothing around but miles of brown grass and a square plot of land protected by white pickets to separate the living from the dead.

She stands with her hands on her hips, a scowl on that flat, oval, wrinkled face. Her nose hooks out like a teapot spout, and each ear protrudes like the handle.

According to Myron, her girlfriend took off a few months ago, fleeing to Bend to be with a younger woman.

Good. She got what she deserved. Stephanie, ever the bull-dyke—hard to believe she's a nurse—has been breaking Parker's balls since he returned four years ago. All he's ever wanted was to be left in peace, but she's constantly on him about the trash in the yard and the late night parties and the occasional puddle of vomit that shows up in her garden. Jesus, if she'd only get a life.

Stephanie Schmidt moved into her house twenty-five years ago. At least that's what his mom told him. After his dad died, Stephanie and his mom got to be great pals, and his mom never let him forget how helpful Stephanie could be.

The last time Parker saw his dad alive was the last time he saw his mom alive, ten years ago, back in the early 2000s. Parker arrived in Seattle on September 10, his two-night visit turning into a week. As soon as the airports reopened and he could catch a flight back to LA, he was gone.

His dad died the following year. After that, he'd call his mother every few months to make sure she was still breathing. Not once did she mention his absence from his father's funeral.

Parker positions the bag of brochures in front of his crotch and says to Stephanie, "What's the matter, too much man for you?"

"Jesus, Parker, it's like living next to a Neanderthal."

"Not my fault they screwed up your sex change."

"That's really clever. Maybe you should write a song. After forty years, something's bound to stick."

"You lousy bitch." He lobs the bag at her, but it catches one of the pickets, tumbles upside down, and sends brochures flying across her yard.

"Damn you, Parker."

Parker chokes with laughter.

"Are you ever going to grow up?"

He's about to volley another rather clever comment about her failed plastic surgery, when a black Ford sedan—a Taurus?—creeps toward the house and stops. The driver stares straight at Parker through the opened window, a young Latino man with a stern, unerring face. Parker is convinced that someone who drives such a shiny car, especially someone so young and wrinkle-free and downright pretty, must be lost, and Parker has no patience for anyone lost, especially when Parker is standing in the middle of his yard wearing nothing but bedroom slippers.

Parker turns his naked and suddenly vulnerable body away from his neighbor and the curious driver and shuffles up his short walkway through the weeds and garbage and broken bottles and climbs the steps onto his front porch, slowing only long enough to announce to Myron that their dragon-lady neighbor is about the nastiest creature he's ever met. Then he stomps into the house and heads to the living room, thinking only about the bottle of Jack on the coffee table and the joint in the ashtray and the pain in his heart that goes far deeper than clogged arteries and failing lungs and a chronic cough that rattles his ribs like the inside of one of those big hollow bass drums bringing up the rear of an endless parade.

Alonzo

Alonzo turns onto Tenth. All he wants is to be done with this ridiculous assignment and back to the office to clear the mountains of paperwork off his desk. He has no intention of losing another weekend playing catch-up.

When he's about to turn on Boxer Way, he spies two women hovering near the large apartment building at the corner. The older woman wears khaki pants and a white sweatshirt and peeks around the building. The younger one hovers in the branches of a thick huckleberry, clutching a billowy black overcoat that erases all but her whitewashed face.

Alonzo drives past the stalking duo and turns onto Boxer Way, where Tenth ends and Cal Anderson Park begins. Parker Davis lives in one of the houses on the left, a few doors down from the apartment building, according to Google maps. A large ancient home sits next to the apartments, with three front doors and a multitude of mailboxes. But the tenants have vacated, as Alonzo well knows, and the house sits empty. Just like he knows about the empty lot next to it, a surprisingly large one, buried in weeds and blackberry bushes and piles of trash and debris. A diamond in the rough to the right investor.

He inches forward. Parker Davis lives in the house next to the empty lot, a filthy, dilapidated tinderbox. The yard is nothing but a continuation of the tangle of blackberry and weeds and trash that define the empty lot, but the Davis property seems worse, as though possessed by a malevolent and particularly sloppy spirit. Perhaps it's the tree, a tall dark maple with a twisted and gnarled trunk, leaning dangerously close to the building.

At least Parker's lot is a good size, as large as the empty one, another rarity in this part of the city, another diamond ready to be mined.

That's when Alonzo sees what he can't believe he's seeing. A decrepit old man stands naked in front of the house, yelling at a woman in the yard next door, on the other side of the white picket fence. He lobs something over the fence. She yells. He laughs.

Alonzo stops the car. The man has a tall, gangly body, twisted with age and misuse. His joints poke at his skin, pulling it into sharp edges. The rest hangs in pale folds that glow in the mellow daylight, his chest sinking into itself like a deflated balloon.

The man shoots Alonzo an angry, hateful look, then stomps off toward the house.

Alonzo drives forward, past the house with the white picket fence and irate neighbor, a real house, a real yard, with trees and a garden, a tiny fortress against her neighbor's looming wreckage.

He glances in the rearview mirror, as though being tailed, a sense of doom, the panic it brings. He creeps through the intersection and parks on Boxer Way up near Twelfth. He draws in three long breaths, then grabs the manila envelope off the passenger seat and walks down to the Davis residence. When he reaches the house, he stands before the fence and again verifies the address on the envelope.

At least the naked man is gone. So is the irate neighbor.

A power line stretches from the house to the street, a coven of crows perched precariously on the wire, beaks poised, talons at the ready, eyes like polished coal.

A crow squawks. Another replies.

He considers running, from the house, the neighborhood, his job, a job he has no taste for, no heart. But family, bills, responsibilities. What good are pipe dreams now?

He opens the gate, but does not step through.

The house looks like it's been hit by a hurricane. Soffit boards hang from the eaves. Siding dangles loose and twisted. Paint bubbles, peels, splits into massive chips of dusty green. The front porch is rotted and warped, steps incapable of supporting a child.

The yard is even worse up close. Garbage covers every inch— paper, plastic, bottles, an endless collection of beer cans—woven

R. H. Sheldon

into fits of overgrown bushes and tall gnarled weeds, spilling into the empty lot.

The maple tree too seems more hideous close up, with its washed-out trunk and twisted, sinister branches. That's when Alonzo spots him, a man with a thick black beard and thick black hair—all jungle-wild and guru-long—sitting cross-legged on the ground and leaning against the trunk. He stares directly at Alonzo, or so it seems from this distance, and strokes what must be a cat, or a giant rat, its fur as mangy and black as the man's grizzly beard and head of hair.

Alonzo is about to reach for the gate when the naked man pushes open the screen door and shouts in a raspy sour voice, "And another thing, *Mizzz* Stephanie Schmidt, I better not catch you spying on me. I know what you're up to!" He lets the door slam and is gone.

Alonzo closes his eyes and prays to the Virgin Mary for strength, although why he would hope for help now is beyond reason, considering how deaf she's been to him in the past.

He steps through the gate and follows what must have once been a walkway, now a dent in the weeds and trash. He climbs the rickety stairs onto the porch, steps over missing boards, tiptoes across those cracked and ready to crumble.

Alonzo glances toward the side of the house. The man under the tree stares without blinking. Alonzo tries not to look at him, tries not to look at anything, except where he places each foot. The house infects him with its dark and sullen mood. He feels a weariness that goes deeper than any he's known since law school. At thirty-two, he should be a lot further along with his career. But finishing his undergraduate degree, then his law degree, were no small tasks, especially with a wife and three kids. He had to take the first job he could get, which meant long miserable hours and an endless supply of crappy assignments. His only hope is that it's all temporary, that he can stick it out long enough—live long enough—to work his way up the company ladder.

He draws a deep breath and knocks on the screen door. The echoes bounce through the house and push back outside. Then silence. He glances toward the tree. The man glares at him with eyes so dark they seem inhuman.

Alonzo knocks again, harder. A shudder passes through the house, out to the porch. He shivers.

"Mr. Davis. Mr. Parker Davis. Are you in there?"

The man under the tree strokes the cat. "I was wondering when you'd get here." His voice is deep and rumbling and grows out of the earth.

Alonzo takes a step toward him. Much of the man's face is hidden by the thick beard and head of hair, by the twisted shadows of dead and gnarled branches. He looks even more sinister close up, almost unnatural. The cat studies Alonzo through slitted eyes, yellow and unblinking, body curled up like a serpent.

Alonzo is about to cross himself—a gesture more from habit than superstition—when the man says, "Of course we're home. Where else would we be?" The voice rumbles through Alonzo like a car woofer pounding out rap on Rainier Avenue.

"You Parker Davis?"

The man considers the question, as though there is no clear answer, then lifts his hand—the short beefy fingers a forest of black fur—and points to the house. "Go in," he says. "Yes, yes, by all means, go in." He throws back his head, as though about to laugh, revealing a single eyebrow as thick as his knuckles.

Alonzo steps back and trips on one of the warped boards. He slams against the door with outstretched arms that slice through the screen, leaving him dangling with his head and shoulders inside the house and the rest of him standing on the porch.

A voice shoots out of the building. "What the hell's going on out there?"

Alonzo struggles to pull out, but the frame snags his tie and pulls it in a chokehold. He tugs. Silk tears. Threads unravel. He catches the sleeve of his white dress shirt, adds a three-inch tear.

He pulls himself upright and clutches his neck. He removes the tie and rolls up his sleeves. He glances toward the tree. The man has disappeared.

The knot in his chest tightens and sucks out his breath. But it's not just the fall, the door, the shirt. He feels the same panic he feels whenever he has to go out like this, whenever he must confront these people in their homes and businesses. Only this time, it's worse.

He pushes up against the screenless door. "Mr. Parker Davis."

No answer.

Alonzo eases the door open and steps inside. A putrid stench closes in, stale beer and cigarettes and marijuana and cat urine. His stomach reels. He takes short, shallow breaths and covers his nose and mouth.

R. H. Sheldon

Before him, battered steps lead up to the second floor, and to his left, an archway into the living room. A dull light filters through the window over the steps. Its yellow glass spreads a sickly haze down the stairs and through the archway. He can barely make out the silhouettes of a coffee table and sofa.

A rustling noise comes out of the darkness, then the flick of a cigarette lighter.

"Mr. Davis?"

He steps into the room. To his left, faint threads of light outline a closed window shade, casting an eerie glow on the nearby chair and the man sitting in it. Smoke twists out of his cigarette and disappears into the shadows.

"Yeah," Parker grumbles, "what the hell you want?" The man reaches toward the window and raises the blind half way up. Wilted lace curtains, stained tobacco yellow-brown, hang limply around the shade, which itself is tattered and torn and bleeding the same sickly colors as the curtains.

In front of the window and next to Parker's chair stands a small round table and upon the table a lamp whose base is shaped like a ballerina—a somewhat chubby ballerina—with breasts swollen far beyond anything he'd expect from a ceramic figurine.

Parker eases back into the chair, a large overstuffed antique, half-covered by a tattered and greasy pink blanket. Alonzo recognizes Parker as the man who'd been standing outside naked, only now he wears a bathrobe several sizes too small, long skinny legs stretched before him. He stares across the room, puffing on his cigarette, seemingly indifferent to Alonzo.

Empty beer cans and liquor bottles and yellow-stained glasses lie haphazardly from one end of the room to the other. Cigarette butts spill out of ashtrays and coffee mugs and flowered soup bowls. Tall stacks of magazines lean against the side of the piano and up against the wall, one stack *Playboy,* another *Hustler,* the others dissolved into mildew and decay.

Parker grabs a roll of toilet paper off the floor and tears off a two-foot streamer. He blows his nose, coughs up a lungful of spit, wads up the tissue, and drops it on the floor next to several crushed-up beer cans. The cigarette never leaves his mouth.

Alonzo steps toward the chair and holds out the manila envelope. "I'm Alonzo Garcia," he says, "an attorney with Higgins, Whitaker & Nye."

Parker blows a lungful of smoke into Alonzo's eyes. He coughs several times, but continues to hold out the envelope.

"Garcia," Parker says, "is that Vietnamese?"

"Mr. Davis, our firm represents a company called Lockhart Investments. Three weeks ago, Lockhart Investments purchased your house at the bank auction scheduled for that day. You should have received numerous notices from the bank about the foreclosure proceedings and sale. Once the sale was final, you had twenty days from that date to vacate these premises. Yesterday was the twentieth day."

Parker pulls the cigarette out of his mouth and flicks the ashes on Alonzo's polished brown shoes. "Aw, your shiny slippers." Parker studies them for a moment, then works his eyes slowly up to Alonzo's face. "You sure are a pretty one," he says. "Ever been a drag queen? You'd make a hell of a drag queen."

"Mr. Davis—"

"I mean, look at you, that dainty little body, those petite features, that silky black hair. Even that smooth maple syrup skin. And those eyes. Like chips off a glacier, so crystalline blue." Parker snickers, puffs on his cigarette. "Man, you in drag would have half the male population in heat."

Alonzo shifts, tries to push his feelings down, away, anywhere but here. "Mr. Davis, this is serious business."

"So is this, Mr. Lawyer. A drag queen with looks like yours can make a lot of money. Can you sing? That helps a lot. Better than all that lip-synching crap. No one wants a phony."

Alonzo bites down and catches a piece of skin. Blood oozes across his tongue. "You have three days to vacate, Mr. Davis."

"You're not one of those transsexuals, are you? You been pumping yourself with hormones, maybe? A few snips and clips perhaps?"

"Three days, Mr. Davis. If you're not out of here by then, we will start legal proceedings." He drops the paperwork in Parker's lap.

Parker stares at the envelope as though it is infected. Then he takes the cigarette from his mouth, leans forward, and grounds it into the ashtray on the coffee table. The envelope drops to the floor.

"Mr. Davis..."

Parker waves his hand before him, as though swatting away flies. "Your mother must be very proud of you," he says. "Very proud."

Alonzo steps back. He's never told his mother what he does, other than to say he's a lawyer. If she knew he spent his days kicking people out of their homes, she would probably disown him. Even his wife doesn't know what he does.

"I'm sorry, Mr. Davis. But it's out of my hands. I suggest you read the information I just gave you. I'll be back Tuesday morning to make sure you're gone." He turns and walks out of the room. The echoes from his ash-covered shoes follow him through the front door, down the steps, and out of the yard. When he reaches the sidewalk, he stops, sucks in a lung full of air, looks back at the house. The sooner it's gone, the better.

He walks up the street and climbs into his car and locks the door. He starts the engine and turns on the stereo. A painfully slow Gregorian chant rolls out of the speakers, like a wide, deep, slow-moving river, haunting and hopeful and sorrowful all at the same time. He shifts the car into gear and eases away from the curb.

At least Davis didn't pull out a gun. That's something.

Stephanie

S tephanie picks up the last of the brochures and drops them into the satchel, then tosses it into Parker's yard.

She scans her garden, a tiny splotch of brick walkways and ornamental greenery, azaleas an obvious favorite. A few trees, too, where she could squeeze them in, mostly laceleaf and coral bark maples.

Winter is coming. She can see it in the lifeless yellow of the leaves, waiting for a good wind to strip them off their branches. Not the rhododendrons, though. Even in winter the leaves remain bright and green. Her largest and favorite is the bush up near the front door. In spring, it blooms large puffy flowers like blue snowballs, planted twenty-five years ago, shortly after she bought the house, back when houses here were worth practically nothing.

Even so, it took all these years to pay it off. She'd sent the final check right before she retired the previous month. A good thing, too. Otherwise, she'd be bleeding her savings dry. She doesn't want to take Social Security until she hits sixty-six, three years away. Until then, she has to survive the best she can, which is the best anyone can hope for.

She steps around the rhododendron near the front door, brushing against the leaves, and enters the house. She still feels it when she steps inside, that sharp intake of emptiness, as though she'd forgotten Georgia was gone. Even though she knew the relationship had long been over—like trying to squeeze water out

R. H. Sheldon

of a dry sponge, she used to think—she still hasn't adjusted to the loneliness, the hollowness of the house, the long, deadened nights. Even after three months.

She wonders if one ever really adjusts to being alone. Sixty-three is a lousy age to find out.

Stephanie enters the kitchen, or more precisely, that area of her matchbox house that contains the refrigerator and stove and sink, just off the area designated as the living room. Hers is a square, squat home with a bedroom, bathroom, and this one large room— low ceilings, uneven pine floors, rough cedar walls, barely enough space for one person, let alone two, let alone eleven years of two.

She grabs the kettle off the stove and fills it with tap water. A cup of tea, then back outside to finish her yard work. She's let things go these past few months, and with winter fast approaching—this already being November—it's time to get back into a routine.

She sets the kettle on the stove and is about to turn on the burner when someone pounds on the front door.

Georgia?

She drops the kettle into the sink and rushes to the door, trying to calm herself and collect her thoughts, but all she can do is fumble for the handle in a fluttering rush of movement. She pulls the door open. She stops. A punch in the gut. Her body deflates. Parker stands before her, wearing the ill-fitting bathrobe that used to belong to his father.

She's not sure what frustrates her more—that it's Parker or that it's not Georgia.

"What is it?" she says.

He pushes past her and stands just inside, bringing with him an aura of cigarettes and stale whiskey. He carries a large manila envelope that's been savagely ripped open. "So this is what it's like in Dykesville," he says.

"I hope you have a good reason to be here."

"Don't get your boxers all in a knot."

"What do you want, Parker?"

He reaches the envelope toward her. She steps back. He pushes it forward. She hesitates, then pinches it between her thumb and forefinger and dangles it before her. She studies the front and back for anything suspicious. She peers inside. All she finds is a thick stack of papers.

What did she expect? A snake?

"What the hell am I supposed to do with this?"

"Read!"

She pulls out the stack and thumbs through the pages. At first, she can make little sense of them, other than references to Lockhart Investments and the law offices of Higgins, Whitaker & Nye, but slowly she realizes what's going on.

"You're being evicted," she says, not quite believing her own conclusions.

Parker nods.

She scans a few more pages, looking for anything that might refute what she's seeing. "I thought you owned the house. Your mother said it was paid for."

Parker shrugs. He reaches for the cigarette wedged in at top of his ear, but catches Stephanie's look and stops. "I took out a mortgage."

"On a house that was paid off? You took a mortgage?"

"Yes, Madame Perfect, I took out a mortgage."

"I'd rather starve than jeopardize my house."

"You do that."

She scans another paper, then another. Finally, she lifts her head. "But why?"

"I got a great deal, if that's any of your business." He reaches into his robe and scratches his crotch.

Stephanie shoves the papers back into the envelope and hands it to Parker. "Good luck, then." She backs up to let him out. He doesn't move.

"You own a house," he says.

"So?"

"You know how this works."

"I don't know anything about this. I pay my bills. I take care of business."

"That's not what I asked."

"You didn't ask anything."

"Christ, don't you ever let up?"

"I suggest you speak with an attorney."

"Apparently, I just did."

"I can't help you. Maybe you should check with that investment company, Lockhart or whatever they're called."

"What the hell for?"

R. H. Sheldon

"What for? They're the ones evicting you, the ones who now own your house." She makes a sweeping gesture that incorporates his property.

"Doesn't matter who owns it if I end up on the street."

"It does if you can stop it."

"What am I supposed to do? Go to the police?

"You can at least do some research. Check online. Make some calls."

"I don't have a computer and I can't find my phone."

She shakes her head in mock pity.

He points across the room to her antique Dell. "You've got a computer."

"Go to the library," she says.

"Don't you care what happens to my place? Don't you care who moves in? You might get neighbors worse than me."

She crosses her arms and shakes her head again.

He grabs the cigarette from his ear and points it at her. "I'm glad my mother can't see how you've turned on me. She'd never believe what she was hearing."

"Your mother has nothing to do with this."

"She has everything to do with this. The house meant everything to her."

He was right. It had meant everything to her. She would have fought with her dying breath to stay in her home.

Stephanie grabs the envelope. "Damn you. Let me see what I can find out."

Parker

You'd never know Parker had moved from his chair, the way he's back sitting here and wearing his father's robe and smoking Lucky Strikes and sipping his whiskey. All of this, the robe, the liquor, the smokes, just like the old man spent his last ten years. The only difference was his dad had been a stump of a man, shorter, stockier, with a frame even more bent and twisted, a carry-over from his custodial custody at Boeing for the better part of forty years.

Music eases out of a fifteen-year-old boom box next to the television, barely a whisper, one of those that plays cassettes or CDs. His dad had it stashed in the basement, along with a collection of tapes from the Big Band era. But it's a James Brown CD that plays, *Messing with the Blues,* James Brown begging in a mournful, sorrowful, soulful voice for his lover to talk to him.

Myron picked up the CD from Value Village. He has a way of finding gems amid acres of debris.

Myron is sprawled across the couch. Sonuvabitch lies on his thighs. Myron pets Sonuvabitch. Sonuvabitch makes an off-key purring noise that sounds like a diesel engine not hitting on all cylinders. Parker is convinced that cat is possessed, no doubt some maleficent spirit set on taking Parker out.

Myron lies with his big bare Hobbit feet pointing toward Parker, the bottoms calloused, the toes twisted in unnatural

R. H. Sheldon

directions, as hairy as his knuckles. On the floor next to him sits the bag of brochures from the Lighthouse Sanctification Church.

Myron holds one of the pamphlets up to the light that filters through the grimy window above the couch. The soft glow spreads an aura around his thick mop of hair, giving him an otherworld quality, almost saintly.

Just what Parker needs, another goddamn Jesus.

Myron pets the cat and flashes a grin at Parker, a grin that is part happiness and part contentment and part street hustler, a grin indifferent to a scorched past and diminished future, a grin that captures his adolescent naiveté and accumulated cynicism, a grin filled with irrelevance and acceptance and self-assured smugness, a grin that makes no sense whatsoever.

Parker hates that grin.

In fact, Parker hates much about his roommate, Myron Trowbridge, an aging hippie and Vietnam vet and suicide survivor who leapt off a bridge only to have his fall cushioned by a mattress that had dropped out of a pickup, an eerie twist of fate that left Myron with a slight limp and smashed-in nose. Myron Trowbridge, a man with nonstop flashbacks that reflect his years of military service and ingested LSD and eerie ability to know things about the past and present and future most mortals are never meant to know. Myron Trowbridge, short, squat, black squeamish eyes, one thick bushy brow, a face scarred by acne and fear, and hair dark and long and beard forest dense, without a goddamn bit of gray, even though he's just as old as Parker, been just as beat up and spit out and left to sink into his own oblivion, an oblivion that, unlike Parker, Myron fully embraces.

Parker pulls the robe tighter and lights a cigarette with the stub of the old one. He exhales long and hard, letting loose another round of dry, hacking coughs. He gulps down beer. He repeats the cycle several more times. He plans to quit the liquor, the cigarettes. Or at least cut back. But every time he tries, something comes up, something makes life more unbearable. And now there's the goddamn house. But he's got to cut back, if for no other reason than the money. Then there are the other reasons. It's time. Perhaps he'll start tomorrow.

Myron scratches Sonuvabitch's head without looking up.

"What the hell we gonna do, Myron?"

Myron's eyes creep over the pamphlet. "What the hell would you like to do?"

What Parker wants to do is tell Myron that it would be nice if he helped out a little more, paid some rent now and then—something more than food once in a while.

"You never asked for help," Myron says. "If you need money, Parker, just ask."

"Yeah, right, you'll be the first person I call."

Myron's mouth slides into one of those grins.

Normally, Parker can let Myron's peculiar ways slide off. But lately, he seems out there more than ever, as though he's reaching into spaces between spaces, digging for something better left unseen. And sometimes he's not even doing that, as if there is no focus, or worse still, he's focusing on the lack of focus, with an intensity unable to bear its own weight. So he travels farther and farther out, tethered by the thinnest of lines, and if those lines were cut, he'd be gone forever.

And Parker is afraid Myron wants to take his old buddy with him.

Myron's smile deepens and he returns to the brochure. "According to this," he says and holds it up higher, "we've completely misread that whole Mayan thing."

"What Mayan thing?"

"The calendar."

"Armageddon already here?"

"It's about dreams," Myron says. "Our dreams and passions and desires and hopes."

"Don't tell me. They're totally fucked."

Myron shakes his head. "They're roadmaps to our soul."

Parker settles deeper into the chair. He feels like the house, every day sinking lower into the dirt. "You believe that crap?"

Myron shrugs. "Doesn't matter what I believe."

"Then why read it?"

"Why play piano?"

Parker sucks in a deep breath, lets out a long, sour hiss. "At what point, Myron, do we give up our dreams? At what point do we let them go, walk away from them forever? Does it say anything about that?"

"How do we do that, Parker? How do we give up dreams?"

Parker wants to cry. Or maybe he wants to remember what it's like to cry. "You don't live in this world, do you?"

"Do you?" His eyes drop back to the brochure.

R. H. Sheldon

Parker leans back. The pain migrates from his lower back into his shoulder blades. "How long do we wait, Myron, before we let it all go? Before we finally accept that all we have left is to wither and die?"

Myron says nothing.

"How long?" Parker shouts.

Myron pets Sonuvabitch. Sonuvabitch lowers his head. His purring grows rougher, louder. He watches Parker with slitted eyes.

Anger consumes Parker, then panic, rising from deep in his guts. His heart flutters and he struggles for breath.

No dreams. No money. No place to go.

He never intended to still be here. He planned to move into the house, get it ready to sell, take the cash, and run. But he mortgaged the place instead, a great bargain he had thought—at least that's what the mortgage company had told him. He planned to use the money to fix up the place. Then the economy tanked. And he tanked. And now he's worse off than when he arrived. Sure, he still works a few nights a week, but when he does, his fingers ache to the point he can barely play. So he takes more pills and drinks more whiskey and smokes more pot and feels his bones and muscles and joints deteriorate. He's too young for Social Security, too young for Medicare, too poor and too sick for insurance, and too old to give a damn one way or the other. If he could just close his eyes and never open them, if he could take his last breath in this chair, if he could accept that after all these years he has failed, that the best parts of his life are gone, that any reason he once had for getting up in the morning has been left on the side of the road, along with his youth and health and enthusiasm and ability to care.

This chair. This place. This moment. Just like his father.

Myron looks up from the brochure. His stare digs into Parker like a burning iron.

"Stay out," Parker says. Myron returns to his reading.

Parker picks up the can of beer, a Bud Light he grabbed from the kitchen earlier, one of three remaining in the house. He should have snatched a second while he was in there. Hell, he should have grabbed all three.

Parker gulps down what's left, drops the can on the floor, grabs the Jack Daniel's, pulls a long draw, feeling the burn in his throat and down in his gut. He clutches the bottle and blinks back the tears.

"What the fuck, Myron? What the fuck?"

Sonuvabitch glares at Parker. Myron fixates on the brochures with a look like Charles Manson.

"How long you gonna read that crap?"

Parker drops the bottle on the floor.

"We need to talk, Myron. We need to figure out what the fuck we're gonna do."

Myron refolds the brochure. The sun breaks free of the clouds and shines through the window, filling the room with a garish glow that turns Parker's skin a deadly yellowish gray. He grabs a Lucky Strike off the coffee table. Myron doesn't move.

Parker is about to light the cigarette, but stops. He pulls it out of his mouth and lobs it at Myron, but it falls short and lands on the floor. Myron turns toward the stack of brochures next to him and pulls out a small booklet, a dozen sheets of letter-sized paper folded in half and stapled at the center.

"Goddamn, Myron!"

Myron gazes up at the window, stares directly into the light. "Not now," he says. "Not ready yet." Then he turns toward Parker, but doesn't look at him. Through him. Through him and into the distance.

If Parker were not so old and tired and sore, if his body could still move and his fists still held strength, if he had not smoked so much weed and guzzled so much whiskey and inhaled so many cigarettes, he would jump out of his chair and bash his useless roommate and his even more useless cat over their goddamn useless heads.

Instead, Parker grabs another Lucky Strike off the coffee table, lights the cigarette, and draws in a lungful of smoke. Then, with it dangling from his mouth, he says, "What are we going to do, Myron, about the house? What are we going to do?"

A quizzical look, buried beneath all his hair, gathers on Myron's face, mostly in the form of a raised eyebrow and a slight softening of his dark stare. "Do?"

"Yeah, you moron. We're getting kicked out in three days."

Myron tilts his head slightly to the left and scratches the cat's neck. He seems to consider for a moment what Parker is asking, then says, "Why do anything?"

Parker reaches to his throat, as though being strangled. He takes a long breath, as deep as he dares. Finally, in a slow, deliberate voice, he says, "Doing nothing is not an option."

R. H. Sheldon

Myron shakes his head and looks down at the booklet.

"Goddamn it, Myron. You live here too. You and that fuckin' cat. For free, I might add." The heat spreads across his face, his scalp, an explosion imminent.

Myron cradles Sonuvabitch in his arm and stands. He shoves the booklet into one of the large side pockets of his cargo pants. He slips his giant feet into his flip-flops and says, "You seem upset. We're heading outside to give you some space." The light through the nicotine-stained glass softens and fills the air with a greenish haze, giving Myron the look of a satyr trekking through the forest, an ethereal look, almost heavenly, a look that really pisses Parker off.

"Fine," Parker shouts. "You do that. Maybe you should just stay the hell out there."

Parker stares at the piano. Myron opens the screen door and steps onto the front porch. The sun moves behind the clouds and the room falls into near darkness.

"Goddamn him."

Parker kicks over the coffee table. Empty beer cans tumble to the floor. The ashtray flies off and scatters cigarette butts across the room. Ash fills the air like Mount St. Helens.

James Brown ends his song about messing with the blues. The CD player clicks off.

Parker sucks on the Lucky Strike and waits for the ash to clear. But it doesn't clear, and before long several coughs erupt from his lungs, the usual sort of hacking at first, the kind that stays with him for a moment and then lets loose with a pop. But this time the coughing grows into something deeper, a choking sensation that pulls the air out of him. His body rattles and his sides ache, his lungs burning with their own fire. A spasm courses through his body, seizing him in a convulsive rage. He struggles against the hacking, the sense of suffocation. He coughs and spits and gags. It continues for many minutes. Hours perhaps. More hacking. More choking. But slowly the spasms ease and control returns. He grabs the roll of toilet paper from the floor. He tries to cough out the pain in his lungs, spit out the heavy poison that sucks up his air. He coughs again, hacks up mouthfuls of phlegm. His breath returns in a series of sputtering gasps.

The pain eases and his chest begins to relax. His coughs now come in short bursts, until he expels one last lump from his lungs. He grabs another wad of toilet paper, spits out a mouthful into the tissue. And that's when he notices the crimson streaks, a bloody mucousy web that bleeds into the paper and onto his fingers and into his heart, where it will settle and spread until there is nothing left of the man that was once Parker Davis, the Boy Wonder.

Stephanie

Stephanie heads to her small desk tucked into the corner of the kitchen area. She carries with her the envelope and papers. She's not sure why she agreed to help Parker. As far as she's concerned, the best thing that could happen is to see his backside for the last time, preferably more clothed than he was earlier this afternoon. And she certainly doesn't want him dropping by again. Ever. The stench of cigarettes and liquor hang in the air like Pepper's Ghost.

Yet she finds it unsettling that an investment company bought Parker's house. Of course, it's not the house they want. It's the land. Even if the house were immaculate, they'd be tearing it down. And the house is anything but immaculate. By the time Parker got his hands on the place, it was already in need of a makeover. Those last few years, his mom could barely keep up. Stephanie tried to help out, but it was simply too much house for a woman her age, living on her own, living on her income. And after Parker moved in, the house went from shabby to shantytown slums, all within four years.

She sits in front of her desk, a solid corner shelf that hangs from the wall, made of smooth and polished maple to match the kitchen cabinets. Georgia built the desk as a birthday present several years back. At the time, Stephanie thought it about the nicest gift she'd ever received. She still does.

Music plays in the background, softly, Mary Black singing about soul sisters. Georgia hated her music.

Stephanie jiggles the mouse to wake her antiquated PC. She rarely turns it off for fear it won't restart.

She opens the email program and checks for new messages, the first time she's done so in several week. Dozens pour in, most of them junk. But one stands out from the others, sent last month by Georgia Plodowski.

Stephanie feels her chest tighten. This is the first communication she's received from Georgia since the morning she left. They both acted so adult that day, so refined. No tears. No anger. No sharp words. A brief hug followed by a brief good-bye. For Stephanie, the tears didn't start until several days later, when she realized just how lonely being alone could be.

She opens the email and reads. But what she reads is nothing worth reading—a bulk email, everyone blind-copied, announcing Georgia's new address in Bend, along with *their* phone number. A brief message describes the couple's cozy new home. Stephanie scrolls down. At the bottom is a photo of a beagle puppy, chewing on socks that look like a pair Stephanie gave Georgia this past Christmas. The caption reads *Bucky, our new baby boy.*

Stephanie hits the Delete button and closes the email program. She wipes her eyes with her sleeve.

I will not let this happen. I will not.

She opens the web browser and searches for Lockhart Investments.

R. H. Sheldon

Alonzo

Alonzo returns to his office in Bellevue—a small, windowless cell on the second floor of one of the suburb's newest and tallest buildings, Lockhart Tower, forty stories of glass and steel brimming with the Northwest skies. The building's just one of the many properties Lockhart Investments has developed on the West Coast and in the Rocky Mountain states. The top ten floors house the company's headquarters. High-tech companies lease most of the others. The law offices of Higgins, Whitaker & Nye reside on the first three.

Alonzo has been with the law firm for nearly two years. The company hired him right after he received his law degree from the University of Washington.

Though it all looks good on paper—the degree, the job with a prestigious firm—the fact is, he's little more than a clerk with a crappy office and crappy assignments and crappy little salary that barely pays the mortgage, let alone makes a dent in the school loans and credit card bills.

What's worse, what he had not anticipated, is how much he hates being a lawyer—shuffling paper, crawling through loopholes, manipulating the lives of everyone involved—carried out under the protection of a legal system that, as far as Alonzo can see, is designed to serve only those who can afford it.

In such a world, what choice does Alonzo have but to strive to be one of those with the money? If he's nothing else, he's a realist.

So he puts up with unrelenting hours and unscrupulous managers and unsavory characters like Parker Davis. All in the name of feeding his family and keeping a roof over their heads.

He thinks about his original interests, those first two years of study—music, art, philosophy—but his father quickly nixed Alonzo's nonprofessional hopes, as did his mother, his wife, and his wife's mother. Even Alonzo understood the fruitlessness of his endeavors.

He plops down in his chair and pulls up to the desk, a slate-colored tin bucket dented and scratched and stained, salvaged from the basement of the old office building. He pulls a stack of papers out of his briefcase and sets them on his desk. He rubs his temples. He sighs.

He plans to use this time to catch up on the backlog of projects that awaits him, perhaps even carve out some free time for himself and his family this weekend.

Buck Lancaster has other ideas, apparent by the way he charges into the office and drops a manila folder on the desk.

Buck is a big guy, rugby player big, with bulging bloodshot eyes and a round ruddy face and a nose shaped like an acorn.

Buck says, "More fun for you, my friend." His voice rolls out in a deep rumble, every word sounding like a threat.

Alonzo says nothing. He knows there's little point. He knows too it's Friday afternoon and he's been trapped once again.

"How did the last one go?" Buck asks.

"He's still in the house. I've served him notice."

"Will he be out?"

"I'm not sure he even knew I was there."

"Drunk?"

"Drunk. Stoned. Hard to say." Alonzo rubs his temples.

"How bad was he?"

"I found him naked in his front yard."

Buck lets out a loud whooping laugh that sounds like a runaway train. "You sure do pick 'em."

Alonzo shrugs. "We'll see what happens in three days." He can't imagine Davis will be out of the house. Then it will move to the courts and the police department and will be out of his hand. All Alonzo cares about is being done with Davis and everyone like him. Why he has to deal with this shit is the real issue. He's a lawyer, for chrissakes, not some lowlife clerk.

"Maybe the next one won't be so bad."

R. H. Sheldon

"Next one?"

Buck points to the folder. Alonzo grabs it and looks inside. He reads the name *Stephanie Schmidt*.

"Lives next door to your last one," Buck says. "Once we have her house, we have most of the block."

Alonzo thumbs through the papers. "Think she'll sell?"

Buck smirks. "Oh, she'll sell."

"Then what?"

"Then they build. And we get a big fat check."

Parker

Parker wakes from his whiskey and weed stupor, the room ablaze, a glare so bright he thinks his house is on fire. But it's only the sun, setting over Puget Sound and the Olympic Mountains. It happens this time of year sometimes, when the sun finds a hole in the clouds and pierces the maple's dead branches and yellow glass over the couch, filling the room with a ghastly glow. He shuts his eyes to ward off the pain.

The window is much like the one over the stairs, what his mom referred to as stained glass, although they're nothing but cheap windowpane tinted yellow. But then, she always referred to his father as a custodial engineer, when in fact he was a floor-sweeping, garbage-toting, toilet-plunging janitor.

"Dreams don't come easy," she used to say, "if they come at all."

A burst of nasally snorts shoots across the room. Parker opens his eyes. Myron snoring, again on the couch, his big ugly feet again pointing toward Parker, Sonuvabitch again sprawled across his thighs. The yellow glow makes the cat look even more sinister, especially against Myron's still and sleeping form, prone in cryptic repose, a casualty of war.

Parker snarls at the cat. The cat hisses at Parker and eases deeper into Myron's legs but never lets loose the way he stares at Parker, and Parker never turns away for fear of what might happen, though nothing has happened so far, but Parker is convinced that the son-of-a-bitch Sonuvabitch is planning something big, the way he always watches Parker and studies him and considers his movements and his proximity to the cat's jumbo black gnarly-furred body.

Myron mumbles, "Where do we go?" but it sounds as though he's shouting because of how quiet the house is, almost too quiet, an unnatural stillness that gathers in the shadows. Then he sweeps his arms across his face to ward off an invisible intruder, but he never wakes and never moves his legs and never does much else but start to snore again.

Parker reaches to the coffee table and grabs the can of Bud Light. The bathrobe pulls at his armpits and up his back. A father too small. A son too much.

Parker eases back into the chair and adjusts the robe. His legs tingle. His ankles ache. Myron moans and snores and swipes at the air. Sonuvabitch hisses and narrows his eyes at Parker.

Parker downs the rest of the beer and lobs the can at the cat, but it instead hits Myron's shoulder and tumbles to the floor. Sonuvabitch dives under the coffee table. Myron sits upright and shakes his head and scans the room with black empty eyes. Then he gasps and jumps off the couch and strikes what certainly must be a battle stance, judging by the way he holds his arms before him and squeezes his hairy knuckles into tight half-fists.

"What the fuck?" Myron shouts. "What the mother-fuckin' fuck?"

Sonuvabitch creeps out from under the coffee table in a painstakingly slow crawl and glares at Parker with a look of retribution. Then he sidles up to Myron and stands in what certainly must be his own posture of defense, his back arched, his head lowered, his half-tail flicking as though he'd been plugged into a socket.

Parker reaches toward the coffee table and pulls one of the Lucky Strikes out of the pack and flicks the lighter several times until a flame ignites and the cigarette catches. He leans back and sucks in a lungful of smoke and sets his feet on the table and waits for Myron to say whatever it is he's going to say next, which could be anything, given that Myron is still asleep.

Myron gasps and his body jerks and his arms flail and he leaps forward and knocks the cigarette out of Parker's mouth and shouts, "The Vietcong!" He stomps out the cigarette with a bare foot and yells, "Always—always—*always* light the end with the label so they can't track you by your American smokes."

Last Stand

Parker grabs another cigarette and lights the label end and takes a long drag and says, "We should be safe now."

Myron looks toward the ceiling and covers his head with his arms as though the cracked plaster is about to drop down on him. Then he raises his hands to the largest crack, fingers spread and palms held upward, and closes his eyes and whispers, "The sun can't shine forever." He drops onto his bed and rolls to his side. He pulls his dog tags from beneath his shirt and holds them in his meaty fist. He closes his eyes.

Sonuvabitch jumps up next to Myron and leans against the back cushion and sticks one of his legs straight into the air and starts licking his balls, all the while watching Parker with a sideways glare that has the look of a psychopathic jihadist. Parker sticks the cigarette between his lips and flips off the cat.

The sunlight flares and brightens the house. Parker looks out to the front hall. For a moment, the gold-plated record glows with a steely light that pierces him with blades of ice. He's got to get rid of that piece of shit, sell it to some looser collector, auction it off on one of those online retailers, like E-Bait or whatever the hell they're called. The sooner the better. The record means nothing now. Why should it? He knows the score. He's nothing but a washed-out, one-hit wonder whose only skill is playing piano and only interest is being drunk.

He long ago accepted the sad facts of his life, facts that have been steadily intensifying by the ever-growing scarcity of jobs and ever-deteriorating condition of his body. And now he's losing his home, a home that's crumbling around him like a decade-long earthquake, extinguishing any glimmer of hope. No longer does he dream of that one break that will put him back on top. No longer does he dream of destiny or recognition or reemergence or a future as bright as the stars.

Four years after he inherited the house, Parker dreams only of surviving this fucked-up hand and doing what it takes to keep that hand from growing worse, despite a bent and wrinkled body that every day sinks deeper into a monochromatic sunset of emphysemic grays.

The room falls into darkness.

Parker forces himself out of the chair, feeling the effort in every muscle, every joint, like the keys of his Mom's old piano, stiff, no spring, life all but extinguished. His knees are the worst—or maybe it's his back—all those years perched on benches and slumped over bars and falling off stools.

He stands before the ballerina lamp, with her wide hips and ample bosom. When he was a teen, plagued by adolescence and testosterone, he would imagine what it would be like if she were to pull a Pinocchio and turn into a fully formed female so he could bury his face in her voluptuous cleavage and breathe in the scent of her perfume and sweat and tight little tutu and squeeze and push and pump and dig into that pile of soft supple flesh.

Parker has been a breast man ever since.

"The light," Myron mumbles. "The light."

"Yeah," Parker says, "the fucking beautiful light."

He erupts into a round of hacking that sets his chest on fire and chokes him with a wad of sludge that explodes out of his lungs and leaves a sour taste in his mouth and a vicious twist in his guts. He stumbles forward and slams into the round table and knocks the ballerina to the hardwood floor, her dazzling breasts split into two identical cones, one tit getting her head, and the other, the tight and tantalizing tutu.

Myron

Myron hears a crash, but can't make out the source. All he sees are hot mists that fold out of the thick underbrush and rise to the top of the trees in gauzy layers that fade toward an invisible heaven.

He opens his eyes. The jungle slips behind the fog and in its place emerges a ceiling cracked and splintered and a yellow glow that deepens the edges of each shadow. Across the room, near the front window, stands an old man hunched over, picking up pieces of broken ceramic, a man too weak and bent to lift up anything, a man that Myron recognizes as Parker.

Myron twists onto his back and props himself up on his elbows, moving his legs as little as possible so not to disturb Sonuvabitch.

Parker turns, a look of guilt on his face. "I've got to get to work." He exits the room and climbs the stairs. His groans and gasps echo through the living room, melt into the walls, burrow into the decaying floor.

Myron wonders how much longer Parker can survive. His cough worsens every day. His breathing becomes more strained. His skin grows more ghostly and gray. Myron also wonders how much longer he'll be around as well. How long anyone will be here when such uncertainty abounds.

He eases back on the couch and waits. Night comes early these days. By the time Parker leaves, the rooms will have already fallen

R. H. Sheldon

into darkness. Silence will creep through the bedrooms, down the stairs, into the heart of the house.

He picks up the booklet he was studying earlier, a small publication put out by the Lighthouse Sanctification Church. He reads about the auric light of human divinity. He reads about the ethereal connection that ties every creature to a universal consciousness. He reads about the profound changes that the world and its people are about to pass through, whether or not they're prepared for what's coming.

Myron finds only vague hints about what one can do to prepare for that coming. Perhaps he should visit the church and talk to the woman who wrote the booklet, this Olympia Culpepper, the same woman listed as the church's pastor.

Myron reads on. At some point—he has no way of knowing how long—Parker creeps down the stairs. He coughs and wheezes and pulls open the front door.

"What happened to the goddamn screen?" He doesn't wait for an answer.

Myron hears Parker step onto the porch and descend its stairs. Sonuvabitch eases deeper between his legs. Myron closes his eyes.

The stillness of leaves, the suffocating heat, above him, jungle skies, canopies of shadow and green, flashes of sunlight. The air is thick with the hot wet scents of the jungle, so stifling he can barely breathe. He watches and waits. And then it happens. The sun explodes into a blinding glare, too bright to look at, too penetrating to turn away. A thunderous clap follows, just like it always follows, filling his skull with echoes that never quite go away.

He opens his eyes. She stands at the foot of the couch, in front of Parker's chair, her eyes burning with the light of a ceiling lamp he never turns on.

"Where is he?" she demands.

Myron grasps for understanding. The light crushes his skull. Sonuvabitch hisses and puffs up his fur.

She folds her arms over her chest. She stomps her foot. "Where is he?" she says. "Where's the man who chased us out of the yard?" Her voice is tinged with a slight Texas accent. In her ear she wears one of those phone devices, the kind that lets her listen and talk without using her hands.

Myron tries to make sense of what she is asking. Parker was in the yard. Myron remembers seeing him outside earlier today. Or was it yesterday? Parker naked, running down the front steps. Not running, more like stumbling, yelling about the devil. Maybe Myron dreamed the part about the devil. Maybe Myron dreamed all of it.

The woman unfolds her arms, places her hands on her hips. She wears the same sweatshirt. *I'm all or nothing.* Myron wants to think about what this means, when the room returns to darkness.

Myron decides to speak, but can't remember what to say.

The woman looks at the brochures on the floor, at the canvas bag that carried them. "Those are mine." She has gray-green eyes the color of Elliott Bay.

Myron holds out the booklet. Sonuvabitch moans.

"Just give me the bag. You can keep the rest.

Myron likes this idea, as though someone has given him a gift. He grins.

"He had no right to do that," she says. "No right at all."

Myron nods in agreement, but does not know what she means. "That must not have been easy for you," he says.

Myron heard this line spoken in a movie. An older woman says it to a younger woman who is divorcing her husband. The younger woman cries and pours out her heart and seems better somehow for having done so.

Since seeing the film, Myron often uses the line when he doesn't know what else to say, and almost always it's the perfect response.

"It wasn't," the woman says. She drops her arms to her sides.

Sonuvabitch eases down into Myron's legs.

The woman says, "I should never have run like that, but when he burst out of the door, naked and screaming, and my daughter there, and him acting like a lunatic…"

"That must not have been easy for you."

She nods and says, "I'm Olympia Culpepper, the pastor of Lighthouse Sanctification Church."

Myron snaps to attention. "You wrote this?" He takes hold of Sonuvabitch, twists around, sits up. Sonuvabitch barely moves. "I have questions."

"Questions?"

He closes his eyes. The light filters through the canopy and spreads on the jungle floor.

Her voice cuts through the dense air. "Do you know where he is? The man who ran out of the house?"

He opens his eyes. For a moment, he has forgotten she was there. "You mean Parker?"

"Does he live here?"

"His house. But he's not here."

"I want to talk to him. I want to tell him what he did was wrong."

"It was wrong," Myron repeats.

She pulls a pen and a small pad of paper out of her back pocket. "Where can I find him?"

Parker

P arker steps off the bus and walks the two blocks to Pike
Place Market. The club where he plays, Oily Tom's Bar
and Grill, sits on the lower level, just off the alley where it
drops down next to the newsstand, around the corner from the
gum wall. The market has a turn-of-the-century look that lends it
authenticity, one of the few places in Seattle that attempts to
salvage the town's heritage, providing an illusion of a past offered
up to tourists and dot-commers like a tattooed virgin at a carnival
sideshow. Even on a Friday night in November, with the stalls shut
down and shops locked up, they still show up for the restaurants
and entertainment. For places like Oily Tom's.

Parker pulls open the glass front door—the windows painted a
dusty gray, like you'd find at a packaged liquor store—and steps
inside. The room is long and narrow, with high ceilings and brick
walls exposed to the past. A few customers sit at the bar, carryovers
from happy hour, slumped over their drinks in a protective stance,
middle-aged men with faces covered in gray stubble and clothes
worked over too many years, with no place to go, no place they
want to be.

More customers are scattered around the tables, mostly couples
talking in low voices and gazing at each other with looks that waver
between disbelief and drunken affection. The place, like the men at
the bar, has a tired and worn look, propped up for too many years
to accommodate late night crowds of tourists and locals and

R. H. Sheldon

drunks who pour in from other bars and restaurants and theaters, not ready to call it a night, not ready to face what waits for them in their daily lives.

But they're not here yet, and won't start arriving for another hour or two, giving Parker a chance to warm up, both inside and out. He stops at the bar.

The bartender, Raphael, looks a lot like the patrons sitting before him, a tired face sagging into pasty folds and watery eyes that protrude from dark bluish-black pockets and a mouth with a fat lower lip that hangs partially open. He nods and says, "The usual?"

"Yeah, the usual. Room on my tab?"

"Barely."

Parker says the same thing every night, receives the same answer. He's notorious here and everywhere else for running up bar tabs that exceed what he earns, despite the discounts and liberal pours and drinks customers send to him throughout the night. But management is happy to oblige. They know that the more he drinks, the more entertaining he becomes and the more customers love him. They also know that if he doesn't drink, he's dull and sullen and irritable and chases people away. The last thing any club wants is a sober Parker.

Raphael pours a double-shot of Jack with a beer back, some weird-ass microbrew that, in Parker's eyes, amounts to little more than pricey swill. But the beer's usually free, as long as he takes whatever they're trying to dump. It's just the whiskey that costs him.

Parker clutches the edge of the bar and downs the Jack. The burn gets worse every day. But it's worth it. Every drop.

He grabs the beer, lifts it in thanks, and heads toward the back of the room. A full-sized upright—about as battered and tinny as a piano can get—sits on a platform raised a couple feet above the rest of the bar. He says nothing to the customers and smiles briefly at the waitress, Francine, a gray-haired Jamaican with tiny arms and tiny legs and a tiny body and an accent that comes and goes depending on the size of the crowd and the amount of flowing tips. Francine has got to be the oldest cocktail waitress in the city.

"You look like shit," she says to Parker, then turns to the young couple at the table behind her. "Anything else?" Before they can answer, she turns back to Parker. "You keep up like this and you'll be dead by winter."

"So I've been told."

He climbs the two steps up to the platform—he refuses to call it a *stage*—and sets his beer on a coaster to the right of the piano keys. He pulls back the bench and sits down. He looks out across the lounge. No one seems aware that he's up here, except Francine, who frowns and folds her Twiggy arms over her chest. Her cheeks glow likes coals in the lounge's dim lights.

How many more nights will he be able to endure this ritual, to force himself to sit up here and play, to listen to the moronic crowds—people here on business, on vacation, visiting friends and family? The local drunks and the late-night partiers. The hecklers. The jocks. The junkies. The fucked up and doped up. How many more nights? How many more inane, insipid, insulting pop-hit songs before he keels over, from exhaustion and boredom and abject failure?

He draws in a slow breath, tries to hold in what air his lungs can handle, and begins to play, a medley of pop hits from the '60s and '70s and '80s. He plunks out the tunes with slow deliberation, turning what were lively songs into a long sorrowful dirge. No one seems to notice.

After several bars of "I'll never fall in love again," he stops and downs his beer. He signals to Francine. She draws up to the platform. "What is it, honey?"

"Another round."

She shakes her head. "You don't need anymore. Especially this early."

He stares into her black eyes. "I do, Francine. I need it."

She studies him for what seems like minutes. There's a weariness about her that extends past this room and building and night, a sadness he's never seen, or never noticed. She turns away and heads to the bar, and soon returns with the Jack and beer, but says nothing.

He plays. He drinks. He watches the room fill—men and women, black and white, gay and straight, young and old, everything in between. Liquor pours. Voices boom. Parker plucks the piano louder and faster.

He learned long ago that the key to performing is to give people what they want, to be an entertainer, a showman, no matter how much he hates it, even if it means pop tunes and show tunes and country tunes and even goddamn Jesus tunes. Three nights a week, selling his soul for a few lousy bucks and some crummy booze and the occasional blowjob in the alley. Well, not so much the blowjobs anymore. These days, he's lucky he can get it up at all, and the one time he tried that fucked-up Viagra, his head erupted in skull-cracking pain that lasted three days and left him wishing he were a eunuch.

The room is packed now. Three more servers and an additional bartender—all women—have been added to the roll. Management is well aware of the benefits of a young, female staff, especially a group of such sexy lithe women, though Parker has to admit that these day, being young is all it takes to be sexy.

It's remarkable that Francine and Raphael have lasted this long, but they've been grandfathered in, so to speak, and the new owners, when they took over a couple years back, realized that the two of them still brought in the regulars. As for Parker, as long as he keeps playing and drinking, they're happy.

The front door opens and a woman slips in and stands next to the bar. He can barely make her out from this distance and in this light, but he has the sense that she's watching him with particular interest, as though she's come here only to see him. There's something familiar about her, but he can't say what it is. No doubt another nut off the street.

Parker turns away, but he can still feel her stare.

He plays, waits for the crowd to loosen up. Soon they'll be yelling out song titles. He can usually predict the requests based on the customers. Tonight, they appear a bit whiter and straighter and older and more suburban than the average crowd, so he expects to be playing "What a Wonderful World" at least three times, excerpts from *The Phantom of the Opera* repeatedly, "Somewhere over the Rainbow"—his record being six times in one night—several James Taylor songs, particularly "You've Got a Friend," a bunch of John Denver crap, including "Country Roads," and anything from Broadway, in addition to *Phantom*. By the end of the night, they'll all be singing in their loud drunk voices and stuffing his tip jar and buying him drinks and telling him that he's the most talented man they ever heard.

He needs a cigarette. Soon as he finishes doling out this melancholy rendition of "Let It Be," another one that will probably reappear before the night is over. He longs for the days when they could still smoke in the bars, when that warm, comforting bluish haze filled the air and turned these places into other-worldly venues, where getting out and away from life really meant something.

Now there's no smoking or spitting or swearing or doing anything that makes being in a bar fun. Before you know it, they'll be outlawing booze.

When he hits the last chord—a bluesy flourish that helps pull the song at least somewhat out of its repetitive mire—an older gentleman steps up to the platform and hands Parker a twenty and asks him to play "Danny Boy." The way he stands, with his eyes averted, acting demure and apologetic, reminds Parker of Mother fuckin' Teresa.

"Can it wait till after my break?"

"If you could before, please. I need to get my wife home. That was our son's name. She wanted to hear..." He glances toward the table, where a withered, white-haired lady sits, barely holding herself upright, her two feet, and much of the rest of her, already well planted into the grave.

Parker studies the twenty. "Sure, but this one's on me." He tries to hand the bill to the man. The man shakes his head and wobbles back to the table.

Parker, of course, knows the song. He hasn't played it in years, but he still remembers every word. It was one of his mom's favorites. Maybe that's why he feels so obliging. Tonight, he'll even sing it. He usually saves his singing till he's had enough liquor to loosen his throat and his pride—and the audience no longer cares. His voice has gotten so dry and crackly, he should give up singing altogether. Especially if he's sober. But something in him wants to make these folks happy, so maybe he's not as sober as he thinks.

He pulls the mike closer and lays his fingers on the keys, feeling that brief sense of peace that comes when he touches a piano, as though he and the keys are meant to be joined, where one can't exist without the other.

He plays the first chord. Even the tinny harmonics sound angelic. A few more chords. Then he lets loose.

> Oh, Danny Boy, the pipes, the pipes are calling.
> From glen to glen, and down the mountain side.
> The summer's gone, and all the roses falling.
> It's you, it's you must go and I must bide.

A soulful, pure quality swells from within him and reaches through his fingers and into the keys and seeps too into his voice so that the sound becomes one smooth, painful melody that mixes

R. H. Sheldon

into a single thought and drifts out to the lounge. And customers must pick up that something different is happening, something profound perhaps, because slowly the room grows quiet and they turn to listen and the waitresses too have stopped working and stand watching Parker as though they've never heard him before. No one moves or speaks or coughs or even takes a drink, caught in their own vortexes of memory and mortality and regret.

He plays and sings, feeling his heart soar with each chord, a sense of wonder he thought no longer possible, not in himself, not in anyone. He plays each note with a careful, light touch that wraps smoothly with his voice and carries the words out. He plays. Sings. Feels sadness. Fear. Moments of happiness. He plays. And the people watch, listen, immersed in each chord, each phrase. He tumbles forward, and they tumble with him, without thought, without understanding, until after what seems like hours of playing he moves toward the song's final moments.

But come ye back when summer's in the meadow,
or when the valley's hushed and white with snow.
It's I'll be here in sunshine or in shadow.
Oh, Danny Boy, oh Danny Boy, I love you so.

He plays a final few bars. They linger in the air, as though waiting for something to happen. Everyone remains still until he hits the final notes, then they erupt in a loud steady applause, unlike any he's heard in years. He feels exposed, embarrassed, not knowing how to respond. He looks over to the table where the old couple sits. Her chin is down and she sobs into her dress. The man helps her stand, and then the two of them, frail and defeated, shuffle toward the front door.

When the room grows quiet, Parker leans into the microphone. "My house," he says, "they're taking my house. My parents' home. The banks. The investors. Everything I have will soon be gone." He stops, studies the faces of the audience. His eyes thicken with tears. "Where do we go when everything is lost? Where do we go?"

Part II

If you think you're enlightened
go spend a week with your family.
—Ram Dass

Olympia

Olympia pushes the papers aside and sips her coffee. She sees little reason to rehash the figures. She doesn't have enough yet to expand into a bigger space. She planned to be further along by now, but dreams come slowly, especially when she's so anxious for them to unfold.

It's these sorts of challenges that most test her faith, when she gets caught in the upheaval of details and forgets the bigger picture. How many times has she told herself to stand back and let the universe unfold? How many times has she preached the same message to her congregation? Just because she's facing a few challenges is no reason to let go of her beliefs. She must have faith that the church will come when the time is right. It's all about faith. If she builds her church based on nothing but brick and mortar, she's already failed.

But enough of that. She needs to work on her Sunday Talk and quit focusing on circumstances out of her control. After meeting with Parker Davis last night—and hearing him play and speak about his house—she knows just what she plans to say. No wonder he was running around like a lunatic yesterday afternoon. She'd do the same thing if she were in his place.

Olympia pulls a notepad out of her desk and grabs a pen from a chipped coffee cup. The cup holds her pencils and scissors and letter opener and an assortment of other pens. Printed on one side of the mug is *Lighthouse Sanctification Church*, and on the other, *We're all or nothing.*

Olympia considers for a moment what she wants to include in her Sunday Talk. Should she start at the beginning, with him running after them naked? That would certainly grab their attention. Or perhaps she should start with her trip to the club last night, which itself might raise a few eyebrows. She likes to hit them in their spiritual smugness now and again.

She removes the Bluetooth headset from her ear and eases back in her chair, comforted by the squeak of rusty springs. She's about to close her eyes when the door flies open and slams into the wall. Bellamy stomps into the room and stands before the desk, huffing like an ailing dragon. She slams a thick copper bracelet on the desk. "It's turning my wrist green. Look, my skin, it's turning this ugly green. Like mold. My wrist is full of mold!"

Bellamy holds out her hand. She must have painted her fingernails last night, when Olympia was down listening to Parker. They gleam with a deadly shade of black.

Bellamy is Olympia's twenty-year-old daughter. Bellamy wears black boots and black leggings and a black blouse three sizes too small. Bellamy wears a black skirt that is practically no skirt at all. Bellamy has six piercings in her left ear, nine in her right, two in her nose, and one in her right eyebrow. Bellamy is adorned with massive tattoos on her left arm, images of the Kama Sutra. The most prominent is a dark-skinned man intertwined with a light-skinned woman, their bodies surrounded by a web of dark and twisted branches and bent into an impossible position. And now Bellamy has black fingernails to match her hair and a wrist to match her green-tinted bracelet.

"Then don't wear it," Olympia says.

"What?" Bellamy's voice booms. She still wears her ear buds, the music loud enough for Olympia to hear. A black wire snakes down from her head and connects to the phone she holds in her other hand.

Olympia points to Bellamy's earphones.

Bellamy pulls them out. The music grows louder. "What was that?"

"Don't wear it."

"You told me to wear it. You did. You said it would help release my psychic energies."

"I said mental."

Bellamy shrugs. "What's like important is that you told me to wear this thing."

"I *suggested* you try it."

"But what happened?"

"Your body must not need copper."

"What does my body need?"

Olympia places her hands on the desk, on top of her notes. She taps her fingers. Stops. "Later we'll do a reading," she says. "We'll let *your* body tell us what it needs."

Bellamy drops into the chair next to the desk. She pushes a pile of papers to the side and leans on her left elbow. The black and white lovers dance across her loose flesh.

At times she looks like such a child, most of the time acts like a child. If anything were to happen to Olympia, Bellamy would be lost. She likes to strut around like a woman, show off all those parts that make her a woman, but forever she remains a little girl, one who likes to play with grown-up toys.

Bellamy's phone dings. She studies the screen and punches out a message. She waits. She giggles. She sends another message and snickers. "Mom," she says, "I like need to raise some cash." She speaks mostly to her fingernails.

Olympia picks up her pen. "Join the club," she says.

"Be serious, Mom."

"I *am* serious."

"Don't you want to know why?"

"Why I should be serious?"

"No, why I need the cash."

"Another tattoo?"

"Mother."

"Bellamy, I have to work."

"You always have to work."

"You should try it."

"What's that supposed to mean?"

"It means I could use some help around here."

"Like I helped you yesterday? Is that what you want? So more ugly old naked men can chase after me?"

"Bellamy, I don't think..."

"I know what he was after, who he was after. He was after me."

"I don't think he was..."

"You forget what it's like to be a woman, to have men want you."

"This has nothing to do with being a woman."

"It has everything to do with it."

Olympia pulls back. The chair squeaks. Maybe she *has* forgotten, at least in the sense that Bellamy is talking about. But Olympia's notions of womanhood are much different than her daughter's—wider, deeper, grounded in the earth. And her ministry ties into that. Now is not the time to lose focus, to become distracted by Bellamy or anyone else. She made this commitment to herself years ago, and she's not about to back down. Even Bellamy's father was no more than a bump in the road, with Bellamy the unexpected detour. But no more bumps. No more detours. She's worked too hard to get where she is, and she doesn't plan to stop now. Her journey doesn't end with a few Sunday sermons—or even a new church. Her dreams are as wide as the heavens.

Olympia says, "I could still use some help around here."

"I don't even know why we were there in the first place."

"Now what are you talking about?"

"Yesterday. That creep's house."

"Someone called and said Parker needed my help."

"Parker?"

"The man at the house."

Bellamy reads a new text. Sends another message. "No doubt a prank call."

Olympia nods. "That might be. But now I have work to do." She returns her attention to the paper.

"I'm pregnant, Mom."

Olympia stares at her notes.

"Did you hear me, Mom? I'm pregnant."

She drops her pen. "You're not pregnant."

"I am."

"You can't be."

"I am."

Olympia studies her daughter, looks for some way to understand, to connect.

"How can you be sure?"

"Mom, I know my own body."

Olympia pushes herself to her feet. She stands, stares at a drawing of her future church, white stone, a spire like a lighthouse.

"Mom?"

She grabs her Bluetooth earpiece. She grabs her pen. She grabs her notepad and smashes it down on her daughter's head. She

R. H. Sheldon

marches out of the room, slamming the door behind her. She exits the church and stands on the narrow strip of lawn in front of the building.

No, it's not a new church that presents the biggest challenges to her faith. It's her daughter. Always her daughter.

Stephanie

Stephanie is about to do something she hoped she would never do again. A trip to the dentist would be nirvana in comparison, a tax audit, Shangri-La.

She climbs the steps onto Parker's front porch and knocks. The inside door is open, but only her echoes bounce out, like a baseball bat hitting a dead tree.

The screen hangs limply, held by a few staples at the bottom, ones Stephanie put in when she fixed the door for his mother. The door, like the house, was already in disrepair when he moved in. Now the place is beyond hope. Even the yard, which was tolerable enough, with its bits of grass and small flowering shrubs, has been transformed into a landfill and breeding ground for rats.

Stephanie knocks again.

Myron appears, Sonuvabitch slung over his shoulder. With his free hand, he lifts the screen and holds it in place and looks through it. "Hello, Stephanie."

Seeing him makes her feel less like a sacrifice. "Parker here?"

Myron shrugs. "Probably upstairs, but sometimes he forgets to come home."

"You don't have to hold up the screen," she says.

"I might fall out."

"Could you check?"

He nods. "You want to come in?"

R. H. Sheldon

Stephanie shakes her head. He lets go of the screen and turns away. She watches him climb the stairs that killed Parker's mother. Sonuvabitch eyes her throughout the ascent. When they're out of view, Stephanie pulls the screen into place and tries to fasten it, but without her tools, there's little she can do.

Parker's voice crashes down the stairs. "What the fuck you want? And what's that goddamn cat doing in here?"

Myron says something about gray skies and a visitor from next door. Parker lets loose a stream of curses. Stephanie swears she hears *dyke* and *bitch* and *neighbor*.

She doesn't have to put up with this crap. She thought she could help. She thought she could save his sorry ass. But nothing can save him. He's past being a train wreck. He's the rusted scraps dissolving into the tracks.

It's probably too late anyway. From what she could find out, Lockhart Investments does own his house. But here's the bigger surprise. Lockhart Investments also owns the lot next door to Parker and the house on the other side of the lot.

Three properties in all. Large lots at that, except hers. Enough to build one of those hideous apartment buildings like the one on the corner, the type the company is famous for.

Lockhart's thumbprint can be found from San Diego to the Canadian border, wherever they can erect cheap, tall, high-density apartments, always pushing the limits in terms of building size and construction quality, getting away with any shortcuts they can legally defend, while leaving in their wake neighborhoods disrupted and changed, if not outright destroyed. Their latest endeavor has been what they call *apodments*, tiny units that command outrageous rents, built without having to jump through many of the hoops that restrict regular apartments.

Parker might be losing his home, but it's Stephanie who'll suffer the consequences. The last thing this neighborhood needs is another densely populated building. The park has been bad enough, with its drug deals and muggings and armed robberies. More high-density apartments will only make it worse.

All because Parker was too stupid to hang on to a house already paid for.

She's not even sure why she came over here. Perhaps she hoped some part of him would rally enough to fight it. Even if he were willing, there's little he can do. It will be up to her to prevent any development. And without resources of her own, there's not a lot she can do either.

She's about to head home when she hears Parker's gravelly voice spill down the stairs. "What'd you find out?" He works his way down one step at a time, clutching the railing like a toddler.

She waits.

He creeps down the last few stairs and shuffles to the door. He wears sunglasses pulled low and his father's tattered, ill-fitting bathrobe.

"Well?"

She tells him what she's discovered about his house and the developers. He stares through the screenless door. He might be looking at her, but she can't be sure. His sunglasses point toward her, but for all she knows, he's fallen back to sleep.

"Your only hope is to get an attorney," she says.

"That's all?"

"What do you want me to say? You're up against a sleazy bunch of developers with lots of money and lots of their own lawyers."

She thinks for a moment he's about to make one of his smart-ass comments—and perhaps he was—but he instead picks at the hanging screen.

Even with his sunglasses, he looks tired and worn, more so than normal. And he looks sick, the kind of sick she'd seen in a lot of patients in the ER, people who entered the hospital breathing, but left as icy stiffs.

"I came up with one possibility. There are a few free legal service organizations in Seattle. Maybe they can help. But you'd have to act fast."

She's about to hand him the list of phone numbers but he breaks into a fit of coughing. His face contorts and he grabs his sides. She waits. He coughs and gasps and coughs some more. When the hacking subsides, he says, "Sign me up."

She wants to tell him to do it himself, but the way he stands there, his body bent, his bony arms sticking out of the sleeves, his skin that ashen gray, she instead says, "Let me make some calls."

He stares over her shoulder. She turns. Her heart races and she feels lightheaded. Georgia walks toward Parker's house. Her short salt-and-pepper hair bobs up and down. Her strong, thick legs carry her proudly up the sidewalk. Georgia. Georgia, home at last.

But it's not Georgia. It's a woman Stephanie has never seen, a woman the size and shape of Georgia, but that's about it.

R. H. Sheldon

She climbs the stairs and says, "Parker, I'm glad to find you home." Then she turns to Stephanie and offers a hand. "I'm Olympia Culpepper."

Stephanie shakes but feels nothing.

Parker raises his sunglasses and peaks at Olympia, then lowers them and says, "You're the woman from the bar."

Olympia smiles. "Is that all you remember?"

Parker rubs his neck and twists his head from side to side. "We talked, right?"

"I'd say."

"We didn't, ah..." He points at her and then at himself.

Olympia laughs, the sound a rusty nail. "Oh, dear, no." She studies him a moment. "You really don't remember, do you?"

Parker shakes his head in a manner that suggests he's already lost interest.

Stephanie feels the same way. "I'm heading home," she announces. She turns, gasps. Myron stands behind her, still holding Sonuvabitch. He's like a midnight fog, visible only when it passes by the light.

Myron glances at the screen door and says, "Back so soon, Stephanie?"

She shakes her head. "I never left."

Myron flashes a wide spread of teeth. His eyes glimmer from their dark depths.

Parker says, "If you'd all excuse me, I have to nurse a hangover."

"We need to talk," Olympia says.

"Hangover first." He turns and shuffles toward the stairs. He grabs the railing and creeps up one step at a time. He wheezes and puffs and coughs with every movement.

"Parker is sick," Myron says.

"He is sick," Olympia says.

Stephanie reaches through the door and pulls the screen into place. This time, she finds a staple dangling near the top, loose enough to pull out one side. She hooks the screen's frayed edge onto the staple, turns, and walks off the porch.

Parker

He takes each step with slow, methodical movements. Even at this pace, he can feel the pull in his lungs, the strain of his breath, wrapping him in a weariness that grows more stifling each day.

Ten years ago, he was diagnosed with the early stages of emphysema and warned to quit smoking and clean up his act. "No more cigarettes," the doctor said. "No more pot. No more liquor. No more pills. Except what I prescribe."

Parker shook his head, rubbed his neck, pulled at his ear.

"But, doctor," he said, "how can Parker stop being Parker?"

That was the last time he sought out medical advice.

He reaches the top landing, stops, clutches the banister, pants like a pit bull eying its prey.

When his air returns—what he likes to think of as his approximation to breathing—he heads into the hallway, a narrow and dark passageway made dingier by the tattered, yellowing wallpaper—a grotesque mix of asters and goldenrod—and the cheap pine tongue-and-groove wainscoting, mottled and faded and nicked up from the last four years of drunken mishaps.

He moves cautiously toward his bedroom. The same bedroom he had spent his years as a small boy and adolescent. The same room he had listened to the Beatles and the Doors and the Rolling Stones and the outrageous electric sounds of Jimi Hendrix. The same room he had slobbered over his father's *Hustler* and *Playboy*

R. H. Sheldon

and beat off until he was convinced his dick would fall off. So often did he masturbate, in fact, that he tried to find books in the library that might explain the risks he was taking and the damage he was doing, but he came across nothing to convince him to let up and saw little choice but to keep at it, just like he saw little choice but to keep smoking and drinking and popping pills and snorting coke and ingesting whatever organic and inorganic substances that came his way.

Parker doesn't consider himself a complete loss, though. Every few months or so, he tries to pull the plug on the liquor and pot and assortment of other substances—or at least ease up for a time—and he's worn so many patches he feels like a quilt. But eventually he falls back to his old ways, all the time swearing to whoever will listen that he can quit at any time and will do so as soon as the mood strikes.

What more can you expect from someone fated to be a rock-and-roll legend?

Parker's bedroom is small and plain. His mother had added the same insidious wallpaper and wainscoting in here as she had in the hallway, all of which happened long after he moved away, long after she removed any remnants of her son, remnants she either threw in the trash or put into boxes in the basement, except the record in the front hall.

When Parker moved back into the house, he took up residence in his old room. Not once did he consider settling into what had been his parents' room and then his mother's. In fact, he has rarely ventured into there in the last four years, and it is still filled with her Penney's clothes and Kmart jewelry and Walgreens perfume. Even her bed remains just as she had left it after she woke up that morning, straightened the covers, and tumbled down the stairs with a basket full of laundry.

Parker sits on his bed, still unmade. The only time he makes it up is when he washes his sheets. And the last time he washed his sheets was sometime in September.

Before Myron moved in, he washed them more often, but for some reason having a roommate seemed to justify a new level of laxity.

Myron started crashing here right after they met. Parker was playing at a club down in Pioneer Square. When it came time for a break, he retreated into the alley for a hit off his pipe. The night was dark and cold and as quiet as a graveyard, with a fog rolling in off the Sound and dampening the noise in the streets. Parker leaned against the brick wall and flicked the lighter and drew in the smoke. Just then, Myron stepped out of the shadows. Parker dropped the pipe and flattened himself against the wall. Myron picked up the pipe and handed it to Parker, despite his invisibility.

"We're living in cottage cheese," Myron said.

Parker puffed and watched Myron for signs of violence. "Why cottage cheese?"

"The curds, man. It's all about the curds." Then Myron disappeared into the shadows.

Later that night, Myron showed up in the club. When Parker finished playing, he bought Myron a soda and bitters. Myron had stopped drinking years before, he said. But Parker had not, so he downed a shot. And then another. And then a few more. When the bar closed, they returned to Parker's house and listened to a Grateful Dead CD that Myron had stashed in his green army fatigue jacket. Parker smoked and drank and grooved with the music. Myron fell asleep on the couch and has never quite woken up.

That was two years ago. And even that seems an eternity.

Parker feels about the same today as he did the morning after he met Myron. His gut rolls and sways and his head pounds like a jackhammer. He grabs a bottle of aspirin from the nightstand. He knows he shouldn't take this shit, not with *his* stomach, but he needs something. Anything.

He digs through the dozen or so bottles, most of them pharmaceuticals, none prescribed to him, finds the aspirin, and sets in on the cap, pushing and twisting and bending it back and forth. It pops off and summersaults to the floor. He reaches down to pick it up. The tablets spill out and scatter across the room, some rolling under the bed, some traveling all the way to the closet. He throws the bottle against the wall.

He reaches down to grab a few pills, but stops. He creeps upright. He stands. He drops on the bed. He feels like an airless balloon, flattened, drained.

He pulls another container off the nightstand, one of those without labels. He's been saving these for a special occasion, and today feels as special as any.

He pulls off the lid and pours four capsules onto the sheet, each a deep blue, with hints of purple, and bold black letters that read *KADIAN 50 mg*, like drops of paint against the pale blue expanse of cotton. He grabs the bottle of Jack Daniel's and swallows one of the pills. Then he swallows another. And another. And another. Until there is nothing left but the sea of blue, a calm soothing ocean that spreads into a horizon as endless and pure as the evening sky. He lies down and stretches across the sheets. He eases his eyes closed. He slows his breath and listens, until he feels the pull of the ocean and the sky and a heaven as long and dark as his past.

Alonzo

When Alonzo left Parker's house yesterday, he assumed—or at least hoped—he would not be returning to this area until next week. But now, in fewer than twenty-four hours, he's back on this miserable street with these miserable houses across from that miserable park—a gathering place for degenerates and derelicts, drunks and druggies, deviants and the assortment of delusional street denizens with no place to go but here.

But Saturday is a good day to present her with an offer. She can take the rest of the weekend to think it over, and he can take the rest of the weekend to have a life. It seems like months since he's had time with his family. Sometimes his girls look at him as though he were a stranger.

Alonzo parks up on Boxer Way, about the same place he parked yesterday, and walks down toward the house with the picket fence. He carries a white, legal-sized envelope that includes the offer letter to Stephanie Schmidt. The letter outlines what Lockhart Investments is proposing and what actions to take. If they can reach a tentative agreement, the official paperwork will follow. With any luck, the mass of details won't scare her away, assuming they can get that far.

He crosses Eleventh, makes a quick detour toward Tenth. All is quiet. No women peaking around the apartment building. No ape-

R. H. Sheldon

man sitting in the weeds. No Parker Davis standing naked in his yard. Perhaps this day won't be so bad after all.

He heads to the home of Stephanie Schmidt. A breeze scurries across the street and scatters debris around his ankles. Voices drift in from the park, but then the air grows still and he hears only the hum of distant traffic. He opens the gate and creeps into her yard, praying Cujo isn't lurking in the shadows.

He stops and surveys the property. The garden has a lush, earthy feel, a tiny Eden, removed from the influences of the park or the street or even her neighbors. Before him stands an assortment of shrubs and trees and female statues, religious artifacts of some sort, mostly naked.

Despite the yard's tiny size, it's still a fine space, quiet and peaceful and a world apart from Parker Davis. Alonzo wouldn't mind having such a retreat. He wouldn't mind having any place he could call his own, even if it were nothing but a room in the basement. But a spot like this garden—that would be ideal.

Too bad it will all be plowed under.

He reaches the front door and knocks. This is the moment he hates the most. He's had people spit at him and sic dogs on him and swing baseball bats at him and point guns at him. Even in cases like this, when making on offer, rather than serving an eviction notice, he's usually greeted first with hostility. If the homeowner likes the offer, civility might follow. But the rest will scoff at the price or dig in their heels for reasons of principle or sentiment or sheer stubbornness.

The front door opens. A woman appears. She wears a red baseball cap. Thin strands of gray stream out from the edges and wrap around large, floppy ears.

"I'm Alonzo Garcia," he says, "an attorney with Higgins, Whitaker & Nye. I'm looking for Stephanie Schmidt."

She eyes him as she would a serial killer. "So you're the one."

He clears his throat. "Our firm represents Lockhart Investments."

"What do you want her for?"

She has a hard face, free of make-up, mapped with heavy lines that spread from the corners of her eyes, a soft blue that contradicts the stern exterior.

"I need to speak with Ms. Schmidt," he says.

She's not a large woman, but with the way she blocks the doorway and glowers down at him, he feels smaller than ever. Being a short man has few advantages, especially as an attorney.

She shoots him a mean look and is about to say something, then stops. She shifts from one leg to the other. She crosses her arms. "I'm Stephanie Schmidt."

He knows the type, can see it in every pore. She can spot bullshit before it comes out.

"Lockhart Investments would like to purchase your home."

"My home?" She drops her arms.

"As you might already know, Lockhart recently purchased the house next door to you."

Her nostrils flare.

"Lockhart has also purchased the lot and the house on the other side of your neighbor's home."

"Get to the point."

He steps back. He thinks about that space to call his own. No jackets. No ties. No stiff-collared shirts.

He wishes for a lot of things these days.

"Lockhart hopes to build an apartment building in this area. If they can acquire your house as well, they will have most of the block on this side of the street, enough room to build a very impressive complex."

"I've seen their handiwork."

"It's a fair offer, Ms. Schmidt."

"Go to hell. I'm not selling."

"But Ms. Schmidt..."

"And you can tell those clowns that I'll do everything I can to fight their development. I know exactly the type of crap that company builds." She pulls back into the house.

"Wait, Ms. Schmidt, please..."

"Get the hell out of here or I'm calling the police."

"Don't you want to hear the offer?"

"No!" She slams the door.

"Seven-seventy-five," he yells. "Seven-hundred-seventy-five-thousand dollars." He stares at the closed door, a rough cedar with a long graceful grain that weaves through the wood.

Several seconds pass. She opens the door slowly and gazes out. "How much?"

"Seven-hundred-seventy-five-thousand dollars."

She leans against the door jam and stares out to her yard. "That much?"

"Lockhart wants to act quickly," he says. "There's a time limit on the offer, of course. Five days."

"That's so much." Her voice has grown wispy and soft.

"Yes," he says. "Plenty for you to move and get resettled. It's a fair offer."

"Fair?"

He hands her the envelope. "Let's talk on Monday. You can think about it over the weekend."

"Yes, Monday." She closes the door.

He turns and heads toward the street, brushing against the rhododendron, a leaf scraping his cheek. He walks up Boxer Way toward Twelfth. He reaches his car and presses the remote and climbs inside. He starts the engine and switches on the stereo. Johannes Brahms. *A German Requiem.* He eases away from the curb and turns right on Twelfth, but pulls over as soon as he sees the ambulance racing toward him.

Bellamy

Bellamy Burns-Culpepper sits on the bed in her tiny bedroom in the far corner of the tiny two-bedroom apartment, which hangs off the tiny brick church like an oblong wart. Bellamy is applying another layer of black lacquer to her fingernails. She wants them to be just right when she adds the finishing touch—an astrological symbol on each finger. She hasn't quite figured out how that will work, though, with twelve sun signs and only ten nails. She can use a couple toes, she supposes, but somehow that doesn't seem right.

Bellamy applies the final touch and picks up her cell phone, careful not to bump the nails. She dials Crystal's number. Crystal is her best friend. They've been best friends since grade school. In high school, they were inseparable, until Bellamy dropped out.

Crystal grew up in a Methodist household but no longer attends church with her family. She now attends Bellamy's church—that is, her mom's church. Most of Crystal's family think Bellamy and her mom and the church are totally weird, but Crystal thinks they're all kind of cool, especially Bellamy's mom, at least that's what Crystal says.

Bellamy would never tell anyone what she really thinks.

Crystal answers. "Hi, Bell."

"Did you watch it?"

"O-M-G. That was like the most awesome video I ever saw. Fondeaux is a genius."

"Ahead of her time. That's what I read online. Way ahead of her time."

"I mean, like the way she uses the dildo for a microphone."

"Not just any dildo. A humongous black one!"

"So amazingly cool."

Bellamy eyes her laptop, sitting on the black midget desk in the corner. The Fondeaux video plays, the sound turned low, a buzzing murmur. Fondeaux grips the dildo with both hands, sings into its wide, bulging head.

Bellamy waves her free hand, blows on the nails.

"I saw a chick on Chaturbate last night do something just like that, but with the real thing."

"Bellamy!"

"You should have seen it."

"I'd never go on that site. If my parents caught me, they'd kick me out."

"Jesus, Crystal, you're almost twenty-one. It's just sex."

"They don't know what that is."

Bellamy switches hands and blows on her fingers. She waits, gives the silence a chance to work. Then she says, "I told her."

"Told her? Told Fondeaux?"

"No, you retard. I told my mom."

"About?"

"Yes."

"O-M-G. How did she take it?"

"It's like she totally freaked."

"*Your* mom?"

"She even hit me."

"What?"

"She hit me."

"Your mom hit you?"

"She got like all majorly pissed. I can always tell. Her Texas roots come out."

"I just can't imagine your mom..."

"Maybe that's why she got like all violent."

"Being from Texas?"

"No, you dumbass. The abuse stuff. She's got all this anger shit 'cause her father abused her. Or uncle or brother or something. I doubt she's been with anyone since my dad."

"You met your dad? Did you get his name?"

If Crystal were here, Bellamy would slap her.

"No, Crystal, I did not meet my father, which means I did not get his name."

"And your mom still won't tell you who he his."

Bellamy switches the phone to the other ear. "All she says is that he wasn't interested in kids. She probably added *Burns* to my name just to piss him off."

"I forget. Why Burns?"

"I've told you a thousand times. My grandmother's maiden name." Bellamy switches the phone back and blows on her nails. "Or maybe my mom was trying to piss off my grandfather for the abuse stuff."

"Then she should have changed her own name."

Bellamy hesitates. Crystal might have a point, something Bellamy seldom thinks about her friend.

Bellamy says, "I hope I don't have a concussion."

"Why would you have a concussion?"

"Haven't you heard anything? My mom beat me over the head."

"She really hit you? Really, I mean, you sure it wasn't an accident? Did she even say anything?"

"Not a word. Slammed me over the head with her book and stormed out of the room. I think she's getting all senile in her old age. You think I should see a doctor?"

"About the baby?"

"About my head!" Bellamy should just hang up on this moron.

"Still, I mean, it doesn't even sound like your mom."

"I've got the scars to prove it."

Bellamy stands and looks into a narrow mirror on the back of the door, trying to decide whether to go for a darker shade of lipstick. She wipes her lower lip with her little finger, careful not to touch the nail. "I just hope the baby's alright."

"You gonna keep it?"

"I am now."

Crystal sighs. Bellamy can picture her sitting there, trying to think up something clever to say, or at least not so dumb. Finally, Crystal says, "But what are you gonna do? I mean, like a baby and all. What will you do?"

Bellamy shrugs and switches hands. "I was thinking of getting a job, save up some money."

"What about adoption?"

"Adoption? Why should I adopt? I'm already having a baby."

"No, Bell, I mean, you putting the baby up for adoption."

Bellamy lifts her skirt and studies the top of her hip. The skin is peeling around her new crucifix tattoo, the wounds and blood the most prominent feature. She places her hand on the tattoo. The heat warms her palm. "I don't know," she says. "I don't think I could do that. Besides, that could be pretty awesome, having a kid around."

"You tell her about the father?"

"We didn't get that far."

"Does *he* know?"

"How could he? After that fight, he swore he'd never come near me."

"You broke his finger."

"He tried to rape me."

"I was there, Bell."

Bellamy drops on her bed and lies against the pillows. "Whatever. All I know is, he hasn't been back to church since. He gave my mom some lame excuse about spending time with relatives."

"I think you should tell her."

"And have her find out we were partying in the church?"

"It was more than just partying."

"Exactly. Besides, what difference does it make now? He's disappeared and she's totally flipped out. It's just me and the baby now."

"A baby."

"Yeah, a baby."

Myron

Myron has not ridden in a car in fourteen years. Myron walks and strolls and saunters and sometimes rides in buses, but he does not travel by car. At least not until now.

After the ambulance came and went, Olympia insisted that Myron ride to the hospital with her, "in case Parker gets admitted, if it comes to that."

"If it comes to what?" he asked.

She started the car.

Myron now sits in this miniature seat, wedged between the door and Olympia, zooming past parked cars and people on the sidewalks.

He does not like the sense of speed or the nearness to the ground. The tight inhibiting quarters make him feel like a cucumber about to be pickled. He pulls in his shoulders and slouches into the seat, hoping the space around him will grow.

Olympia speeds south on Eleventh past Cal Anderson Park to Pine Street. She runs the red light, races to Pike, runs the stop sign, races to Union, runs the next stop sign, and flies around the corner toward the hospital.

"They're taking him to the Elliott Bay ER," she says. She still wears that device in her ear, a small blue growth on her lobes.

"Elliott. I like that name."

"Elliott Bay," she says.

R. H. Sheldon

"Hospitals make people sick."

She turns toward him, but doesn't slow down. "How did you know? He never said anything."

"Know?"

"How did you know something was wrong with Parker? What tipped you off?"

Myron tries to make sense of her question, but the rush of curbs and sidewalks and parked cars makes him think of being sick at a carnival.

When they reach Broadway, Olympia zooms across. Luckily, the light is green. At the next intersection, she curves to the left and then to the right, following the main flow of traffic onto Seneca, slowing little when she passes through the intersection. Car horns honk and a man on a bike yells out that she's a goddamn lunatic.

"How did you suddenly know Parker needed you? What did you hear?"

He peers out the window toward the top of the trees. He doesn't know how to answer her. He doesn't know how to explain a room that loses its air. He says, "It's what I didn't hear."

The sound of a harp echoes through the car. Olympia touches her earpiece and speaks into the windshield. "I can't talk right now." She pauses. "What was that? Puke? Duke? Oh, rebuke." She listens. Myron hears only a buzz. "No, I shouldn't think so. Have him do the breathing exercises I showed you." Olympia glances in the mirror. "Fine, we'll discuss it tomorrow."

She touches the earpiece again and hits the gas. The apartment buildings blur into a wall of brown and gray, reminding him of a military compound. She picks up speed. A hazy light shimmers through the trees. He closes his eyes. The light pokes at his face like a thousand miniature needles.

The car swerves. Tires screech. His eyes pop open. A truck is stopped at the intersection, where Seneca crosses Boren, its bumper inches from their car. Olympia waves, smiles, continues across Boren. The hospital looms large on their left. She pulls over to the right and parks.

"You have any quarters?" she asks.

"In my pocket I keep one," he says.

She digs through her purse, pulls out a fist full of coins, and climbs out of the car. He follows and stands next to her. He looks down at the concrete. He makes an offering to the sidewalk.

They rush across the street, toward the emergency room entrance.

"I'm going to do something about this," she says.

"Good," he replies.

"A call to action."

"Yes," he says, "a call to action."

"We can't let them get away with this."

"No, we can't." He looks up at the surrounding buildings, towers of concrete and glass, holding the sky at bay, a shield against the encroaching horizon, everything in check, at least for today, at least for now.

R. H. Sheldon

Stephanie

Stephanie spots Myron as soon as she walks into the waiting room. He sits by the huge aquarium, his face glued to the glass, standing out like Jerry Garcia at a Young Republican's convention.

The room is fairly crowded, about what she'd expect on a Saturday afternoon, the assortment of sick and injured, their friends and families, all waiting to be seen and heard, some with desperate, confused looks, others, merely impatient.

Large double doors mark the entrance to the ER, protecting the space where Stephanie spent the better part of twenty-five years. Well, not exactly *this* space. The ER got moved around a couple times. But wherever it was, it long enough.

She hasn't been back since her last day of work.

She wonders whether she could take the pace of the ER now. Even after so short a time, the thought of that constant barrage of injuries and ailments, the ODs, the drunks, the verbal assaults, the physical threats, the puke and blood and urine and shit—all of it. By the time she left, she was ready to give it up. She just hadn't expected to face retirement so alone.

Myron must have seen her reflection in the fish tank. He stands and waves his arms above his head and calls her name. Those near him turn and stare. He smiles with an oblivious look.

Stephanie works her way through the flutter of people and stands before Myron.

He says, "Hello, Stephanie," and sits down.

The woman she met earlier—Olympia?—sits next to him. In this light, she doesn't look anything like Georgia. Yet there's something about the way she sits, the way she holds herself, the proud certainty, an air of smugness, that seems somehow familiar. In the right circumstances, at the right distance, Stephanie could easily make the same mistake again.

Myron says, "He's in there," and points toward the doors.

"We haven't heard anything yet," Olympia says. "But they know we're waiting. We checked in at the desk. I told them twice we're out here."

"Yes, they know," Myron says. "And now you're here. Isn't that right?"

"Yes, Myron. I'm here."

"Good," he says and grins at the fish.

When Stephanie worked in the ER, she saw every imaginable type of patient, from those living in the streets to high-tech billionaires. They came in all shapes and sizes and ages and races, some models of good health, suffering a temporary setback, others barely breathing or thinking or remembering, many not leaving alive. But throughout all that, she never met anyone like Myron. Nowhere, in fact, has she ever met anyone like Myron. One moment, he seems as simple as a child, at other times, as deep and wide as the Mississippi.

Stephanie pulls a chair over to the other two and sits down. She still has no idea who this Olympia is or where she came from or what's she's doing here now. Perhaps she's one of Parker's groupies from back in his heyday. Or maybe he owes her money, like he does most everyone else.

"She belongs to the church," Myron says. Then he turns toward Olympia. "I have questions for you about what you said in that little booklet of yours."

"Parker goes to a church?"

Olympia frowns. "It's nothing like that."

"The Lighthouse Sanctification Church," Myron announces. He speaks the words slowly, as though reading them for the first time.

"Yes," Olympia says, "but no, Parker does not come there. And I don't think now is the time…"

"It's not far from where Parker lives," Myron says. "Not far from you. From me. In the Central District, across Madison. Isn't that right, Olympia?"

Olympia taps a finger on the arm of the chair. "Perhaps we can find out what's going on with Parker."

Stephanie stands. "Let me see what I can do."

She heads toward the ER and pushes through the large doors. The bustling complex assaults her senses, the glaring lights, overflowing cubicles, nurses racing from bed to bed, station to station, the rush of techs and aides and physicians, the beeps and whirls and hum of machines, the clanging metal, screams and moans, the IVs, the carts, the gurneys and wheelchairs.

What was she thinking? She doesn't belong back here, not any more. But here she is, amid the frightened patients and racing technicians and sour antiseptic smell that permeated her clothes and nostrils for all those years.

She weaves through the rushing bodies and equipment and lands at the central desk.

Roger stands behind the counter, a nurse she worked with for many years. When he sees her, he flashes a frenzied smile. "Stephanie, my long lost chum. What brings you back to Never-Never Land?"

"I've returned."

"No! You haven't given up already?"

She chuckles. "Not to worry. Just forgot my place for a moment."

"A lot of that going around." He nods toward one of the doctors, a baby-faced intern with an officious, nervous look.

"Some things never change."

"So what does bring you back, Steph, ol' girl? Feeling nostalgic? Or did you decide to renew your license and give it another go?"

She laughs. "License still good. I can nurse forever."

"Must be nostalgia."

"Only for you."

"I should have guessed."

"But I could use your help, Roger."

"Ah, now we get to it. That will take more flattery."

"While I try to come up with a fitting retort, perhaps you could get me an update on one of your patients. Parker Davis. Showed up in the last hour or so."

Roger lets out a *tsk, tsk, tsk,* glances over his shoulder, and feigns a conspiratorial look. "I shouldn't, you know."

"I know."

He grins and plugs the name into the computer. "Behind door number two. Let me see what I can find out that I'm really not finding out because that would be less than professional, not to mention illegal."

He smiles and moves out from behind the desk and heads toward the second station, then slips through the closed curtains.

The ER spins in a whirlpool of activity. She'd forgotten what a circus this place could be. How could she have spent so many hours here, so many years? It certainly doesn't evoke any sense of nostalgia, nor does she feel any regret for leaving, only gratefulness that she was able to get out when she did. She has friends who could never quite adjust to retirement, but she'll never be one of those. And being here now only reinforces her decision, not only because of the chaotic pace, but also because of how out of place and obsolete she feels standing here. It doesn't matter what her life had been like or how important a part she had played. That time is over and she must accept it, and acknowledge she was ready to make the change.

Even so, she can't help feeling she's been put out to pasture.

Roger squeezes out from behind the curtains and returns to the desk. "Not much new. Still unresponsive, though he seems stable for now."

"Any idea what's going on?"

"He took something, but no one knows what or how much. Some type of opiate, we think. Alcohol, too. We've pumped his stomach and found evidence of what looks like a time-released narcotic. Got any ideas?"

"With him, it could be anything. And everything."

"So we wait."

"Yeah, we wait."

She returns to the fish tank and tells Myron and Olympia what she's learned. Olympia asks why Parker would have taken the pills. Myron shrugs. So does Stephanie. She has no idea why Parker does anything. Certainly, he was aware of the risks of mixing narcotics with alcohol, but she can't imagine Parker doing himself in. He's much too ornery.

"There's no telling what he was thinking," Stephanie says, and then the conversation moves to the situation with the house, and Stephanie tells Olympia what she learned about the law firm and the investment company.

Olympia pulls out a small pad and jots down a few notes. With each stroke she grows more agitated. If she wrote any harder, the paper would ignite. In a flurry of motion, she slams the pad shut and leaps to her feet. "No sense me waiting here, too. I've got things to do. If you learn anything, please let me know." She shoves a business card into Stephanie's hand and races for the door.

Stephanie nods and sets the card next to the fish tank. Myron picks it up and studies it and sticks in it in pocket. Stephanie still has no idea what that woman was doing here, but can't help feeling a sense of relief that she's gone.

Stephanie asks Myron if he knows what Parker took.

"Pills," Myron says. "He took pills."

"What kind of pills?"

"Pills he should not have taken?"

"Did you see them?"

Myron closes his eyes. His lids flutter slightly and he shakes his head. Then he opens them and says, "Parker should rest. For a long time, I think."

"Maybe that's what he had in mind."

Myron looks at Stephanie as though he's just discovered a new species. "Are you going to sell, Stephanie? Are you going to sell your house?"

"But how—"

"Are you?"

She turns toward the aquarium. "I don't know what I'm doing." A tropical fish the size of her hand, covered in iridescent blue and green scales, flicks its tail and scoots beneath a pile of rocks, leaving behind a trail of bubbles.

Alonzo

A t last, Alonzo gets to spend a Saturday afternoon at home, the rest of the weekend, in fact—no files, no paperwork, no phone calls.

He's down in the basement, in what they call the family room, with his three daughters and year-old boxer, Roscoe. Roscoe chews on a Barbie doll, the one with spiked heels and elegant evening wear and long blond hair piled on her head like a beehive. Elena, the seven-year-old, cries and pulls at the Barbie. Roscoe growls and shakes his head and digs his teeth deeper. Julia, nearly ten, yells for Elena and Roscoe to shut up so she can watch her movie about vampires and werewolves in the murky woods of western Washington. After Julia turned nine, she announced she would have nothing to do with dolls, and now rolls her eyes whenever Elena mentions anything to do with Barbie. Teresa, twelve-years-old-going-on-twenty, says nothing. She's pouting because she wants to go to the mall with her friends, but Alonzo is making her stay home to have family time with him and her screaming sisters.

Three girls, each one with striking dark eyes and dark hair and skin the color of molasses, each one spoiled and pampered and a handful in her own right, each one a joy and blessing and a reminder of why he works as hard as he does, why he sacrifices so much—so they can know lives better than what he knew, what Isabel knew, what their parents knew.

R. H. Sheldon

He tried to get his wife to stay home as well, but ever since Isabel turned thirty, she's become distant and secretive and treats him like an intruder. When he suggested an afternoon of family time, she insisted on visiting her sister in Seattle. She needs my help, Isabel said, but he knew she mainly wanted to get away from the kids and the house and him.

Teresa decides to break her silence. "Daddy, you promised me my own cell phone."

"When did I promise that?"

"Well, it wasn't exactly you. It was more Mom."

"Why do you need a cell phone?"

"How can you even ask? It's like all the kids have their own phones. At least all the kids whose parents care what happens to them."

"Teresa, honey, you know how expensive those things are."

"Everybody's got one. I'm about the only girl in middle school without a cell phone. Do you know what it's like to be different from everyone else?"

Elena screams. Alonzo turns toward her. The dog shakes his head wildly. Blond curls stream through the air. "Roscoe, let go of the doll."

Julia yells, "If she's getting a phone, I want one too!"

Roscoe runs to the far end of the room and then back, trying to get Elena to chase him.

"What if there's another one of those school shootings, Daddy? How would you feel then? Everybody calling home to tell their parents they love them, and I'd get shot before I could tell anyone anything."

"Teresa, please."

One day, she'll make a fine lawyer, much better than he'll ever be.

"Mom said I could have one."

"We'll see," Alonzo says. "I can't promise anything."

"Don't forget me," Julia shouts. "Now everybody be quiet."

"But Mom said..."

"We'll see."

She crosses her arms and drops back into the chair, her face resuming its pointed pouting.

Elena screams again, pulls off her shoe, and whacks Roscoe over the head. The dog yelps and lets go the Barbie. It's covered in dirt and drool.

"Yech, look what he did to my doll." She lobs it across the room and Roscoe chases after it.

"Shut up," Julia shouts. "Everybody just shut up."

"Elena. Julia. Let's all settle down."

"Why can't I go to the mall? It's Saturday. All my friends are at the mall."

"I thought we could do something together," he says. "Maybe go to Marymoor Park. Play Frisbee or something."

"That's so lame," Teresa says.

"I want to watch my movie. I don't want to go to the park."

Elena sings, "The park, the park, let's all go to the park."

Teresa leaps up from the couch. "I am *not* going to the park. I am *not*." She runs up the stairs and stomps across the kitchen and flees to the second floor. Her steps echo through the basement like a beating drum.

"The park, the park, let's all go to the park."

"I don't want to go to the park. I want to watch my movie." Julia turns up the volume.

Elena grabs the Barbie and throws it across the room. Roscoe barks and sprints after it.

Alonzo's cell phone rings. The tones are like the bells at St. Louise Church, where they attend mass every Sunday. He checks the caller ID. Blocked. He shouldn't answer it. He knows he shouldn't. But what if it's Isabel? What if she needs his help?

He takes the call.

A woman says, "I'm looking for Alonzo Garcia." She has an official sounding voice that sends an icy wave up his spine.

"I'm Alonzo," he says. His throat feels like rubber.

"Well, *Alonzo*, I'll have you know you'll not get away with this. You won't."

"Away with what? Who is this?"

"You'll soon find out."

"Is this about Isabel? Where's Isabel? Let me talk to Isabel."

"Don't try to stall me, *Alonzo*. I know how your type operates. Rest assured that I'll do anything I can to stop you. *Anything!* People like us will not put up with people like you any longer. You're nothing but parasites. Pariah. Do you hear me, Mr. *Alonzo* Garcia? Do you hear me? Your days are numbered!"

Part III

I thought how unpleasant it is to be locked out;
and I thought how it is worse, perhaps, to be locked in.
—Virginia Woolf

Olympia

The next day, Sunday, Olympia stands at the lectern before her congregation, waiting for Clara Winnable to finish playing "This Land Is Your Land," one of about a dozen old folk songs she digs up for the service every week, her voice as off key as the strings on her guitar, like a sparrow choking on a grasshopper in mid-warble.

Clara wears a pink hijab that covers most of her sparkling red hair. Last month it was dreadlocks. The month before, a black hoodie.

One day, Olympia will have a church big enough to support a real choir, maybe even hire a director and bring in a couple musicians. But she has much yet to accomplish.

That's not to say she hasn't made progress. More people show each week, and each week she raises more money, putting as much of it as she can in the new building fund. But she still has far to go, too far to allow herself to get mired in the immensity of it all. She just needs to hang in there and not think about it too much. The faithful keep coming, more than ever. That's all that matters.

She looks around the church, at the expectant faces, full of hope, full of faith, trusting in what she says and how she believes. She can feel nothing but gratitude from such a response, even a sense of honor, infusing her with optimism and hope. But she's a realist. She knows too they'll leave here unchanged, except for one or two perhaps, and those one or two are the reason she keeps at it.

Today, however, she needs more from them, from all of them. Today she has to move more minds, more hearts, more mountains.

Bellamy sits in the back row, barely visible behind the people squeezed into the pews. She snuck in right after the service began, with a look as guilty as her father used to get. It was that look, more than anything, that convinced Olympia it was time for him to leave.

But Olympia can't focus on Bellamy right now. No matter how stupid her daughter's behavior, Olympia has to let it go. Let her go. It's time she learned to act like an adult, especially with a baby coming. Jesus. Even the thought makes Olympia cringe. But she's got to forget all that right now. She's got to stay on her mission. They have only a small window of opportunity.

"Friends," she says, "I want to tell you a story about a man I met last week."

Some in the congregation sit up straighter, exaggerate their serene smiles and peaceful countenance.

"The man I'm talking about lives in a small house not far from here, a house that has been in his family for generations, a house that is falling apart all around him—because of age and neglect and lack of money.

"The man I'm talking about is sixty years old. He's in failing health and can't afford doctors or tests or medications or treatments. He can't afford utility bills or food bills or any other bills. He especially can't afford his mortgage.

"The man I'm talking about is close to losing his home. Through no fault of his own, the bank has pulled it out from under him and sold it to a big developer whose headquarters are in *Bellevue*." She waits for the looks of disdain, held in check, but there.

"The developer is now kicking the man out of his home, his family's home, even though he has no place to go. In three days, he must be out. Three days. That's all the time they've given him to move. Imagine being told you have three days to move. Imagine being sick and broke and alone and forced from the place where you grew up. Imagine."

The congregants remain silent, focused, heads nodding in quiet ascent. Peace fills Olympia like a ray of sunshine, pouring through them and into her heart. A purpose fulfilled, at one with her surroundings.

"The developer plans to tear down the man's house and the houses that surround it. The developer plans to build yet another high-density high-rise apartment building, without regard to the

R. H. Sheldon

people living nearby or what will happen to their neighborhood. And this man, a man about to lose his home, a man without money or a place to live, a man in ill health who can't afford medical care, will be forced to live in the streets. Where else is such a man to go?"

This is where the pause is most critical. Give them time to think about the question, imagine the answer, a trick she learned years ago, back when she was first ordained, from a crusty old minister who hated the idea of women in the pulpit, but happily accepted them in his bed.

It's a tricky balance, though, these lengthy pauses. Go too far and they start coming to their own conclusions.

"Without his neighbors to help him, to save him from this cruel injustice, the man will likely take his last breath in a gutter somewhere close to here. And we, my friends, will be just as guilty as the banks and the developers and the lawyers who put him there. We will share in the responsibility for their crimes. We will have the same blood on our hands, the same scars on our hearts."

That hit home. She can see it in the flush of their faces, the downcast angle of their eyes. The spirit surges through her, courses through her veins, nerves tingling with anticipation, filling her with a newfound sense of direction and purpose and hope. She wonders if Joan of Arc felt this way when she heard the voice of the angels and saints.

"My friends, the time comes in all our lives when we must take a stand against the injustices of the world around us, when we cannot continue to sit by complacently while our friends and neighbors are treated in such an undignified, uncaring, and undeserving manner.

"My friends, I have prayed and meditated about this man and his condition for many hours, and I have heard the voice of the Divine, the voice of the greater universal truth that guides all of us. And what I heard came through as clear as the ring of a lone bronze chime on a crisp winter morning.

"My friends, no longer can I sit idly by while the wheels of injustice roll over the weak and disadvantaged and innocent. No longer can I pretend to care but do nothing to show that care. No longer can I swear by a compassionate heart, but hold that heart clenched in fear. I must stand up for what is right. I must stand up for the greater good. I must stand up against all who would spread injustice and fear and greed."

Olympia draws in a long deep breath, lets out the air in a measured rhythm, counting the heads in the first row, another old trick she learned in divinity school. Keep them waiting, ready for the next.

One more breath.

"Such a stand is not easy, my friends. I have to hold firm to my spiritual resolve, yet maintain courage in the face of those who would overthrow that resolve. But I can find courage in the people who fought bravely before me and who stand beside me now, those who have faced the same struggle but have resolved to be true to their higher selves as they served the needs of the greater good.

"My friends, I ask of you now something I've never asked before. I ask that you stand beside me in our struggle against those who would darken all our spirits. I ask that you march with me to fight for the rights of people like this man so they can keep their homes and receive medical care and be free from lives of poverty. Make no mistake. A war is being waged against the poor and the infirm and the underprivileged. A war that makes poverty and sickness and disability a crime.

"I ask that you join me in this fight against injustice and fear, march with me arm-in-arm against corporate greed and corruption of the soul. But do not join me out of hatred and fear. Join me carrying the torch of truth that has blessed all of us. Tap into your own universal consciousness and use the limitless love available to everyone in order to aid our fellow human in his time of need. Only together can we move with one voice and one heart and show the world that our power is not only in numbers, but also in the truth and beauty and the universal love that is an innate part of everything we are.

"My friends, let us help this man. Let us help this Parker Davis. Let us show the world that a new age is upon us and the old ways no longer have a place in our hearts or in our minds or in our souls. Let us act in the name of righteousness and freedom and truth. I am heading into battle, my friends, and I need each of you by my side."

R. H. Sheldon

Parker

P arker wakes. He gazes through slitted eyes over his blanketed toes and across the room toward a half-opened door. Snot-colored walls glare with the harsh fluorescent lights, spilling down into an icy spread of linoleum tiles that flow out of the room. Even the dull blue blanket is an assault not to be endured.

Parker's sluggish brain kicks into gear long enough to deduce that the bed in which he lies is not his own and is in fact strikingly similar to the sort of bed one finds in a hospital. To add credence to his observation, Parker also realizes that next to the bed stands not a particularly thin barmaid, but rather a tall, mechanical-looking IV pole that holds a bag of clear solution and from that solution runs a tube that winds down toward the bed and disappears beneath a wide bandage on his arm. Parker notices too the plexus of wires twisting out from the covers and connecting to the nearby monitor, its beep lethargic and slightly irregular.

I must be alive, he thinks, feeling neither indifference nor concern. What he does feel is a balloon wedged in his skull, inflated enough to dull his senses and inhibit the sharp intake of thought, but not enough to ward off what continues to be one hell of a monster headache.

A man pushes open the door and walks into the room, a nurse it would seem, and glances at the monitor and then at the IV and finally at Parker. A lumberjack in pajamas, the same blue as Parker's blanket.

"You're awake," he says.

"Perhaps," Parker replies.

"How do you feel?"

"Like the inside of a garbage truck."

"Never been in one."

"Nothing to write home about."

The nurse takes Parker's wrist, a twig in comparison to his bear claw. "You remember anything?"

"I remember a killer headache," Parker says. "I remember lying down for a nap."

"Anything else?"

"I think I was flying."

"You do a lot of flying?"

The nurse slips a plastic sheath over an electronic thermometer and sticks it into Parker's mouth. The plastic is thin and tasteless and soon covered in slime. In a few seconds, the thermometer beeps and the nurse removes it.

"Am I alive?"

"Barely."

"Good enough. But a cigarette would be nice."

The nurse chokes out a three-syllable laugh. "Yeah, you bet. I'll get right on that."

"Lucky Strikes."

"Lucky you. But first, you happen to recall taking some pills?"

"Pills?"

"Before you went beddy-bye."

Parker wipes his hand across his chin, feeling the scrape of bristles in his palms. "Something with a K?"

"That narrows it down."

"Kaspian?"

"As in the sea?"

"Kadian?"

"Ah."

Parker pulls at one of the wires connected to his chest. "And that would have been when?"

"Before you laid down for your nap. Before you were brought here."

"Where's here?"

"Elliott Bay. You got a room with no view."

Parker glances out the window. Rooftop, vents, stretches of tar. "Lovely."

The nurse checks the IV.

"Then how did I get here?

"By ambulance, I imagine. Sometime yesterday."

"Yesterday?" Shit. That means he didn't make it to the club last night. That means he lost a whole night's wages. That means he probably doesn't have a job.

"You recall anything else about yesterday morning?"

"Of course. I mean, I remembered the pills."

"And you took those because?"

"As I said, killer headache."

"And the liquor?"

"Got rid of my headache, didn't it?" Parker snickers. He can't tell whether the nurse is disinterested or disgusted.

"And why would you have done that, booze on top of pills?"

"Be hard not to."

"You do that often?"

"You mean drink? I've had a few in my time."

"I mean liquor and narcotics."

Parker shrugs. How's he supposed to remember every little thing he does? He's lucky he remembers to get up in the morning. "What's going on here? Why all the questions?"

"Just making sure we know what happened."

"Sounds like you know more than I do."

"That's how it usually works."

Myron

Myron sits on the front porch, his feet bare, planted on the first step, icy against the wet plank, Sonuvabitch in his lap, purring like a hurricane. Myron can feel it coming, a stirring in the air, like a cool breeze that drifts off the mountain. Before him lies the sidewalk and beyond that the road and its assortment of parked cars and beyond the cars Cal Anderson Park, the usual mix of students and street kids and junkies and parents and toddlers and pets.

Stretching out from his feet stands a mix of dried weeds and blackberry brambles and beer cans and deteriorating shreds of unopened mail and composting trash. Yet what he sees are not the objects themselves, not exactly, but the moments that make them possible, the brief push of life that culminates in wood and paper and metal and concrete and grass and rock, fleeting gasps no more substantial than the air before him.

Myron sits, his feet firmly planted on the splintered wood. He sits and waits and watches.

The clouds thicken, bloom, spill in from the west. The wind gusts in spurts, stirring the leaves and trash, then falls silent. A smell he does not recognize fills the air, not the smell of ozone, as he might expect, but something heavier, thicker, like the smell of an oil drum burning on the side of the road.

R. H. Sheldon

Stephanie steps out from her yard and moves toward him. She, too, can feel the change. He can see it in the way she walks, her body bent forward, as though rushing into the space before her.

When she reaches him, he says, "You can't move that way."

"What way?" Her voice sounds tired, tentative. The air around her vibrates in a subtle shift of colors, almost imperceptible, visible only from the corner of his eye.

She says, "I called the hospital. Parker is awake and stable, or at least as stable as can be expected."

"I know," he says.

"How do you know?"

"I know."

"You always know, don't you, Myron?" The air pulsates around her like ruffled feathers.

"No one always knows," he says. "I don't always know. I don't never know." His eyes sparkle, grin. Sonuvabitch lifts his head.

"You knew about my house. How did you know that?"

"You always ask the wrong questions, Stephanie."

"What should I ask?"

"Hell if I know."

She shakes her head. "But you did know about the offer on my house. I didn't even know till yesterday morning. Were you out in the yard? Did you hear us? I bet you heard us. That must be it. You must have been somewhere nearby." She relaxes her shoulders.

Myron looks to the west. The clouds pile deeper.

"There's a storm coming," he says.

She glances up. "Just supposed to be overcast. Maybe a few showers. That's all."

"Okay," he says.

"What are you going to do," she asks, "if they take away the house?"

He shakes his head, feels the sense of the jungle close in. "What is there to do?"

"And what about Parker? You think he can last out there? In his condition?"

"None of us will last."

The air around her shifts again, and for an instant, grows dim.

That's not what I meant," she says.

"You have to decide, Stephanie."

She is about to protest, but stops.

"Do you want the money?"

"It would make life easier."

"Would it?"

"I don't know what I want."

The gust lifts a newspaper out of the weeds and wraps it around her legs.

"I think I should visit Parker," Myron says.

"Good idea."

"Wanna come?"

"No."

"Come anyway. You can walk with us." He moves Sonuvabitch from his lap to the porch. The cat moans. Myron stands. "I'm ready to go," he says.

Bellamy

When the service ends, Bellamy slips out the front door and heads to the side of the church to wait for Crystal. Crystal has this adoration thing going for Olympia and always hangs out after the service and gagas over her like she's some virgin saint. And now with all the talk of rescuing this Parker Davis guy, Crystal will be in there forever. What's worse, it's the same perv that chased them naked down the street. Like, this guy should be locked up or sent to prison or something, not turned into some friggin' hero. What the hell is her mom thinking?

Too bad Crystal didn't see the way her mom behaved yesterday morning. Imagine a woman hitting her own daughter like that, a minister no less. And Bellamy about to have her grandchild.

Bellamy should have known she couldn't count on her mom. When has she ever been there when Bellamy needed her? She always has time for the people in her church and her neighbors and even total strangers, like the loser with the house, but she never has time for Bellamy. No, never for her daughter.

Why couldn't she be related to someone like Fondeaux, a superstar genius, cool and hip in all the right ways? Maybe they've got some unknown connection through Bellamy's dad. Maybe they're like stepsisters or cousins or something really cool like that.

Bellamy huddles up to the building, surrounded by shadow. She doesn't want anyone to see her, talk to her, torture her with all that love and light crap. Doesn't matter, though. No one is coming out.

By now, they should be walking down the street and climbing into their cars and driving away. But they're still in the church, jabbering with her mom about being righteous and being concerned and saving this Parker Davis creep.

Bellamy should just get the fuck out of here, leave both of them guessing about her whereabouts. As if either of them would care.

She moves to the edge of the sidewalk, waits another ten minutes. Then another. A fine mist falls, diminishing the light even more. People start pouring out. She squeezes back into the shadows. Crystal finally appears, buried beneath that bulky North Face coat. Makes her look like a bedspread. But she can get away with that crap, being as skinny as a twig and all, the way most guys like it.

Crystal steps into the shadows.

"Thanks for rushing out here," Bellamy says.

"No problem."

Bellamy would like to shove her face into the wall. "What did you do to your hair?"

"You like it?"

"Looks sort of, ah, old."

"It was like I needed to do something different, so I chopped away and added some color."

"You call gray color?" Her hair looks disturbingly like that of Bellamy's mom.

"I'm making a statement."

Bellamy shakes her head, picks at the brick wall. "What went on in there?"

"A plan of action. We're meeting at the guy's house on Tuesday morning. We're staging a protest. We're not going to let the banks kick him out."

Bellamy shakes her head. Crystal's enthusiasm makes her want to puke. "Let's get the hell out of here."

"I'm ready. We should hit Seattle Central."

"What's there?"

"The Occupy folks. They've moved onto the campus."

Bellamy has no clue what she's talking about. What has a college to do with anything? "Occupy?"

"You know, like those dudes camped out in New York, protesting all those rich white guys. Don't tell me you haven't heard of them."

"Yeah, I've heard of them. I just didn't know that's who you meant."

R. H. Sheldon

They work their way to Twelfth and follow it north along Seattle University until they hit Pine Street. They turn left, past the police station, past Cal Anderson Park, and onto the college grounds, where they find about a dozen tents pitched in the grass near Broadway Performance Hall, crowded into a tiny encampment that reminds Bellamy of the photos in her mom's office, some Third-World village in Africa or Colombia or someplace, where she was in the Peace Corps.

Scattered about are people talking and sitting and standing and generally just hanging out like they're having a party. One guy wears an American flag draped over his shoulders. Another wears an Uncle Sam costume and tries to talk to those who pass by. A woman stands in the center of the encampment and plays a recorder, the sour notes mostly lost in the racket that surrounds her. A nearby listener holds a cardboard sign that reads *Occupy Wall St.org*. On the ground lie dozens of more cardboard signs, unreadable from where Bellamy stands.

Most of the people are close to her age or a little older. They wear knit caps and berets and sweatshirts with hoods that cover most of their faces. Some have on flannel shirts and rain slickers and army fatigue jackets. Most are dressed in black and brown and gray, a post-grunge street look with hippie overtones, but a couple guys wear shirts and ties. Corporate drag must be part of their protest strategy.

Crystal flashes pictures with her phone. "This is so awesome, so exactly what your mom was talking about. It's like a global movement or something, everybody coming together for justice against all that corporate greed." She snaps more pictures and wanders over to the cardboard signs lying on the ground.

Bellamy heads toward a group of campers on the other side of the tents. She weaves through the small encampment and stands near the edge of the gathering. She tries to listen to the individual conversations, but it's difficult to hear any one person, so she steps closer to the man crouched down near several chairs, the sexy one with the long sandy dreads. He talks about the General Assembly and their move here on Friday. He talks about the dynamics of yesterday's protests and about the protests planned in the coming days. He talks about taking down the systems of free trade and deregulated banking and the Wall Street greed machine. He talks about standing strong and holding true to their vision and returning the power to the people.

Bellamy could listen to him all day. She doesn't care what he says. As long as she can hear him. And watch him. Mostly watch. He stirs something in her, something deep, something almost mystical. She's been with plenty of guys, but this one is different. She can feel his energy pulsate through her, an excitement and enthusiasm she never feels.

Maybe it's something to do with all this Occupy stuff, though that seems unlikely. Too much like the shit her mom dishes out. Crystal might fall for it. Crystal will slobber over an emoticon. Not Bellamy. She knows how life works, how people think, how they treat each other. Yet she's got to admit she's feeling something new, something that goes beyond just a sexy guy. And there *is* something about this scene that's pretty cool. Just look at what's going on—all these dudes camping out, coming together, being together. All the really cool people. The street kids and saggers and protesters and watchers. The guitars and packs and hair and skateboards. The hoods and signs and sick, crazy talk. All of it. All of them. Nothing like her mother's church. Nothing like those dull, middle-aged and ultra-aged guru types who don't know anything about what it means to live in the streets, to live on the edge, to fight for a cause worth fighting for—to feel what it means to be alive.

The stuff her mom hands out, the stuff people like Crystal eat up as though they're starving, seems so dull, uninspired, pointless. But these Occupy people are different, what they're saying is different. Sure, maybe this is a little like the feelings her mom and those church people get, except that this Occupy stuff is real, not like what goes on at church. Bellamy can feel it, moving her in a way she's never experienced. It might seem peculiar, coming on so fast, but she can't help it, especially the way this guy talks about it, this yummy, handsome, sexy, inspiring guy. She could occupy him right here and now.

The man continues, his face bright with passion, awareness. The others murmur their approval, stare with admiration, respect, taking in every word. Bellamy is so caught up she can barely make out his words. But she listens. She watches. She waits. A thrill passes through her, then another, and then another, like the early urgings of a sexual encounter, the vague spark igniting, burning through her flesh, piercing her heart, but less physical and more emotional, almost spiritual. It sounds crazy, she knows, and she'd never admit it to anyone. Not Crystal. Not her mom. Nobody.

Sure, maybe she's just being silly, like she's still in junior high or something, but the longer she stands among this small group, the more she feels their sense of community, their camaraderie and fellowship and common purpose. Here is the truth her mother always lectures about. Here is the commitment and willingness to risk everything—home, possessions, even freedom—in the name of something greater. None of that phony and pretentious crap her mother is always peddling. None of that safe ivory tower liberal bullshit that keeps people frozen in fear and righteousness and inaction. Bellamy has found something with meaning, something she can believe in, something with purpose and direction.

She pulls out her phone. "At last," she texts Crystal, "I am home."

Stephanie

Once again, Stephanie is doing exactly what she doesn't want to do. Why she agreed to accompany Myron is beyond her. But here she is, heading with him to the hospital to see Parker, ready to escape at the first opportunity.

Myron can be a difficult man to refuse.

They wind through the corridors and up the back staircases to Parker's floor, routes she's well familiar with from her years working here.

When they arrive at his room, they find two other people standing near the bed, looking as though they're at a funeral.

Parker's corpse-like appearance does little to dispel the image. His face is drawn, ashen, his lips cracked, his eyes sunken, his arms pale, his fingers white. If someone who looked that bad had shown up in the ER, they would have had the morgue on stand-by.

Myron squeezes up between the two visitors and grins, "Francine," he says. "Raphael. Parker took pills."

Parker moans. "Thanks for pointing that out, Myron."

"You're welcome."

Parker of course does not bother to introduce the other visitors. Stephanie moves in closer. "I'm Stephanie," she says, "Parker's next door neighbor."

How can one simple sentence carry so much weight?

Raphael stands with drooping shoulders and a sour look, packed with middle-aged fat and abuse, a shorter, squatter version of Parker. He grunts a greeting, focuses on the roof outside the window.

Francine smiles, nods toward Parker. "Thought we'd check in on this guy. See what trouble he's gotten into this time." She has a slight Jamaican accent, a woman as old as Stephanie, a lean body, face, with a tough look, hardened. Yet her eyes are different, a gentle, smooth quality, like down.

"I don't deserve you," Parker says.

"Just get yourself better and get back to work."

"I still have a job?"

"Depends on you, I expect."

"I'll be fit as a fiddle come next week."

Francine shakes her head. "Don't expect miracles." Her face shines with humor, though she doesn't smile. "Anyway, we're off. Come on, Raphael. Some of us have to work."

Parker pushes his pillow around, tries to sit more upright. "Give my regards to the gang."

Myron says, "Goodbye Francine. Goodbye Raphael."

Raphael grunts. Francine says, "Come visit us, Myron. Haven't seen you around for a while. And make sure you get that friend of yours to work on time next week."

They leave. Parker readjusts his pillow. Myron sits on the chair near the bed. Stephanie stands next to Myron, wishes she were home, pruning those nasty blackberry bushes creeping in from Parker's yard.

Parker says, "They think I was trying to do myself in."

"Who thinks? Francine and Raphael?"

"Them? Nah, they're used to me. The hospital people."

"Were you?"

"I had a headache."

"I get aches in my head," Myron says. "Explosions of light. But not only explosions."

Parker stares at his roommate.

"Sometimes it's more like bullets of light."

"Jesus, Myron, can't you give a sick guy a break?"

Stephanie shakes her head, tries not to focus on how sick he really does look. She says, "Any word when you'll get out?"

"Maybe tonight. Probably in the morning."

"So soon?"

"Unless they decide I belong in the psych ward."

She forces a smile. "Try not to act so much like Parker."

Myron says, "He can't help acting like Parker."

"Thank you," Parker says.

Myron cocks his head.

Stephanie says, "Do you want to get out?"

Parker shrugs. His shoulders poke at the hospital gown. "Might be better to stay, given what awaits. Let them lock me up."

"Not much of a solution," Stephanie says. "Once you head down that road, there's no turning back."

"You know a lot."

"I know what I know."

Parker rolls his eyes. "I doubt they'd keep me anyway. Soon as I told them I had no insurance, all they could talk about was my leaving."

Stephanie imagines what the discussion must have been like among the nurses and doctors. They saw the condition he was in and no doubt got a sense of his lifestyle—the alcohol and drugs being enough of an indicator—and concluded that there wasn't much they could do. A man bent on destroying himself. Whether intentional or not was of little consequence. If they could be rid of the burden, so much the better. No doubt he'd be back in the ER before long, but until then, he wasn't their problem.

Even if they didn't discuss it outright, that's what everyone was thinking.

Stephanie stands. "I'm getting coffee. Want anything?"

"I need a cigarette. These goddamn patches don't do shit."

"Can't help you there."

"What about you, Myron? You got a smoke for your old buddy?"

Myron shakes his head. "I don't smoke."

"I know you don't smoke, you moron. I asked if you had a cigarette. I thought you might have brought some along for me."

"I don't smoke," Myron says.

Parker curses.

Stephanie turns to leave, but discovers Olympia standing in the doorway.

Parker says, "You got a cigarette?"

"I don't smoke," she says.

"Christ, I feel like I'm at Bible camp."

Stephanie turns to Olympia. "I'm going for coffee. Need anything?" There she goes again, doing what she absolutely doesn't want to do.

"I thought you were going to call me about Parker's condition."

"You're here, aren't you?"

"I had to call the hospital."

Stephanie is about to protest, but Olympia holds up her hand, as though stopping traffic, and signals for everyone to be still. She taps her earpiece.

"Can't talk long." Pause. "I'll know more tonight. Call me then." She taps the headset again.

Stephanie feels the hairs on her neck rise.

Olympia steps toward the bed. "We've got to act," she says.

Parker raises his eyebrows.

"All of us," she says. Then she looks around the room.

"Yes," Myron says. "We must act."

"I've spoken with members of my congregation. They want to help."

"Should I know what you're talking about?" Parker turns his head toward Myron. "Should I know what she's talking about?"

Myron draws circles on the tile with his toes.

Stephanie backs away from the bed. The heat in this room is stifling, the air almost too thick to breathe. Sweat trickles down her neck, onto her back.

Olympia moves closer to Parker, her face glowing with defiance. "Tuesday morning, right? That's when the lawyer said he'd be back?" Parker shrugs. She turns toward Stephanie. "That right?"

"I guess." Stephanie eyes the door.

Olympia leans into Parker. He pulls back. "We'll be there. At your house. We'll show them they can't keep running over everybody who gets in the way of their bloody greed."

Myron says, "We'll show them."

"We'll gather in front of your house. We'll be there when the lawyer arrives. We'll draw our people together. We'll protect you and your home. We'll gather our forces just like Gandhi and Mandela and King."

"You mean Elvis?"

"Martin Luther."

Stephanie inches forward. "What the hell you talking about? A demonstration? Outside his house? Outside my house?"

Olympia puffs out her chest and projects her voice as though addressing a crowd. "We must stand together. We must be unified. We must be a force of one."

"What a bunch of crap. I don't want some lunatic circus camped out on my front lawn."

"We're not talking *your* front lawn. We're not talking *your* house. It's Parker we're trying to help. It's Parker we're trying to save."

"Really? And have you asked Parker what *he* wants?"

Parker gazes at the ceiling. "Sounds fine to me."

Stephanie pushes in toward the bed. "And you'd let some religious whacko just roll on in and call the shots? Is that it?"

Olympia spins around. "Religious whacko? Is that what you said? Sounds to me you're the one with the problem. What is it? Afraid to have your perfect little life disrupted? Afraid to take a stand or get involved? Afraid to assist someone in need because you might get your hands dirty?"

Stephanie wants to shove Olympia's head into the toilet and use that frazzled mop to scrub out the stench. "I know exactly how your kind works, how you latch on to causes, never caring about anyone but yourselves—how important you'll feel, how you can pat each other on the back for your services. You're nothing but a hypocrite who cares as much about Parker as you do all your other liberal causes. Anything to make you feel less guilty and more righteous. No matter who you have to use to get there."

"I don't know what your problem is, but no one is forcing you to help or do anything. The last thing Parker needs right now is all your negative energy. And the last thing we need is some bitter, mean-spirited old woman whose misplaced anger and light-sucking life force serves only to bring the rest of us down."

"Yeah," Parker says, "lighten up. Nothing's even happened yet, and you're already getting pissed. Besides, it's not like *you've* come up with any solutions."

"Why, you...you bastard."

"Why, you...you bitch."

She steps toward him. Stops. Backs off. Turns. Rushes to the door, kicking a chair out of the way. She stomps out of the room and marches down the hall. She stomps down the stairs. She pours out of the hospital, shakes her fists, yells at the sidewalk, feels the frustration of that moment, the last few days, last few months, like poison chewing at her insides.

Let them do whatever the hell they want. She tried to help Parker, and this is how he pays her back. She should have known better. A snake is a snake. Period.

R. H. Sheldon

Alonzo

They walk out of the Saint Louise church in single file, the same way they leave church every Sunday, first Elena, then Julia, next Teresa, then Isabel, and finally Alonzo. And always Alonzo receives the same comments. "What a fine looking family." "What lovely girls." "God has really blessed you." Some, of course, usually the older men, stroke their beards or mustaches or gray stubble and say, "Three girls, Alonzo. What are you going to do with three girls?" Or maybe he'll hear, "Just wait till they're teenagers. Just wait, Alonzo. You wait and see."

Isabel walks without looking back. He catches whiffs of the fresh soapy smell from her hair, soft black waves, long and thick, like strands of silken thread, all a perfect rich flow, except for a thin streak of white that winds down the left side. He asked her once why she didn't dye it or even cut it out. Mistake. Big time. She flashed him a deadly gaze, marched out of the room, and didn't speak to him for the next three days. He never mentioned her streak again.

If she were to stop talking to him now, he'd hardly notice. Even this morning, when they were preparing for church, she barely spoke a word, and yesterday, too, ever since returning from her sister's. She doesn't seem angry, nor is he aware of any recent incidents that would cause her to act so withdrawn, but something in her has shifted, and that shift keeps widening the distance between them.

When they reach the parking lot, the girls break formation and scramble ahead, bursting forth like a fountain. Somewhere along the way, the family had adopted the unspoken rule that the parking lot was their free zone. Behavior could be relaxed. Obligations met.

He loosens his tie and steps up next to his wife. "Let's do something fun today."

She stares straight ahead. "I was thinking of going to my sister's again."

"Sure, we could do that. Go home, change, head back out."

"Just me. I meant just me. I told her I'd help her unpack the rest of the boxes. I promised. I did."

"Maybe we could all help."

She lets out a quick snort. "You?"

"Yes, me."

"It's just that—it would be easier, that's all, without the kids around. If you could watch them again..."

"Why can't you do this during the week, when the kids are in school? You've got plenty of time then." She shoots him a look that sours his stomach, a look he's become well familiar with. "I just meant...it might be better then. That's all."

"You know how busy Lita is with school. And work. And taking care of Lucas. You know that. And you know how difficult it is for her to do it all alone."

"Then she shouldn't have had the kid in the first place!"

Other parishioners glance his way.

Isabel narrows her eyes. "She's my sister."

"And I'm your husband."

"Then act like one."

"What's that supposed to mean?"

"It means that if I had wanted to marry a clerk, I would have."

He kicks a rock across the parking lot. The girls look back, then continue with their play.

"Perhaps if you knew how to be more supportive."

"More supportive? What do you call all those years while you were in school?"

He's already lost, and if he says anymore, he'll only get himself in deeper. He hates what has happened between them, hates the resentment, the bitterness, the stringing words. But he hates just as much how much time she spends with her sister, especially these last few months. He's convinced that Lita is the reason Isabel has turned against him. Lita is eight years younger. She's working

R. H. Sheldon

on her master's degree. She's raising a kid on her own. She lives in the middle of the city, dresses like someone in the streets. Isabel's always been so stable, so reasonable—a good mother, a good wife. But lately...

His phone vibrates in his jacket pocket. He takes it out. Isabel shakes her head and turns away. He looks at the caller ID. Blocked, just like yesterday. He answers. He can't help himself.

"You better be ready, Alonzo Garcia. Your time is up."

"Who is this?"

The caller hangs up. He pockets the phone, pockets any sense of hope, and follows Isabel to the car.

"When do you plan to take off?" he asks.

"As soon as we get home."

"That soon."

"Yes, that soon."

Bellamy

Bellamy stands amid her new friends at the Occupy encampment. The sidewalks flow with people rushing from one destination to the next, most talking on cell phones, texting, plugged into headsets, many of them Sunday shoppers, heading home from downtown, carrying their Macy's bags and Gap bags and Old Navy bags. But the camp itself, though crowded in its own right, provides an oasis from the pedestrians and traffic and general buzz typical of Broadway and Pine.

The man standing next to Bellamy, the sexy one with dark blonde dreads and scraggly beard and tanned cheeks and brand new Enjoi Rasta Panda skateboard, points toward the sidewalks. "Man, just look at those fucktards. Carloads of consuming cattle keeping the corporations content. Those pathetic losers." He takes a drag off his hand-rolled cigarette. "This can't go on, I tell you. It's like we buy all this shit and use up all the resources and never know when to stop. Man, it's just so like we're dogs chasing our own tails. And what for, I ask you. What for?"

The others nod, including Bellamy. His voice is like the street, restless and deep and pushing the edge.

"And while they're all shopping and buying and consuming, while they're shelling out their cash and running up their credit cards, while the bankers and board members are getting fatter and richer and out of control, more people lose their jobs, more people lose their homes, more people lose their health insurance, more

R. H. Sheldon

people go to bed hungry. Man, like that's why we're here. That's why we've got to force change, because change won't happen on its own."

Bellamy bursts out in applause, but she's the only one. The others nod, listen, act cool. Bellamy stops, hoping it's not too late, that they haven't already decided she's not one of them, one of the hip. She'd never recover from that. It's bad enough to be here by herself. Crystal disappeared hours ago. The last thing Bellamy wants is to look even more pathetic and out of place.

Two women approach—Hispanic or something—one younger, closer to Bellamy's age, sort of cool, in a revolutionary kind of way. Except she doesn't wear makeup and her clothes seem sort of ordinary, jeans and a plain brown jacket, a slight military look, but still, there's something unusual about her, maybe the brown skin or dark brown eyes or being here with a kid, a toddler, balanced on her hip, while standing strong and proud. Defiant, almost. She nods a greeting to several in the small circle, an understanding, an invisible handshake.

The other woman is older, definitely older, clothes too neat, too perfect. A long blue-gray Columbia rain jacket, buttoned at the collar, pressed designer jeans, lightweight black leather boots with inch-high heels. She has long black hair, a thin white streak on one side. Her eyes dart around the crowds, the camp, a look of discomfort, almost disdain. Must be from the suburbs, just out of church or a PTA meeting. She doesn't get it. Bellamy can tell. Is it an age thing? Does something happen to people when they hit thirty that makes them quit thinking? That makes them act like everyone else?

The man next to Bellamy smiles toward the younger woman, a sheepish embarrassed grin. "Lita," he says, "you came. Sweet."

A smile touches her lips and she says to the other woman, "That's Casey. The one I told you about."

He grins. "You were talking about me?"

Lita says, "My sister, Isabel." She nods toward the other woman. "You camped out here?"

Casey beams with pride. "You bet. It's like, where else would I be?"

The toddler squirms. Lita holds firm.

Bellamy turns slightly toward Casey. His desire is almost palpable, the way he watches Lita, forces his nonchalance. He puffs on the butt of his cigarette, flicks it on the ground. Sparks fly off, glow briefly, and fall dark.

Bellamy feels an ache in her stomach, rising into her chest. Why'd these two bitches have to show up? Why'd they have to ruin everything?

The only bright spot is that Lita doesn't act all that interested in Casey, more like amused. She's definitely not putting it out there.

Knowing men, that's probably why Casey's flipping out over her.

Bellamy shifts her weight, moves closer to him.

"I just heard something like that," Bellamy says. She squirms, feels like a buffoon.

The others gaze at her, Casey with a look almost of impatience.

"What you were saying, ah, Casey. Just this morning. I heard about a man losing his home. The bank is kicking him out. Gave him three days. He's like really sick and poor and old and stuff. No place to go and not a cent to his name. Just like that, they're throwing him into the streets. Right in this neighborhood, in fact. Not very far at all."

Casey shakes his fist. "That's exactly what I mean. Those bastards are killing us. They're taking it all and leaving the rest with nothing. That's why we're here. To stop those motherfuckers." He pulls out his tobacco and rolls another cigarette.

The others shake their heads in disgust, except Lita and Isabel. Lita wears the thinnest of smiles. Isabel just stares. The toddler giggles and squirms and reaches for his mother's breasts.

Casey watches Lita as though he's reading a dinner menu.

"We plan to fight them," Bellamy says. "That's right. We're organizing this awesome protest in front of his house. We're gonna stop those bastards." She shakes her fist just like she saw Casey do. "We won't let the banks get away with this. We won't let them kick him out of his house. We won't let him end up sick and dying in the gutter." She stops and looks around. Mostly she looks at Casey. "We're going to *occupy* his yard. That's what we're going to do!"

Part IV

Home life is no more natural to us
than a cage is natural to a cockatoo.
—George Bernard Shaw

Parker

L ate Monday morning. Parker at home, feeling the effects of being up too early. A hell of a lot earlier than what's normal—or civil. The hospital released him a couple hours ago. Myron was there. The powers that be checked Parker out, seemed happy to expel him, and he and Myron left, got lost in the maze of corridors, found their way to the bus stop, stood in the rain, climbed aboard. Parker fell asleep on the short ride home.

He wouldn't feel so exhausted if the hospital had let him rest, but every time he fell asleep, someone woke him—to check his temperature or pulse or take blood or give meds and do whatever else they could to make him as miserable as possible.

And now Parker sits in his living room, in his chair, and Myron lies on the couch, the soles of his feet facing Parker, just like they've faced him a thousand times. Myron reads church brochures and pets Sonuvabitch. Parker half-watches a black-and-white movie on the semi-color TV, a video that belonged to his mom.

They used to have cable, until Comcast discovered their illegal hookup. He's convinced Stephanie called them. Who else would have turned him in?

After that, Myron connected a pair of rabbit ears he found in the basement, but they were no match for the digital age. So instead of TV, they watch movies on the VCR, all part of his mother's collection, mostly classic black-and-whites filled with actors long dead: *Sunset Boulevard. All About Eve. The Philadelphia Story. Mr. Smith Goes to Washington.*

He's seen most of the movies so many times, he's lost count. But he's usually stoned when they're on, so when he's not too buzzed, like now, they have an eerie not-quite-familiar quality.

Casablanca plays, the part where Ingrid Bergman has just flown off and Humphrey Bogart is acting all, well, Bogart-ish. But the sound is turned down and Parker only half-heartedly watches the picture, mostly just to keep from looking at Myron's feet.

There's something oddly comforting about all this, their little family back in the nest, as though nothing happened in the last few days. But today is the deadline. By midnight he's supposed to be out of the house. Yet with no place to go, his only choice is to wait. Perhaps Olympia's plan will work, though he doubts a handful of New Age fruitcakes can do much, except perhaps buy him some time. In the end, he'll still have to move, and with no money or time to raise it, his options are few. And none of them look too pretty.

Parker reaches for the bottle of Jack, intent on the last few swallows. He lifts it to his lips, catches the vapors, starts to choke. He returns the bottle to the coffee table.

Myron looks up from the brochure.

Parker glares at him. "Did you want something?"

"Nothing," Myron says. "Just stretching my eyes."

"What do you think about all this?" Parker says. "About what Olympia wants to do?"

"What does Olympia want to do?"

"What do you mean, you cretin? You were at the hospital. You heard what she said."

"Oh, that."

"Yes, *that.* Any thoughts?"

For a moment, Myron looks like a small boy caught stealing from the corner store. He nods, pats Sonuvabitch on the head, and says, "Not really."

Perhaps it's the last few days in the hospital, the lack of alcohol, the disrupted sleep, the reported brush with death, but something in Parker relaxes and he feels perfectly fine with Myron's response, perhaps even finds a bit of comfort in it, that stalwart lackadaisical indifference that so defines his friend's existence. After all, when has Myron ever given a useful answer about anything? Most of the time, Parker might as well be talking to a wall. And now is no different. Only now he doesn't care. Only now he cares little about anything. Even cigarettes and booze seem to have taken a back seat. Maybe it's the patches or having barely escaped an otherworldly fate, at least for now. The same thing with losing his house. It seems less important somehow, as long as he has a little time. If nothing else, he'll find some fleabag hotel until he can get himself settled. All he cares about is a place to crash. That's what matters.

What he needs now is sleep. As soon as he can gather his strength, he'll head upstairs. Tomorrow he might be out in the streets, but today he still has a bed. It's probably one of the meds he brought home from the hospital that explains his indifference. He has no idea what he's taking, some long generic names he never heard of, but one of them seems to be working, or at least chilling him out.

And you never know, perhaps Olympia will make something happen. He wants to believe she will, but he's not sure he can. All he knows is that he's got nothing to lose at this point. Everything he had hoped for or thought he was or might become is gone. Even his three-night-a-week gig might have disappeared. He has nothing. Nowhere to go. Nothing to leave behind. Perhaps Olympia can give him enough time to figure out what to do next. He needs so little, really. Just a space to sleep.

But what about Myron? What's he going to do? He acts as if there's no problem, as if they can live here forever.

Myron looks up. "Nothing's forever, Parker."

Parker closes his eyes. Now that, he thinks, is too much.

Olympia

Olympia shivers and pulls on her sweatshirt, sleeves long, bulky, a dwarfing comfort.

She sits at her desk, before her, paper, pen, morning coffee, steam rolling like fog. She grabs her pen, writes, thinks, writes, note after note, page after page. She writes large. Always has.

She grabs her mug, the first sip a dagger. There is much to do. People to call. Signs to make. Flyers to print. And she must arrange food—sandwiches or burritos or something cheap. She'll get someone to run to Costco. Perhaps she can take up a collection.

At nine tomorrow morning, they'll meet in front of Parker's house. She gave them the usual warnings. Dress warm. Wear layers. Be prepared for rain. And no matter what, keep it peaceful. "We have the upper hand," she told them. "Let's not lose that."

She'll repeat her message in the morning.

The key to all this, of course, is the press. Getting them there won't be easy. Most reporters are over-worked grunts with little interest in small Seattle protests, especially if there's no significant trouble. For that, she'll need the police. Only they can supply the type of full-fledged confrontation the press will eat up.

But she won't do anything yet. She wants to get there tomorrow and have a chance to better assess the situation. A lot will depend on when the lawyer arrives—this Alonzo Garcia—and what he does when he gets there. Legally, he can have Parker evicted almost

R. H. Sheldon

immediately, but that will involve the police or sheriff's department or somebody—perhaps even a court order—and there's no telling what he'll be expecting when he gets there and how prepared he'll be. Tomorrow will be a gathering of forces, a chance to prepare the troops, a time to finalize their plans.

Until then, she'll focus on the groundwork—call in other supporters, spread the word to nearby churches, and get the food lined up. It will be hard to pull in much of a crowd, especially on a Tuesday, but a free meal will at least help to convince those who do show up to stick around.

This will all come together. She's sure of it. She's been down this road before. It's been a while, certainly, but it's like welcoming an old friend. She feels energized in a way she has not felt in years, inspired and enthused, ready to take on the world. At times like this she feels closest to her mission in life. Ready to lead. Fight. Bring about change. That's what she was put on this earth to do.

She's about to jot down a note about sign-up sheets, when she hears a scratch at the door. Fingernails. She looks up. The door crawls open. Bellamy sticks in her head.

"I could use your help," Olympia says.

"You still throwing your protest tomorrow?"

"It's not a party, dear."

"I only meant..."

"Can you make some signs?"

"Not right now."

"When?"

"When I get back."

"Where you going? How long will you be gone?"

"Just forget it."

Bellamy pulls out of the office and slams the door. Olympia knew better than to ask her daughter questions like that, but they've got to figure out a way to get past this crap, especially given Bellamy's latest exploits. A baby, for chrissakes. You'd think in this day and age she'd know better. She probably got pregnant just to spite Olympia, to prove once and for all she's her own person. All she's proven is what an ass she can be.

Olympia drops her pen. It rolls across the desk and falls to the floor. She closes her eyes and rubs her temples and eases back in the chair. The springs squeak like a distant cry, someone too far away to help.

Stephanie

Until this past Saturday, Stephanie never considered selling her house, but now, all she can think about is getting the hell out of here. And it's not just Parker and his crass and callous ways. This area has grown way too congested, too trendy and hip, too urban and mean—and it's only getting worse. Cal Anderson Park has been the biggest disappointment. At first, she thought it was a great idea, covering the reservoir, opening up the space, adding the fountain and reflecting pool. But the number of unsavory characters grows larger every day, and with them come the drugs and alcohol, the parties and trash, the late nights and unrelenting noise, a comfort to Parker perhaps, but for the others living around here, it's getting unbearable.

Yet even the neighborhood isn't motive enough to flee. Now that she's considered selling, she realizes how ready she is to get out of this house. Too many memories, too many reminders, too many dreams never to come true.

She used to think of her house as an extension of herself, a place that expressed parts of her personality that could find no other outlet—the garden, the artwork, the general love and care. That's no longer the case. The house breathes its own life, makes its own claims, leaving her feeling more an extension of her home than the other way around. What was once a labor of love has become a tedious process of frustration and obligation. Like anything she's tried to possess, she ends up the conquered and the fallen.

R. H. Sheldon

She digs out Alonzo Garcia's business card and dials his number. He answers right away, but sounds apprehensive and cautious.

"This is Stephanie Schmidt," she says. "I'm calling about the house."

"Oh, the house, yes, yes, the house."

"I didn't wake you, did I?"

"Wake me?" He lets out a forced laugh.

"I've decided to sell," she says. "I've decided to sell my home."

Saying it brings a rush of emotions, and she feels herself start to choke up. Not all memories are bad. But they're just that—memories. She clenches the phone tighter.

"Yes," she says, "the sooner the better."

Garcia says nothing for a moment, then mutters, "Fine, fine. I'll stop by tomorrow with the paperwork."

"Not a day too soon." She hangs up.

That's that, then. Now to decide what to do with the rest of her life.

She walks outside and stands in her garden. The plants have that semi-dormant look you find this time of year, stalks brown, dry, leaves infused with yellow and gold and shades of dusty green, a brittle look that defies the steady brush of fall moisture. Even the rhododendrons and camellias, with their perennial green leaves, have less of a luster, after the summer peaks but before the real rains wash out the gray hues. But they'll be coming any time now. Once November hits, anything is possible. They've already had a few good dumps, but the relentless storms have yet to descend. Once they do, everything will be soaked and will stay that way for the duration of the winter.

She wonders whether she could live anywhere other than the Northwest. She's been here all her life. She knows the seasons, the moods. She knows how the fall storms move in, how the sun breaks out on a cold winter day. She knows the idyllic summers, the dreary winters. Perhaps she knows too much.

Maybe she should head to the desert, where she knows nothing.

A sense of excitement surges through her, a sense of vast horizons and open highways. She's been so steadfast in so many aspects of her life that she's never considered other possibilities. But now the time is here—and consider she shall.

"Yes," says the voice. "Yes, yes, yes."

She jumps. Myron stands at the fence, leaning into her yard.

"Myron!"

"You've decided," he says.

"I've decided. And good riddance, I say."

"Good riddance," he repeats.

She doesn't know how to take this. She doesn't know how to take anything he says.

The clouds open for the sun and a beam lands on Myron's face, turning his features young and impish. She wonders whether she'll miss him—his weird, unpredictable ways. He's a fixture in his own right, an odd, unpredictable, slightly skewed fixture.

The sun slips back behind the clouds and drops the garden into a long gray shadow.

"You never did tell me," she says, "what you'll do if you need to leave."

"I won't *need* to leave, Stephanie."

"Fine," she says, "but if you do find yourself seeking refuge in a place other than Parker's house, where would that place be?"

A look crosses Myron's face that suggests he's never considered such a possibility.

"Does it matter, Stephanie, what I do? I will still be here. I will still be there."

Stephanie sighs. "You don't belong in this world, Myron."

"Who does?"

"Who, indeed?"

Myron sweeps his big hand across the tops of the picket fence, touching each post with his palm while swaying gently from side-to-side. He studies the garden. He glances across the street. He looks up to the sky. Finally, he says, "Winter is coming."

"It's that time of year."

"We should have a celebration."

"What would we celebrate?"

"Life."

"We should celebrate life."

"Or death."

"Why celebrate death?"

"Or life. Either way."

"Myron."

"I better check on Parker," he says.

"I better start packing," she replies.

He smiles and waves.

R. H. Sheldon

Stephanie feels a few light raindrops on her face, more of a mist than anything. She turns and walks toward the house. Today feels all askew, good, bad, everything in between. Like a blister, something needs to pop.

Myron

Instead of going inside, Myron heads to the tree. The fall is his season and he likes to be with it while it still visits. And Sonuvabitch will be waiting for him. The cat left earlier on his afternoon walk and always returns about now. He loves crawling through the weeds and stalking his prey and pretending he's a great jungle hunter. He always comes back smiling and ready for a nap.

Myron loops around Parker's house, cutting through the weeds and piles of trash. He stops just to the left of the steps and looks at a dark spot in the brush, darker than the surrounding shadows. He pushes aside the weeds. A crow with wide dead eyes stares up, body lifeless, twisted in a stiff and agonized death.

Myron looks up. A lone crow stares down, balancing on the wire, swaying slightly back and forth. The bird lets out a squawk, cocks its head.

Myron turns toward the dead bird and pushes the branches back in place, then heads to the giant maple. He drops to the ground and leans against the trunk. A light mist falls, barely noticeable, but enough to let him feel fall all the more. The weeds are fringed with green, glistening with moisture, but they still have a hard brittle look, much of the stalk brown and dry. Dead leaves hang from the lower branches, their edges crumbled and torn, waiting for a good wind to pull them down.

R. H. Sheldon

On days like this, he can sit out here for hours, studying the way summer tries to linger while winter reaches its tentacles and drags the world forward. Fall lives at the crossroads, pulling day into night, a dance as mighty as the tides that hold the ocean's rhythms. On such days, he feels massive and small, eternal and as finite as a flame's brief flicker.

Sonuvabitch creeps out from the weeds. A rat with a stunned look hangs from the cat's jaws, its tail winding down like a snake.

"Let go, Sonuvabitch. You're just playing with him."

A muffled peep squeaks out of Sonuvabitch.

"No lap time if you have a rat in your mouth."

Sonuvabitch lets out a huff and drops the rodent. It looks up stunned, then scurries off into the weeds. The cat sits on the ground and licks his fur, behaving as though he had intended to let go of the rat all along. When he finishes, he crawls onto Myron's lap, curls into a small ball, and closes his eyes.

Myron pets Sonuvabitch with long easy strokes. The cat purrs, loud, rough. Myron can feel it in his fingers, a tiny engine, running and running. He wonders why only cats purr, what it is that makes them so special. What if all creatures purred? What if humans had small motors they could switch them on whenever they felt content? Or wanted to feel content? Myron wonders which comes first—the purring or contentment. Or maybe it's something else. Maybe he's asking the wrong question, just like Stephanie always asks the wrong questions. Just like Parker. Not Olympia, though. She's not asking the wrong questions. She's not asking any questions. And that's what concerns Myron the most.

Bellamy

Bellamy sits huddled with Casey and the other Occupiers beneath the canopy. Rain drizzles against the tarp, one of many showers rolling in and out with no particular pattern. The clocks got turned back yesterday, and night comes earlier than ever. Only seven o'clock and already it's been dark a couple hours. The lights from the school and shops and street lamps glisten on the damp pavement and brick walkways, giving the world a magical mystical feel.

A breeze brushes off the Sound, carrying with it the cool smell of the ocean. The air cuts through her, chills her to the marrow.

At least that skank Lita took off, along with her bitch sister. No one left to distract Casey. Sure, the woman with the recorder is hanging around, no longer playing, but holding it on her lap should the need arise. With that toad face and wide-load hips, there's no competition, and the other two girls are snuggled up to their boyfriends. Bellamy's already scoped out the tent situation. Casey's got one to himself.

It's all like a dream for Bellamy—sitting in a camp in the middle of the city, surrounded by traffic lights and glaring storefront windows and flashing neon signs, yet feeling like she's out in the wilderness, striking out in new directions, seeking out new forms. All she's got to do is get Casey to invite her into his tent.

She studies the surrounding area, a rush of pedestrians, a steady stream of cars, the few remaining cops, standing off to the side, watching and saying little. She wonders if they'll be out there all night. Just them and the campers. And Bellamy.

Of course, Casey's done nothing to indicate whether he wants her to stay, but he hasn't done anything to suggest she leave. In fact, he hasn't left her side in the last hour. Yet she refuses to make any moves. If he doesn't give her a definite sign, she won't do anything. The last thing she plans to do is act desperate. At least not yet.

Maybe those two couples will get him feeling romantic. Every minute they seem to move in closer and speak softer and draw into themselves even more. Just as long as all that affection doesn't make him think about Lita.

Only the recorder lady remains attentive. She sits on Casey's other side, slithering toward him little by little, acting as though his every word is coming down from heaven and pretending she doesn't care about getting him naked. Every chance she gets, she spurs him on so he keeps talking and she can keep listening and acting like there's no one else but him.

Bellamy knows that trick. She's used it a hundred times. The more she gets a guy to talk about himself, the happier he is. Just ply him with questions and sit back and listen, nodding on occasion, cocking her head with interest. Eventually, he'll wear himself out and be ready for something more.

The recorder girl leans in closer. "Casey," she says, "if they break up our camp, what do we do?"

"I won't leave."

"I won't either," she replies, "but they still might try."

"Then let them arrest me. I refuse to budge."

"So do I." The musician moves another inch closer.

"I won't either," Bellamy announces.

Casey and the girl stare.

"What I mean, when I get my tent down here...When I *get* a tent, then I won't budge either. Let the cops come."

She looks out past the campers, toward where the police stand. One of them, a tall Chinese guy with thick legs and wide shoulders and a narrow waist and a strong, stern face, stands apart from the others, just at the edge of the light, staring in their direction with a gaze so fixed he looks like a statue, the kind with holes for eyes, empty, dark, impenetrable.

Bellamy has never had sex with an Asian or a cop. She's never been drawn to either, but this guy's pretty fucking hot. She imagines what it would be like to be inside Casey's tent, the two of them going at it, knowing that the black-haired god stands outside, watching, listening, aware that at any moment he could storm the tent, drag Casey out, take her right there. Nothing could stop him.

A shiver runs through her, the thrill almost palpable.

"You're cold," Casey says and wraps his arm around her shoulders. "Here, squeeze in closer."

She scoots up next to him, feels the touch of his leg, his chest, his arm, feels his lean muscles against her soft flesh, feels his strength, the comfort, the command. The cop stares, his face set in stone. The musician's eyes fall to the ground, and she heaves a sigh nearly inaudible in the rising breeze.

Alonzo

He stops reading the brief—part of a lawsuit related to a land acquisition from last year—and reaches behind his head to prop up the pillow. Isabel is hiding in the bathroom. Every few minutes she turns on the water and lets it run. The house fills with a loud whining screech that seems to go on forever, until she turns off the water, causing the pipes to clank several times. This has been going on at least an hour, turning on the water, letting it run, turning it off. Then she waits, the bathroom still, the house creeping in on itself. Then the water on. Then off. Then on. Then off.

He closes his laptop and eases his head against the pillow. The edges puff out and cover his ears, deadening the latest round of whining. She must have been the last to use this pillow. The slight smell of lotion rolls off the case—lemon and roses—almost a dream, the way it fades when he tries to hold it.

He opens the computer's lid and returns to the brief—another case against Lockhart Investments. The plaintiffs insist they had been misled prior to the sale, that they would never have sold if the buyers had not misrepresented the zoning and development ordinances and their impact on property values. Alonzo knows the plaintiffs have no case. Their evidence is flimsy at best, and the sellers had every opportunity to vet the issues themselves before taking the cash. No doubt some sleazy attorney filling their heads with easy fortunes.

Damn, Alonzo hates this profession.

The bathroom door eases open and Isabel slips out. The light glares behind her, surrounding her head with white light, giving her an angelic look that further complicates the sadness in her face.

He pats the bed next to him, balancing the laptop on his thighs. "Come on, Is. You look tired. Lie down and I'll rub your back."

"I look tired?"

"I only meant..."

"My back is fine."

She marches across the room and snatches up the blue terrycloth robe off the foot of the bed. She acquired it last week after visiting Lita, a huge monstrosity that covers her like a blanket. When she slips it on, it snags the hem of her peach nightgown and pulls it up to her waist. Her pubic hairs catch the light from the bathroom and glisten with a soft haze. She pulls on the robe quickly and turns away, like one of the girls caught in a lie.

He says, "Won't you be too hot in that?" He wears nothing but his boxers.

"I'm going downstairs to watch TV," she says.

"Watch it here."

"You're working."

"I'll stop."

"You don't know how to stop."

She pulls the robe tighter and pushes her feet into her slippers, large and floppy, the same color as her nightgown. She heads for the door.

"Isabel, wait." He closes the lid on the laptop.

She stops but doesn't turn. The back of her robe droops into thick folds as she empties her lungs. The robe must be three sizes too large. The shoulders hang halfway down her arms, the bottom nearly touching the floor.

"We need to talk," he says.

"You need to talk."

"If you'd just tell me. If you'd open up."

She turns. Her eyes land on him like an executioner's axe. He pulls the spread across his legs and up to his chest.

"Is that what you want? Really?" Her voice swells with frustration.

"I need to know."

"I expected more. I hoped for more."

"From me?"

"Who else?"

"Does this have to do with the clerk comment? Is that what you think of me?"

"You went to school. I dropped out so you could keep going. I took care of the house. I took care of the kids. I worked in between so we could make ends meet. And look at us now."

"I got a job. I'm doing the best I can."

"Exactly."

Alonzo feels the punch in his guts. He wants to lash out. He wants to crawl into a hole.

"And running to your sister, that's the answer."

"At least she knows who she is, what she wants."

"And I don't?"

"You have a family, Alonzo. You have commitments. It's time to face facts. You're not a writer or an artist or a musician. You are an attorney. Act like one."

She holds his gaze for a moment, lets out a huff, and stomps out of the room. Her muffled steps cross the hallway and fade down the stairs. The light clicks off. He hears her move through the kitchen, toward the basement. The door opens and closes. A rush of silence follows her down the stairs.

He considers going down there, but then his cell phone rings. He grabs it from the desktop. Another blocked call. The third one today. Like the first two, he doesn't answer.

He sets the phone on the nightstand, then his laptop, and clicks off the light. He stares through the doorway and into the hall, but all he can make out are the thin layers of shadow, an ethereal gateway to another place, another time, when his heart carried more than despair, more than this hopeless empty yearning.

Part V

For what do we live, but to make sport for our neighbors
and laugh at them in our turn?
—Jane Austen, Pride and Prejudice

Bellamy

Horns blast. Tires squeal. A garbage truck rumbles. Another honk.

Bellamy opens her eyes, looks for the car, the truck, sees nothing but a confused mix of shadows. She can still feel the horn, whooshing through her, like the shock waves after an explosion. She struggles against the knot of blankets, the cold stretch of nylon. Each movement tightens the noose.

Around her the space melts into a bluish haze, the light so soft it seems no light at all. She pulls one arm free and rubs her eyes. A seagull squawks, screeches, inches from her head, so close she expects to be covered in bird shit. A squabble follows, filling the air with flapping wings and painful cries. Then she remembers— Seattle Central, the Occupy camp, the tent, Casey. It's not a blanket that binds her, but a sleeping bag, built for one person, shared with a body so lean, so hard, she could cut herself on its edges.

She feels his breath on her neck, a mere whisper slow and deep, his chest rising against her spine, flesh to flesh, pore to pore, the movement so subtle she'd forgotten it was there, a fit so natural she can't imagine life without it.

But she has to pee, in the worst way, and that means pulling herself out of his arms and out of the bag and out of the tent and into the dreary Northwest morning. Nothing but a bloated bladder could do that.

She turns slowly away from him while at the same time trying to unfurl the bag from beneath her hip. Doesn't matter they never zipped it up, the bag so twisted she can barely move. Not surprising, though, given their affectionate interludes in the middle of the night, a bonus after their initial encounter—a profound experience in itself, despite her disdain for sleeping bags *and* tents.

She frees herself enough to slip halfway out of the bag and flips over and aims her face directly at Casey's, their lips so close she can taste the sex and sweat and Indian food.

"Casey," she whispers and strokes his cheek with the back of her hand, his beard like the soft bristles of a toothbrush.

That's what she needs. Her toothbrush, about the only thing not in her pack. She has tissues and candy and condoms and Kotex, but no toothbrush. And she won't need the Kotex for a while. Or the condoms. Not that she'd use them anyway. Condoms ruin it for her, that sense of having a man inside, feeling him move in her, through her, the way *nature intended,* a phrase her mom is always throwing at her. And what could be more natural than sex?

Bellamy nudges Casey on the shoulder. "I need to pee."

He mumbles, but never quite wakes.

"Casey."

He lets out a long breath, a field of garlic, then stillness, almost eerie, an animal's last breath. Like it was when Pan died, their thirteen-year-old Siamese, his kidneys failing, appetite gone, weight nothing, growing more listless every day. One night he lay on Bellamy's bed. She stroked his head, talked to him like she always did. He let out a long sigh and never breathed again.

"Casey!"

He bolts upright, his body a silhouette against the tent's bluish glow. "What...what...what the hell?"

"I thought..." Her heart pounds. The blood surges through her temples.

He grabs her arm. "What is it?"

"Your breathing. The way you stopped..."

"What?"

"I thought..."

"You were worried?"

She can hear the slight mocking tone, almost impatience, but without being able to see his face, she can't be sure. She nods.

He chuckles, wraps his arms around her and pulls her down. "Come back to bed."

"I need to pee."

"The honey buckets are near the steps."

"They're the only option?"

"What's wrong with them?"

"They're just so..."

"How early is it?"

"Early."

"Try between the performance hall and school. No one should be around."

"Outside?"

"If you've got to go..."

"But outside? It's so, like, public."

"Maybe one of the coffee shops is open. Just not Starbucks. Too corporate."

"Their toilets?"

He says nothing and she thinks he might have fallen back to sleep. She unzips the tent and crawls out, but leaves the flap open. An icy mist laces the breeze, burrows into her flesh. The morning hangs heavy, barely begun. The first light, a dull gray glimmer, edges through the low clouds.

She considers one of the honey buckets after all, but even from here she can smell their stench, and she's not going outside. She looks toward the intersection. Nothing of use. And Starbucks isn't even a choice. The nearest one is at the other end of Broadway. There's a Safeway on Pike, just a block from here. They must have a restroom. She just won't tell anyone, in case they're also too corporate.

She heads in that direction, her bladder about to explode.

That's when she sees the cop from last night, as focused and mean as he looked then, standing near the sidewalk, exactly where he was when they crawled into the tent, even the same stance, the same focused gaze, the same sense of power, purpose, strength.

She walks past him toward Pike, smiles as she goes, hoping her face isn't too contorted from the need to piss.

He says nothing. He stares into the space before him, as though he hasn't seen her, but he has, she can tell by the slight glint in his eyes, the way he stands a bit straighter, how his fists tighten into thick muscled balls of fury.

She walks by him but doesn't look back. She thinks he's watching her, though she can't be sure. Yet she feels it somehow, his hardened gaze, his secret thoughts. He's waiting for something. He's waiting for her. Why else would he still be there?

Stephanie

She's not sure how to feel. How she's supposed to feel. She worked years to make this house hers, putting into it everything she could afford. Yet when it came time to make a decision, it was like jumping into a pool of cold water—the initial resistance, uncertainty, until she plunged in headlong, and suddenly it was no decision at all.

She sets the kettle on the stove and opens the curtains. Nearly nine. She never sleeps this late. Even when she worked swing shift, she was up at seven. She couldn't have slept in if she wanted to. Pissed Georgia off big time. She preferred late nights and late mornings.

Perhaps her new girlfriend is more accommodating.

Stephanie pulls the jar of tea out of the cupboard, genmaicha, Georgia's favorite. Not much of the tea left, a few pots, maybe. Stephanie would be happy with Lipton's, or better still, a strong cup of coffee, but she can't see wasting what's already been bought. What *she* already bought. Stephanie carried most of the household expenses when they were together, with Georgia contributing only when she had a few dollars to share. But Stephanie didn't mind that part of their relationship, at least not too much. Georgia didn't make as much money, and Stephanie was ready to help. That's how partnerships work.

She stands in front of the stove, waiting for the water to boil. Already, the kettle rocks, emits a mild hiss, rumbles like an empty stomach. It will be whistling in no time.

She's about to reach for her mug when someone pounds at the front door.

What the hell? The attorney isn't supposed to stop by till late morning. She turns off the burner. It better not be Parker.

When she pulls open the door, she discovers two women and one man, all three pushing seventy, all three wearing khaki pants and pullover sweatshirts and paper name tags covered in plastic, the sweatshirts each a different color, with large black letters. *I'm all or nothing.*

Ida, tall and bone thin, wears a canary yellow sweatshirt. Louise is a short chunky duck and has on a powder blue one. Bert, whose size and shape falls somewhere between the other two, wears a moss green sweatshirt that's two sizes too large.

"We're here about the house," says Louise.

Stephanie looks beyond them for a *For Sale* sign. "The house?"

Ida lets out a distinct *ahem* and says, "We're here to protest."

At times, Stephanie has the sense that the world is assembling itself before her, as though reality is defined moment by moment and doesn't always get constructed fast enough and she's left to piece the rest together.

Once she does, she says, "I think you want next door." She points at Parker's house.

The three turn to the lot next door. For them, too, reality seems to have just assembled itself because their eyes grow wide and jaws drop open and faces draw into themselves, as though only now they've started to shrivel.

Louise says, "That can't be."

Ida says, "Just look at that place."

Bert says, "There must be a mistake."

Stephanie bites down to keep from smiling. "Afraid not," she says. "Be sure to knock loud, though. They're probably still asleep—if they went to bed at all."

She closes the door and waits to hear them shuffling off the porch. Then she heads to the stove and turns on the burner.

Before long, she has a steaming mug and a slice of toast layered with too much butter and clover honey—along with a sprinkle of cinnamon—and is sitting next to a wide laceleaf maple, the remaining leaves thin and crinkled, glistening with moisture, hanging by what are essentially threads. Snippets of cool, damp air puff up from the Sound. A thick slate ceiling looms low above her, as though it could turn to fog at any moment, her butt freezing against the seat's icy wrought iron.

What would it be like, she wonders, to be sitting outside this time of year without wearing twelve layers of clothes, without the socks and shoes and long pants and extra shirts and jackets, just for a few minutes of fresh air?

Choices are never so easy, though. She knows that. There is much she would miss about the Northwest, especially the late winter and early spring when the mass of flowers starts to appear, the daffodils and crocuses and plum blossoms, brightening the gray days.

Her favorite is winter daphne, with its balls of white and pink flowers and leaves like long tongues and a scent as sweet and rich as a young forest. They show up in mid-February, just like the sweet box, another of her favorites, the flowers not as rich as the daphne's, but their fragrance extraordinary, like spring in a bottle, except more elusive, more subtle, so subtle in fact, it's hard to sniff them directly. She'll catch a whiff when she walks by, right when she's least expecting it, but as soon as she tries to hold in the scent, tries to get closer, make it her own, it's gone, as though it never existed and she's left with nothing but an empty space.

A car pulls up in front of her house and parks in front of the gate, a small Toyota or Honda, this one old, a faded, dusty red, full of rust and dents and paint scraped off to raw metal, beat up more times than those drunks who used to come into the ER.

Can't be the lawyer. A lawyer would never drive something like that.

Then *she* pops out, the same awful woman from the hospital, taking the only available parking spot. Stephanie jumps out of her chair and races to the fence, near the corner of her lot. A tangle of blackberry branches snags at her wool socks, reaching through the gate from Parker's yard.

"Excuse me," she says.

The woman wears khaki pants and a white sweatshirt, a backpack slung over her shoulders. She carries a stack of fluorescent orange traffic cones. The headset still sticks out of her ear. She talks in a loud, excitable voice. "We need two tables. What's the big deal? Just stick them in your car." A pause. "Get Marty to drive." Another pause. "Then wake him!"

"Excuse me."

Olympia glances at Stephanie, first with a look of annoyance, then one of uncertainty, and finally comes the recognition.

"Oh," she says, "it's you."

Stephanie tries to free her sock, loses her rubber clog. She balances on one foot and points to the car. "Would you please move that?"

"What in the world for?"

"I'm expecting a visitor. She should be here any minute."

"She can park around the corner."

"Or you can move your car. There's space right in front of Parker's."

"We're reserving that."

"You can't reserve the street. Just move your car."

"Why should I move? It's not your street."

"It's in front of my house."

"So are the sewers."

"Just move that piece of shit."

Olympia scans the heavens with rolling eyes and shakes her head in disgust. She's about to speak, but then her phone rings—the sound of a harp, coming from her jacket pocket. She touches the earpiece.

"Where are you?"

She stares toward the clouds when she speaks.

"We'll get the flyers later. Just get your butts down here." She stops, listens, talks more, all the time wandering toward Parker's house, having forgotten, it would seem, that Stephanie still stands there.

Someone needs to take this imbecile out.

Stephanie pulls her clog out of the bramble, slips it over her wet wool sock, and heads for the gate. She makes sure Olympia is turned away, distracted by her call, and steps out on the sidewalk. She creeps out into the street and to the far side of Olympia's car. She crouches down by the back tire and twists off the valve cover and pushes in the pin with her thumbnail. Air gusts out, smelling of rotten old shoes, then settles into a soft hiss. The car eases downward until the tire is flat.

She lets loose the valve and puts the cover back on. Then she peaks through the car windows to make sure no one is watching. She pushes herself up slowly, her knees cracking and popping, until she's standing upright.

"Hello, Stephanie."

She nearly jumps out of her clogs. When she turns, she finds Myron. "Damn it, Myron. Quit sneaking up like that."

"What are you doing, Stephanie?"

She averts her eyes. "I, uh, thought I dropped something."

"What, Stephanie? What did you drop?"

"Forget it. It's not here."

"Look," he says, "the car has a flat tire."

She rushes back to her yard and into her house.

"Of course," she says. "Of course he'd show up."

She drops into the chair near the front window. Pants. Fumes. Glances outside, but sees no one. The phone rings. Maybe it's the lawyer? The phone rings again. It could be another sales call. She waits for the answering machine to pick up. She hears the click, followed by her short greeting: "I can't take your call. Please leave a message." Then the beep. Then the caller speaks. "Stephanie, it's Georgia..."

Parker

Parker sits up in bed, kicks off the covers, lies flaccid, an amoeba, melting into the sheets. Slits of light creep through the blinds and slice his naked legs. He must have slept at least twelve hours, maybe more. He spent the better part of yesterday falling in and out of naps, most of the time in his chair, until sometime in the evening when he wandered upstairs. Whatever they gave him sure did the trick. Or something did the trick. Maybe just exhaustion. Until this morning, he'd forgotten what it was like to get decent sleep.

He squirms back under the covers and closes his eyes, but his bladder and joints demand action. He pushes off the covers and climbs out of bed and reaches for his robe, only to discover that he still wears it, at least partially. The tail has crawled up his back and hangs in a twisted knot, tugging at his shoulders like a heavy weight.

He pulls the right sleeve part way down his arm, dragging his T-shirt with it. The shirt tightens around his neck. He tugs harder, choking himself with cotton. The robe tears along the seam, right at the shoulder—now at his elbow.

He doubles his efforts. The sleeve rips from the robe and snaps off his arm. His T-shirt bounces back and eases the hold on his neck. The robe hangs limply from his shoulders. He dangles the sleeve before him like an exterminated rat, then drops it to the floor.

He reaches behind him with his exposed right arm and untangles what is now a loose knot. Then he pulls what remains of the robe around his narrow chest and searches the floor for his slippers, but instead finds a field of aspirin, spread across the wood like dots of cotton. When he kicks them aside, he stubs his right big toe on a loose floorboard. Pain shoots through his foot and up his leg.

He limps into bathroom to piss, plopping his tired old ass on the toilet rather than trying to endure the aches that go with standing, although squatting down and then pulling himself up are no less a nuisance. He washes his hands, splashes water on his face, dries them all with a soiled towel that he last washed when he did his sheets.

He shuffles through the hallway and stops at the head of the stairs. He grabs the railing and starts to hobble down, wincing each time he puts weight on his right foot. But it's not only the throbbing toe that slows him. Or any of the stiffness and aches that greet him each day. It's something else, a weariness that digs deeper than his OD and hospital stay and loss of the house, not that any of these aren't enough—and no doubt they're playing their parts—but whatever he's feeling goes beyond them, as though something inside him surfaced when all those pills got flushed out, something deep and abiding, a sense of dejection and loss and fear that he's managed to keep in check all these years.

Mostly.

He creeps steadily downward, clutching the banister with both hands, the arthritis in his fingers like needles, growing sharper every day, his knuckles red, swollen, tender to the touch.

When he reaches the bottom, he stops, breathes, releases the banister in a surge of trepidation. He moves into the living room. Myron's gone, his bed a couch, the blankets folded and set in the corner, pillows on top, like every morning. The house creaks and groans, a rotten echo, deep in the walls, pulling at his heart.

What he needs is a distraction, but how does he find that at such an ungodly hour? He'd watch TV if he could, but that's not an option, and he's not in the mood for another old movie. Music, perhaps?

He heads for his dad's fifteen-year-old boom box next to the television, picks up one of the Big Band tapes, decides against that as well.

He eases toward the piano, an instrument he's barely touched since moving back into the house. A stack of *Playboy* covers the bench. He shoves them aside, sending most to the floor. He sits and pushes open the cover. He plucks out a few notes. He winces. He tries a chord. Even worse. Not just out-of-tune, but sour, harsh, brutal as the morning sun.

He plays, trying not to listen too closely, a simple melody, a tune he wrote several years ago, before he moved back, when he still believed reemergence was possible.

Halfway through, he hears knocking at the front door. He plays. More knocking. He plucks the keys harder. Another round at the front door. His playing grows louder. On the fourth set of knocks, he slams out one more chord and pushes away from the piano. The bench screeches across the wood floor like claws. He heads to his chair and locates his slippers. He sits, pulls on the left one, then the right. His toe throbs, his ankles like blowfish.

He hobbles to the front hallway. Stops. Maybe it's the lawyer. The last thing he needs is that asshole. It can't be much past nine. The only time Parker's up at this time is if he hasn't gone to bed yet, and usually then he's too wasted to know the difference. Starting the day in this way is unnatural, like stirring up dust before it's settled.

He turns toward the steps, considering an ascent, and glimpses his solid gold hit.

The knock again. Louder.

He sighs. More a hiss. A car radio in the middle of Nebraska.

He opens the door and stares through the screen. Three shriveled up old farts. No gender. No class. No distinction. Just old. Even the clothes. A Walmart nightmare.

He scratches his bare arm, then his armpit—a clear advantage to being sleeveless—waits for them to speak, this aging trio, with their rainbow sweatshirts and matching pants and name tags, this Ida and Louise and Bert, this Mo and Larry and Curly.

One speaks. He can't tell which. "Mr. Davis?"

The screen dangles by a single staple. They shift, watch him through the door, their faces pixelated by the weave, a Monet in ruins.

"Parker Davis," the short one says in a toadstool voice, "we're looking for Parker Davis." Louise, that's her name.

R. H. Sheldon

Parker coughs up a wad of phlegm, pushes open the door, spits past their heads. The three step back, like soldiers practiced in retreat.

He sees Olympia out on the street in front of his house. She places orange traffic cones several feet out from the curb and talks into space. She wears an old army backpack that makes her look like an aging hippie in search of a commune.

Beyond her, also out in the street, Stephanie crouches behind some beat-up old shit of a car, acting as though she's trying to hide. Myron approaches her. She jumps. They exchange words and she rushes into her yard. Myron saunters onto the sidewalk, past Olympia, through the gate, and toward the house.

Bert clears his throat. "Perhaps we have the wrong place."

Myron steps up on the porch. Sonuvabitch appears out of the weeds and hops up after him. The three start. Bert holds his hand over his heart, his name tag.

"Right house," Myron says, his grin like fire. Sonuvabitch hisses, belches up a hairball onto Ida's sneakers.

Parker pulls the screen door closed and says to Myron, "Parker, these nice folks are looking for you." He shuts the inside door and retreats up the stairs, his breath no more than a memory.

Alonzo

Isabel still has not returned from taking the kids to school. Not unusual, Alonzo knows that. She often stops at the store or runs errands or visits her mom, who lives only a few blocks from here. Today might even be the day Isabel volunteers at the church. He can never remember when that is. But whatever she's doing, he dare not call and ask.

He lets Roscoe in from the backyard and leads him into the laundry room. He pats the dog on the head. Roscoe stares with a grief-stricken look and lowers his head in defeat. Alonzo shuts the door and rushes out of the house.

He climbs into his car, starts the engine, and clicks on the music, Mozart's Requièm Mass in D minor. The car fills with the long mournful tones, a movement deep, rich, filled with an eloquent sorrow that pulls at his heart, like an ancient river, its depths hidden in darkness. He thinks of the look in Roscoe's eyes.

Alonzo turns up the music and pulls out of the driveway, searching one last time for the minivan.

Isabel hates Mozart or anything like it. She prefers Mexican country music—*norteño*—with its whiny accordions and ill-tuned *bajo sextos*, like strumming strings over a tin can, the kind of music they play at those cheap Mexican restaurant chains, Denny's with tacos. Doesn't matter she can barely understand Spanish, let alone speak it. Lately, she won't listen to anything else. Before, she

R. H. Sheldon

used to play it only sometimes, said it reminded her of her grandmother. Now it's every chance she gets.

Alonzo heads onto I-90 and drives across the floating bridge into Seattle. Though it's almost ten, traffic is still backed up, bumper-to-bumper going into the tunnel. It's always backed up driving into the city, unless it's three in the morning.

He cranks up the stereo. *Sequentia, Dies Irae.* Full orchestra. Full chorus. Flowing through him like a rushing river.

The traffic pushes forward. He eases into the right lane, crawling until he reaches his exit, Rainier Avenue, northbound. Better to get off here than try to skirt downtown.

He'll visit Davis first, then Schmidt. He doubts Davis has made any progress. People seldom do in three days. He's been surprised in the past, but rarely have those surprises made Alonzo's life easier. Like the man who burnt down his own house. It should have expedited the process. But the investigation and court case put them sixth months behind schedule.

He drives down Twelfth until he hits Boxer Way. He turns left and parks. No sense trying to get any closer. Even if there were a spot, he prefers keeping his car at a safe distance.

He turns off the engine. Mozart dies.

He climbs out of the car, grabs his briefcase from the back seat, and heads down Boxer Way toward Eleventh. A light shower falls, almost imperceptible, like the inside of a cloud. He crosses Eleventh, passes Schmidt's house. A beat-up old CRX is parked in front, the hatchback covered in bumper stickers: *Free Tibet. Love Your Mother. Eat Organic. Arms Are For Hugging. Kill Your TV. Simplify Your Life.* The largest of them is white with giant black letters: *We're all or nothing.*

He moves toward the Davis ruins. Stops. A small band of people stand in front of the house, amid the tangle of weeds and piles of trash and empty beer cans and whiskey bottles, huddled like a group of pilgrims preparing for winter.

The only one Alonzo recognizes is that dark grizzly guy from last Friday, lurking near the others, but standing a step back, watching, his finger in his ear, that cat at his feet, sentry-ready, the others—four of them—wearing matching outfits, sweatshirts different colors. A geriatric crowd, except one, a middle-aged woman, with a look of purpose, impatience, a lioness ready to pounce, the queen of her pride.

She says, "More will come."

The other three nod, their eyes darting from the house to the yard.

Alonzo feels that twist in his guts and flutter in his chest. The tension rises whenever he makes these calls, whenever confronted by the unexpected.

The dark-haired man, the wild one, sees Alonzo, his look one of delight, anticipation, his eyes locked in their own fire, burning dark, deep, untouchable.

"He's here," the man says in a rumbling voice.

The woman, no doubt the leader, the way she stands, gazes past her comrades, aims a deadly stare at Alonzo. The three clones turn toward him, shift from one leg to the other, sharing the same look of consternation, controlled by a single switch.

"You must be the attorney," the leader says, a voice almost familiar. "Alonzo Garcia."

He steps back. "Yes, but..."

The dark-headed man picks up the cat, drapes it over his shoulder, moves closer to Alonzo, though he doesn't seem to actually move, but grow larger, a shift in perspective, like camera trickery in a B-grade horror movie.

Alonzo feels his throat tighten. "My business is with Parker Davis."

The leader steps toward him. Her three cohorts huddle closer, like chicks looking for shelter.

"Your business is with us now."

The wind kicks up a pile of leaves and sweeps them toward the empty lot. A shiver crawls up his back and through his shoulders, a clammy sign-of-the-cross.

"I'm here to see Parker Davis."

"Parker Davis is still recovering from his trip to the hospital, caused in no small part by your last visit."

Big Foot aims his stare at Alonzo. "Parker is sick."

The woman continues. "You tell your bosses they won't be getting this house. You tell them they've lost this one. You tell them that they either rein you in or we'll do it for them."

She means business, Alonzo is sure of it. And that means trouble. For Lockhart. For Higgins, Whitaker & Nye. For Alonzo Luis Garcia.

Fuck.

R. H. Sheldon

Alonzo tries to keep his voice as even and indifferent as possible. "Please tell Mr. Parker that I will be contacting the sheriff's office and he will have to deal with them."

"The sheriff?" Her voice brightens. "You do that. The sheriff is exactly what we need. And the press. Let's be sure to include them." Her chuckle comes out harsh, sinister, full of smug satisfaction.

One of the older women, the short one, pulls out of the leader's shadow. "Yeah," she says, her voice thin and shaky, "you bring the sheriff."

The leader smiles, pats the woman on the shoulder. "We're not leaving, Mr. Alonzo Garcia. You tell your bosses that. You tell them that the Reverend Olympia Culpepper and the members of the Lighthouse Sanctification Church plan to camp out here for as long as it takes. You got that, Mister Alonzo Garcia? You tell those bosses of yours they better be prepared for battle. You and your kind have ruined enough lives."

Alonzo turns and walks out of the yard. He will not look back. He will head up the street and climb into his car. He will return to his office and prepare the paperwork that the courts will require to have Parker Davis evicted. The reverend and her misfits can huff and puff all they want, but he has the law on his side, and there's little they can do to stop that.

He walks toward Twelfth, thinking only about getting into his car and getting the hell out of here. Someone calls his name. He resists the temptation to turn. When he hears it again, he gives in. Stephanie Schmidt stands at her white picket face.

"I can't talk right now," he says.

"But what about my house? You said you'd stop by this morning. You said we'd talk about the sale."

"I have other problems."

"So do I."

"Until we sort out the situation with your neighbor and his friends, there will be no sale."

"You mean those wackos from the church?"

Alonzo nods. A pain shoots through his neck.

"Something needs to be done about them."

"Yes, something does."

He marches up Boxer Way, climbs into the car, and starts the engine. Mozart comes to life. *Offertorium, Domine Jesu Christe.*

Olympia

As far as she's concerned, the law is exactly what they need. He'll bring the cops. She'll bring the press. More people will join the protest. And that will lead to more cops.

She's played this game before, though it's been a while, a part of her life she thought long gone. She hadn't realized how ready she was to be a player again. And the time is ripe for taking a stand, not just here at the house, but across the city, the country, around the world. Never have people been so ready to confront the inequalities that keep millions in poverty, without jobs, without healthcare, without futures. Never has there been such a willingness to come together to take back control. Look at Tunisia. Look at Egypt. Look at the Occupy movement.

But she must gather more forces—and quickly. If the cops show up now, they'll laugh. Her group can't do much resisting with only a handful of people. Sure, a few voices are better than none, but they need to make enough noise to get the authorities to act and react. But they haven't much time, and she expects Parker to be of little help.

Olympia points to a car parked in front of the empty lot, a blue-green Saturn a bit rough around the edges. "We need to find the owner and get that car moved. We need the spot cleared so people can see our stage." She turns to her three protesters. "Have you spoken to anyone else? Do you know who's coming?"

R. H. Sheldon

The three shake their heads, puppets on one set of strings. Ida says, "Do you think he was serious? About bringing in the sheriff?"

"I hope so."

"But the police," Bert says.

"We need to stir things up."

Olympia turns toward Myron. "Know anyone who wants to help out? Friends ready to join the cause?"

Myron tilts his head. "Friends?"

"Yes," she says, "friends, people who can help protect your home."

"Not my home." He picks up Sonuvabitch and drapes him over his shoulder. The trio steps back. Olympia swallows her impatience. She needs to stay focused, in control.

"If there's anyone you can ask, Myron, please do. The more of us, the better. How about Parker's friends? You know any of them?"

Myron looks off toward the dead maple tree, scratches the cat's head.

Olympia follows his eyes. Too bad there wasn't time to cut it down. "They'll be free food," she says. "Tell your friends that. We'll have plenty of free food."

Myron grins, emanates an eerie sense of knowing and acquiescence.

Usually she can read people, know their motives, what they're really after. But not Myron. He's like a vacant lot whose weeds hide a buried treasure—or Pandora's Box.

Myron says, "I'll go look."

"Look?"

"For friends."

He steps around the others, places Sonuvabitch on the porch and whispers to him. The cat lets out a short meow and twitches his tail. Myron strolls out of the yard and crosses the street to the park. He walks with a lumbering, swaying rhythm, in tempo with the cat's tail.

Olympia grabs her backpack off the porch—a beat-up Army carry-over from her college days, fatigue green, frayed at the seams. She reaches inside and retrieves a roll of plastic garbage bags. She peels off a bag and hands one to Louise, does the same for Ida, then Bert. Holds one out for herself.

"Let's clean," she says.

"Clean?"

That's Louise, never inclined to bend over if she doesn't need to.

"Make the place look better. At least get rid of the trash. We want a sympathetic public."

"Good idea," Ida says.

Bert nods in agreement.

Olympia smiles at Louise. "You think you can find the owner of that car? Knock on a few doors and ask them to move?"

Her smile is one of relief. "I can do that."

"I've left several cones down by the curb. Soon as the car's gone, set those out in the street."

Louise nods and scurries out of the yard.

Olympia turns to the others. "Start with the recyclable stuff—the bottles, cans—then we'll hit the trash."

They go to work, weeding through the weeds for bottles once filled with Budweiser Light and Jack Daniel's and Diet Pepsi-Cola and a few Snapple teas, an inexplicable quirk best not to question. Plenty of beer cans, too, the type found on sale at Safeway—Pabst, Schlitz, Miller, Schaefer, National Bohemia, and of course, Bud Light—along with a collection of food cans, mostly Campbell's chicken noodle soup, some potato, a few minestrone, the cans filled with an oily mucky dirt, scraggly weeds pushing out of the mulch, like mini-terrariums, micro-ecosystems that drip and ooze and emit a foul smell of mold and mildew and something akin to a dead animal.

Sonuvabitch watches from the porch, sniffs the air, feigns disinterested curiosity as only a cat can do, even such a snarly miserable creature as this one.

Olympia stuffs her bag full, grabs another from her pack. The others work with steady slow movements, accompanied by a few grunts and groans, but they seem contented enough, relieved perhaps by having a purpose, satisfying a desire Olympia has seen in a lot of older people—the need to feel as though they're part of the world around them, that they're still viable participants and contributors—little to ask for, yet few ever get it.

Ida and Bert fill their bags quickly, surprisingly so, and all this from the small space in front of the house. Olympia hands out more bags and returns to stuffing her own bag. She reaches for a bottle buried in the weeds, blackened with dirt and rot. Her arm snakes through a tangle of dried stalks and withered leaves. She digs deeper, her fingers nearly reaching its goal. She stops. Not a bottle. A dead crow, eyes a bottomless well.

She pulls back, straightens, kicks soil over the bird.

She's about to start in another spot when a blue Chevy van pulls up, an old one, as old as her car, almost as beat up. The vehicle slows, then parks near the corner, next to the *No Parking* sign. The driver turns off the engine. It rolls over several more times and ends with a gasp and a puff of black smoke. Four people climb out—Janice Ying and Digger, her live-in boyfriend and the van's driver, and a man and woman Olympia has never met, all four about the same age—late thirties, early forties—all four in that awkward phase of still wanting to appear young but no longer able to pull off those twenty-something fads—what Bellamy calls that semi-grunge, semi-street kid, semi-skater, semi-stoner, semi-urban look—and all four seeming more at home here than her elderly compatriots ever will.

They shuffle toward Parker's house. Digger tips his fedora in that streetwise, condescending way he has, and leads the group into the yard. Digger plays guitar in a blues band, and Janice reads tarot cards and interprets astrological charts and cleanses people's auras, when she can get the work. Janice has been coming to the Lighthouse Sanctification Church since Olympia first opened the doors and has shown up for every service since, except when Digger was in the hospital from a knife wound.

Janice hugs Olympia, then hugs Ida and Bert. When she spots Sonuvabitch, she climbs onto the porch, cracking one of the boards, and bends over the cat. Sonuvabitch leaps to his feet, snarls, hisses, and coughs up another hairball, then runs off into the weeds on the side of the house.

Janice is unfazed. She scans the yard and the house and announces from the top of the porch, "This place is a dump!"

Digger laughs, brushes his beard. "Worse than the house we had in Rainier Valley."

Olympia steps forward. "And who are your friends?" She reaches to shake their hands, but neither responds, as though they don't understand the gesture. Instead, they step back, nervous and guilty.

Janice jumps off the porch. "Olympia, this is Gavin and Harmony." The woman starts at the sound of her name. Gavin stares at his leather boots. The two shake slightly, hang back, hide their faces, him beneath a scraggly red beard and low hanging stocking cap, her beneath an even larger wool cap, pulled partially over her eyes, both faces drawn, pale, in search of the next buzz.

Ida and Bert return to their garbage duties, say nothing, poke through weeds. Louise appears with a middle-aged woman in tow, hints of gray and osteoporosis. She looks around in confusion, climbs into her car, and pulls away. Louise places the cones in the street just as instructed.

"Glad to meet you," Olympia says and reaches for her pack to grab more bags.

Janice says, "Where is everybody?"

"Just getting started. Thought we'd clean up a little to make the place more presentable."

Digger lets out a croaky, sour guffaw. "Pick up trash? No way in hell."

Janice aims a cool gaze in his direction. "Give me a bag," she says. Olympia does. Janice goes to work, pulling trash out of the weeds, along the porch, near the sidewalk, never slowing, never stopping long in one place, mixing bottles and trash in the same bag—beer bottles and Styrofoam cups, aluminum cans and cellophane wrappers, plastic spoons and piles of junk mail. The same bag!

Olympia turns away just in time to catch Digger flash a wry smile at Gavin and Harmony, the two like gold fish staring out of their bowls into the waterless void.

Alonzo

B ack in his office, waiting to face Buck. A battle rages in his stomach. A battalion fires in his head.

Buck will be furious. He expects these situations to wrap up quickly, without his intercession.

Alonzo reads email, not really reads, scans the Inbox, feigns interest, tries to ignore the blast of acid in his guts.

Buck charges into the office, fists against desktop, face scarlet, veins in his temple about to explode.

"What the fuck happened?" His voice ricochets through the office.

"I don't know."

Again, the fists.

"You don't know?"

"No, I don't know. I don't know what happened."

"How the fuck could you not know? You went there, didn't you?"

Buck leans in closer, his breath steamy, full of salami and beer.

"Yes, of course. I mean, I was there. But so were the protesters, in front of the house."

"Protesters? What the hell were they protesting? Fucking whales?"

Alonzo picks up a pen—a Pilot retractable fine point, blue ink. He clicks it several times, taps it against the desk, his palm. Buck rips it from his fingers and throws it across the room.

"Us," Alonzo says. "They're protesting us and the bank and Lockhart."

"So what if they protest? Why should we care?"

"They could make trouble."

"Let 'em. Get the cops. Have 'em evicted. It's our house now." Buck scratches his belly, drops into the chair, leans back. "How many protesters?"

Alonzo stares at the pen lying into the corner. "Five, I guess."

Buck snorts. "Five? You let five fucking freaks stop you?"

Alonzo nods. He feels like one of those dolls with the bobbing head.

"And what did the owner, ah, past owner, have to say about all this?"

Another squirt of acid against his stomach wall. "I didn't talk to him. He wasn't out there."

Buck stabs Alonzo with his stare. "You're telling me you didn't even speak to him?"

Alonzo feels himself crawl into the hole that is his nothingness. "He was inside. I didn't get past the protesters. They—"

"Where are your goddamn balls, man? You had one simple little assignment. Any jackass could have handled it."

"I know, but..."

"Quit being such a goddamn pussy and get back there and tell that goddamn loser sitting inside the house laughing at you that he better get the fuck out of there. Now!"

Buck springs to his feet. Alonzo can feel the heat from the massive hulk. "You better get yourself a backbone, boy. Before you can't even stand upright."

Parker

P arker wakes, climbs out of bed, steps on a wayward aspirin, and crushes it into powder. He winces and limps out of the bedroom and descends the stairs. He pulls open the front door and steps out onto the porch in his underwear and torn bathrobe and gray stubble and eyes permanently locked into light-resistant slits, the foggy haze of cataracts creeping steadily across his horizons.

Parker stares at the three old people picking up garbage and the one not-so-old girl picking up garbage, her skirt no more than a tattoo, her skin-tight blouse an open invitation. Three others stand at the gate, uninvited spirits, too cool to speak, too hip to help, too stoned to do anything but linger. Not that young, but young enough, and Parker has grown weary of the young—their assumptions, their prejudices, their unwillingness to bend. He'd like to think it was different when he was that age, but it wasn't. Mass foolishness. Mass ignorance. A generation with their heads up their asses.

Little has changed from what he can see. But who cares what he thinks? He doesn't even care. In fact, that's probably what differentiates his older self from his younger one more than anything else—his recognition of his own inconsequence.

Olympia taps her earpiece, ends her call, steps toward the porch. "Parker," she says, "you've decided to join us."

"Some of me, at least."

"Better than nothing."

"Perhaps."

She points to the young woman picking up trash. "Janice." She waves a hand toward the man in the fedora. "Digger." She nods to the other two. "Gavin and Harmony." Then she aims her finger at the three elderly cleaners. "I believe you met them. Louise, Ida, Bert."

Parker wonders why she would provide him with this information. It only makes him want to retreat back into the house that much sooner.

She's not about to let him.

"Thought we'd do a bit of cleaning."

"Suit yourself."

"Perhaps you'd like to join us. Might do you good."

He's genuinely surprised by this assumption and the logic that might lie behind it. "What for?"

"The better the place looks, the more people will come."

Perhaps it's the drugs or the hospital stay or the years of cigarettes and booze or his general mental condition, but he really has no idea what the hell she's talking about and all he can think of to say is, "What people?"

And, of course, she doesn't miss one syncopated beat. "All people."

So he says, "Why should they come?"

"They don't want it to happen to them."

"It already is."

"What do you mean?"

"What do *you* mean?"

Parker quickly tires of this game, like he gets tired with Myron. Where *is* Myron, anyway? Jesus, this day makes no sense whatsoever.

"I'm going back to bed," he announces.

"And miss all the fun?"

He's about to open the door when he notices out of the corner of his compromised eyes the march of a dozen street-occupying denizens led by his furry and freaky friend, Myron, the troop scurrying across Boxer Way toward his house, about two-thirds of them men, about a third women, and one who falls somewhere in between. They wear ill-fitting clothes. They walk with limps and bent backs. They are smudged with dirt and street grime. They

R. H. Sheldon

carry duffel bags and giant plastic garbage bags. Some push carts. All need a shave.

They follow Myron into the yard and stop in front of the porch. Myron says to Olympia, "My friends."

Parker smiles. Parker snickers. Parker giggles. Parker laughs so hard tears stream down his wrinkled and sallow face.

The three aging musketeers scurry toward Stephanie's white-picket fence, near a thicket of blackberry bramble, and huddle close together. Janice says, "Sick." Digger sucks on his cigarette and strikes a *seen-it-all* pose. The two tweakers, Harmony and Gavin, twitch and sway and look up to the sky for redemption.

Olympia draws in a deep breath. Myron waits. The street denizens hover nearby.

Myron says, "They're hungry."

Olympia shakes her head. "The food isn't here yet."

Parker reaches for the door with his bare arm. His head feels suddenly light, fluttering in the breeze. He grabs the door for support, misses, pushes through the screen. The house swallows his arm. He tries to stand upright. The screen tears into his flesh. A wave of nausea surges through his guts.

When he finally disentangles himself, the screen comes with him, hooked on several threads that dangle from the robe's shoulder.

Myron says, "My friends are hungry."

Parker holds up a bloody finger. "Let them eat cake."

"We have cake?"

Parker feels a bubble in his guts. "I think I'm gonna puke." He places his hand over his mouth.

Olympia eyes him for a moment, then turns to Myron. "The food won't be here for another hour at least." She returns her attention to Parker. "Maybe you *should* lie down. You're looking a bit pale."

He pulls his hand away from his face. "I always look that way."

Digger crosses the yard and stands next to Janice, who's stuffing a piece of soggy cardboard into the bag.

"I need cigarettes," he says.

"Good, go. You're only in the way here." She never looks up from the trash.

"I won't be long."

"No hurry."

Digger retraces his steps, stops before Gavin and Harmony. "Up for a ride?" Harmony shrugs. Gavin stares into space.

"Come on," Digger says. "Then we can run that *other* errand."

A spark flickers through Harmony's eyes. She makes small gestures with her fingers, as though gathering the psychic forces that have spilled out.

Gavin grabs her hand, not in an affectionate way, but as one would lead a stray dog to the pound.

Janice picks up a potato chip bag and shoves it in with the other trash.

Digger tips his fedora and he—along with his two zombie comrades—head toward the van. But before they can reach it, a clamor erupts from across the street, from within the park, somewhere beyond the small hill and cone-shaped fountain, like a gang of football revelers in search of a tailgate.

Parker doesn't like this, not a bit. He wants out now. Myron climbs on the porch. The noise grows louder—the singing and cheering and yelling and *whooping*. Parker backs up toward the door.

Myron says, "Where you going, Parker?"

"Straight to hell." He opens the screenless screen door.

A crowd appears, heading straight toward them, the din growing louder, more confused, until from its center rises a steady chant: "Ninety-nine. Ninety-nine. Ninety-nine percent." The street fills with marchers, their faces a mix of anger and party-ready excitement, voices young and strong and full of defiance.

"Ninety-nine. Ninety-nine. Ninety-nine percent."

They stop in front of Parker's house, most of them in the street, between the two rows of parked cars. Thirty at least. Passionate and ready to be pissed.

Parker recognizes one of them. Olympia's daughter. It's got to be. Standing at the front, clad in black and raising a fist over her head, the free hand clutching the hand of a young man—a kid— who raises his own fist.

Digger and his accompanying tweakers back away from the van, join in the shouting.

Olympia moves toward the sidewalk, tries to talk to her daughter, but the girl continues to yell.

The chanting grows louder. Cars pull up at the intersections at either end of his block. People empty out. They shout. They sing. They carry signs. *Save Parker's house!* Some push their way through the crowds and into the yard. Others join the protesters in the street. More shouting, more chanting. At first, Parker can catch only snippets of what is said, but it must catch on because soon everyone is yelling the same thing. One voice. One message. "Occupy Parker's. Occupy Parker's. Occupy Parker's."

Parker slips inside the house, pulls the screenless screen door closed, and pushes the inside door closed. He locks the door and reaches for the railing. He climbs the stairs one step at a time. He catches his breath at the top.

In his room, he kicks off his slippers and peels off his torn robe and climbs into bed. He stares at the cracked plaster above him, trying to ignore the shouting, the chattering, the buzz of the crowd.

He grabs his high-priced sound-cancelling Bose headphones, slides the iPod into the charger, and cranks up an endless shuffle of jazz, a classic mix that ranges from Cab Calloway to Rosemary Clooney to Thelonious Monk.

The iPod and headphones are the only real pieces of technology he owns. The iPod was gifted to him by a drunk friend and bar patron who insisted upon sharing his music collection with Parker because of his "extraordinary talent." Whether his grateful buddy had intended to leave the iPod with Parker indefinitely, Parker will never know. Shortly after insisting that Parker listen to the classic collection, the patron walked out of Oily Tom's and stepped directly in front of a Metro bus. Parker did not hear about the incident till the next day, but as a tribute to the fallen jazz enthusiast, Parker invested in the headphones and the charger, a worthy outlay given the abundance of free music.

And never has he appreciated them as he does at this very moment.

Stephanie

Stephanie sits at Victrola's, a coffee shop on Fifteenth, at the top of Capitol Hill. The tables are packed, mostly young hip types looking fashionably unfashionable, hair perfectly deranged, tattoos and piercings en masse to show their independence. Most of them stare at laptops or cell phones, headsets plugged in, their attached detachment complete. Those not electronically impeded speak in loud, rapid voices, the word like peppered throughout their sentences, each one ending with that question-like inflection that governs most of their dialogue. They remind Stephanie of sitcom characters, intent on making an entire generation sound incapable of rational discourse: it's like, that's like so, he was like, I was so like...

Aargh!

She should never have agreed to meet here. They could be sitting in her garden right now, or at least someplace a bit less trendy, like one of the thousand Starbucks scattered around, but Georgia wanted to meet here and here they are, sitting across from one another like long lost pals, both sipping weak genmaicha tea and pretending it has flavor.

"I had a few things in storage," she says. "Thought I'd drive up before we get any closer to winter."

"You should have let me know you were coming."

Georgia fidgets with her cup, stares over Stephanie's shoulder, toward the front window.

R. H. Sheldon

Stephanie says, "How long you in town?"

Georgia shrugs. "Not sure yet. Have some business to take care of. Get the rest of my things out of storage and load my truck. It's not much."

How odd to hear her say that—*some business*. They used to share everything, even the most mundane of details. That's where relationships lie, it seems, in the mundane.

But theirs is a relationship no more. Times change, like it or not. Georgia even looks different, hair shorter, a few pounds lighter, the lines in her face more pronounced, especially those around her lips and the ones that push her eyes into perpetual sadness. Or maybe Stephanie's not remembering exactly. Three months. An eternity. Still, there's something different. She looks haggard, a bit pale. The drive, perhaps, has depleted her resources.

"You have a dog," Stephanie says.

Georgia stretches her mouth into an uneven grin. "Yeah, Bucky. A beagle pup. She's our little baby."

There it is again, the *our* word. Always *our* or *we* or *us*. Does she do it intentionally?

"Must be a handful."

"We couldn't live without him."

Stephanie pushes back from the table. "I better get going. I have an appointment this afternoon."

She does not, of course, but sees little reason to prolong their meeting. She should never have agreed to come.

"There was one other thing." Her struggle not to look at Stephanie is almost comical.

Stephanie hunches forward, grabs her mug, squeezes.

"I also came to see a specialist."

"Specialist?"

"Oncologist. Gynecologic oncologist."

"Georgia." The espresso machine hisses. Dishes clang. Customers chatter, their incessant *like, like, like*. The air feels hot, muggy, almost suffocating. "What's going on?"

Georgia studies her empty cup. "Some odd symptoms— bloating, back pain, tiredness, upset stomach. Even lost some weight. Didn't you notice?" She tries to smile.

"But those could be..."

"Anything, I know. But I had an ultrasound. It showed a mass in one of my ovaries."

Stephanie gasps, tries to recover, curses herself for her reaction. She needs time. She scans the coffee shop, looks everywhere but across the table. The last thing she wants is for Georgia to pick up on her fear. Stephanie knows what a mass can mean. She knows too much. She tries to look at Georgia. "But nothing's been confirmed, right?"

"That's why I'm here. One of the top doctors on the West Coast is in Seattle. And I'm still a resident in Washington. My insurance is still here. It just makes sense."

Stephanie nods. "What happens next?"

"Exploratory laparotomy, not sure when. I meet with the doctor tomorrow."

Stephanie touches Georgia's arm. "I'm so sorry. If there's anything I can do..." The words feel hollow, broken.

"I just wanted you to know, that's all."

So that's what's going on—the weight, the color, the muscle tone—everything, just a little off.

"Where are you staying?"

"With Danny and Virginia."

"Those nuts? They drive you crazy."

"They've got the room."

"So does the Woodland Park Zoo."

"And they're not too far from the hospital."

"Either am I."

This doesn't seem to register with Georgia, at least not at first. She cocks her head, her face filled with questions. Then understanding comes and she frowns. "What are you saying?"

"You're staying with me."

"You'd put me up?"

"Of course."

She shakes her head, drops her eyes to the table. "No, I can't."

"Why not? I'm a nurse, for chrissakes."

"You know why not."

"Don't be daft."

A hint of a smile crosses her face. "Daft? Where did you get that?"

"I have my moments."

Georgia seems to fade from the room, as though she stands in a different time and place.

"Your girlfriend can stay, too," Stephanie says, "BJ, if you want. I mean, if she ends up meeting you up here." She tries to sound lighter than she feels. "Hell, you can even bring Bucky."

Georgia glances up. Her eyes catch the light from the window, the start of tears glistening.

"BJ doesn't handle this sort of thing very well."

Stephanie considers for a moment what to say next, but instead jumps to her feet. "Come on," she says.

"Where to?"

"To get you settled in my place."

"I thought you had an appointment."

Stephanie feels the guilt spread. "I'll cancel."

"But—"

Stephanie forces a grin. "Didn't you learn anything from our time together?"

Georgia pushes herself to her feet, holds the table for stability. Stephanie feels something crack within her.

Georgia says, "You sure about this?"

Stephanie places a hand on her shoulder. For a moment, she can feel the tension ease, and all she wants to do is hold her in her arms and tell her everything will be okay.

"Yeah," she says. "I'm sure."

Myron

Myron stands to the side, considers the crowd. They creep. They devour. They conquer. Shifting as an organism, indifferent to its parts, relying on those parts to survive. Too much jungle. Too much.

He moves toward Olympia in short furtive steps. He stands beside her, taps her on the shoulder. She talks into the air. "And get the food here," she says. "And more signs." She touches her earpiece, turns toward Myron. He's about to speak, but she holds up a finger, then taps her earpiece again. "Barclay? You and the others might want to get down here. And where's Mark? He's supposed to be shooting the photos." She stops, starts again. "Yep, the Occupy group. A lot of them landed here." Stop. Start. "Well over fifty last I counted." She touches the earpiece.

Myron points to her head. "Where does that end and you begin?"

She frowns. "I don't know. But I'd be lost without it."

Myron says, "My friends are very hungry." He nods toward the small group, huddled near the far corner of the porch.

"Soon. Very soon." She looks past Myron toward the street. "I see they've arrived."

Myron follows her eyes. Several cops stand near the curb in front of the empty lot. They survey the crowd, the way it spreads along the sidewalks, spills into the street, over to the park. One of the cops sees Myron, stares at him across the fence, across the

R. H. Sheldon

weeds, across the bramble of blackberry, big and tall and solid as a truck. Myron decides to take a walk.

He slips into the gangway between Parker's house and Stephanie's white picket fence, a narrow tunnel of wall and brush. In the backyard, he finds several young male protesters sharing a pipe. They stop when they see him but decide he's no threat and continue to puff. He steps over the chain-link that was once a fence, rusted and split into pieces. He follows the gravel to Eleventh.

Myron wants to go to the far end of Cal Anderson Park, but the crowds stand in the way. He heads north on Eleventh, walks up John, follows Twelfth to Olive, then down to the park. A giant loop. An unbroken circle. A way of quiet and peace.

When he reaches the park, he ventures no further than the cluster of trees near the sidewalk, where the ground rises up gently from the cement, wedged between the playfields and the playground. Brown-yellow leaves cling to the branches, many already fallen, scattered across the ground, shimmering with their collected moisture, the grass, too, wet with the day's mist.

Myron savors the quiet oasis of grass and trees, the stretch of idle playfields, like a clearing in the jungle. He's finished with the crowds and the police. He'll return to Parker's house later tonight. Sonuvabitch will want to see him.

Myron doesn't get along with the police, mostly because they don't like him. At least that's how it used to be, especially with the white ones. Always telling him where to stand or sit or walk. Sometimes they'd push him around, hit him with their sticks, but he never knew why, never knew what he might have done. And he never knew which ones it would be.

It's not so bad now that's he's older. These days, they treat him more like a cartoon, a funny dark joke. But before, after he returned home, he was no joke. The cops back then reminded him of a lot of the soldiers in the jungle. The heat, the dense air, the thick canopies—they did something to people, made them forget who they were. Cops with sticks sometimes forget who they are.

Myron sits under the tallest tree and leans against the trunk. The bark scratches through his shirt, the ground cool, damp, infused with sacred scents as old as the earth, rich, musty, teeming with life.

He listens to the distant moan of traffic, the sirens, the horns, the thrust of engines, the crowd near Parker's, like a river, cascading through the forests. Quickly the jungle mists close in, the call of birds wild and exotic, animals unseen, the sun falling in patches on the thick vegetation, its rays swirling in gray.

Then he hears it, the bleat of the chopper, distant at first, but soon hovering over the canopy. He looks up through the trees, sees the splotches of sky. The noise grows louder. A shadow passes over. He squeezes against the tree. Giant blades slice the air, the glint of metal, the screaming in his head. He covers his ears. Squeezes his eyes shut. Not again. Not ever again.

He falls over, holding his ears, whimpering like an abandoned puppy.

R. H. Sheldon

Bellamy

Bellamy eyes her mother up on the porch, talking into space, amid the rush of voices and eruption of protester cheers. She must be really pissed about this—Bellamy rounding up more people than she could. She must be out of her friggin' mind with jealousy and rage.

"Where's your mom now?" Casey asks. He leans against the fence, his hands in his pockets, his face elfish and glowing. Probably the weed.

Bellamy points toward the house.

"She organized all this?"

Bellamy groans. "Still mourns the Sixties."

His eyes widen, whites like roadmaps. "She's *that* old?"

"Old enough to be influenced by it, I guess. She's like always saying she should have been born sooner."

"Oh, I get it," Casey says. "It's like all this apathy now. Your mom sounds so totally awesome."

Her mom is anything but awesome, and she's the last person Bellamy wants to be talking about. She should never have suggested they come here. She never would have if she knew Casey would bring half the Occupy forces with him, including that Lita bitch, still carrying her kid around, still dragging Isabel along, and Isabel still acting like she's too good for any of them.

They showed up at Seattle Central right as the group was preparing to head up to the house. Casey insisted that the sisters join in, acting like a schoolboy with a crush on his teacher. Maybe Lita will get run over by a truck.

The only good part about all this was seeing the look on her mom's face when they arrived. And seeing too how impressed Casey was by her mom's activism. With any luck, he'll assume it runs in the family. But now it's time to get away, just the two of them, in a camp all their own.

Casey stares up at the porch. "Pretty sick your mom's into this shit. My parents are locked in their corporate offices in Redmond, securing the software empire."

Bellamy glances at Lita—too close for comfort.

"Want to meet her?" Bellamy grabs his hand and pulls him through the gate and thicket of protesters squeezed into the front yard. The crowd has doubled since they arrived, more Occupy people, more from the church. A small group of street types hover near the far end of the porch, not like those hip dudes hanging around the camp, but the kind who've been doing it too long, who never gave up. That part of the porch serves as a table for the food her mom had shipped in, mostly Costco-type crap: turkey wraps, crackers and dip, corn chips and salsa, meatballs, rice rolls, cupcakes and muffins. The usual commercial shit. What would Casey think of her mom now if he knew she was the one who ordered it?

They climb the rickety steps and stand next to Olympia. She shouts into the air. "Not sure how long we'll go tonight." Pause. "Some police. Not many yet." Another break. "Yeah, that's great, but when will Channel 7 get here." She scrunches her face. "Channel 5? Yeah...yeah. I don't know about them. Newspapers even relevant anymore?" She reaches for her headset, ready to disconnect. "Okay. Fine. And get the photographer here. Now!" She touches the earpiece, frowns at Bellamy.

"Quite a crowd you brought."

"I thought you'd be happy."

Her mom flashes a phony smile, something out of a Target ad.

Bellamy says, "Mom, this is Casey, one of the Occupy campers. He's the one who sent out the tweets, got the people to come."

"Guess we have you to thank," she says. "I'm Olympia." This time her smile is real.

"Very cool what you're doing here," Casey says. "The world is changing."

"I hope so," Olympia replies. "None too soon, either."

R. H. Sheldon

"Awesome."

"How did you manage to get so many of the Occupy people here? Aren't they needed at the camp?"

Casey smirks. "Plenty still there. More at City Hall. The Occupy forces are a lot bigger than you realize."

"Excuse me." She touches her earpiece. "Where are you? We expected you an hour ago. Tomorrow is too late. We want those photos online by tonight. Hold on." She turns to Casey. "How did you say you got people here?"

He snickers again. "Tweets. A bunch of them."

"Tweets?"

"You know, Twitter, tweets, the social networking site..."

"I know what Twitter is."

"I just thought..."

"If we can get some photos online, can you tweet their links? Maybe include a few messages?"

"Yeah, sure, I just—"

"The more the better." She stares into space. "Mark, we need those pictures online as soon as possible, before the crowds start to thin out." She sighs. "Bring them along. A couple kids will give it a family look. Just hurry." Finger to the earpiece.

"Casey, I'll let you know as soon as we're good to go. What's your cell number."

"My cell..."

"Never mind. Bellamy, have him call me so I have his number." She spins around. "Louise. Ida." Her voice carries through the crowd. The two women turn, flash tired smiles, work their way toward her.

Bellamy turns to Casey. "Let's get out of here."

"You mean leave? With all this shit going down? Look, more cops just showed up."

Bellamy stares out into the street. Two arriving squad cars. Then she spots the cop from the camp, standing off to the side, still as tall and dark and hot as ever—and once again staring straight at her.

She smiles slightly, just enough, then turns away. "Maybe you're right," she says. "Let's stick around. But no need to hang here. You've seen what *she's* like."

"Yeah, what an amazing woman. Just the sort we need on our side."

"But..."

"It's nice to know there's cool people like that around, especially older ones. I'd so like given up hope."

Bellamy kicks a pebble at Casey, but it goes wayward. The whole thing feels like a backed-up toilet. "Less crowded in the street," she says. "Let's go there."

They weave through the throng until they reach the curb. Casey gravitates toward Lita, despite Bellamy's attempts to lead them further along.

Landmines everywhere.

More people have arrived and even out here the crowds have thickened and push well into the park. Some hover on top of the hill, more by the fountain. A number of makeshift signs, all saying the same thing—*Occupy Parker's House*—while half the protesters chant, "Occupy Parker's. Occupy Parker's."

Isabel now holds the child and Lita stands next to them. Isabel's eyes flit across the crowds nervously and she squeezes the child close in. The toddler squirms and waves his arms, but Isabel doesn't relent. Lita seems indifferent to his struggle and stands with her hands in her pocket, easy and relaxed, as though she spends every day among crowds of protesters. Casey stares ceaselessly at Lita, shifts his weight from one leg to the other, all the time tapping out a rhythm on his hip.

Lita says, "So why here?"

Casey shrugs. "Opportunity."

Bellamy snaps to attention. "What?"

Casey grins, half guilt, half amusement. "A good chance to join forces, that's all I meant."

Lita sends him a cool smile. He looks away.

The chanting grows louder. The crowds squeeze in. Bellamy becomes aware of the sound of rolling thunder, growing steadily louder. Soon the street fills with a pounding roar that echoes against the buildings and carries into the park. Bellamy looks up. A helicopter approaches, low on the horizon.

The others notice, too. Now they all stare at the sky, their chants softening in the din.

"A news chopper," someone says.

Casey shouts, "About fucking time."

Bellamy turns toward the front porch. Her mom stares into the sky, her smile as wide as the Grand Coulee Dam.

R. H. Sheldon

Alonzo

A lonzo parks a couple blocks away, on Eleventh, near the south end of Cal Anderson Park. He climbs out of the car. A lone figure emerges from the trees, his walk stumbling, confused. Another drunk. Or another junkie. Then Alonzo recognizes the wild mane, the shadowed eyes, the single eyebrow. The man stops, gazes toward Alonzo, not at him exactly, but through him, around him, as though what Alonzo thinks of as his corporeal self is no more than a mist.

A shiver passes through him.

The man glances over his shoulder, up toward the sky. A squadron of seagulls circle and squawk. His eyes glaze over, grow wild with fear. He drops to his knees and covers his head. He lets loose a violent *yeeeeaaaoooowww,* then jumps to his feet and sprints off from the direction he came, waving his arms and screaming "minions of the devil" over and over.

Alonzo hears the thump of helicopter blades. He looks up and sees Chopper 7 news, hovering over the park. He rushes up Eleventh, grows aware of the shouting, the buzz of the crowd. He is soon upon the hordes, squeezed into the street, moving into the park. He approaches Boxer Way. Several cops stand around the traffic circle at the intersection, their backs toward him. They watch the protesters, faces like steel.

How do they do it, stand there like that, with so much enmity directed toward them? With danger lurking at every turn? Alonzo would make a horrible cop.

People carry signs and yell out epithets against banks and Wall Street and developers and lawyers.

He crosses the street to the side opposite the park and creeps toward the traffic circle. When he arrives, he stops next to one of the officers, a man twice Alonzo's age, standing with his arms crossed, his face stern, unyielding.

Alonzo says, "What's happening here?"

Shouts erupt from the crowds, an incoherent mix of chanting and yelling and song. Then he hears it, "Occupy Parker's. Occupy Parker's." The chants grow unified, stronger, over and over, "Occupy Parker's. Occupy Parker's."

"This can't be..."

The cop's fingers twitch and his fists tighten, but his face remains still.

Alonzo moves to the sidewalk, pushes through the crowd, through the sweat and grime and stench. He must find Parker Davis, talk some sense into him. The crowd squeezes in, shoves up against Stephanie Schmidt's white picket fence, bending it toward the yard.

His chest tightens, squeezes out his breath. He tries to worm through the protesters, but the wall is unrelenting. Everyone is shouting now, with voices that border on screams. "Occupy Parker's. Occupy Parker's."

He reaches the spot where Schmidt's fence abuts Davis's infested yard. A slit in the crowd opens between him and Parker's house. The woman from the church stands on a platform, just in front of the fence, yelling into a megaphone, "Occupy Parker's. Occupy Parker's." She sees him and stops. Delivers an icy stare. Points. "There he is! One of *them*." Those near to the stage turn toward Alonzo. His heart flutters and sweat pours from his armpits. "There!" she yells and waves her hand. "Listen, everyone, listen." The chanting softens. More protesters turn toward the stage. She continues to point, her face filled with anger and hate. "Alonzo Garcia, attorney at large." The megaphone buzzes, whistles. "Alonzo Garcia," she shouts. "Remember that name!"

More of the crowd turns toward Alonzo. He tries to step back, but the protesters have closed in. His knees weaken and head grows light.

"Alonzo Garcia, notorious villain from Higgins, Whitaker & Nye. A *Bellevue* law firm. The legal representatives of Lockhart Investments. They're the ones who built that monstrosity on the corner. They're the ones who want to build another monstrosity right here. They're the ones who are kicking Parker Davis out of his home, into the street, into the gutter." Her face reddens; her fingers squeeze into a fist. "You, Alonzo Garcia, are the one who should be thrown into the street. You, and everyone like you!"

The crowd jeers and boos and closes in tighter. He pushes against the corner of the fence. A spike digs into his back, another into his side.

The protesters move in so close he can feel their breath, see the looks of revulsion and hate, frustration and rage. He looks for the police, but they're invisible from here. He's trapped so completely it would take an army to pry him out.

They start to chant, almost a moan, low, steady. "Occupy Parker's. Occupy Parker's."

Alonzo squeezes against the fence, the pain sharp, like spikes of fire. The protesters close in. Their chants grow louder, faster. He pushes back with all his strength. The fence gives. He tumbles backwards, into a tangle of blackberry. A half-dozen protesters fall next to him, on him. Dozens more spill into the yard. The crowd pushes harder, knocks over more of the fence. Others fall, pinning Alonzo against the bush. Barbs poke through his shirt, scrape across the flesh. He struggles, fights, becomes more entangled.

Minutes pass. Maybe hours. Suddenly, the pressure eases, a collective shift in bodies. Alonzo acts quickly. He pulls against the bramble, tries to tear himself free. His clothes rip, his skin bleeds. He tugs with all his strength. The branches release him and he rolls to the side. He looks up. No one notices him. He crawls away in short spurts, squeezing through legs and twisted bodies. He grabs air when he can, ignoring the torn flesh, the sting of his sweat.

The crowd rushes to fill in the gap, more fall into the bushes, their shouting louder, their numbers greater, another wave of bodies, no longer aware of him, of anything. He races on his hands and knees toward Schmidt's house, grabs the corner of the building, and pulls himself to his feet. He squeezes up to the rhododendron near the front door, struggling for breath. A late afternoon sun breaks out across the yard, invigorates the crowd. They laugh and shout and sing. No longer focused on anything, or perhaps focused on the sun or the crowd itself, but not on Alonzo. Or so he hopes.

He creeps toward the far corner of the yard and along the side of the house. The scratches sting and burn. He reaches the gate in the back and slips into the alley. When he emerges on Eleventh, the cop at the intersection turns, as if by instinct, eyes Alonzo for a moment, long enough for his skin to crawl from his toes to his scalp. The cop turns away.

Alonzo circles around the protestors, walking blocks out of his way to get back to his car. His legs ache. His heart pounds. His stomach wages holy war. When he reaches his car, he stops, pants heavily. Sweat stings his cuts, his eyes. He wipes his brow with his sleeve, now all bloody and torn.

He's about to climb in when he hears his name. Too late to run, he turns. "Isabel!"

Lita and her kid stand next to her.

"You all right?"

"But how—how?"

Lita says, "He must be okay. Let's head to my place."

Alonzo feels his insides empty out.

Isabel glances at Alonzo and then at her sister.

Lita shakes her head. "So you're not just a clerk. You also kick people out of their homes."

Isabel wears a look both sad and confused. "You told me you practice real estate law."

Alonzo looks around, searching for help. He clears his throat. "Where are the girls?"

She hesitates, glares. "At my mother's."

"Shouldn't they be home, with you?"

Isabel is about to speak, stops, turns away. She flips her hair over her shoulder, white streak and all.

Alonzo watches her and Lita walk up Olive, heading toward Twelfth. The helicopter grows louder and appears over the trees, stopping directly above him, its thunderous roar shaking the ground like the final days of the Apocalypse.

R. H. Sheldon

Stephanie

The first thing Stephanie spots when she turns off John onto Eleventh is the string of people hovering along the sidewalks near Boxer Way, hovering much too close to her fence and yard. Beyond them stand a handful of police, their cars parked across the intersection in a haphazard blockade, and beyond them, a gaggle of bicycle cops, straddling their rides like a renegade cavalry, poised for an attack.

She slows, checks for Georgia in her mirror, and turns into the alley behind her house. She parks and waits for Georgia to pull in next to her. They climb out of their cars.

The air rings with the sounds of a helicopter bleating and crowds rumbling and the amplified voice of a lone speaker spewing out a string of garbled words.

Georgia stares with a look of bewilderment. "What the hell's going on?"

"Long story," Stephanie says. "But you can guess who's at the center of this mess."

"Parker?"

"Parker."

Georgia hates Parker even more than Stephanie. She hates everything about him—his lewd comments, rude behavior, late-night parties—everything. More than once their confrontations nearly ended in fistfights, with both storming off in child-like tirades. Parker would retaliate by flinging more beer cans and whiskey bottles into the yard. Georgia would return the favor by pounding on the front door with a bag full of trash, first thing in the morning when she knew Parker would be sleeping.

Parker was the one issue they could always agree on.

Georgia says, "Maybe this isn't such a good time to stay here."

"It will blow over. I'll fill you in on all the gruesome details when we get inside." Stephanie feels much less confident than she tries to sound, and Georgia looks a lot less confident than Stephanie feels. "Besides," she continues, "I'm not sure Danny and Virginia will take you back. They seemed a bit miffed about your change of plans."

"You think so?"

Stephanie grabs the pack from behind the front seat of Georgia's truck, a Toyota Tacoma, white, like new. Nicer than anything she had when she lived here.

Stephanie heads toward the house. Georgia follows. Her suitcase rolls over the stone walkway, rattling like a toy train about to derail.

When they reach the side of the house, Stephanie stops. A mob has taken over her yard. They laugh. They shout. They squat on the ground amid shredded azaleas and ruined maples and a trellis destroyed.

She drops the pack. She gnashes her teeth. She huffs and puffs. She storms the crowd with waving arms, screaming for them to leave. She runs in circles and threatens them with sticks. She curses and pants and swears an undying revenge. She rushes to the far corner of the lot and yells at the police standing in the street. "Why the hell aren't you doing anything? These vandals are destroying my property! Stop them! Don't just stand there!" She runs back to the intruders. "Get the hell out of here! Out! Out! Now!" She pushes the ones closest to the downed fence. She grabs others. She screams louder. Curses more. Shoves and elbows and knees. She runs back to the far side, again calls out to the police. "Do your goddamn jobs and get these criminals out of here!" She returns to the damaged corner. She grabs them by their collars, threatens louder, pushes and pulls and pushes and pulls.

The protesters respond slowly, but in the end offer little resistance, a reluctant herd moving to the next pasture. A young woman calls Stephanie a corporate Nazi and another says she's a fascist tyrant, but in the end, most of them move along.

Only one man stands his ground, hovering near the broken bench in his prerequisite stocking cap and North Face jacket. He grabs a small statue of Diana and lobs it at Stephanie, but in his juiced-up, activist state, he sends the sculpture soaring over her head and into the street. Diana's outstretched arm nails one of the cops in the thigh and sends him tumbling to the ground. Several of his cohorts shout, "Officer down, officer down," and charge into the crowd waving batons and aiming rifles loaded with canisters of pepper spray and rubber bullets. The news helicopter quickly zooms in.

The vortex that surrounds the police sucks away the nearby protesters, including the Diana-lobbing assailant, and sends them running with the rest of the mob, leaving Stephanie standing with a broken branch in one hand and a wrought iron bench leg in the other, panting and cursing and ready to attack whoever comes next.

Out in the street, protesters scream and cry for help and flee into the park. The cops chase them down. Knock some to the ground. Others fall. Many get trampled. Gas flows. Batons swing. Rubber bullets fly. Chaos ensues.

Georgia approaches from behind and places a hand on Stephanie's shoulder. Stephanie jumps.

"Easy," Georgia says.

Stephanie pants.

"Come on," Georgia says, "let's get inside."

Olympia

Olympia doesn't know how the riot began. Sure, she might have pushed the envelope somewhat when Alonzo Garcia showed up, but that resulted in only a minor scuffle. This time it's different. One moment she's talking to the protesters about justice and taking back control, and the next moment the police are storming the crowds and people are running and screaming. Then sticks start flying, followed by rocks and bricks. And now protesters are going after windows in nearby cars and in the abandoned house and in the apartment building on the corner. More cops arrive, dressed in riot gear, hiding behind shields. Sirens blare. Bullhorns scream. Pepper spray fills the air.

Some try to stand their ground, locking arms, chanting, taking the brunt of clubs and gas, even hits by rubber bullets. Bellamy stands with them, her arms locked with Casey's, yet hers is not an expression of resolve like the others, but instead one of confusion and fear.

A canister drops near Bellamy's feet and a bluish cloud rises from the ground. She screams, gasps, falls to the street. Police rush in. They grab her. She struggles and cries. The cops club her and drag her away, like a bag of dirty laundry, along with her boyfriend and several others. The news helicopter hovers lower. Another arrives. More press on the ground. Cameras. Shouting. Screaming. Bedlam from curb to curb.

R. H. Sheldon

Olympia jumps off the porch and tries to reach Bellamy, but the crowds rush toward the house to avoid the pepper spray and sticks. An impenetrable wall squeezes in and drives her back to the stairs. They follow her onto the porch, flatten her against the cracked siding and peeling paint, along with those nearest her, struggling to escape the sudden chokehold. She tries to raise the bullhorn and call for calm and level heads, but it gets knocked from her hands.

Pepper spray penetrates the crowd, burns her eyes and nostrils. She struggles to breathe. The crowd pushes toward the porch. She can't move her legs, her arms. Something sharp digs into the back of her thigh. An elbow burrows into her chest, bony Ida, Louise and Bert pushed face-first into her. Louise lets out a whimper.

A board snaps. The porch rumbles, shifts, lets out a loud crack, then gives way in a sudden *whoosh*. Olympia tries to grab for the wall, the door, the peeling paint, instead goes down in a rush of splintering wood and tumbling bodies. People scream. Arms flail. Legs kick. Then a brief silence, followed by a swell of moans and cries for help. A cloud of moldy dust puffs up from the debris, filled with the years of beer and urine that had soaked the undisturbed dirt.

Olympia reaches for her earpiece, not sure whom to call, but finds nothing but a lobe. That and a handful of blood.

Part VI

Fame was thrilling only until it became grueling.
Money was fun only until you ran out of things to buy.

—Gloria Swanson

Parker

Six-thirty Wednesday morning and Parker is awake, a remarkable feat given that he's not been out of bed this early in all his adult life. Even yesterday seems like sleeping in compared to this misfortune. But what choice does he have? After his brief jaunt outside yesterday afternoon, he returned to bed, plugged in the headphones, and listened to music throughout the night. He must have gotten up to pee a time or two—at his age, how could he not?—but all he remembers is a dark room and a quiet house and a desire to get back in bed and back into the music.

When he opens his eyes this time, he quickly notes the ungodly hour, marked as it is by the deadbeat clock radio that belonged to his mom. He'll never fall back to sleep now. He pushes off the covers and pulls off the headset, bringing to a halt Sarah Vaughan and her promise to deliver come rain or come shine.

He pulls himself out of the bed amid an orchestra of squeaky springs and creaky floorboards and knee joints that sound off like the Boston Pops.

He stands. He wheezes. He coughs. He steadies himself against the brief spell of dizziness. He pulls on his father's torn bathrobe and locates his father's failing slippers. He creeps down the dilapidated steps through a dim gray light that oozes through the tiny window over the staircase.

When Parker alights on the ground floor, he shuffles across the short hallway, past his solid-gold hit. The front door stands slightly ajar. He tries to close it, but the frame is skewed to one side, just enough to prevent the door from shutting all the way. He pulls it open. The screenless screen door is not to be seen. He sticks his head outside. The porch too is among the missing, replaced by a pile of rotted and splintered wood and a whole lot of nothing. He curses the debris fervently, mostly because he'll now have to use the back door.

He scans the front yard. It must have been one hell of a party, judging by the trash, the flyers, the fallen signs, and of course the porch. Then there's the police tape, crisscrossing much of his yard. Even Stephanie's fence was taken out, a sight worth a solid-gold record in itself.

Parker pushes the door closed as far as it will go, but it still leaves a two-inch gap. He'll have to stuff the opening with a blanket or something, when he gets time, but for now he wants only to get his carcass to the chair.

He heads into the living room and finds it empty. The bed is a couch, blankets in the corner, pillows on top. No sign at all that Myron was home last night. Maybe he's up and out already, even on a dreary dark morning like this. Parker has no idea when Myron normally rises. Before Parker, that's all he knows. Perhaps Myron stayed out all night. The crowd was already getting big when Parker went to bed. It must have grown even larger. That would have been enough to send Myron running for the trees.

Parker flops into his chair. A thin cloud of dust puffs out of the cushions, mingles with the cool air that pushes in through the doorway. He eases into the dust.

A voice calls through the front door and rattles the room. "Parker? Parker Davis?"

He wraps the robe tighter, feels a slight tear in the remaining sleeve.

"Parker, are you in there?" Wood creaks, groans, knocks against the house. "Parker? You in there?" More scuffling. Scraps of board snap. The front door creeps open. "Parker?" He catches movement to his right, the play of diminished light.

Olympia soon stands in the hallway, puffing slightly, her face locked in that annoying look of self-righteousness, sculpted by an unwavering certainty in her own perceptions and opinions and causes. What makes it worse is the bandage on her head, wrapped

R. H. Sheldon

around like a Civil War veteran, her hair flaring out as though she's been shot out of the rebel's cannon.

Parker studies his bare right arm. Both patches gone, no doubt rolled up in bed.

"Damn early," he says.

"I wanted to catch you before the others arrive."

"Others?"

"Have you seen the news?"

"Last year."

She moves into the living room, rustling the air when she passes, a smell not quite patchouli, and sits on the couch. Myron's bed. The cushions let out a muffled scream.

"We made quite the splash," Olympia says. "Today's protest will be bigger still."

"Remind me again?"

She passes a wane smile, impatient, martyred. "Twenty-six arrests. Seven people still in the hospital, including Ida, Bert, and Louise. Six officers suspended, an investigation under way. And Bellamy..."

"Bellamy?"

"My daughter."

"Thought it was a condition, like acid reflux."

"Pregnant. Helpless. Pepper-sprayed. The press ate it up." Her smile lingers.

"I need food, I think." His stomach gurgles and feels like a grease trap. He can't recall when he last ate.

"You have anything here?"

He shrugs. "Ask Myron." He picks at a bit of adhesive left by one of the patches. "You seen my cigarettes?"

His eyes rest on the coffee table, where his ashtray once sat. Myron must have removed it, along with the carton of Lucky Strikes. No Jack Daniel's, either, or beer cans or any signs of a joint. What the hell has Myron been doing?

"Where is he, anyway?"

"Who?"

"Myron."

She responds with an indifferent gaze. "Haven't seen him since yesterday."

Parker feels a slight nudge inside, swallows it down. "The crowds," he says. "Probably too much."

Olympia sits up, leans forward just a bit, her eyes wide and focused, each movement practiced, considered. "We need to talk about you, Parker. We need to strategize."

No wonder he never gets up this early. The world makes no sense. Alice must have dropped down her rabbit hole at seven in the morning. "Strategize?"

"About you."

"Me. What the hell for?"

"What for? So you know what to say. So we're acting together. So we're speaking with one voice."

"I need a cigarette."

"You're an overnight sensation, Parker. The whole city's talking about you—about you being sick and uninsured and about to lose your house. We've got to leverage the momentum, Parker. Speak while they're still listening."

Parker chuckles. "And how long will that be? An hour? A day?"

"A minute is better than no minute."

"Christ. Where do you pick up that crap?"

"Facts are facts."

"And when that minute's gone?"

She shakes her head. "We can't worry about that. We take what we can get when we can get it."

"I've tried that already."

She sighs in a way that ensures he can hear it, but made to seem as though she's trying to hide it. She's good, he'll grant her that. He could have used an agent like her back when he had *his* hour.

She leans forward. Myron's bed squeaks. "Do you want to save your house, Parker? Is that what you want? Because this could be your last chance."

He tries to laugh, but it hurts, and not just in his chest. "This could be the last of a lot things."

Sonuvabitch jumps into the front hallway and steps tentatively into the living room. He saunters over to Parker, stares him straight in the eyes, waits, inches forward. Then he rubs up against Parker's leg.

Parker clutches the arms of the chair. "What the fuck? Where the hell is Myron?"

R. H. Sheldon

Stephanie

Stephanie surveys the damage. The yard lies mostly in shadow, a dull gray, diffused by the early hours and an offshore haze, typical of this time of year, yet even in this light, she can see the downed fence, the trampled bushes, the slaughtered plants, the debris from hundreds of trespassers.

At least it seemed like hundreds. When she blew up at them, she hadn't been thinking, let alone counting. She flew through the yard like a raving lunatic. And then the riot followed, erupting from here, but fueled by a frenzied crowd, an anxious police force, and that bitch minister who brought all this upon them. Yeah, she's the one to blame, and Stephanie will damn well make her pay.

Olympia's car is still parked out front, unscathed by the crowd's wrath, unlike all the other cars, with their newly delivered scrapes and dents and broken windows. From what she can tell, the apartment building too saw its share of damage, most of the windows taped or boarded, at least those she can see from her yard.

It's hard to tell what damage the park might have sustained. The low mists erase most of the details, except the outline of the hill and the tip of the fountain. A few cops linger near the intersection—the street still closed and the public barred—but she tries not to look at them, tries not to associate herself in any way with what occurred.

Yet Stephanie has been lucky, in a sense. The worst of the chaos—the pepper spray, clubs, screaming protesters—stayed out in the street or pushed into Parker's yard or into the park. But the crowds avoided her property after her blow-up, not that she necessarily attributes their absence to her response. It no doubt had more to do with most of the cops being at this end and the crowds instinctively fleeing in the opposite direction.

After Georgia got her inside and calmed her down, the two stayed in the house. Outside protesters screamed, sirens blared, bullhorns blasted, helicopters hovered until even the squirrels left. But all Stephanie could think about was her yard. Her beautiful, wonderful yard. Occasionally, she and Georgia looked outside, but mostly they stayed away from the windows, kept the lights low, and waited.

It took a couple hours for the streets to settle down, and several hours more before most of the police left with their amplified voices and blaring radios and racing engines and armored vehicles. And now it's morning, with order restored and those left behind having to contend with the aftermath.

Stephanie examines the fence, where it broke off at the posts. She thinks she can stand it upright, at least temporarily. She has to. According to this morning's news, more protests are planned for today. For now, she'll brace it with scraps of wood until she can do something more permanent. Most of the damage is to the front fence and the corner near Parker's. The sides remain pretty much intact.

A salty ocean smell fills the air, mingling with damp Northwest mildew. She kicks a piece of the iron bench and heads to the shed. She pulls out the hammer, skill saw, extension cord, and a glass jar filled with twelve-penny box nails. She also grabs a hatchet and a pair of gloves. At this point, she's concerned only with fortifying the fence, not with aesthetics, not with long-term. Hell, she doesn't even know what long-term means anymore. The house. The sale. And now Georgia.

Her appearance muddles Stephanie's life even more. And no matter how much she tries not to let the situation affect her— Georgia being here and Georgia being sick—Stephanie's been shaken to the core.

She tries to focus on the project at hand. The first thing she's got to do is clear some of the blackberry bushes that continue to creep in from Parker's yard. She pulls on the gloves, hacks away at the

R. H. Sheldon

brambles, tosses branches onto his property. She clears just enough to work. At some point, she'll come back and finish the job, hacking off every tentacle. If she still lives here. If she's still alive.

Now onto the fence. She stands a section of it upright and wedges in several temporary braces. She saws, she hammers, she raises more fence. The cuts are rough, the work sloppy, but soon thick braces of unfinished wood angle into the posts and span the corners, each ill-fitted with a heavy rough-hewn look. But they'll work for now. In fact, the fence is stronger than ever. All it needs is one more touch.

She returns to the shed and pulls out a giant roll of barbed wire she bought last year at Lowe's. When she saw it on sale, she had this freaky brainstorm about running it along the fence between her place and Parker's, just to teach him a lesson, get back at him for his late-night garbage dumps and party overflow. She imagined him leaning over the fence to puke into her bushes or grabbing on when he tosses over his trash, only to discover his torn shirt and bloody palms. But after she brought it home, she thought about Myron and Sonuvabitch and other animals around here and decided against it. But now she was at war. And war called for an end to all rules.

She starts at the corner nearest the intersection, weaving the barbed wire near the top of the fence spikes, along the runners. She works her way toward Parker's, every few feet, stopping to hammer sections of wire, using the same twelve-penny nails she used on the braces.

She moves along the fence with slow, deliberate motions, inching ever closer to Parker's home. When she reaches the gate, she decides to continue without a break, emphasizing her decision by sinking several nails into the posts so the gate won't open.

She continues until she reaches Parker's lot, turns the corner, and works steadily toward the back of her yard. She's surprised at the sense of satisfaction she feels, almost a sense of serenity— rolling out the wire, braiding it into the fence, nailing it in place one step at a time, over and over, each movement part of a private rhythm that drives and sustains her. She should have done this years ago, taken the definitive step that would sever all ties with her miscreant neighbor. The sooner she's done with him, the better.

"Isn't that a bit overkill?"

Georgia stands next to Stephanie, her eyes sliding up and down the fence.

"Depends which side you're on."

"And which side are you on?"

Stephanie shakes her head. "No side. Just trying to keep you from running out." As soon as the words come out, she regrets what she said and quickly unfurls several more feet of barbed wire. "Actually, I was just thinking I should have done this long ago. Good neighbors and all that."

"You would have had my support. Remember that time Parker fell over the fence in the middle of the night? Started screaming like a banshee? Remember? Couldn't find his way out no matter how hard he tried."

Stephanie smirked. "Yeah, you nearly stepped on him after he crashed out near the azaleas, his arms wrapped around Aphrodite."

Georgia chuckles. "I think he tried to take advantage of our little goddess that night."

"I doubt he could have gotten it up. Even back then."

They laugh.

Stephanie tries to remember the last time she felt like laughing. She's amazed at the ease she feels being around Georgia, despite everything that happened—her leaving, the new girlfriend, her reappearance, her health—slipping back into the house as though she'd never left.

Last night, after the streets calmed down, they ate, watched a movie, fell into bed. No sex, but the closeness was still there, still the same, yet so very different, that sense of too much having happened, too many miles together and apart.

Perhaps that's where the comfort lies.

Georgia places her hand on Stephanie's shoulder. "Think I'll make some tea. Want some? Or would you prefer waiting till you're done with your great wall?"

Stephanie studies the fence, what she's done, what's to come. "I'm ready for a break."

Bellamy

Bellamy spots Crystal in front of Parker's house, near the makeshift stage, a small platform on the sidewalk, in front of the fence, directly in front of that gnarly dead tree, looming like some hideous ogre. Her mom stands at the center, a couple feet off the ground, talking to those around her, no doubt barking out orders. She still wears that lame bandage, a crooked halo wrapped too tight around her head.

Crystal stands next to the stage. She wears something pink, late '50s, early '60s. Hollywood retro, sort of, but more a punked-out Barbie doll.

The crowd's already double what it was yesterday, the entire block packed, people flowing into the park, spreading across the lawn, moving up the hill and closing in on the fountain, a dense, pulsating crowd, shifting, buzzing, flowing in waves, so juiced they can hardly stand still. The cops had planned to keep everyone out— at least that was the official announcement—but too many protesters poured in, arriving by foot, by bike, by car, and not just her mom's churchgoers or all those Occupy types—or Occupy wannabes, as is more likely the case—but all sorts of folks, people who've had their own run-ins with the banks, union members and laborers, office and warehouse workers, the unemployed, the uninsured, anyone fed up with what's going on and what's happening to people like them. Something about Parker's story touched them in a deep way—his health, his finances, his house—

or maybe because he used to be some kind of pop star, years ago, back in the '60s when they were writing all those stupid protest songs. Perhaps they all think rubbing up against Parker will make them celebrities.

No doubt her mom had a hand in all this. She still knows how to handle the press, even after all these years. And Casey was tweeting all night, once they got released from prison. But Bellamy doesn't want to think about any of that. It was all so humiliating, the way the cops treated them, like caged animals, like dirt under their feet.

They held everyone in a big room, taking hours to get their names and IDs, and this was after gassing them and chasing them and hitting them with clubs.

A total outrage!

As soon as they got out, Casey went to work. He tweeted about the brutality and the arrests, about the unprovoked attacks and the violence, about the porch and the old people in the hospital, about a pregnant woman victimized, assaulted, attacked. He was especially incensed about that one, and so were his Twitter-ites. And he was totally cool about her being pregnant, like he was almost happy about it. Even her mom suddenly acted like it was the sickest thing in the world. In an interview to the press, she condemned the cops for the riot and the collapsed porch and the assault on her pregnant daughter and future grandchild, announcing to the world how awesome Bellamy was, how proud she made her.

Bellamy pushes through the crowd toward the stage and yells for her friend in a shrill voice. "Crystal! Over here! Crystal!" Half the crowd turns.

Crystal jumps with excitement. They rush toward each other, meet in the street, in the thick of the crowd. They hug. They smirk. They laugh. They giggle.

"O-M-G," Crystal announces. "I can't believe you got arrested."

"And pepper-sprayed. And beaten with a club." Bellamy pulls up her left sleeve, exposes a bruise about the size of a dime. "Then they arrested us and hauled us off to prison. It was way so terrible." She swoons.

Crystal acts like a puppy needing to pee. "I looked for you. I was here, by the fountain. That's when the riot started. I ran till I couldn't breathe. In those stupid boots!"

"You've got no fucking idea what it's like being busted like that and rounded up."

"Oh-my-god! Oh-my-god!"

"It wasn't just the arrest, though that sucked big time. It was like the way they brutalized me. The tear gas. The clubs. The way they pushed me, knocked me down. I thought they were going to kill me! And all the time my eyes burned and my lungs burned and my heart burned and I could barely breathe. Me, a pregnant woman. Pregnant! Imagine!"

"Oh, Bellamy..."

"Did you see the news?"

Crystal shakes her head.

"They got a video of the police pepper spraying us, hitting us with their sticks, though it was a lot worse than how it looked on TV. The *Seattle Times* has a picture of me on their front page, with one of the cops standing over me with his club, though the headline sort of sucked. Called me a pregnant teen."

"Teen?"

"I know. I could have killed them. Freaked Casey out. Had to show him my ID."

"Casey?"

Bellamy slips her a sly smile. "Why do you think I haven't charged my phone?" Crystal's eyes grow wide, and Bellamy lowers her voice. "He's where I spent the last two nights."

"Two nights? You friggin' whore. Tell me more."

Bellamy feigns a wistful look. "He screwed the shit out of me. I'm lucky I can walk."

They break into uncontrollable giggles, not stopping until Bellamy points toward the stage, where Olympia leans toward Casey. "There he is, talking to my mom."

Crystal doesn't spot him at first, but when she does, her head jerks back. "Him?"

Bellamy nods with pride.

"But I thought..." She fidgets with her phone.

Olympia shouts from the stage, calls for Bellamy to join them, waving her arms like a demented demon.

"Got to go," Bellamy says. "The press wants to interview us about yesterday." They hug and Bellamy weaves her way toward the stage.

When she draws near, Casey puts his arm around her waist and pulls her in, his arms like magnets, his body, home.

Alonzo

Alonzo stands naked before the bathroom mirror. Ugly red scratches crisscross his body—his legs, arms, chest, face. His back too, he can see, if he turns enough. Little of his skin untouched, scourged as he was by the unrelenting mob.

He spent a good hour yesterday evening cleaning his wounds and taking a shower—being as gentle as possible, though it still pummeled his body—then applied peroxide, dabbing each wound, the sting, the foam, reaching his back as best he could.

The house sat empty then, just like now, a cool tomb, disturbed only by the hum of the refrigerator, the building settling on its foundation. The kids, he discovered, are staying at their grandmother's the rest of the week, prearranged by Isabel the day before, not a word said to him, nothing to suggest he was part of the family, all under the guise of helping Lita get moved, get settled, get a life.

The house feels exceptionally empty this morning, without the girls scurrying about, getting ready for school, Isabel rushing them along, reminding them to bring their books, homework, coordinating dance and soccer schedules, pushing breakfast like a dealer. Every morning the same routine, the same battle as the day before, but not today, the quiet almost haunting, a specter of silence, yet not all of it unwelcome, a surprising reprieve, in fact, a chance to breathe, think, reflect. He should be more concerned about Isabel's absence, about everything with Isabel, but the

R. H. Sheldon

solitude is too enticing, especially now. Never has he felt so depleted, never has he longed for such oblivion, distanced from real estate law and real estate attorneys, from the demands of work and house and family and debt and the myriad other forces that conspire to keep him imprisoned in a lifestyle of frustration and unhappiness, a lifestyle Isabel wants him to embrace, to excel at, if only to pull them out of their mire of debt.

He wraps a towel around his waist, trying not to touch the wounds, and moves into the bedroom. The bed is unmade, something he's not given much thought to before. Isabel has usually straightened it by now, somehow fitting it in as she runs after the girls.

He clicks on the TV and flips to CNN. The newscaster—a young white woman made up like a sixteen-year-old hooker—talks about a riot in Seattle, her report filled with terms such as *arrests* and *pepper spray* and *police brutality* and *Occupy Seattle*.

A queasy feeling settles on Alonzo. He tries to convince himself that this has nothing to do with him, that it all happened at Seattle Central or City Hall or down at Westlake Plaza. But then he hears the name *Parker Davis*. And next the name *Lockhart Investments*. And finally *Higgins, Whitaker & Nye*.

He drops onto the bed.

The Seattle Police Department, according to the sexy reporter, is alleged to have forced a group of protesters up on a porch, threatening them with pepper spray and clubs and rubber bullets. The porch gave way under their weight, sending numerous protesters to the hospital, including three in their seventies. The cops are also alleged to have gassed and beaten a young pregnant woman who was doing nothing but standing in the street.

The station displays a close-up of a fuzzy photo with the pregnant woman kneeling on the ground, succumbing to the pepper spray, her face streaked with black make-up, her eyes filled with tears, a beefy cop standing over her, about to bring his club down on her head. Or so it would appear.

The report ends with an aerial view of the riot, taken by one of Seattle's news helicopters. The police charge. They shoot pepper spray. They wield clubs. They chase after the scattering crowds. The video switches to a half-dozen bike cops chasing down a group of young black kids and cornering them near the basketball court. The cops draw guns and raise clubs and shout out orders and herd the kids into a waiting van.

The video returns to the front of Parker's house. A group of protesters run to the porch for cover. The chopper closes in. The protesters crowd up to the house, squeeze onto the porch like cattle. It disintegrates beneath them. They drop, tumble, fall one on top of the other. And then, in a surreal gesture from CNN, music replaces the bleat of helicopter blades, an old folk song, a '60s sound, vaguely familiar. The lyrics are difficult to understand, something about there being one last chance to take a stand. A stand against what? The song never says.

Alonzo flicks off the TV, pushes himself up from the bed, his body stiffer and sorer than ever. The scratches pull at his skin. The deeper ones burn, though better stiff and scratched than not to have made it out at all.

He dresses, grabs his computer bag, and heads to the car. Then he sees Roscoe, still outside, staring at Alonzo through the gate, his head cocked to one side, confused by the change in protocol.

Shit. Alonzo doesn't dare leave the dog outside—or locked up all day again.

He cuts across the front lawn and opens the gate. Roscoe bounds out, leaping around like a jackrabbit.

"Alright, alright, settle down."

Alonzo opens his car's back door. Roscoe stands with a look of confusion. He's never been allowed in this car before. Alonzo prods him along. The dog crawls in, as though about to be beaten. Alonzo climbs into the front and starts the engine. The music of Erik Satie floats out of the speakers. He closes his eyes and leans back. Each note floats effortlessly from one to the next, as though a piano is meant to be played this way, the music merely a reflection of what music should be—effortless, harmonic, played out in a calm, smooth rhythm that eases and invites, like a silken thread woven through air.

Roscoe barks. Alonzo jumps. Panic rises. The dog stands in back wagging his tail.

Alonzo turns up the stereo. He puts the car in gear and drives, trying to hold the music within him, against the traffic, against the noise, against the impending visit to the office.

He reaches downtown Bellevue and pulls into the lower level of the Lockhart building. He parks. He leaves the windows cracked for the dog. He takes the elevator to the second floor. He enters his office.

Buck is waiting. He watches Alonzo, his mouth locked into a grim snarl, a look sinister and hateful, his face more flushed than normal, a psychotic Santa ready to blow. He sits in Alonzo's chair, clutching a newspaper. Alonzo swears he can hear Buck's grinding teeth.

Buck drops the paper on the desk. Alonzo reads the headline. "SPD Gases Grannies, Pregnant Teen." A photo fills half the page. The same one he saw on CNN: the kneeling woman, her black tears, the cop with the club. In the background, an out-of-focus crowd.

Buck says, "You couldn't have fucked things up any more if you tried."

Alonzo studies the picture.

"Well?"

Alonzo looks up. For a moment, he has forgotten about Buck, about almost everything. "Well, what?" Alonzo can feel the heat pour from Buck's face.

"What the hell you got to say for yourself?"

Alonzo's eyes drop back to the paper, to the young woman with the black streaks running down her face. "Too much make-up," he says.

Buck slams his fist on the desk. "This is no time for games!"

Alonzo is not certain what has overtaken him, not the anger or frustration that he usually feels, that he would expect, but a sudden indifference, a giving up. Yet even that doesn't quite describe it, as though his feelings don't belong to him, but to someone no longer invested in the world, in anything.

He picks up the paper, shuffles through several pages. "Wow, I hardly ever read a newspaper anymore." He continues to browse, one page after the next, until he lands on a full-page Macy's ad. "Look," he says, "a sale." He sets the paper before Buck, points to the ad. "Today and tomorrow. Wouldn't want to miss that."

Buck sweeps the paper off the desk and jumps to his feet. He fills half the office with his bulk, his face a massive cherry.

"I will not put up with your bullshit, you little twerp. Pack up your crap and get the hell out of this building. You're finished!"

Alonzo laughs, a fitful guffaw from deep in his guts, from deep within the intruder who possesses him. He holds his sides and drops to the chair. Buck waves his arms, shakes his fists, tries to speak, but what comes out is gibberish, a clownish attempt at words, and then his right arm drops to his side, as though fallen to sleep, and he tries to step forward, but his right leg gives out and he goes down with a loud *thump*, his words a mixed jumble, his eyes locked in confusion, the look of someone who cannot understand what he sees, what he feels. His right arm lies on the ground, moves slightly, almost a twitch, his right leg, too, on permanent holiday, twisted to the side, no longer in his control, no longer related to him in any way. He tries to signal with his left arm, but the motions are uneven, inexact, as though disconnected from his brain. He speaks, but all that comes out is a jumble of meaningless babble tangled in his drool.

Alonzo considers whether to pick up the newspaper.

Buck stops moving and stares with half-opened eyes that look at nothing. Alonzo should probably do something about Buck, tell someone, but all he can do is watch him lying on the floor, drooling from the side of his mouth.

Alonzo picks up the newspaper and sets it on his desk. He stands, steps over Buck's hefty frame, and tries to open the door, but Buck partially blocks it, a beached whale, a hijacked hippo. Alonzo pushes Buck out of the way with his foot. Buck whimpers.

Alonzo exits his office, which is just off the reception area. Katie sits at the front desk, rifling through files, a bright young intern not yet jaded by the realities of law. He steps up to her station, catches her attention.

"Good morning, Mr. Garcia."

"Katie," he says. "You better call 9-1-1. I think something's wrong with Mr. Lancaster."

Parker

Parker dresses in a tired pair of jeans and a T-shirt from a bar in Tucson, Two-Eyed Jacks, where he played many years ago, nearly arrested for getting high in the parking lot with an underage high school girl.

He pulls on a wool sweater, dull charcoal, itchy as shit, but warm like thick socks.

He returns downstairs and glances out the narrow opening where the front door stands ajar. A crowd has congregated in the street and stretches into the park. He tries to shut the door, remembers it won't close. He needs to get that fixed, keep out the cold, shut out the mindless din.

He stumbles into the living room, cooler and damper than ever. Sonuvabitch rubs up against his leg. Parker pushes him away with his foot. Sonuvabitch returns. Parker pushes again.

Where the hell is Myron?

Parker moves into the kitchen. Sonuvabitch follows and stands next to the refrigerator and lets out a short squeak.

"What the fuck?"

Parker's tempted to kick the cat across the room, but Sonuvabitch sits and waits and stares at Parker with hungry eyes. "Oh, all right." He pulls open the refrigerator, jerks back, a putrid smell that sours his stomach, the stench of rotting flesh.

Sonuvabitch steps up on the lower shelf, sniffs the air. "Goddamn it, cat. Get the hell out of the way." Sonuvabitch doesn't move. Parker reaches over the cat's head and pulls out an opened can of Purina Fancy Feast—flaked chicken and tuna—and sets the can on the floor, next to a bowl filled with a half-inch of some watery brown mixture. He rinses out the bowl and fills it with water and places it on the floor next to the food. Sonuvabitch eats like a lion with his prey.

Parker opens the back door and slips outside, the air cooler and damper still. He coughs. Waits. Coughs again. Splotches of blue spot the sky, the marine layer starting to break up. The weather is guesswork at best this time of year. By noon, it might be pouring.

He steps down into the yard, amid the weeds and trash. No one there. The preacher has managed to keep the protesters in the street, away from the back of the house, which suits him just fine.

He heads toward the alley, following Stephanie's white picket fence. Each step pushes the aching up his legs and into his hips. He wobbles, sways, grabs onto the fence. A sudden pain stings the soft flesh of his palm. He grabs the fence with his other hand. Another sting. He pulls back. Stares. A string of barbed wire runs along the top of the pickets.

"That bitch."

He kicks the fence. His big toe tears through the sneakers, connects with wood, catches a splinter, burns.

"Goddamn dyke."

He bought the shoes four years ago, on sale at Walmart. Now he'll need another pair. He limps out to the alley.

Sonuvabitch scurries out of the house, runs up to Parker and meows. Parker says, "Go away." The cat sits on the gravel and stares at him. Parker shrugs. "Fine, then help me find Myron." The cat scurries toward the side of the house.

"I don't want to go that way."

Sonuvabitch returns and lets out a demanding meow.

"Not over there."

The cat meows again.

"Fine."

Parker follows him with reluctant, painful steps, tightening his hands in fists to ward off the stinging.

He moves cautiously along the side of the house to avoid being seen by the protesters or that maniac preacher.

Blackberry bushes cover most of the yard over here, the leaves barely hanging on, but the barbs locked on strong. Over the last couple years, Myron has staked out a path and managed to keep it passable, but Parker needs to stay low, not an easy feat for a man whose height will so readily betray him.

He creeps forward. The branches snag his sweater, his jeans, but he manages to get near the tree, where Sonuvabitch sits waiting. Parker glimpses the crowd through the gnarled branches. The protesters have gathered in full force, chanting and hollering in between speeches.

He crouches as low as his knees will let him and semi-crawls toward the trunk.

Sonuvabitch sniffs the air and then digs through the dried leaves and fallen weeds. He pulls something metallic out of the mulch, attached to a thin chain, dull and tarnished. Dog tags.

Parker reaches out from the bushes and grabs them from Sonuvabitch and reads. *Trowbridge, Myron H.*, followed by what Parker assumes is a serial number, then another number of sorts, and finally Myron's religion, listed as Quaker.

"I'll be damned."

Sonuvabitch moans.

Parker pockets the tags and backs up through the blackberry bushes, catching his sweater again. The thorn pulls out a long strand of wool. He returns to his yard, toward the back door. He grabs onto the railing and eases up the steps. He passes through the kitchen and into the half bath squeezed under the stairs, a tiny room permanently infused with the stench of urine and infested with wild strands of Myron's black hair. Parker pisses into the toilet, mostly hits the bowl, flushes. And then he sees it, his bottle of Jack, sitting on the floor under the sink. He grins and grabs the bottle and carries it outside. He eases himself down onto the steps and twists open the cap and takes in the fumes and grins again. He drinks. Sonuvabitch approaches, sniffs the air, crawls onto the porch and onto Parker's lap. Parker is about to push him off, but instead pets the knotted fur on his head and takes another swig. Sonuvabitch closes his eyes and purrs. Parker closes his eyes and thinks about his fabulous luck in having found the bottle. The bottle that Myron had hidden.

Goddamn him. Where is that boy, anyway?

Olympia

I t's time to get this show going. She put out the word earlier that the rally would start at noon. And she plans to stick with that schedule. The last thing Olympia wants is for people to lose interest and wander off.

She brought the PA system from church, not the greatest, but it will do. Good thing Parker still has electricity. Perhaps Lockhart Investments is now paying to give her movement voice.

The street is packed and so is this end of the park. The ones in back will never hear anything. But word will get around, and that's what's important. As long as they have plenty of people and plenty of press, they'll be fine.

She plans to start off the rally today by introducing Casey. He's already got the Occupy ear, and they'll be an easy crowd to rev up. Mention banks and developers and lawyers and everyone will be in a frenzy. And with Casey's boyish good looks and naïve enthusiasm, he'll easily bring others on board. He's got just what she needs, a natural political savvy and simplistic moral compass that crowds love. This is no place to examine nuances or debate subtleties. He's the type who can speak with a level of sincerity that crowds respond to. Olympia got a taste of it this morning, watching him work the kids nearby. People listen to him, respond to him. He'll go a long way, whichever direction he decides to take.

Bellamy will speak next, or try to speak. She's just the opposite of Casey, not the type people respond to, and usually ends up

R. H. Sheldon

making a fool of herself. Perhaps in this case, Bellamy's propensity for exaggeration and dramatization will work in their favor. The helpless victim. Pregnant. Clubbed. Pepper sprayed. Hauled off to jail. Makes good copy, as long as she can stay on target.

Too bad she's dressed like she is. Always too bad, really. Within the span of two days, she's gone from that peculiar funereal look to something protester-like, in a semi-Occupy sort of way—black hooded sweatshirt, low-hanging cargo pants, Converse sneakers, and a dark knitted cap that sits to the side—all of which on her looks warped and unbalanced, thrown together in desperation, the end result clownish and overbearing.

But maybe even that might work in their favor, the misdirected outcast, too pathetic to know how to dress herself.

Olympia will follow after Bellamy, mostly to lay out the facts, let people know where things stand—with the arrests, the investigation, the folks still in the hospital—bringing everything back to Parker's house and the guilty parties and then tying it larger issues. She's pulled together some notes, mostly statistics that point out the bleak status of homelessness and poverty and healthcare in this country. All easy targets. All true.

And then she'll introduce Parker. He's the one she worries about the most. He's a loaded gun, yet the public needs to see him. So far, most of the focus has been on the crowds and the riots and the pepper spray and the clubs and the arrests and the collapsing porch, with Parker staying in the background.

It's time to turn that around. And quickly. She has no way of knowing how long this surge will last, and she intends to make the most of it while it's here. The Occupy forces can pretend the movement will go on forever, but Olympia knows how the real world works. She's seen more efforts fail than most of these kids can imagine, or would ever want to hear about.

She looks out at the crowd. They cover the sidewalk, the street, the lawn across the street, spreading halfway through the park. They talk and laugh and shout and play. They carry signs. Dozens read *OPH*—Occupy Parker's house—the catch phrase of the day.

The Occupy forces have thrown themselves fully behind Olympia's cause. So has her congregation. But countless others have arrived, too, many from out of town, a good-sized contingency from Portland, more on their way. And the protests have made the national news, setting off a landslide of celebrity tweets, calling for an end to injustice, for action against the banks, for an investigation into the police. Not bad for a couple days work. Not bad at all.

Olympia steps up on the platform that she calls her stage. Casey and Bellamy stand nearby. He's a fit of energy, she, a cauldron of nerves. Olympia taps the microphone, clears her throat, leans in closer.

"Welcome, Seattle!"

The protesters cheer and applaud and stomp their feet and shake their signs and chant "OPH, OPH," over and over and over again.

Olympia waits, smiles, feels the pulse of enthusiasm surge through her veins. Like coming full circle, like coming home. Finally, she signals for quiet, but does so gently, a mother calling to her children. The chanting and hollering subside. Not completely, but enough.

"As some of you know, I am Olympia Culpepper, the pastor at Lighthouse Sanctification Church." The crowd explodes into a long round of applause. Some wave their arms. Others shout her name. She gives them their time. "Thank you. Thank you." She draws in a breath, smiles, but not too much. They can't lose sight of the seriousness of the situation.

"Last week," she says, "I met Parker Davis and learned about his house and his health. I found a man up against a system that pitted him against the banks and developers and attorneys, a system that saw him as an expendable cog in a merciless, unyielding wheel."

Many boo, jeer, rail against the system. "Fuck the banks. Kill the lawyers. Burn down the government."

Olympia holds up her hand. "But look at us now. Look at all you beautiful people out there. All of you, every last one, willing to stand here in the face of injustice, the face of greed, the face of evil. You've put aside your jobs and your schedules and your activities and your many commitments to be here today, to help protect the rights of Parker Davis and everyone like him. Your presence fills me with joy. You are what I've been praying for. You are the miracle that brings hope in the face of adversity and injustice. You are what gives me faith in our futures!"

The crowd erupts in an even longer and louder round of applause that she can feel through the ground and into her little stage. They holler and scream and clap and shout out over and over, "OPH. OPH. OPH."

Olympia lets it go on, flashes a benevolent smile, full of good-natured gratitude and pride. Then she signals for quiet, ever so gently. When the roar subsides, she continues, "Despite the uphill battle we face, we can take comfort in the knowledge that there are so many dedicated individuals willing to fight for the greater good. In the last couple days, I've had the great honor of meeting one of these people. He's been instrumental in bringing the Occupy movement to Seattle and in bringing you here today. Ladies and gentlemen, I want to introduce Casey McDonald, a man I'm happy to call both a colleague and a friend."

The crowd bursts into another round of frenzied applause. Casey steps up on the platform. Olympia hugs him. He returns her embrace. Onlookers hold up their phones, snap pictures, take videos. The press stands to the side, their cameras poised, waiting for something real to happen.

Olympia steps off the stage. Casey jumps right into crowd control. "What do we want?" His voice screams out of the speakers.

Half the crowd yells, "Change!"

"When do we want it?"

"Now!"

He shouts louder still. "What do we want?"

This time everyone joins in. "Change!"

"When do we want it?"

"Now!"

He brings the mike closer. "That's right. Now! And there's no stopping us. We are united. We are one." The crowd screams, claps, roars. A nearby group chants his name: "Casey. Casey. Casey." He raises a fist in solidarity. "We're the ninety-nine percent and we're mad as hell." The protesters break into a chorus of feverish cries against the banks and Wall Street and the politicians in DC.

Happy with his performance, Olympia slips away from the stage and heads toward Parker's yard. The press huddles by his fence, not just local, but AP, Reuters, even CNN. But she won't talk to them yet. Not out here, where there are so many distractions. She set up a news conference for this afternoon, after Parker has spoken, after she's had time for any damage control.

She slips into his yard and tunnels along the side of the house, the din from the crowd like a relentless surf driven by wind and tide. She feels a strange detachment back here, as though the protesters are no more than the neighbor's TV, a background annoyance of reruns and cliché plots, founded in make-believe.

The gangway spills out into the backyard, a small weed-infested enclosure that flows out to the alley, filled with liquor bottles and beer cans and debris piled in clumps and entangled with weeds.

Olympia finds Parker sitting on the back step, with that nasty cat in his lap, staring off into space. He turns toward her. "You seen Myron?"

"Not yet." Olympia reaches to her ear and tries to make a phone call. All she finds is flesh.

"You ready?" she asks.

"Ready?"

Sonuvabitch hisses.

"For your talk, you know, just a few words, let folks at the rally see who you are."

He glances toward the alley, into Stephanie's yard, the empty lot on the other side. "When was that?"

"Soon, Parker. Bellamy is next, then me, then you. Remember what to say?"

He shrugs, glances again toward the alley.

"Just tell them what you told me—how you tried to contact the bank, the runaround they gave you, how the lawyer showed up with no warning and told you to be out in three days. And don't be afraid to talk about your medical issues. Give them some totals of how much you owe the hospital. Most importantly, tell them you have nowhere to go and no money to get there."

Parker wears a wooden stare.

"Got it?"

He salutes.

Olympia backs away, just when the crowd lets out a long round of cheering and applause.

Stephanie

At least they're staying out of her yard, Stephanie can be grateful for that. But Boxer Way is stuffed with people, a mob ready to explode. Protesters push up against her fence. Some lean against it, but as soon as they discover the barbed wire—either eyeing it or feeling its consequences—they pull away quickly, only to be replaced by the next wave.

As long as the fence holds, that's all that matters. At least there are plenty of cops around if it doesn't. There must be at least twenty, standing at the intersection, watching with stone faces, clad in full riot gear—black vests, military pants, helmets, face shields, massive nightsticks—both creepy and reassuring at the same time.

Their presence seems to be keeping the crowd thinner at this end of the block and preventing stragglers from hovering along Eleventh. She and Georgia should have no problem slipping out of here for the doctor's appointment.

"Would you please come away from the window?"

Stephanie turns. Georgia sits at the small counter, sipping another cup of tea. The white tile, infused with the tiny green ivy and tumbling bluebells, shimmers in the pale light.

"Your bladder must be the size of a bowling ball."

Damn, wrong thing to say again.

Georgia seems not to notice. "You're just jealous 'cause of that pea-sized one of yours. Now get away from the window. Staring out is not going to help."

"You don't know that."

Georgia sighs, but it's a friendly, feigned exasperation, an agreement between the two that what's past is past and that all those habits and idiosyncrasies and peculiar ways that drove each other crazy are inconsequential now, fodder for amusement and affectionate recollection.

Stephanie glances out the window. Georgia shakes her head and sighs.

"You hear those morons out there? They sound like animals."

"Just a little rally. You used to like them."

"What time is your appointment?"

"I've told you a half-dozen times."

"Two?"

"Yes, still two. Just like it was an hour ago and an hour before that. And I also told you I can get there on my own. No need to waste your time too."

"I'm a retired old lady now. All I have is time."

"Lady?"

"Something new I'm trying out."

"Besides, I know how much you hate to leave with all that's going on outside."

"Yes and no. I'll only drive myself nuts sitting here."

"Too late."

Stephanie grabs a pillow from the chair and lobs it at Georgia. It goes wide and lands on the floor.

"You always were a lousy shot." Georgia picks up the pillow and studies the picture of the Space Needle. Parker's mom gave it to Stephanie, a souvenir from the Seattle World's Fair in '62.

"That was just a friendly warning. Next time you won't be so lucky."

Before long, they're heading out back to the parking area by the alley, where Stephanie's car is parked, a '93 Chevy Beretta, another gift from Parker's mom. The crowd emits a steady ocean of sound.

"I can't believe you still have this piece of shit."

"It runs."

"Is it safe?"

"As safe as ever."

R. H. Sheldon

They climb into the car. Stephanie drives to Elliott Bay Medical Center and parks. They head into the first building and maneuver the maze of corridors and offices, until they find a cavernous reception area that represents the first phase of an intake process that involves insurance cards and IDs and signing forms that absolve the medical center of any responsibility whatsoever for anything that could possibly go wrong at any step along the way, no matter how or why or who or what or when. Sign here, the forms say, because if you don't, you're screwed, and if you do, well, you're screwed, too.

Georgia takes her place at the registration desk. Stephanie retreats to the corner and sits on an ill-conceived chair next to a small end table covered in magazines—*People, Us, InStyle, Better Homes & Gardens*—about as useful as a TV sitcom.

She picks up a copy of *People* and scans through pages filled with celebrity photos that accentuate the pointless lives of the rich and famous, made all the more pointless by the likes of such magazines. She returns it to the table, hoping that retirement means more than a descent into pop culture masturbation.

Georgia steps away from the registration desk, appearing even frailer than before. Or perhaps Stephanie is noticing more. Or reading more into what she's seeing. Jesus, she can drive herself crazy.

Still, Georgia's movements *do* appear slower, more labored, the fatigue becoming more apparent with each step. Perhaps the reality of being here has sunk in. It's one thing to drive up from Bend, have some idea of what might be coming, but it's a different creature once entangled in the system. Stephanie has seen it thousands of times in the ER, people arriving scared, uncertain, sick, their reserves depleted, their concerns exacerbated by the whirling machinery and callous indifference and a system that chews up patients the same way it chews up the people who care for those patients. Even those who try to retain some measure of humanity can't help but succumb to the weight of unseen forces— an army of bottom-line bureaucrats who read patients as dollar signs and ailments in terms of profit. Now that she's out of here, she wonders how she could have stayed on as long as she did.

And Georgia is about to be recruited into that system. What she thinks or feels will have little bearing from this point forward. She'll be at the mercy of tests and charts and statistics and medications and insurance company agreements that will treat her as little more than a second-class citizen, if she's accorded even that much consideration.

Georgia sits next to Stephanie. "So it begins."

"You ready?"

"How bad could it be?"

Even in jest, Stephanie dares not answer. Too many booby-traps. The illness. The treatment. The system that's just sucked her in. The debt if she's around long enough to pay it off.

"That bad, huh?"

Stephanie tries to smile, places a hand on Georgia's knee.

The irony of all this is that Stephanie should be one of those outside Parker's house protesting with the rest of them. It's not just the medical system that's screwed up. No institution seems immune to cataclysmic failure and taking everyone down with it. But there's something about all those protesters acting so socially aware and self-sacrificing that drives her crazy, how easily they're swayed by any shiny object, willing to jump on just about anything that appeals to their trendy sensibilities. They walk around with their cell phones and computers, indentured to the latest fashions and haircuts and pricey tattoos, basking in their entitlement and self-righteousness, while following each other around in herds, more susceptible to the prevailing winds than a ship sailing open waters. What she doesn't see among all those suddenly conscientious protesters are the people most battered by the system, those with few resources and even fewer allies, forever removed from the equation, discarded because of age or illness or disability or poverty, the kind of people who show up in the ER routinely, usually as a last resort, usually with no place else to go. Not anything like the crowds outside of Parker's house. How can Stephanie stand beside such a volatile, self-absorbed lot? How can Stephanie stand beside Parker, that perpetual adolescent who's been handed more than just about anyone she's known and still managed to fritter it all away?

Alonzo

He flees the office as soon as the paramedics remove Buck's hulking and mostly comatose body. He takes his laptop and a large box filled with books and paperwork and the framed picture of Isabel and the kids. He also takes the unopened bottle of Glenlivet that was stashed in his drawer for the past year, a gift from a grateful, yet insignificant, client.

He doesn't tell anyone where he's going—or even that he's leaving. He just goes.

When Roscoe sees Alonzo approaching the car, the dog bounces between the front and back seats until he sets off the alarm, which quickly turns him into a whimpering mass that slithers to the floor. Alonzo aims his remote and clicks. The garage falls silent.

He loads the box into the trunk and climbs into the car. The dog quickly returns to his tail-wagging over-the-top self, sticking his nose in Alonzo's ear in between barking at the parked cars.

Alonzo drives out of the underground garage and heads toward Seattle. He cruises across the I-90 floating bridge and exits at Rainier Avenue and drives to Parker's neighborhood—Capitol Hill—but does not go to Parker's house. Instead, he heads toward Lita's apartment. He wants to find Isabel. Tell her about Buck, about losing his job, about everything that just happened.

He heads up Fourteenth Avenue and travels north, winding around traffic circles and easing through stop signs. When he reaches her building, an ancient gray brick throwback to the '30s, he stares up to the second floor, toward her window, beaten and broken as the frame that surrounds it. He waits. Sees nothing. Does nothing. Then he drives on.

He continues up Fourteenth, past Millionaire's Row and into Volunteer Park. Yellow-brown leaves cling to the trees, many already fallen, but the evergreens remain full, soaring like furry green giants. He parks near the old water tower, a massive silo, cylindrical, brick, varying tones of dark red and brown, an impressive structure, all too real.

He opens the car door and climbs out. Roscoe jumps over the seat and zooms past him, running for the curb to pee. Alonzo grabs the bottle of Glenlivet from the trunk and crosses the street. Roscoe follows. They climb the concrete steps to the tower's base and stand before the entrance, protected by two massive columns and a frame of stone.

He crosses the threshold into the tower. The dog slips in behind him.

An enormous water tank consumes most of the inside, the tank gray, made of thick metal plates, held together with giant rivets. Circling the outside of the tank, a steep metal staircase spirals up along the inside of the brick walls. He follows it up with his eyes, realizes that this is one of two staircases, each following a path opposite the other, like massive DNA strands twisting toward heaven.

Alonzo steps onto the staircase, letting loose thunderous echoes that bounce against the tank and fills the space above them. Roscoe whines and whimpers and barks. Alonzo climbs. The dog hesitates, sniffs, creeps up after him, his ears laid back, tail between his legs. Each step sets off a new round of echoes, causes Roscoe to crouch lower. Alonzo picks up the pace. The tower breaks into laughter.

The ascent is long, steep, marked by narrow windows carved into the thick brick wall. Gray slits of light seep in and cast a hollow glow against the massive metal tank. He climbs up the circular tower, feeling the echoes in his chest, the stir of rising ghosts. Sweat beads up on his forehead. His heart races. Roscoe whimpers.

Alonzo stops midway up and pounds on the tank several times. A deep cavernous sound chimes across the tower, filling Alonzo with dread. Roscoe yelps and cowers next to Alonzo's feet. Alonzo continues to climb.

When they reach the top, they find a large round room, filled with the last of the fading echoes, stirring within Alonzo a feeling he can't quite grasp, a memory, perhaps, a forgotten dream. There's something familiar about the space, though nothing he can point to—a round brick room with a domed ceiling, the top of the water tank fenced off from visitors, a tall, white chain-link barrier, the windows screened and barred, like a prison, a lonely tower where even memories are too much to bear.

Roscoe bounces from window to window, fully recovered from his terrible ascent. Alonzo stands before a window that faces west, the views obscured by low clouds hanging heavy over the landscape, the skies and water gray, horizons nothing but vague outlines. A cool wind gusts through the tower, chills the sweat beneath his shirt. He pulls the tails out of his pants, lets them hang in all their wrinkled glory, the T-shirt too, released from its confines. He loosens his tie and undoes the top button.

Several wooden seats are backed up against the fence, cheap park benches, out of place in this damp cold prison. He sits on the nearest one. Roscoe sniffs at the air coming through the windows.

Alonzo stares out the one nearest him, at the gray abyss outside. How strange, he thinks, that he should end up here, in some tower, alone, away from everyone and everything he knows, trapped in one of Elena's cartoons.

He feels the same uncertainty he knows wherever he goes, that ever-present sense of not fitting in, not belonging—not here, not at home, not at work. A permanent condition, like eczema or herpes, always there, always waiting. The more he tries to make himself fit in, the more alienated he feels, until he doesn't know who this Alonzo is. Husband? Father? Lawyer? All without meaning, all a game, one he always assumed he had to play, one he always felt he was losing. But he *does* have to play. He's got kids and a wife and a home worth substantially less than what they owe. And today he lost his job.

Alonzo eases against the fence, opens the bottle, and swallows a long swig. He hacks, chokes, feels the fire in his guts. His eyes water and burn. He closes them and rests his head against the fence, letting the silence wash through him, not out of desire, but necessity, a need almost frantic to think nothing, feel nothing, if only for a moment. He waits, listens to the stillness of the space, lets his breath soften, until all he knows is his breath, his lungs filling, deepening like the water tank behind him, emptying into nothing, catching that instant before the next breath, a moment between life and death, between everything and nothing.

He takes another swig.

He's about to doze off when he hears the metallic steps of someone climbing the tower. He should have known he wouldn't have the space to himself for long. He's lucky to have found it empty at all.

With each step the echoes grow louder, but the rhythm stays steady, almost painfully slow, stretching the inevitable into a sustained sense of dread. Perhaps he should leave, escape down the opposite staircase, but the echoes are so confused it's impossible to know which one is empty. All he can do is wait.

Roscoe backs away from the window, scoots up next to Alonzo, shivers. The intruder continues to ascend. The echoes grow so loud Alonzo can barely pick out the steps. Each sound bleeds into the next. Those that fade give birth to those newly formed. The whole tower seems to shake, the room charged, the air like static. Alonzo grips his seat.

A voice ascends the tower, muffled, deep, no more than grunts, a few muttered words. The echoes grow unbearable. Roscoe shrinks to the floor.

And then he appears. The man Alonzo saw at Parker's house and saw later walking the streets. The wild dark-haired man who sits under dead trees and cowers at helicopters. The man who Alonzo is sure is a certified nut case and has now come looking for him.

Alonzo leaps to his feet and adopts a defensive posture, his feet spread, his knees slightly bent. If he only knew what to do with his arms.

Roscoe doesn't move.

The man looks up. Recognition spreads across his partly exposed face.

"I'm Myron," he says and grins.

Alonzo steps back.

"Now I know why I'm here," Myron says. "Olympia told us you're Alonzo Garcia, the lawyer trying to take Parker's house."

Alonzo backs into the fence. "I don't want trouble."

Myron steps closer. "I thought you like trouble." He says this in a low rumbling voice, but not as a threat, almost as a question, as though trying to understand what's going on.

"I was just leaving," Alonzo says.

"Yes," Myron replies. "Me, too. So is Parker. So is everybody."

"Parker is leaving?"

Myron flashes a quizzical look that turns into a long penetrating gaze.

Alonzo shivers and scoots sideways.

Myron looks down at Roscoe. "A doggy!" He drops to the floor, sits crossed-led, reaches out his hand. Roscoe sniffs, wags his tail with a tentative swish. Myron pets his head. Roscoe rolls over. "Big crowds at Parker's house. Too many people." He scratches Roscoe's belly.

Alonzo inches forward. "They're still there?"

"More than yesterday."

Alonzo shakes his head. "What a mess."

"We'll see," Myron says, much too cryptically for Alonzo's tastes. "It's not my concern anymore. That was my past life."

Myron shakes his head, reminding Alonzo of a wolf stalking its prey. "They don't go away," he says.

"The crowds?"

"The past lives."

A jet flies low over the tower. Alonzo takes a long draw off the bottle. Then he turns toward the window, stares at the top of an alder. Its leaves hang limply, those that remain, a dried patch of gold and brown waiting to drop. "In school, I took a class about Hinduism. We learned about Maya, the world of forms, the sensuous world that surrounds us. It's not real. It's all an illusion. At least that's how I remember it."

"An illusion?" Myron chuckles, stands. "Yes, that works, too. An illusion. I like that." He laughs deeper now, quietly at first, but then it grows into a loud boisterous snort that echoes through the room. The tower seems to shake again, and for an instant, Alonzo thinks they're having an earthquake.

Myron drops onto the bench, holding his sides with laughter.

Alonzo considers fleeing, but he can't. He won't. He instead steps over to the window and gazes through the bars. From up here, he has a clear shot of the space needle, its top barely scratching the clouds. Beyond it, the cool waters of Puget Sound spread to the west, the horizons washed out by a low-level marine layer that locks the distant shores in gray, and past that, nothing.

Bellamy

Bellamy didn't expect to still be standing here, but Casey is going on forever, and the crowds love him. He could shout horseshit and they'd cheer. He's a lot like her mom in that way, his ability to move people, make them think the way he wants them to think. And just like her, he loves it. He must have been up there thirty minutes already, and he's still going strong.

Okay, so like here's the truth about all this. She hardly remembers what he said, outside the usual anti-bank, anti-Wall Street, anti-whatever stuff. It's like the same shit said over and over again, just in different packages. No one seems to care, though, and that's all that matters.

The tough part for Bellamy is trying to follow his act. Speaking before the crowd sounded fun at first, but now she feels like a rabbit about to be fed to the wolves. And she's not all that sure what to say, outside what she's already said a thousand time, about the cops and their nightsticks and pepper spray and being dragged off to jail.

Her mom once told her that talking to a crowd is easier if you imagine everyone naked. But that's the worst thing Bellamy could do. She'd either be totally grossed out by all the fat and ugly and old people, or she'd be looking for Casey and trying to figure out ways they could sneak out of here and crawl back into his tent and spend the rest of the day fucking.

R. H. Sheldon

She glances toward the intersection at Eleventh. About twenty cops hover near the traffic circle. The tall dark Asian guy is back, staring in her direction. She thought he might have been one of the cops suspended after the riot. Now she's not even sure he was here when it started. In fact, she can't remember much from yesterday. After the pepper spray flew, she could hardly breathe, let alone see. She has no idea who grabbed her, except for recognizing the uniform. But she felt the club—or felt *something*—and the next thing she knew she was being hauled off to prison.

When Casey announces her name, she jumps. Her stomach groans and turns sour. She searches for her mother.

He tells everyone to be cool and listen to what she has to say. "Bellamy," he shouts, "is the daughter of the remarkable Reverend Olympia Culpepper. Bellamy, following in her mother's footsteps, put herself on the line of fire yesterday, here in the streets, right where we stand. Please welcome her now as she tells her story."

The protesters clap and shout and yell "OPH" as though they're doing it for the first time. Casey grabs her hand and helps her to the platform. He puts his arm around her waist and pulls her closer, then pushes the microphone into her hand.

She returns his hold, feels his lean frame through his clothes, the touch of land after sailing a stormy sea, but then he detaches himself and leaps off the stage. A shudder runs through her. She gazes out at the crowd, at the expectant faces, the waving signs, the restless gestures. For a moment, she forgets why she's up here, feels nothing but their heated stares, and when she lifts the mike toward her mouth, all that comes out is a raspy whisper. "I'm Bellamy Burns-Culpepper," she says, "and I'm here to tell you my story."

Shouts come from the crowd. "Louder. More volume. We can't hear you."

She pulls the mike in closer, feels her throat tighten, the squeeze on her chest like a suffocating ocean.

"I, um..." Her knees dissolve into gelatin. "Wall Street," she says. "Ah, we got to get Wall Street." She hesitates. "Yeah, the ninety-nine percent. I mean, one percent. We got to get them."

Protesters stare, shift from leg to leg, mumble to each other. Shouts of "OPH" ring out, but even those die quickly.

Bellamy glances behind her toward Parker's house. Casey is gone. Her mother has still not returned. The press huddles near Parker's fence, about a dozen men and women, a handful of photographers, talking among themselves, mostly staring at the house, pointing. No one looks at her.

"Yesterday," she says, "I stood in this very spot...well, not like this very spot, over there a few feet." She points. "I stood...we stood...and we were all like—"

More calls to turn up the volume, speak louder. She pulls the mike nearer to her mouth, practically swallows it, feels herself choking as it goes down. The protesters grow restless, no longer look at her, turn instead to talk to friends and compatriots. Chat, joke, forget Bellamy.

She shouts into the mike. "So, we're standing there, like waiting for the protesting stuff to start, when suddenly the cops spray their pepper spray or tear gas or mace or whatever it was." She raises her voice louder. "We were all like minding our own business, being peaceful and all that, just getting into all this energy stuff, and the cops practically blind us with their gas, totally unprovoked. All we were doing was standing there! I couldn't see anything, couldn't tell where I was, what happened to the others. I had no idea what to do and how to get away. I thought they were trying to kill us!"

Their eyes are back on her, no more chatter, no turning away. Now she gets it. Now she knows what to do. She's got to scream like a raving lunatic.

"And after they sprayed their gas, they kicked us and pushed us and hit us with their clubs, and we like never knew what they wanted, why they wanted it, or where they wanted us to go!"

Protesters boo, shout for retribution. Anti-cop epithets swirl through the crowd.

Bellamy feels their energy pulsate through her, like an infusion of Red Bull with her vodka, jacking her up and giving her life. "Those of you who were here yesterday," she says, "you know how it was. How awful and humiliating. How terrible. I know. I was there."

A commotion erupts off to her left. Her mom comes out of Parker's yard, followed by Casey and by Parker himself. The reporters close in like a bunch of groupies. She hears their voices, but can't tell what they say.

The crowd strains to see what's going on. They push in closer toward the stage, toward Parker's house. Parker stands taller than everyone else, but doesn't look tall, his height diminished by a frame bent and frail, hair gray, skin an ashen sheen.

R. H. Sheldon

Bellamy's only hope is to push forward. She grips the mike tighter and yells out to the crowd. "So like there I was. They gassed me. And clubbed me. And manhandled me. And blinded me. I couldn't see! I couldn't breathe! I had no idea what was happening to me, what was happening to any of us!"

She stops to take a dramatic pause, just like she learned from her mom. Someone in the crowd shouts, "When do we get to hear Parker?" Someone else yells, "Yeah, where's Parker?" Several others scream, "We want Parker." And suddenly, as if being led by a conductor, the crowd breaks out into a screeching chorus of "Parker. Parker. Parker. Parker." They stomp their feet each time they say his name, until the whole street shakes, broadcasting a horrific echo against the nearby buildings, until all anyone can hear is "Parker. Parker. Parker. Parker."

Bellamy screams into the mike. "They blinded me! Choked me! Beat me! Assaulted me!"

"Parker. Parker. Parker. Parker."

"All I could think about was my unborn child. My baby. My little baby." Bellamy pants and clutches the front of her sweatshirt. "My baby! All I could think about was my baby!"

She shakes, shivers, cries gumdrop tears.

The crowd grows louder, the stomping fiercer.

"Parker. Parker. Parker. Parker."

Bellamy moves closer into the mike. "My baby! My baby!"

"Parker. Parker. Parker. Parker."

Olympia rushes up on the stage, places a hand on her daughter's shoulder.

"Bellamy," she says, "perhaps we should let Parker speak. Might be easier." Her voice is calm, assuring.

Bellamy won't fall for it. "Go to hell!"

Olympia reaches for the microphone. Bellamy pulls back. "My baby," she shouts.

"Yes," says Olympia, and tries to grab the mike.

Bellamy resists. They struggle. Olympia loses her balance, almost topples over, but rights herself, takes the offensive. She shoves Bellamy with her shoulder and pulls the mike away.

Bellamy stares at her empty hand, then out to the crowd, and finally back toward Casey. He stands off to the side, shaking his head in disgust. She slumps off the stage and heads through the crowd, toward the corner of Eleventh, tunneling through hordes of young hip protester types and old broken church types and forgotten confused worker types and all the uncertain hopeful idealist types, mostly white and middle class and looking for something to give their bland lives a little meaning and purpose.

She hates these people. She hates everything about them.

When she reaches the edge of the crowd, she brushes past the cops, stopping before the tall dark one. "Forget it," she screams. "I don't care how hot you think you are, you're never gonna have me!"

The cop shows nothing on his sun-glassed face.

Bellamy pushes past him and the other cops and works her way to John Street and follows it up the hill to Fourteenth, where she turns north and keeps walking, not sure where she's heading or what she'll do when she gets there.

R. H. Sheldon

Alonzo

Alonzo turns from the window. Steps ascend the tower, slow, tentative, a woman's sighs, caught in the harsh echoes. Roscoe hovers near Myron. Myron pets him with long reverential strokes.

When she reaches the top, she stops, catches her breath, holds the rail for support, a young woman, awkward, almost attractive. Her eyes move in fear.

She's dressed a lot like those kids he saw near Parker's, but on her, the black hooded sweatshirt and cargo pants don't quite work, something from Nordstrom's Cool Kid department, and the dark knitted cap only makes it worse, sitting precariously to the side, pinned in contrived angles.

Roscoe moves toward her, wagging a tentative tail. Her face softens. She crouches down and pets the dog, then hugs him. A tear crawls down her face, trailing a black streak.

And that's when Alonzo recognizes her, from the newspaper picture. Why her? Why now? Another of God's jokes?

Myron says, "I saw you at Parker's house. You're Bellamy, Olympia's daughter."

Does Myron know everybody?

Bellamy stands, looks startled, then disappointed. "Don't mention that woman to me."

"She can't help herself," Myron says.

"What?"

"You're mother gets forgetful."

Bellamy turns toward chain-link, flipping her head in a way that suggests disgust and anger. "What would you know about my mother?" She stomps around the tower to the other end, on the opposite side of the fence.

Myron says to Alonzo, "That's Bellamy. Olympia is her mother. Olympia is having protests at Parker's house." Myron twists in the bench and calls to Bellamy, "This is Alonzo Garcia, the attorney who told Parker he had to move out of the house."

"You're the attorney? You're the one who started all this?" She lets out a distinct *harrumph*. Alonzo never actually heard someone harrumph before and isn't quite sure what it means. "My mom hates you," she says. "She thinks you're scum." Her face remains obscured by the fence's crisscrossing pattern.

Alonzo knows he should retreat from this gloomy tower and these people right now, but he doesn't move, his gaze torn between them and the misty horizons through the narrow windows, as though an unseen force propels him to stay, the same force that possessed him to act like he did with Buck, to flee from the office without a word, to climb the tower in the first place. He must be possessed.

"I'm not doing that anymore," he says.

She steps around the fence. Anger flashes through her eyes, and her face takes on a hard, sullen look. "Too bad. I'd love to see someone put Parker and my mom and the rest of those fucks in jail. All those shithead protesters, too. They deserve whatever they get."

The world shifts again. He returns to the window, stands before it, but doesn't look out. He feels disoriented, lightheaded. He lifts the bottle and takes another drink, then sets it on the floor. He never could handle his liquor.

Bellamy says, "I used to come here a lot, back when I needed a place to hide from my mother. She never figured out where I went."

Myron says, "I like to come here, too. It stretches my head up."

Bellamy frowns.

Alonzo turns back toward the window and rolls up his sleeves. He holds his right arm up to the light. One of the scratches stretches along the inside of his forearm, the skin red, inflamed. He places his left palm on the wound, a palm much too dainty for a man's hands, too small and unassuming, able to cover only half the scratch.

Heat percolates through his skin.

R. H. Sheldon

Bellamy says, "I don't know why I came here. Something drove me. Like a wind pushing me."

Myron says, "No helicopters."

Bellamy says, "No mothers."

Alonzo says, "No picnics."

The other two stare at him. "Picnics?" That was Bellamy.

Alonzo walks to a different window, looks out on the park grounds, toward the art museum and conservatory. Off in the distance, he can just make out Husky stadium. "Picnics," he whispers. That's when he remembers, the time when he was a little boy, when his family came here on an outing, eight of them in all, his parents and the six kids. He was fourth in line, arriving long after children stopped being a novelty for them. He remembers little about that day, being here, a recollection of faces, a flash of memories—grass, food, games—the image of a boy looking for a space of his own, a moment of quiet against the never-ending onslaught of family. He fled up the stairs of the tower. He can't recall actually being up here, only the escape, the need to be away. But that hardly explains his sudden uneasiness—and mounting sense of doom.

He turns from the window. "A picnic," he says. "We should have a picnic. That's just what we need. I have whiskey. What else do you bring to a picnic?"

A malevolent spirit—that's what has taken control. Maybe it's this tower. The ancient feel of brick and mortar. The hollowness of the tank. The echoes that never quite die.

"Yeah, whiskey," Bellamy says. "That's exactly what I need."

Roscoe steps up to Alonzo, leans against him. Alonzo crouches down and pets the dog with long strokes. "I've not been on a picnic since I was a boy."

"I don't drink whiskey," Myron announces.

Alonzo starts. "You don't?"

Myron shakes his head, his great mane caught in the bluish light filtering through the windows. "I don't drink beer, either."

"That sucks," Bellamy says. "So like what *do* you drink?"

"Water."

She harrumphs again. "Not me. Fish fuck in water."

Alonzo says, "No water for me either." He stands and picks up the bottle.

Myron springs to his feet. "Let's go visit the conservatory." He grabs Alonzo by the arm, pulls him toward the stairs. Roscoe follows.

"I'm coming, too," Bellamy says. "I'm done with this place."

Roscoe barks. The echoes gyrate against the metal tank and spin up through the tower. The dog squeezes up next to Myron.

They descend the stairs, first Myron, then Alonzo, then Bellamy, their movements slow, steady, steps in rhythm. Roscoe creeps down after them.

"It's like we're off to see the friggin' wizard," Bellamy says.

Alonzo had been thinking along the same lines.

Parker

P arker hasn't heard a crowd shout out his name since he was in his early twenties, when he was still riding the "Last Stand" wave. Back then, audiences would wait in line for hours—sometimes overnight—just to hear him play, just to hear that goddamn song.

And now, after all these years, this sudden popularity, filling him with an odd sense of nostalgia, a fair amount of regret, and even a bit of a thrill, softened perhaps by his awareness of the absurdity of the situation and even greater absurdity of his life. "Last Stand" was little more than a cheap, schmaltzy protest song like so many of that era, made popular by a naïve audience too stoned to decipher talent from the emotional pop-culture frenzy that defined his generation and every generation to come.

And now he's out here on a miserable gray day in the even more miserable Northwest about to deliver some half-assed diatribe about his terrible life and all the forces that have contrived to make it so terrible.

Still, he is, if nothing else, a showman, despite the years of battle scars and battle fatigue and time in the trenches, and being faced with such an enthusiastic audience invigorates him and spins him into a ready-made performance machine. Granted, the Jack he discovered in the downstairs john didn't hurt. A few healthy gulps provided just the motivation he needed to face the crowds, enough to turn what was lining up as a treacherous afternoon into something that might be fun, at least for a bit. And what a great opportunity to stick it to Olympia. With every passing minute, she annoys him that much more, so why not annoy her back? Why not give her a performance she'll remember? Besides, he's had to perform under worse circumstances, like that time in LA when he showed up at the wrong club on the wrong night and played show tunes to a loud aggressive audience made up of NRA delegates. Compared to that night, today's rally is nothing. And who knows? This ridiculous gesture might help defer his inevitable eviction. It's coming, he knows, but the longer he can put it off, the better for everyone, especially him. Until then, it can't hurt to have a bit of fun.

Olympia now stands on stage, her daughter having fled into the crowds. The reverend manages to quiet the protesters, at least somewhat, with a few well-placed smiles and gentle hand signals, all delivered with the professionalism of a practiced speaker, someone who also knows how to work a room. Then she announces in her strong alto voice, tinged with a bit of Texas southern drawl—which also sounds a wee bit practiced—that the man they've been waiting to hear, Mr. Parker Davis, feels strong enough to talk, to tell his side of the story, a story few have been willing to listen to until now. "He has, in fact, come to believe it's his civic duty to share his tale, so without further delay, please help me welcome Mr. Parker Davis."

Parker moves toward the stage. His buzz makes him feel unsteady, even a bit woozy. Several bystanders help him up. Olympia takes his hands in hers, guides him gently along, hands him the microphone, and in general treats him like a demented ninety-year-old ready for a diaper change.

He holds the microphone and waits for her to leave. She picks up on his psychic nudging and slips off the stage, leaving him to face the adulating crowd alone.

He looks around, catches the eyes of numerous people in the audience, let's his gaze linger on several of the young women. He takes a deep breath. The crowd grows quiet. He speaks.

"Well, goddamn, look at all you sons-of-bitches out there!"

The crowd could not be happier. They laugh. They scream. They wave signs. They clomp feet. They chant and sing and applaud. Even the older in the crowd, those not given to such unbridled enthusiasm, smile and clap hands and try to act cool like they remember it from their younger days.

He laughs into the mike. "Hold on. Hold on for chrissakes. I haven't even said anything yet. Not a goddamn thing." He grins. "Not that I've got anything to say. Shit, when's the last time anybody said anything worth hearing? To be honest, if you're all standing here listening to the likes of me, I'm more concerned about you then I am about me."

They explode in mirthful applause. Audiences love a funny old guy.

"No, no, stop. You're killing me. Not a good thing for an ancient fart like me. What the hell's the matter with all of you?"

More clapping. More grins and laughter. More gleeful joy.

Parker smiles. He feels twenty again. Or forty, anyway.

He pulls the mike in closer. "Besides, we need to go after bigger game. Like those goddamn bankers. And asshole developers. And shithead lawyers. Especially them. And all those motherfuckers on Wall Street!"

The applause is continuous now, so is the shouting.

He raises his voice. "A dozen or so Uzis should do the trick, don't you think?

Some cheer, others glance around, nervous, a shudder of uncertainty. A small gang of dark-hooded thugs hang along the curb near the corner, eye Parker with suspicious looks, then whisper among themselves.

"No, no, just kidding. Don't get your panties all in a bunch. Do I look like I could really handle one of those things? Christ, I'm lucky to get to the toilet in time."

The mention of a toilet seems to appease them. They clap, smile, their concern relieved. Those on-board all along scream out his name.

He's enjoying himself immensely, more than he ever imagined. He didn't think it was possible to still have this much fun.

"Okay, enough screwing around. Time to get down to business. So why would you be standing out here on a putrid Seattle day to listen to some dried up old codger who's drunk too much whiskey and popped too many pills and smoked enough weed to knock all of you on your ever-lovin' asses for the next year?"

The mention of weed pushes the audience into a frenzy of hooting and hollering that could be heard in Bellevue.

"I'll tell you why you're here. Because if this shit can happen to me, it can happen to any of you. There are no safeguards any more, no protection for any of us. You might look at me and see nothing but a shamble, but I tell you, none of you motherfuckers, *not one,* is immune. We've been forsaken by our government and all those goddamn rich folks who run it. You know the score. You don't need me to tell you. Corporations have more rights than all of us together. We've become a country of the boardroom, by the boardroom, for the boardroom."

This sets them off big time, just as expected. He watches, smiles, lets them have their fun. And then it happens. A cough erupts from deep within his lungs, right on cue. He keeps the mike close. The hacking rings out, the exaggerated gasps for air. He lets it go on, as long as he dares, then he pulls a chunk of soggy toilet paper out of his pocket and spits up a wad of phlegm, buries it into the tissue. He waits. He makes them wait. Olympia steps toward the stage, but he waves her away. He shoves the tissue into his pocket, lets his breathing return.

"See," he says, "I told you it ain't pretty.

A hushed discomfort spreads through the crowd. No one moves. Distant traffic ruffles the air. Voices filter across the park from the playfields on the other side. A few young guys hover close to the stage, looking stylish, confident, ready to take on the world.

"You," Parker says, eyeing each of them, "you stand there with your young strong bodies, barely out of diapers, full of ideas and attitudes and cum, just like me at your age, just like a whole generation of us. You have no idea what's coming. How could you? How could any of us? But this is what awaits you." They move uneasily, their eyes to the ground.

Parker points to himself, waves his hand up and down to emphasize the sickly frame. "You don't believe it, do you? That's okay, 'cause even if you don't, hear this. If you think what the banks and insurance companies and attorneys and politicians and Wall Street are doing now is bad, you just wait. Wait ten years or twenty or thirty. It will get worse. I promise you. They will take more control. They will take more money. They will take everything they can take and keep on taking. Unless you do something now. Right now. It might be too late for people like me, but if you hope to protect yourselves in the future, you better not wait till you're standing where I am today. You can't just keep talking about your problems and holding a few little protests and expect everything to change. You've got to act. Really act. Not this chanting and preaching and sign-waving and camping-out bullshit. I mean, do something real. Because if you don't, you're all fuckin' screwed—

R. H. Sheldon

and no amount of protesting or occupying or whining will change one goddamn thing!"

For a moment, no one moves, but then a few start to clap. Soon others join them and before long the entire crowd is applauding and shouting "Parker, Parker, Parker, Parker" until the proverbial cows come home.

Parker coughs again, this one unplanned, and steadies himself as best he can, not an easy feat, given he has nothing to hold on to. Might be time to head to bed.

He studies the crowd, the varied shapes and sizes, mostly kids, but not completely. Doesn't matter though. He always loved a good audience. But in the end, this is a young man's sport, a game made for and given to youth, and there's no going back—for him or anyone. Still, it can't hurt to have a little fun now and again. For Parker, working an audience is like meeting a sexy lady, the chase, the climb, the anticipation of conquest.

"I need a drink," he announces.

Olympia reaches into a cooler behind the stage, pulls out a bottle of water.

"Not that shit." He turns back to the crowd. "No one's got a bottle stashed in his pack? Jesus, what's happened to this generation?"

One of the guys he singled out earlier pulls a fifth of Jack Daniel's out of his bag and waves it before him. Parker feels a canyon-wide grin spread across his face. "Bless you, my son. And my favorite, to boot. You'll be going to activist heaven for sure."

Parker takes the bottle and twists off the cap and pulls a long, hard draw, feels the burn, welcoming every fiery blast.

Olympia moves closer to the stage, signals to Parker to finish up.

"Almost done." He gulps down more. She frowns. He lifts the microphone to his mouth. "Man, talk about manna from heaven." He grins. "Okay, folks. I gotta start winding up. I'm about to get booted out of here."

The crowd boos, shouts out his name.

"That's alright," Parker says. "It's almost time for my nap."

They laugh, applaud.

"Besides, that Olympia chick will have my balls if I don't get the hell off here."

He turns toward her. She flashes him a grizzled look.

He grins at her. "Just about done here, darling." Then he turns back to the crowd and speaks in a loud voice, his words slightly slurred. "It's not about my house or about me or my petty little problems. It's about you. It's about the future. Your future. You've thought about what to do and talked about what to do and beat off over what to do, but if you're going to make a difference, you've got to move now. If you're going to act, act now. If you really want to see change, make that change happen now!"

He takes another swig and hands the bottle back to the young man. The kid takes a drink, passes it on to his friends, all of them pleased to have been singled out, each staking claim to his moment of fame.

A cop shows up from nowhere and pushes up next to the guy with the bottle and demands that he turn it over. "No alcohol," he yells. "No alcohol."

Parker knows an opportunity when he sees one and draws on the last of his reserves. "This is just the kind of shit I mean. Exactly. Look at these cops, pulling the same crap they've been pulling for centuries. Who were these boys hurting? Huh, Mr. Poo-*leece*-man. Who the hell were they hurting?'

Several more cops push through the crowd, stand next to the first one.

"Give us the bottle," one of them yells.

Parker shouts, "Hold your ground! Hold your ground!"

The kid with the bottle glances at Parker, backs away from the cop. "Go to hell," he shouts. "This is mine. Paid for with my money."

Those nearby cheer. Shouts ring out. "Leave him alone! Mind your own business! Get the fuck out of here!" A chant spreads through the crowd. "Leave. Leave. Leave. Leave. Leave."

One of the cops grabs the pack, still on the kid's back. The boy falls, struggles to hold on. The cop battles him for the bag.

Parker screams into the mike. "My God, now they're attacking him. Just like they attacked us yesterday. What next? Assault rifles? Listen everyone. We can't let this happen. We've got to stand fast. We can't let these cops roll over us again."

Olympia tugs on Parker's jeans. "Get down from there," she whispers. He pushes her with his foot.

Protesters close in on the police. Additional cops arrive. Voices rise. More chanting. More shouting. More threats. People in the park try to push into the street, fuel the crowds already there. The police drop their face masks, lift their shields, raise their clubs.

A banana peel flies off the hill, lands on one of the cop's helmets. More recruits arrive. The crowd squeezes in.

R. H. Sheldon

Parker yells, "We've got to stop them. It's our last chance. Our last stand against tyranny. Our last stand against a total police state. We must not give in to these fascist Nazi pigs!"

The crowd rumbles, shakes, roars. Garbage flies. A rock hits one of the cops in the shoulder, another in the head. More cops. More clubs. Blue clouds of pepper spray. The press comes to life. They snap pictures, make calls, jump up for better views, squeeze into the crowds.

"My God, look at what they're doing. Look at how they're clubbing those kids, spraying them with gas."

Parker pauses, watches, waits. He's amazed the police haven't come after him. Have they not been listening? Do they have any idea what's going on? What choice does he have but continue? "Fight, goddamn it. Stand up and fight! There's a hell of a lot more of us than there are of them!"

And it's true, the police are far outnumbered, and this fact must hit home because some sort of groupthink descends upon the crowd and they come at the cops all at once with sticks and bottles and bricks and rocks, and the police are soon on the ground, despite their shields and canisters and nightsticks.

More protesters close in and strip the cops of their clubs and go after car windows and car taillights and car headlights until their focus lands on the giant apartment building on the corner near Parker's house, where they break windows and pull down siding and tear apart fencing and knock down small trees. The mayhem becomes even more frenzied, turning the protesters into a mob of lunatics, screaming and threatening and destroying everything in close range. Near the corner of the park, the group of dark-hooded young men huddles in a small circle, their looks furtive and grave. Then one of them emerges, wielding a chunk of burning wood. He runs toward the deserted house and lobs it through one of the windows. Flames quickly shoot out of the broken glass, followed by more hollering and screaming and running in circles. Fire alarms clang and sirens blare and dozens more cops arrive. Protesters scatter like seeds on the wind. Clouds of pepper spray erupt throughout the park, spread out into the streets. The area surrounding the stage is now all but deserted, except for Olympia and the press, with their cameras flashing and phones recording and faces flushed with joy.

Parker steps off the platform, feeling the weight of the day, the months, the years. He hands the mike to Olympia. "It's all yours, honey." Then he slips past the press and into his yard and around the house and into the back door, where Sonuvabitch sits waiting.

"Let's go take a nap," he says.

Sonuvabitch meows and the two head into the living room. Parker stops at the front door and wedges his slipper beneath it to keep it closed. He ascends the stairs. Sonuvabitch follows.

In his bedroom, Parker strips off his clothes and crawls between the sheets. Sonuvabitch jumps on top of the covers and heads to the foot of the bed. He circles several times, then settles into a black gnarled hairball and is quickly asleep.

Parker can hear Olympia outside. She shouts into the microphone, calling for calm, reason, a peaceful resolution. He puts on his pricey Bose headphones and cranks up the jazz, then drifts into his own world of slumber, marked as it is by his fantasies of fame and fortune and females and a fifth or two of that fine Tennessee whiskey.

R. H. Sheldon

Bellamy

O kay, so she realizes this Alonzo guy is like a total nerd and in no way her type. Shit, he still wears that lame jacket and tie, like they're out at the friggin' opera. And he's seriously way too old. Sure, she's been with old guys before, like her baby's father, but Alonzo seems old in other ways, deeper and darker somehow, not like your typical perv.

She follows him anyway, down the stairs, out the water tower, to his car. Because underneath all that weirdness and nerdiness and attorney-ness is a pretty hot guy, that smooth dark skin, epic black hair, and a face a million times more handsome than shit-ass Casey. Sure, he wears that cheap wedding band, but like when did being married ever mean anything?

She waits until Alonzo puts the dog in the car, then follows him toward the conservatory. Myron goes first, then Alonzo, and finally Bellamy, still walking in a line. She follows close enough to see the grit on his stiff white collar and smell his bug-spray cologne, more of his nerdy features.

They walk past the Asian Art Museum, with its looming, windowless stone walls, two massive camels, one on either side of the doors.

Across from the museum sits the giant donut—a dark marble sculpture that's supposed to represent the setting sun—overlooking the Space Needle and Puget Sound. The rain has let up some, and the sky's not as dark, but it's already getting late in the afternoon, and it won't be light much longer.

A streak of blue breaks out to the west and light shines on the Needle and the Sound, giving everything a glimmering sheen, almost mystical, the way the shrouded mists, still in darkness, try to squeeze out the light.

When they reach the conservatory, Myron steps aside and waits for Alonzo and Bellamy to enter. Alonzo shoves the bottle inside his jacket, holds it with one arm. Myron follows them in.

They move to the left, along a narrow aisle squeezed between two rows of rich foliage, one running along the windows, the other an island stretching through the long narrow room. The air is warm, moist, perfumed with an assortment of fragrances, fertile, sweet, exotic. Ferns everywhere, the occasional palm, light and airy, then the flowers, each with their own tiny signs—aroids, hibiscus, begonias. The best are the brugmansia, peach-colored trumpets dangling from their branches. The colors vibrate and shimmer, like she's just started peaking.

They stop at the end of the aisle, near a small pool of water, surrounded by more ferns and something called Mexican breadfruit, large leaves, heart-shaped with long slits cut out the sides. Bellamy squeezes up next to Alonzo. Myron stands right at the corner, staring at the plants, rotating slowly. He lets out short grunts and groans and long deep sighs that make the air seem even more stifling.

Then he stops, his eyes wide, his body shaking. "Not good," he shouts. "Not good for Myron." He twists around and bumps into Bellamy, knocking her into a palm. She stumbles, trips, falls toward the pool. Her outstretched hand, with its green wrist and black nails, lands in the water and hits a slick layer of slime. She slides forward until her face, along with the rest of her arm, sinks into the water.

Alonzo grabs her and pulls her upright. She gasps for air, clutches his jacket for support, the tears ready to flow. She wipes her face with her dry sleeve, but there is too much slime, too much wet. Alonzo produces a handkerchief, soft, white like fresh snow, and dabs her face. Outside, Myron shouts, "No more jungle!"

"Let's get out of here," Bellamy says. She grabs on to his free arm, the one not clutching the bottle.

They pass through the glass entry, move outside, the slap of cold on her face, the smell of Northwest damp and Northwest mists.

Alonzo escorts her across the street to the bench that looks toward the intersection, toward the statue of William Henry Seward and the steamy glass windows of the conservatory. Myron has disappeared.

"You okay?" Alonzo asks.

So considerate. So unlike any of the others.

"I hope the water wasn't poisoned. How do I know if it was? I mean, what if I start getting some weird disease like herpes or something?"

"You'll be fine," Alonzo says, his voice the same honey-taste of his skin. "I'm sure they make certain the water is safe."

She nuzzles up toward him. He draws back, but only slightly, and pulls the scotch out from under his jacket. He unscrews the lid and takes a swig. He looks pretty lame, drinking from the bottle in that way, like a twelve-year-old smoking a cigarette.

Alonzo offers her the bottle. When she grabs it, she wraps her fingers around his, feels her skin ignite. He retrieves his hand and looks away.

She pulls the bottle toward her mouth, the rim cool against her lips. She expects the usual burn she gets from whiskey, in her throat, her stomach, but what she gets is a smooth woody taste. There's still some fire, but not like she's used to.

She swallows long and hard, smacks her lips when she's done. "Good shit." She's about to take another drink, but feels her stomach grumble. She looks down at her belly. "Oh my god!"

She lets go of the bottle and it crashes to the sidewalk. Glass and scotch shoot in all directions.

Alonzo jumps to his feet. Bellamy jumps to hers.

She shouts, "What the fuck's the matter with you? Why you feeding liquor to a pregnant woman? Oh my God. My baby. My baby. You killed my baby!"

Horror spreads across his face.

"My baby. My baby." Bellamy waves her arms and races around in small circles. "You beast. You animal. How could you do this? I'm pregnant! I'm having a baby! Don't you care? Doesn't that mean anything to you? Oh, my baby, my baby. What am I going to do?"

She is about to say more, but then she spots them, those two skanks, Lita and Isabel, standing at the curb, the toddler crouching next to Lita, holding her hand.

Bellamy yells, "What the fuck you two want?"

Fury gathers in Isabel's face. She steps toward Alonzo. Glass crunches beneath her boots. "You better explain yourself, Alonzo. What are you doing here? And why are you hanging around with this little tramp?"

Bellamy stomps toward Lita. More crunching glass. "Tramp? Who the hell you calling a tramp?"

Isabel pokes Bellamy in the shoulder. "You listen to me, you pathetic slut. You come near my husband again, you're dead."

Bellamy slaps Isabel's hand away. "He's married to you? No wonder he's so miserable."

"Why you little…"

Lita leaps forward, takes Isabel by the arm and pulls her back. A dumbfounded look descends on Alonzo. His left eyelid twitches.

Bellamy screams, "Fuck all of you. I don't need this shit." She throws the handkerchief into Alonzo's face and stomps off across the broken glass and heads in the direction of the water tower. Why does she always end up with these losers?

She cuts past the donut, down the steps, and around the reservoir. When she gets to the park entrance at Twelfth, she stops, reaches into her pack, and pulls out her phone. She's about to call Crystal but discovers her phone is dead. Fuck. She'll have to go to a coffee shop to charge it. She rifles through the pack, but can't find her charger. The last time she recalls seeing it was when it fell out in Casey's tent.

She searches her pack more seriously, pushing aside the tissues and make-up and combs and pens and paper, but still turns up nothing. Her only choice is to head back to the camp. And now is probably as good as time any. Casey's no doubt still at the rally and the Occupy camp mostly deserted. She just hopes no one's there who witnessed her pathetic performance.

She heads down Broadway and follows it south toward Seattle Central. The street buzzes with the usual assortment of panhandlers and tweakers and queers and shoppers rushing about from one spot to the next. Music pours from several shops, hard, pounding noise, most of it so yesterday, not like all the cool stuff at some of the clubs, at least the ones she knows about, when she can bullshit her way inside.

The evening closes in quickly, though it's not much past four.

She creeps into the camp, all stealth and caution. Few occupiers occupying, huddled in the center. A break, finally.

The camp looks far more decrepit than she remembers. Tattered tarps, tents, trash strewn about. And the Honey Buckets reek worse than ever. Even the traffic—the coarse diesel engines, rubber on wet pavement—seems disturbingly loud.

She tiptoes toward Casey's tent, tries to swallow her regret, focus on her scorn. The front flap is partially unzipped, no one nearby. She kneels, leans in closer. She grabs the zipper and drags it one click at a time, trying to muffle the sound with her fingers. A car honks. Brakes squeal. She starts. Catches her breath. Waits. Then she peels the flap open and sticks her head into the shadows.

Suddenly movement, then a quick groan. A lantern switches on. Not one body, but two. Casey and that cop who'd been watching her, his body a massive sea of smooth and pulsating flesh, folded into the sleeping bag, his arms wrapped around Casey's lean and hungry frame. The cop glares. Casey grins. Bellamy flees the camp and runs toward the street and never for a second looks back.

Stephanie

After their long hours at the medical center and Georgia's snippet of time with the oncologist, after their drive to Ballard and their exchange about a broken medical system and arrogant doctors, after their walk on the beach at Golden Gardens Park and continued conversation about bureaucracies and their bureaucratic minions, after their early dinner at Ray's Boathouse and ongoing discussions about procedures and preparations, Stephanie and Georgia drive from Ballard to Capitol Hill, slowing briefly past the Fremont Troll, and head toward the house, only to find Tenth and Eleventh blocked by police cars with lights flashing red and blue against the night sky and the wet roads glistening with the pulsating colors.

Stephanie slaps the steering wheel and groans. "Now what?"

She drives up John, turns right on Twelfth, and heads to Boxer Way. A cop car blocks this intersection as well, leaving Stephanie with a queasy feeling that brings up the salmon she had for dinner.

"Maybe it's a block party," Georgia says.

Stephanie is in no mood for humor.

She turns onto Boxer despite the barricade, but a cop stops her and signals for her to roll down her window. A tired and rust-colored officer announces the street is closed.

"But I live here."

"You'll have to park up the hill. No cars allowed back in yet."

"When?"

R. H. Sheldon

He shrugs.

Stephanie swings the car around, zooms across Twelfth, and parks close to Thirteenth. A nearby street lamp highlights the fine mist drifting through the air. They head down the hill. If Stephanie were on her own, she'd be running to the house, but even a slow pace is a challenge for Georgia.

After they cross Twelfth, the same cop stops them and asks where they're going, giving no indication he's seen them before.

"We...I live here," Stephanie says.

"I need some ID. The block's closed off to all but residents."

Stephanie pulls out her driver's license. Georgia does the same. "I live here too."

Stephanie tries not to attach any significance to Georgia's license or pronouncement, attributing it to Georgia's lack of organization, an issue that came up between them often.

The cop studies their IDs with his flashlight, then shines it in their faces. Stephanie feels her skin crawl, an odd sense of helplessness and frustration.

"How bad is it?" she asks.

The cop remains stone faced. "Quiet now." His lips barely move.

"But it must have gotten bad earlier," Georgia says. "Right?"

"Bad enough."

The officer hands them their IDs, ushers them along.

They continue down Boxer Way, the streetlights dark, buildings hidden in endless shadow. Window frames glow through drawn curtains and tightened shades, a town hiding its lights for fear of an air raid.

The closer they get to Eleventh, and the longer their eyes have to adjust, the more debris they see around them—boards and bricks and rocks and broken glass and overturned garbage bins and cars with smashed windshields and headlamps and taillights. Then Stephanie notices a burning smell, like the remnants of a campfire, making her want to run more than ever.

When they near the intersection, they discover that the park too stretches into one long shadow, the surrounding buildings like ghost ships on an empty sea.

The only real light comes from a police car parked in front of Parker's house, its spotlight sweeping the yards, the street, this end of the park. Then the light hits Stephanie's garden. The fence she fortified this morning, the front corner near Parker's lot, is nothing but burnt stumps, with large chunks of charred pieces lying on the ground. What little vegetation survived yesterday's onslaught has been fully trampled, the front yard now looking like a bed of weeds, not much different from her neighbor's, maybe even worse.

Stephanie rushes toward the yard. The spotlight takes aim. She shields her eyes. A voice blasts from the car's loudspeaker. "Hold it right there."

She freezes. Georgia steps up beside her.

"Both of you. Don't move."

The passenger door opens. The police radio squawks. A cop steps out, a shifting silhouette, boots against asphalt, the scrape of rubber. The officer moves into the harsh light, face half shadow, hard.

That's when Stephanie recognizes her. "I know you." She feels herself relax.

The cop studies Stephanie, a slight softening. "The ER."

Stephanie nods, flattered that the officer remembers her. She used to show up in the ER on occasion, usually in the later hours, dealing with a domestic dispute or violent crime or other unsavory incident. Stephanie always had her pegged as a dyke, and not a bad looking one at that.

"This is Georgia," Stephanie says. "She's, ah, visiting from Oregon." Then she turns to Georgia. "And this is Officer Edwards."

"Rocky," she says, and turns toward the car, signals with a brief wave that everything is okay, turns back toward them. "And what brings you gals out on this fine evening?" Stephanie was right. All dyke.

Stephanie points a thumb at her house. "My place." The reminder of her house brings her back to the present.

"You just getting home?"

"Yeah," Stephanie says. "We've been gone since early afternoon. Looks like things got a bit exciting."

"Hold on a second," Rocky says. "Let me grab a flashlight. I'll help you check it out." She trots back to the car, speaks to the driver, returns with a flashlight the size of a nightstick.

They climb over the remnants of fence. Rocky aims the light at the strips of barbed wire curling across the ground. "Odd."

They move through the trampled plants. Stones and bricks cast long shadows, take on enormous proportions. Rocky shines the light across the yard, breaks apart shadows, builds others, in front, along the sides, every bush and tree destroyed. The house itself, though, doesn't look too bad, some markings on the side, giant letters on one wall, *OPH,* written with a charred piece of wood, a few other comments about bankers and occupying and the one percent.

"Christ," Georgia says, "as though your tiny home represents the wealthy and elite."

Stephanie lets the comment drop.

They circle the house once, confirming that most of the damage is confined to the front. That's when they discover the glass, the largest of the windows, shattered, broken inward, jagged shards wedged into the frame.

Rocky switches the flashlight to her left hand, pulls the gun from her holster, shines the light into the house. Glass is scattered across the floor, the chair, as far as the counter. Off to the side, Georgia's pack sits untouched, nothing out of the ordinary, so damned normal, in fact, Stephanie shivers. Then she sees an unfamiliar shadow, a great lump off to the right, wedged into the corner, just a shade darker then the surrounding shadows.

She taps Rocky's arms, points to the heap. Rocky aims the beam. A mass of hair, black, scrambled. Myron and Sonuvabitch, sleeping like babies.

Myron

At first, all Myron can see is the beam of the flashlight, vague outlines behind it, three people perhaps.

Someone calls his name, distant, maybe in his dream. A wide meadow brown with fall, clear skies, pulsating sun.

Sonuvabitch screeches, flees into the shadows, Myron's arm marked with the cat's claw.

"Ouch."

"Myron, what are you doing?"

Is that Stephanie? Floating in the shadows?

A flick. The sudden glare of lights. Stephanie stands by the wall, her hand on the switch, the ceiling a white pumping glare, like his dream. No meadow.

Stephanie before him, next to her, Georgia. Then the one with the flashlight, a female officer of the law, her frown like a clay pigeon's. She continues to aim the flashlight. And the gun.

"That must have been difficult," Myron says.

Stephanie pulls away from the wall, closes in on the cop. "It's okay. He's our neighbor."

More frowning. "What's he doing here?"

Stephanie says, "What's up, Myron?"

He shakes his head, tries to recall. "The window." He points to the broken glass.

Stephanie crouches down, their faces on the same plane. "What happened?"

R. H. Sheldon

Myron shrugs. "Saw the broken window. Sonuvabitch thought we should wait here, watch over the house." He scans the room. "Where's Sonuvabitch?"

"Ran outside," Georgia says.

"Hello, Georgia. How are you feeling?"

She shoots a look at Stephanie.

"I didn't say anything."

Stephanie takes Myron's arm, helps him stand. "Thanks, Myron, I appreciate you two watching my home. If it weren't for you, I might have been robbed."

Myron tilts his head, listens. "I better go. Parker just woke up."

The officer eyes him suspiciously, but he's used to that. He slips out the door into the cool night, dark as a forest. He feels the mist on his face, a tonic, waking, real.

He winds around to the back of Stephanie's house and heads into the alley. He shuffles across the gravel and turns into Parker's yard. Sonuvabitch waits on the back porch, lets out a quick squeak. Myron pets his head. Sonuvabitch follows him into the house.

Myron knows the kitchen, can maneuver in the dark. When he reaches the living room, he finds the tiny brass lamp on the piano turned on, just enough light to pull the corners back into the room. Only the light gives form. In the dark edges, the world no longer exists.

Myron is about to drop onto the couch when he discovers another person stretched out on the cushions, covered with his green wool blanket. A slight snore puffs out each time the blanket falls.

Sonuvabitch meows.

Myron says, "I don't know who's in our bed."

Sonuvabitch rubs against his leg. The stranger lets out a low grumble, the sort that comes from dreams.

For a moment, Myron thinks Parker is crashed out down here, but then he hears movement above, the shuffle of feet, the creak of floorboards, the footsteps on the stairs. When Parker appears in the entryway, Myron says, "It's not the you I thought."

"It never is." He drops into his chair. "Where the hell you been?"

"Visiting Stephanie."

"For two days?"

"No, Parker, of course not."

Parker glances at the couch. "Who's that?"

Myron cocks his heads and steps nearer to his bed. A slight nervous smell. Hints of patchouli. "Olympia Culpepper, the preacher from the Lighthouse Sanctification Church."

"What the hell is she doing here?"

"I don't know, Parker. Would you like me to ask her?"

Parker rolls his eyes. "Yeah, old buddy, you do that."

Myron pokes her shoulder. "Olympia Culpepper, what the hell you doing here?"

A low moan oozes out from under the cover.

Myron leans closer, pokes again.

Olympia rolls over and pulls back the cover. Their noses practically touch. She opens her eyes. Starts.

"Olympia Culpepper," Myron says, "Parker wants to know what the hell you're doing here."

Olympia blinks, pulls back, bolts upright. She stares with a look Myron has often seen in others, a jungle look, uncertain, scared, senses betrayed.

"I'm Myron," he says.

She blinks again.

Myron eases to the floor, near the end of the coffee table, next to Olympia's feet. He crosses his legs, waits for Sonuvabitch to crawl onto his lap. The cat squeaks, jumps onboard, curls into a ball, purrs.

Parker searches the floor near his chair. "Not one goddamn smoke. What'd you do with my cigarettes, Myron?"

"I don't smoke, Parker."

Parker grumbles.

Olympia pulls herself upright, turns, places her feet on the floor, her face yellowed by the dim light on the piano. She turns her head toward Parker, stares with a brittle gaze, the blanket still pulled up to her shoulders.

"You," she says, "what you've done."

She points an accusing finger, like the Ghost of Christmas Future, without moving her hand, but Myron sees it, as sure as he sees the fear in her eyes. She doesn't understand that there is no control, no order. Only the jungle.

"I thought you would be in jail," Parker says, "with your comrades."

She lets the blanket fall. Her sweatshirt is streaked with mud, torn at the shoulder. "Do you have any idea of the damage you've done?"

R. H. Sheldon

"Just having a bit of fun."

"A riot is fun?"

She leaps to her feet, but not really.

Parker shrugs, turns to his right, reaches to the floor, toward the broken lamp, and picks through the bits of ceramic. "Not one goddamn butt. Jesus, Myron, what are you trying to do to me?"

Olympia stands, this time for real. She pulls on her jacket, her stocking cap with the giant *LSC*. "What was I thinking, wasting my time on someone like you?"

Myron says, "You were probably thinking about all the people who would hear you talk."

Olympia glares at Myron. "You're just as crazy as him."

Myron strokes the cat's head. "Are you done with our bed?"

Olympia stomps toward the front door, stops, turns, heads into the kitchen. Myron hears the door open, her anger on the back steps.

He studies the couch, thinks about a dream he had three nights ago, giant parrots, massive green wings, mountain-sized shadows.

Parker says, "Myron, buddy, I really need a cigarette. What'd you do with all my smokes?"

Myron does not recall what he did with Parker's Lucky Strikes. Myron is not sure he did anything with them. When he's about to tell Parker this, a loud explosion erupts outside the house. Gunfire. A single shot. Followed by a brief scream and the even briefer words, "Oh my God."

Part VII

A home filled with nothing but yourself.
It's heavy, that lightness. It's crushing, that emptiness.
—Margaret Atwood, The Tent

Alonzo

He's convinced his brain has swollen to twice its normal size. What else would explain this jackhammer in his head? And his tongue feels like boot leather, his eyes encrusted with centuries of sand.

He lies on top of the white duvet cover, staring through slitted lids at the shadow-dimmed ceiling, a creamy wave that spins in slow spirals and churns his stomach. He still wears his jacket, the tie a slack noose, shoes tight against swollen feet.

So this is what a hangover feels like. He could have happily died without ever knowing.

The liquor leaves more than just a shattered body. The hollowness has grown, taken a permanent home, a hunger beyond food or family or comfortable bed.

If Isabel were here, if she could see him on the bed with his filthy clothes, doused in grime and reeking of scotch, she would storm out in disgust. But she's not here. She's either still with her sister or at her mother's. Or maybe somewhere else. But he doesn't mind so much, at least not at the moment, in fact, takes comfort in the quiet that pervades the house, too much comfort perhaps, as though quiet were an addiction.

The last time he saw Isabel was at Volunteer Park, by the conservatory. She screamed. Lita glared. He listened. Sort of. Mostly he stared at the shards of glass and scotch-soaked concrete. Then she ran off, just as she would now if she saw the bed.

He tries to sit up, his body stiff and sore, a beaten-up feeling, battered and betrayed. After Isabel and Lita stomped off, he returned to the car and climbed into the back seat with Roscoe, and the two curled up and slept for several hours. He woke in a nauseous fog and stuck his head out the door and puked along the curb, then drove home to the empty house.

He crawls to the edge of the bed and sits. Roscoe appears in the doorway and wags his tail, his eyes too bright and full of glee.

"You probably want to go out." Alonzo can barely speak, his throat a dried-out rubber band.

He stands. A sharp pain shoots through his head and breaks across his temples. He drops back to the bed. Roscoe barks.

"Argh. Stop. Bad dog." Alonzo grabs his head with both hands to keep his brains from spilling out. Roscoe sits.

Alonzo coughs out a "good boy." He stands once more, still holding his head, and shuffles toward the door. Roscoe leaps to his feet, quivers, bounces from paw to paw.

"Not one bark."

Roscoe obeys, but the bark still hangs there.

Alonzo crawls down the stairs, through the kitchen, the utility room, opens the outside door. Roscoe runs past him, knocks Alonzo into the cabinets. He bangs his head against an open door. His skull explodes in a swirl of Tide and Shout and Downy.

He hangs onto the dryer for a moment, then picks his way into the kitchen, into a room too bright, and sits at the counter, next to his phone and keys and a brochure from the Volunteer Park Conservatory. He has no idea when he acquired it.

The phone buzzes. He jumps, grabs the counter to keep from falling.

Another unknown number, this time Bellevue. He pushes the phone away, swears not to answer. The buzzing stops. He rubs his temples, avoiding the spot that whacked the cupboard. The phone buzzes again. He reaches, grabs it, intent on tossing it into the trash. The same number. He answers.

"Yeah." He holds the phone several inches away.

"Alonzo?"

"Who's calling?"

"Dartmouth here. Harold Dartmouth."

Dartmouth? The senior partner? Calling Alonzo? "Yes, sir, Mr. Dartmouth. This is Alonzo."

Alonzo slips so easily into his obsequious role that he forgets for a moment his brain feels like a muddy soccer field. But a bark at the door pulls him back, reminds him of his pain, the liquor that caused it, his disappearance from the office.

"Listen, Alonzo, I know you're upset about what happened to Buck. We all are." He has the voice of an archbishop, all control and practiced confidence, a gentle cover over his seething power. "Buck would always tell us how close you two were, how well you worked together. 'He's my right arm,' Buck would say. I can only imagine how you're feeling now, Alonzo. And normally I would tell you to take a couple days off, collect yourself, regroup, take your family on a little vacation. Christ, you've earned it, after all."

Dartmouth must not know Buck fired Alonzo. Of course, he doesn't. How could he? No one knows. Who could Buck have told?

Alonzo clears his butchered throat. "We all have to bear up, sir."

"Exactly, my boy. And we need you to bear up more than ever."

"Sir?"

"This situation with the Parker Davis house. It's out-of-control. And now the shooting."

"Shooting?"

Alonzo pushes himself to his feet, shuffles around the counter, grabs a glass from the cupboard, one of the kid's Disney cups, and fills it with water from the refrigerator door, cold, filtered, liquid silver. He gulps and slurps and wants to puke.

"Last night. A cop shot one of the protesters."

Alonzo stops drinking, pulls the phone closer to his ear. "Davis?"

"No such luck." Dartmouth sighs. "Our clients are furious. They're demanding answers."

Alonzo gulps more water, feels little but indifference and nausea.

Dartmouth must have taken the slurping as a sign of protest. "Now don't you worry, Alonzo. I know you were following orders. The truth is, Buck could be a bit of a bulldog, a useful trait, most of the time. But now we need someone to take charge who has a more diplomatic touch, someone like you, Alonzo."

"Me?"

Dartmouth hardly knows Alonzo. They would greet each other at the annual Christmas party, but Dartmouth and the other partners rarely broke rank, and at gatherings of any sort, an entourage of aggressive associates groveled and surrounded them with an impenetrable wall, leaving attorneys like Alonzo on the sidelines, sipping wine and chewing on smoked oysters.

"Yes, you, Alonzo. Don't think your efforts have gone unnoticed. And this situation with Davis is going to take more effort than ever. It's beyond being a powder keg. It's a war zone. And we need you to negotiate the treaty."

Alonzo has no idea how to reply.

"I know what you're thinking," Dartmouth says. "'What's in it for me?' And I don't blame you. Buck's not coming back, you must realize that, and we need someone to take his place, someone who understands the ins and outs of the cases you've been working on. That would be you, Alonzo, stepping into Buck's shoes. You keep up your good work, and someday there'll be a partnership in it for you, something to make your people proud."

His people?

He sets his glass on the counter, returns to the stool.

"Thank you, Mr. Dartmouth. You're very generous."

"Call me Harold. And don't thank me. Just get the job done."

"You can count on me, sir."

The call ends. Too bad Isabel isn't here. She'd be overjoyed. At least he thinks she would. He just hopes she gets over whatever she's going through soon so they can get back to normal.

Alonzo drinks more water, swallows several ibuprofen, lets Roscoe inside, fills his bowl with kibble, feels almost human. He dresses and locks Roscoe into the laundry room, ignoring the dog's famous look. He exits the house and climbs into a car that smells of dirt and wet canine and the faint remnants of scotch, sour, almost putrid.

He starts the car and clicks on the radio, hoping to catch news about last night's shooting. He needs to get up-to-speed fast, figure out what it will take to resolve this situation. Actually, he knows what it will take. He just needs to know how much.

He switches channels until he hears the name Parker Davis. "After forty years," the announcer says, "the song is still as relevant as it was then. Here it is, folks, for the third time this morning, 'Last Stand.' Let's keep the calls coming."

Music plays, a folksy sound, more piano than guitar, the voice okay, young and silly, the tune just typical '60s nonsense, with lyrics to match, the usual insipid adolescent angst.

We are a frightened species behind our shuttered doors.
We turn to war and promises, do battle with the poor.
The answer isn't money or politics or fame.
Together we must take a stand to raze this wall of shame.

Alonzo wants to switch channels, but feels compelled to stick with it through the end, despite the simplistic mire and pounding refrain, like falling into the rabbit hole with Dr. Seuss.

A stand we must, a stand we can
Our last, our only, lonely stand.
One last stand, one last for man,
Our last hoorah, our lonely stand.

After singing the refrain alone several times, Parker is joined by a full chorus and orchestra, repeating it over and over, twenty times at least, maybe more, the music grating, repetitive, unimaginative. The perfect pop song, then and now.

The announcer returns. "Amazing stuff," he says, his voice almost weepy. "Across the country, the song has shot up to the number one slot, and here in Seattle, I plan to do everything I can to keep it there. We're at a crossroads, people, and the time has come for all of us to get up off our butts and do something about it."

He plays another song, "The Times They Are a-Changin'."

Alonzo clicks off the radio, shifts into gear, and pulls out of the driveway. The times are changing, all right, and there's not a blasted thing anyone can do about it.

Bellamy

At least she has a working phone this morning. After that bullshit at Casey's tent yesterday, Bellamy marched to a Radio Shack and bought a new charger. She has no intention of returning to that stupid camp. Ever. It was worth the thirty bucks just to be done with that asshole. She only hopes she can talk her mom out of enough cash to cover the bill.

After she bought the charger, she snuck into the house, shut herself into her room, and switched on the TV. She didn't check messages or texts or anything. She plugged in the phone and turned down the volume and forgot all about it. Before long, she fell into a long fitful sleep.

Images of the horrible mix of dreams still flash through her head—standing naked before a booing crowd, Casey pointing at her and laughing, cops chasing her down the street and bombarding her with raw eggs and flash-bang grenades. As soon as she woke up, she checked her body for slime.

She grabs the phone and turns up the volume and unplugs it from the charger, letting the cord plop to the floor. The screen shows a number of new texts and emails and voice messages, probably mostly from Crystal, or maybe her mom begging for her help again.

Bellamy launches the Twitter app, types *#occupyseattle,* and scrolls to last night's tweets—hundreds of posts, talking about a riot and arrests and a curfew and shooting. Bellamy scans through them briefly, part of her wishing she hadn't missed all the action, at the same time glad to be done with all those jerks.

She scrolls down further and comes across hundreds more tweets featuring *#parkerdavis,* how cool he is, how funny, how honest and real—just more bullshit—but then she discovers her name, referenced simply as *#bellamy,* just like *#modonna* or *#ellen* or *#fondeaux.* A rush of giddiness rises through her, and she considers the possibilities that fame might bring: money and travel and men all around the world. But then she realizes the tweets are all dissing her, calling her names like *pathetic lard-ass* and *loser retard* and *inbred bitch ignoramus.* They poke fun at her hair, her clothes, her face, her boots, the way she talks and walks and blows her nose, *a dying heifer letting off gas, a munchkin-land reject that makes the tin man look like a brain surgeon.*

Bellamy searches on her name. Reads a hundred or so more tweets. Reads them a second time. A third. Then she stops, stares at the phone, at the scratched surface of the glass, the chips on her lacquered nails. She huffs, shrieks, and flings the phone across the room, then buries herself under the covers.

She considers ways to take herself out. A bullet to the head? Too messy. Poison? Too sickening. What about gas? She could lock herself into the kitchen and turn up all the burners and jack up the oven and pull its door wide open.

Except the stove is electric.

Maybe she can use her mom's car. Run a hose from the exhaust to the window. Or perhaps drugs. Enough downers and booze and she'd be done. She'd go out like all those famous people, like that Kurt Cobain guy or what's-his-name with all the hair. Then she'd show them. Every last one of them. They'd realize how terrible they had treated her, suffer for years with torturous guilt, knowing they were instrumental in her demise, knowing that each of them was in part to blame.

She can see it now. She'd tweet what she was doing right after she took the pills, let them read for themselves the effects of their cyber-bullying. She'd tweet and tweet until her fingers stopped working. By the time they found her, it would be too late, but her tweets would live on in Internet infamy. They'd be all over the news and the guilty would be arrested and everyone would learn that they couldn't treat people like they treated her. People would view *#bellamy* as a savior, the heroine that went to her death as a sacrificial lamb they'd all been waiting for. Over and over #bellamy would fly through the airwaves. *#bellamy. #bellamy. #bellamy.*

Her phone lets out a sound like broken glass. A new text message. She pushes back the covers, retrieves the phone, and climbs back into bed.

A message from Crystal. *U home or at hospital?*

Bellamy types. *Home. Why hospital? U hi?*

On my way.

Bellamy pulls the covers up to her neck.

Crystal must have been outside because she arrives before Bellamy can text a reply. She pushes open the bedroom door and sits at the bottom of the bed. She wears cargo pants and a sweatshirt and looks just like Bellamy's mother.

Bellamy holds her arm up to her forehead and lets out a long, sorrowful sigh and says, "My life is ruined."

Crystal's phone dings. "Just a sec." She responds, her thumbs like greyhounds.

"Oh, Crystal, what am I going to do?"

Crystal sends her text and looks up. "Your mom will be fine. She's a fighter."

"My mom? I'm talking about me, Crystal."

"Geez, Bellamy. It's not like you got shot." Another ding.

"Shot? What the hell you talking about? I got gassed and clubbed, not shot."

"Hold on." Crystal replies.

"Goddamn it, Crystal. Why did you come over here if you're just going to play with that thing?"

"Huh?" Crystal glances toward Bellamy.

"I need sleep. I'll call you later maybe."

Crystal finishes the text. Her eyes let loose the phone. "But what about your mom?"

"What about her?"

"Aren't you going to the hospital?"

"Why do I want to go to the hospital? I'm fine. The baby is fine." Another ding. "Don't you know? It's been all over the news."

Bellamy feels as though the elevator's dropping too fast.

"What do you mean, Crystal? Tell me what you mean." She pushes the covers back, sits up.

"I can't believe you don't know."

"Know what?"

"Your mom. She's in the hospital. A cop shot her last night."

The elevator shimmies and shakes and slams into the ground.

Olympia

Not only did Olympia end up at the same hospital where Parker had done his stint—the Elliott Bay Medical Center—but it appears she landed on the same floor, in a room very close to his, judging by the rooftop spread of tar and air vents.

Her shoulder is still pretty numb from the late-night surgery. Damage around the rotator cuff, according to the surgeon, nothing that couldn't be repaired. The main challenge will be wearing this damn sling for the next two months. Even with all the painkillers, she's ready to tear it off. And the dressing on her head doesn't help, any more than the fact that she'll have to rely a great deal on Bellamy, a pregnant twenty-year-old with all the sense of a turnip.

At least it was a cop who shot her. She couldn't ask for a better setup. She and her church have received national attention. Well-wishers from around the country have been calling the hospital since early this morning. The room is stuffed full of violets and roses and lavender and dozens of other flowers, exuding a tropical aura, exaggerated by the room's excessive heat.

The nurse's assistant, a young man who claimed to have never met a real celebrity, told Olympia that the press had been camped out downstairs all night, waiting for word on when they can see her. She's already had visits from the Seattle Police Department, the FBI, and the CIA, all asking questions about what happened last night, and she told them all the same thing, that when she walked out of Parker Davis's house, a cop shone a floodlight in her face, called for her to stand still, then shot her. At first, she thought someone had knocked her over with a club, but then the blood flowed and the pain followed and the lights flashed. Cops gathered, yelled, called for backup, searched the area around the house. Parker showed up. So did Myron. And next came Parker's neighbor—Stephanie?—acting all professional and concerned, a nurse, as it turns out, one who evidently knows her way around blood and trauma. Then the ambulance arrived and whisked Olympia away to the ER, where she received an IV and oxygen mask and an onslaught of questions about medications and allergies and past injuries and sexual habits.

News about the shooting must have gotten out quickly, because members of the press were at the hospital in no time, along with scores of Occupy folks and people from her church, all squeezed in the waiting room, poking in their heads for news, badgering anyone they could for information. The hospital had quite the time, in fact, controlling the crowds, which only grew as the evening stretched into the late night hours.

Between all that and this morning's flood of visitors, all Olympia wants is a little rest. Just ten minutes of quiet without anyone to disturb her or poking at her or asking her questions.

"Mom!" Bellamy rushes into the room, tears tattooing her cheeks, her body writhing with sobs. "Oh my God. Oh my God. I just found out what happened." She drops to her knees and tries to bury her face into the blankets, but the bed sits too high and her pose wavers between mournfulness and clownishness, as though feigning tears to generate laughter.

"I'm fine, Bellamy, really. You can get up."

Bellamy sobs louder, her words chopped and broken. "When...I...heard..." More cries. "I...could...not...believe..." She gasps. Twice. "If...only...I...had..."

She drops to the floor, a broken warhorse. All Olympia can see is the wild mane of hair, jet black, a thin strip of light roots.

Crystal stands at the doorway, fidgeting with the molding.

Olympia says, "You can come in, Crystal. I'm not contagious."

Bellamy rises from the floor with a ritualistic flare, lets out a weepy sigh, and drops into the chair next to the bed. Crystal creeps into the room, places her palm on Bellamy's shoulder. Bellamy pats her friend's hand, taking comfort in the dramatic touch.

Olympia says, "You'll be happy to know I'll probably make it. Inconvenient, but not fatal."

Bellamy and Crystal stare.

"Honest."

Bellamy whimpers. "What about your head? They shoot you there too?" More sniveling.

Olympia touches the bandage. "That's from the other day, Bellamy, when the porch fell. Don't you remember? I was wearing it yesterday."

Bellamy shrugs, a heavy motion that conveys the unbearable burdens the world has placed on her shoulders.

Crystal scoots closer to the bed, flashes a slight nervous smile, teetering on psychosis. "You're like so amazing, Olympia. Organizing all those protests, being in the middle of the crowd when the porch collapsed, and now this. So like awesome. They should erect a statue to you."

Bellamy's eyes flutter as though she has just woken. "What about me? I was the one tear-gassed and clubbed and hauled off to prison."

Crystal barely looks at Bellamy. "Yeah, but you're okay now. It's not like *you're* in the hospital after being plugged full of bullets."

"It was only one bullet, Crystal, and it went through my shoulder. Missed my bones completely. I'll just be a little sore for a while."

"But imagine how bad it could have been. Look how close it was to your heart. A few more inches and you'd be dead!"

"Really, Crystal, I don't think we need to..."

"You're so brave, Olympia."

Crystal lowers her head in reverential silence. Thankfully, Bellamy has no other close friends.

Olympia scoots up in the bed and tries to sit up straighter. "But I will need your help," she says. "The surgeon says it will be tough going for a few weeks. I need to keep my shoulder completely immobile. In a sling, like this." She nearly lifts her arms to show them. Stops. Repositions herself again.

Bellamy says, "You don't know what it was like, Crystal. *You* weren't sprayed. *You* weren't beaten. *You* weren't hauled off to jail."

"I only meant, you're okay now. But your mom has a *real* injury."

Bellamy leaps to her feet. "What do you know by real? What have you ever done that's real. Have you ever been beaten with a club? Sprayed with a poisonous gas? Have you ever been in prison?"

"You know I haven't, Bellamy. Just forget it."

Olympia rubs her temples with her free hand, gazes across the rooftop, toward a horizon hidden by brick and concrete.

"And pregnant on top of it. What do you know about that, Crystal? What do you know? Christ, you haven't even been fucked."

Olympia turns back to the room. "Bellamy, perhaps..."

"You too, mother?" She flings her head back. "I don't need this shit." She grabs her pack off the floor and marches out of the room.

"Bellamy, wait!" Crystal chases after her.

Olympia closes her eyes and thinks of Jephthah, an Old Testament judge who led the Israelites into battle against Ammon. Jephthah vowed to sacrifice the first person from his house who greeted him, should his team return victorious. They did. Upon his arrival home, his daughter and only child rushed out to welcome him back. The rest is Old Testament history.

Parker

P arker tried to convince Myron that they should take a cab to the hospital, but Myron insisted the bus was better. And given Parker's financial straits, he could hardly argue. But he did anyway, even though Myron is not someone you argue with. Myron is someone you simply get used to.

That doesn't mean Parker has to like it. He doesn't have to like any of it, especially coming to visit Olympia, even if it seems best to go along with Myron on this one as well. Myron insisted, and Myron never insists on anything. He just does. But Parker *was* feeling a bit remorseful about the whole thing, as though in some odd way he was responsible for Olympia being shot, and that's why they're standing in front of the hospital, about to pass through its foreboding entrance of steel and glass.

A crowd is gathered before the front doors. They stand silently, heads bowed. Many hold candles, none of them lit, perhaps because of the falling mists. Most have that Occupy look, stocking caps and stylish street threads, entitled revolutionaries. Church people too, mounting a khaki campaign, a rainbow of *LSC* sweatshirts.

Parker pushes through the front door. Myron follows, all the while watching the crowd with their unlit candles. Inside, they work their way through the cavernous waiting room, aiming for a distant reception desk. They weave through groups of young and old, sitting, standing, talking, walking in Zen protest circles. More

R. H. Sheldon

churchgoers and occupiers and members of press, holding cameras or talking to peers or staring obsessively at their portable electronic devices.

One of the more graceful and stylish of the press, the only one in fact, a woman who fits in with none of the others in the room, a woman of enticing youth and poise, her skin the same tawny brown as the chair on which she sits, rises gracefully and stops Parker in mid-stride with a suggestive smile and a flirtatious pose and a voice like ripe and swollen honeydew.

"Mr. Davis," she says through fluorescent cherry lips, "our viewers are anxious to know what happened last night, when the shooting took place, who was there, what you saw." She waves to a man on the other side of the room, her look a demand for obedience. He slings the video camera up to his shoulder and pushes through the crowd. Others in the press notice. They squeeze in, wave cameras and phones, yell out questions, about the shooting, about Olympia, about his house. "What next, Parker Davis? What next?"

The occupiers occupying the floor near the front doorway catch on that their man of the hour is within proximity of their protestations and squeeze in around the reporters.

"Parker. Parker. Parker. Parker."

The churchgoers quickly join in, adding an offbeat clap with each call of his name.

The woman reporter—did she say CNN?—pushes in closer and waves a mike tauntingly in front of his mouth.

"First the shooting," she says. "Tell us what happened."

Parker knows what they want—blood, gore, horror. And a tale of reluctant heroics.

"There I was," he says, feeling the crack in his throat, "in the house with my roommate." Parker glances around. Myron has vanished. "Olympia...Reverend, ah, Culpepper had just left."

"What were you talking about?" This came from an old guy, older than Parker, probably one of those washed-out geezers they use on the local news, just to feel good about their diversity and loyalty to their viewers.

"We talked about our favorite sexual positions. What the hell you think we talked about?"

"Mr. Parker," says the enticing reporter with the syrup-stained eyes, "we're just trying to make sense of what happened."

Parker would love to be a pair of her jeans.

"You're right," he says. "Sorry. I'm just a little tired. We were talking about what had taken place yesterday, how out-of-control the scene had become, how sorry we were that it had happened."

"Are you saying that the protesters got out-of-control? That it was all their fault?"

Smart and pretty. Parker is in love.

"No, ma'am."

"You're saying it was the police?"

"I'm not saying that, either. All I'm saying is that we both wished things had turned out differently. No one benefits from the type of chaos that ensued yesterday."

She pulls herself in closer. "Mr. Davis. Some are suggesting that Lockhart Investments might actually be liable for the collapsing porch, since they claim ownership of the building."

"They'd be liable? You mean, everyone who was on the porch could sue?" Parker gives them a glimpse of a smile. "How about me? What about my emotional distress?"

The room grows eerily silent.

The reporter who Parker plans to marry heaves her voluptuous breasts and moves her sumptuous mouth closer to the mike and says, "Did you make any plans at that point? Decide on a course of action?"

Parker reaches for the mike, wrapping his fingers around hers, suddenly stricken by the contrast between his arthritic knuckles and aged-stained hands and her soft and youthful flesh. He lets go.

"No. No plans."

A different reporter, no doubt also there as a result of a local diversity program, says, "And that's when Reverend Culpepper left?"

Parker nods. "She left. We heard a shot. We ran outside. Police poured in from every direction. Kind of creepy, really, the way they all showed up so fast, as though they were waiting for something like this to happen."

Parker's not sure why he said this, why he even thought it. Where the hell did Myron go?

"What did she look like?"

"Look like?" Jesus, what do they want from him? "She looked like a woman who'd been shot."

"Was there much blood?"

"Was she in much pain?"

"Was anyone else there?

"How did it make you feel?"

"Did you try to help?"

"Were you scared?"

"Did she say anything? Yell anything?"

Parker leans toward the mike, speaks in a low voice. "You know, I think she said something about being with her maker, that no matter what happened, she prayed that she had made the right choices, that she had struck a blow for justice and liberty, that all she wanted was to help. I can't be sure of course, but it was something like that, I'm sure."

The reporters stare with looks of rapture. The rest of the crowd closes in. Some sigh. Others applaud. Many cry. They hold up their cell phones, snap pictures, shoot videos. They text like demons. The noise from the crowd grows. They yell out their disgust with the police, with the system. The press continues with the questions, closing the circle even more.

And that's when Parker sees her, Olympia's daughter, coming from the elevators, oblivious to the crowds.

Parker shouts, "There she is. That's the one who will know what's going on. Olympia's daughter, Belfry."

"You mean Bellamy?"

"Yeah, that's the one."

The crowd turns on her, aims microphones, cameras, phones. They explode with questions.

"How's your mother?"

"How is she feeling?"

"Will she survive?"

"Were you there when she was shot?"

"Will you press charges?"

Bellamy freezes, her face covered in fear. Reporters close in. Others follow. More photos. More videos. More texts.

"Tell us, Bellamy. Tell us."

Her lips quiver, tears fill her eyes. "My mother. They shot my mother." The cameras zoom in. The microphones push in. She disappears in a sea of flannel and wool and cotton-clad flesh.

Parker moves toward the elevators.

"Mr. Davis."

He turns. It's that kid from yesterday, one of the first to speak at the rally. A regular Music Man.

"Mr. Davis," he repeats. He springs toward Parker, wielding his skateboard like a weapon. "I'm Casey. I met you yesterday." His dreadlocks drip with rain.

"Casey, yes."

"I just want to say how impressed I am with what you're doing, taking on a system like this, standing up for what's right. I mean, someone of your generation."

Parker tries to keep from choking. "Yes, well, we all have to take a stand some time."

"Awesome!"

Parker jumps back. Casey holds up his skateboard. A bulky blue pack hangs from his back. "This is for you, Mr. Davis! And for everyone like you!"

The crowd spins toward Casey. Bellamy sees him, turns a peculiar shade of pumice.

Casey waves his skateboard, nearly slamming it into Parker's head. "For you!"

"Yes," Parker says, "we seem to have established that."

Casey turns toward the room, holds up his skateboard in both hands, high above the altar. "First thing tomorrow, I take off for Portland. On my skateboard." He beams proudly. "From now on, everything I do, every action I take, I do to raise awareness of the plight of Parker Davis and everyone like him."

Some applause. More pictures. Much more texting.

"Tomorrow! Portland! For you, Parker Davis." Casey kisses the skateboard, places it on the tiled floor, hugs Parker like an old comrade. More pictures.

Bellamy bursts out of the crowd, "No, Casey, no. Don't do it. I know I should hate you. But I can't. I need you. I can't have anyone else I love harmed." She falls to her knees.

Casey reaches down, takes her hand, lifts her to her feet. "We have to do what we have to do." He kisses Bellamy on the forehead. She folds to the ground in a heap of tears.

Reporters watch, take notes, snap pictures, looks of glee plastered on their faces. Group masturbation at its finest.

Parker wipes his brow, coughs, and heads toward the elevator. He'll save his laughter for later, when no one is looking.

R. H. Sheldon

Myron

Myron climbs the back staircase he discovered when he visited Parker, concrete and steel echoes and bone-colored walls, like a tower without a tank. Parker wasn't shot, though. Olympia was shot, but Parker is still full of holes, like the guys in the jungle, the ones in the streets, Olympia and her daughter.

Myron too. Holes he doesn't see. Invisible holes. Individually invisible. Maybe that's how they all survive.

He reaches the landing and opens the door. Warm hospital air rushes past him, full of sour and sterile smells, the clanging of carts, the swarm of hushed voices.

He emerges on the same floor where Parker had stayed. Myron doesn't know what floor this is or what it is about this floor that differentiates it from the others, but he's certain this is the floor. Where else would Olympia be if not here?

He follows the fluorescent corridors past walls of closed doors and scuff-free tile, moving steadily into busier hallways where double-takes and scoffing stares serve up a collective scorn, broken infrequently with greetings more gentle and looks less cool and wrapped in fear.

The hospital heat stifles beyond normal heat, a suffocating jungle, made worse by climbing the stairs. He pulls off his fatigue jacket, pulls back his snarled hair, lets his neck cool, his armpits feel the air. People in the hallways, staff and patients alike, stand aside like a parting sea.

When Myron reaches Olympia's room, he pushes past the half-opened door, hangs his coat on the back of the chair, and sits down. "Hello, Olympia. How is your shoulder?"

She stares. "How did you find me?"

"I walked here to your room."

"But the staff have instructions not to give out my room number."

"That's why I came here."

"But how did you know?"

"I followed my feet."

"Yes, I see that, still..." She shakes her head.

Myron says, "Your shoulder will be fine, Olympia."

"So I'm told."

"Did you have a nice visit with Bellamy?"

"Bellamy? The usual disaster...But how did...You must have seen her in the lobby."

Myron taps the arm of the chair. *Rat-a-tat-tat-tat.* He thinks about reality, how difficult it can be. How different.

"Parker is coming," Myron says.

"Good. I want to talk to him. We need to strategize."

"Yes, we need to strategize."

Olympia glances toward the hallway, toward the rush of hospital sounds.

"When will he be here," she asks.

"When will *who* be here?"

Olympia frowns, sours, winces with pain. "Parker Davis."

"Parker Davis arrived at the hospital when I arrived. We took the bus. Parker wanted to take a cab, but I like buses. Parker has no money for cabs. And I like buses."

"Where is he then? Where is Parker?"

"Parker was downstairs playing with the reporters, but he's done playing. Parker is trying to find you."

Myron stands, sniffs the air. Something bitter, tired. He sticks his head out into the hallway and waves his arms. "We're down here, Parker." Parker looks up, shakes his head. Others look and turn away.

Myron returns to Olympia's room. Parker soon stumbles in after him. "Ah," he says, "so here you are."

R. H. Sheldon

Myron once rode on a ship in the Gulf of Thailand, along with thousands of men with holes the size of the Grand Canyon. Where are Myron's holes? Where?

Myron says, "Olympia wants to strategize, Parker."

"Nice to see you, too." He grabs Myron's jacket off the chair, hands it to Myron, and sits down. The fake leather crinkles and lets out a soft *whoosh*.

Olympia says, "I'm fine. Thank you for asking."

Myron says, "But Olympia, Parker didn't ask."

Parker shakes his head, sticks a finger in his ear. "As far as I can see, Rev Baby, you and I need each other. Together, we can rule the world." He snickers, belches long and loud.

"God help us," Olympia says.

"It could be worse."

"Perhaps. Unfortunately, I suspect you're right on both counts. The issue now is how to proceed."

"The issue," Parker says, "is to decide what we want."

Myron slips out of the room and works his way back to the stairway full of echoes. He drops down into the cavern and soon emerges in the lobby. When he sees the hordes of people, he heads outside. The vigil is in full swing, though the candles remain unlit.

Off to the side, sitting on a concrete bench, alone, afraid, sobbing like a three-year-old girl, sits Bellamy Burns-Culpepper, her cheeks streaked with mascara, her hair a Sonuvabitch mop, her face as mopey as a hung-over Parker.

"Bellamy," Myron says, "you look sad. Maybe you need a holiday."

"I need something," she says between sobs.

"Yes," he says, "we all need something, Bellamy."

She sniffles, cocks her head like a sheep dog.

"It's the holes," he says. "It's always the holes."

"What?"

"The holes, Bellamy."

She leans away from him.

He sits down.

"Leave me alone."

"I can leave you alone. But can you leave you alone?"

Bellamy jumps to her feet. "I said leave me alone."

"Is that what you want, Bellamy? To be left alone?"

"Go away."

"Where shall I go?"

"Just leave."

He sits.

She grabs a rock from a nearby planter. She waves her arm in a threatening pose. He stands. She steps back. He steps toward her. She throws it at him. He ducks. The rock hits a window next to the front door. The window cracks. The vigil people scream and scatter, their unlit candles tumbling to the ground. Four security guards descend on Bellamy. She cries out like a dying hyena.

Time to go home, Myron thinks. Time for something.

Stephanie

Stephanie pulls the filter out of the teapot and sets it in the sink. Green tea always smells a bit like seaweed, even genmaicha, with its grainy overtones.

She pours a cup for Georgia, one for herself, then sits next to Georgia at the counter, their backs to the broken window. A draft pushes through the cracks, puffing out the plastic, each crinkling gust a reminder of her first chore today, boarding up the window.

Georgia scoops honey into her tea, drips it on the bottle, the counter, the sides of her mug, just like usual, oblivious to the mess she leaves for others to clean up. But the honey is trivial compared to the mess that waits behind her.

Stephanie managed to sweep up the bulk of the broken glass last night, but shards had flown everywhere, and the room still needs a good cleaning, especially with all the mud and debris they tracked in. Then there's what's left of the window itself, splinters wedged into the frame, buried in the gully that once seated the glass.

She has plenty of boards in the shed to provide a temporary patch, but it won't be pretty, and it will make it damn gloomy in here, especially with the droopy weather and shortened days. Too bad Georgia isn't her healthy self. Stephanie could sure use the help. Still, Georgia is looking better today, her cheeks less gaunt, her face less tired. Perhaps the drive had been part of the problem after all.

Georgia says, "You gonna jump on the window first thing?"

"Soon as I finish my tea."

"Glad you had some of the genmaicha left. My favorite."

"I remember."

Georgia says, "I need to run a few errands this morning, take advantage of the lull in the action."

"You talking about the protests or the doctors?"

Georgia chuckles. "Both I guess."

She might as well stay busy. There's little she can do until the laparotomy next week. And she'd been planning to use this time to get a few things out of storage. She also said she had other business to tend to, but didn't elaborate.

Stephanie says, "If you wait till I finish here, I can help you."

"I'll be fine. Besides, it's not like I have anything else to do." She stirs, sets the spoon on the counter. Drops splash across the tiny flowers in the tile. She slurps her tea.

Stephanie knows what will happen. Georgia will race out of here, leaving her cup on the counter and the honey jar open and her mess all over the tiles. And she'll leave her clothes strewn across the floor and her suitcase in the middle of the room and her wet towel bunched up on the bathroom floor. She'll never pick up or clean up, let alone offer to help with the window.

Georgia, in fact, is the only consistent and predictable thing in Stephanie's life right now.

Stephanie clicks on the TV. Pete Sizemore looms large. He's the morning anchor, a sincere, middle-aged white guy whose daddy owns the station. Stephanie listens to him most mornings. She doesn't watch, but she listens. It's the only channel she gets since the airwaves got digitized and she had to get one of those high-tech converters.

Thinking about that whole conversion scam still frustrates her. Politicians can't make health care or social services or education work in this country, but dangle shiny new televisions in front of everybody, and suddenly governments and communities and businesses from coast-to-coast spring into action, with subsidies and government programs to provide universal access. What crap.

She turns up the volume.

Pete announces that they're going live to the Occupy camp at Seattle Central Community College, where field reporter Anita Franklin is interviewing two of the protesters. Then the camera

R. H. Sheldon

switches to Anita, a young African-American woman with a sincere smile and bright, ambitious eyes.

"Thank you, Pete. Today I'm interviewing Garfield Singley and Melody Voronin, both camping here at Seattle Central." The camera pans the two guests, each dressed like an REI castaway. Anita welcomes her guests and quickly turns the discussion to yesterday's riots and last night's shooting and the plight of Parker Davis.

Stephanie slams her mug on the counter. Tea sprays out, splashes Georgia's arm.

"I can't listen to this crap."

Georgia wipes her arm with a cloth napkin. "You turned it on."

"Besides the point."

"Give it a minute. That Anita is kind of sexy."

Stephanie clutches her mug and gulps her tea.

Anita says, "I just came from the Elliott Bay Medical Center, where Reverend Culpepper is being treated. Have you had any recent updates?"

"Not in the last hour," Melody replies. "But we'll continue our vigil outside the hospital until she's released, and we plan to hold another one in front of Parker's house."

"And Parker Davis? Any recent updates from him?"

This time Garfield replies. "All we know is that he's way like upset. The Rev got shot right outside his home, where she'd been visiting."

"That's what others have said as well," Anita replies. "But according to the Seattle Police Department, the incident is still being investigated. We've had no official word on what happened."

Garfield shouts, "Those douchebags. I'll tell you what happened. I tell you what's still happening. The cops are out-of-control henchman, government Nazis, like they're everywhere, minions of Wall Street and Big Business, just like all those politico types."

Melody quickly adds, "But we don't condone the type of violence we saw yesterday, on anyone's part. We believe in using only peaceful means, including civil disobedience. Our methods are always nonviolent, even in the face of such adversarial behavior as we saw yesterday."

"You mean on the part of the police?"

"I mean no one should behave how people on either side were behaving yesterday. But I guarantee you, no one committed to the Occupy movement participated in any of that violence."

"Yeah, man, it just ain't cool to be destroying property and hurting people, even cops. That's not like what we're all about."

Anita pushes forward. "What are you about?"

"We're about the ninety-nine percent, man. We're about fairness and justice for all. That's why we like joined in the cause for Parker Davis. He represents everything that's wrong with this country, everything we're fighting against."

Stephanie gags on her tea and has to cover her mouth to keep from spitting out.

Georgia laughs. "I couldn't have said it better myself."

Melody jumps in. "I think what Garfield means is that Mr. Davis represents the type of victimization experienced by millions around this country. What's happened to him is happening to far too many people, and it must be stopped."

Anita pulls in the microphone. "Speaking of Parker Davis, we just learned that a producer from Dive Rock Studios plans to bring together a number of well-known performers to record 'Last Stand.' All proceeds will go to Mr. Davis and others in similar circumstances."

Melody says, "Wow, that's amazing. Such a timeless song."

Garfield claps and *whoops* and says, "Way to go, Parker."

Anita says, "In fact, we're about to play the original song right now, for our viewers back home."

"Awesome!"

The camera switches back to the studio. Pete says, "Here we go, Parker Davis singing his 1960s hit 'Last Stand.'" The camera switches to an ancient photo of Parker holding his gold record, grinning while his lips clench a cigarette. Then the music begins, a few soft bars on the piano, a suggestion of a snare and bass, followed by Parker's adolescent, slightly off-key voice.

Stephanie clicks off the TV. "I'm not listening to that crap."

Georgia grins. "Maybe Parker will give us his autograph, if he'll even talk to us little people anymore." She stands. "At least you were there to help last night. It could have turned out a lot worse if you hadn't been."

Stephanie turns away, talks to the broken window. "The ambulance was already on the way. I hardly did anything."

"Why do you do that? Always undercut yourself?"

Stephanie shrugs. "Habit, I guess."

"In that case, I'm off."

Georgia grabs her coat, gulps down the rest of her tea, and rushes out as though off to a fire, and once again, Stephanie finds herself alone in the house with sticky counters and dirty dishes and broken glass.

She finishes her tea, sets the cup on the counter, and lugs Georgia's suitcase and backpack into the bedroom. Then she picks up several socks and shirts scattered on the floor. Next she rinses the mugs and wipes the honey jar and the counter. Now she's ready to start on the window.

She slips on a jacket and pair of gloves and heads out to the alley, where she retrieves the large garbage bin. Thankfully, the trash was picked up a couple days ago, so there's plenty of room. She hauls it back to the house and pulls it inside. She peels the plastic off the window, careful not to bump the dangling glass. A steady flow of cool air pushes through and sends a chill through her body.

She shoves the plastic into the garbage bin and starts picking at the glass, pulling long shards out of the frame and dropping them into the container. The biggest ones she breaks carefully inside the bin.

Although this is the largest window in her house, it's only about five feet wide and four feet high, not so insurmountable a task to consume the entire day. It's not the labor that concerns her, but the loss of the view into her now-destroyed garden, the loss of light in the house, the loss of relative comfort and safety she once felt in her home. Plus, the cost of a new window.

She's about to pull another shard out of the frame when someone hammers on the front door. She drops the glass on the floor. It splinters into a thousand pieces. Well, at least a hundred.

"Damn!"

More knocking.

"Hold on."

She tiptoes around the glass and opens the door. Rocky the cop stands before her, dressed in civilian clothes, jeans, blue rain jacket, black leather boots. In daylight, she looks yummier than ever, a strong lean face, short brown hair like dark honey, a few strands of gray, deep-set eyes, hazel with flecks of emerald green.

Rocky says, "I took off in such a hurry last night, I didn't get a chance to say good-bye. And I wanted to check on how you were making out today."

Stephanie opens the door wide, feels another chill, but this one from nerves. "Where did you come from? I never saw you enter the yard?"

"I snuck around the back."

"Just for fun?"

"And a little discretion."

Stephanie signals for Rocky to enter. "As you can see, I still have a ways to go."

"Perhaps I can help."

"Help?"

"Yeah, cops aren't completely useless." She smiles, a bit awkwardly. So adorable.

Stephanie feels her scalp flush. "I can use all the help I can get."

"Where's your girlfriend?"

"Girlfriend?"

"The woman with you last night. Georgia?"

"Oh. Her. She's out running errands. But she's not my girlfriend. She was, but..."

Rocky nods. Stephanie has no idea what to make of it. Then she realizes that Rocky returned today not to see her, but to see Georgia.

She should have known. This is how it always was when they were together, everyone hitting on Georgia, looking at her, fawning over her. As the years progressed, Stephanie grew increasingly invisible, to the point she hated going anywhere with Georgia. It didn't help that Georgia could be a bit of a flirt—what she liked to call *friendly*—making suggestive comments to other women, openly teasing them in front of Stephanie. Maybe some of that was going on last night, in the short time Georgia and Rocky were together. Stephanie was so focused on the window and her house—and then the shooting—she had little time to think about anything else, let alone evaluate the dynamics between the two women.

Stephanie says, "You know, it's really not that big a deal, I can easily take care of this."

Rocky smiles. "I'm glad to help. And I even came prepared." She pulls a pair of gloves out of her pockets and slips them on.

"Great," Stephanie says, but knows Rocky is merely biding her time until Georgia returns home.

Alonzo

When Alonzo arrives at the Higgins, Whitaker & Nye law offices, Katie at the front desk greets him with slightly more deference than she has in the past and says that he should go directly to Mr. Dartmouth's office. "He was insistent," Katie says with a professional air. "He came out here personally to make sure I told you."

Alonzo thanks her and proceeds up the back staircase to the second floor offices. He stands before Dartmouth's door and straightens his tie. He knocks and waits. When no one replies, he knocks harder. A soft voice penetrates the massive wooden door, instructing Alonzo to enter.

He steps into the large office, sparse, almost monastic. The air is hot, moist, filled with incense and lemon-oil furniture polish. Off to the right, on a low shelf of polished teak, sits a small statue of the Buddha, fat and happy in his meditative pose.

A dim light sifts through heavily tinted windows and casts soft shadows across the furniture's clean lines. The desk itself is orderly and as clutter-free as the room, the teak a hushed luster against the filtered light.

Dartmouth sits in a black-leathered chair, precisely at the desk's center, his carriage stately, regal, emitting an aura of confidence and calm. He has a thin frame with a full head of well-trimmed gray hair and deep-set eyes that stare out like bullets.

Alonzo wonders whether he should genuflect.

"Come in, Alonzo. Come in." His words flow out like silk, his voice warm, paternal, not too loud, not too soft. He points to one of the lush leather chairs positioned in front of the desk.

Alonzo sits, careful not to move the chair for fear of violating the *feng shui*. "Thank you, Mr. Dartmouth."

"Please, call me Harold. I asked you to call me Harold."

The reminder feels like a slight chiding. "Yes, Harold," he says. "I understand you wanted to see me."

"I did. Thank you for coming by."

Alonzo shifts in his chair, glances at the Buddha. The scratches beneath his shirt start to itch.

"First off," Harold says, "you're being moved to Buck's old office. We've already had it cleaned and his personal possessions boxed up. As sad as this situation is, there's no sense pretending that he'll be back."

Alonzo considers asking about Buck's condition but sees little point. Alonzo is perfectly happy that Buck won't be returning. And Buck's office is almost as nice as this one. Sure, Buck had it filled with all sorts of crap—football trophies, beer steins, photographs of him in uniform from his days in college and in the marines. Once that stuff is out of there, it will be a great space.

But first Alonzo wants to hear what else Dartmouth has to say. After all, it was just yesterday Alonzo was ready to tell all of them where they could shove their job.

Dartmouth flashes a fatherly smile. "I want you to get settled as quickly as possible so you can focus on this Parker Davis matter."

"Of course, if you think that's the best course."

The one thing Alonzo learned from Buck was to agree with whatever his superiors said. Didn't matter what Alonzo was really feeling. Just agree. That lesson has come in handy on many occasions, especially with Buck.

"I know this is a lot to ask from you, Alonzo, but we're in rather a difficult position. Lockhart is furious and screaming for blood. He called me at three this morning, demanding that we get this mess cleaned up. I realize you were close to Buck and what happened to him is nothing short of a tragedy, but we cannot deny that because of him, we find ourselves in the current situation."

"No, sir."

Alonzo is not sure how it has been decided that all the blame fall on Buck, but he can see the wisdom of this strategy. Not only is Buck incapable of defending himself, but his health can also be cited as a reason for his lack of judgment. Whether Dartmouth actually blames Alonzo—or at least holds him partially responsible—is hard to say. In all likelihood, he didn't know who Alonzo was until yesterday, and whatever he might think, Alonzo is the only one who's up-to-speed on this case. No doubt Dartmouth would sacrifice Alonzo in a minute, but for now, the situation presents a golden opportunity.

"Mr. Dartmouth, I mean, Harold, may I speak frankly?"

Dartmouth rests his elbows on his polished desk, and places the tips of his fingers together, as though warming up to prayer.

"Please do," he says.

"Although I was extremely fond of Buck, as you have pointed out, I was concerned about many of his decisions lately, particularly with regard to the Parker Davis situation. Yet I felt enough loyalty to him and the company to have faith that he was leading us in the right direction."

"That's very admirable, Alonzo."

"But given the current circumstances, I, like you, believe we need to take a different approach."

Alonzo draws in a deep breath, eases back into the chair. The leather emits a soft *whoosh*. If he were alone, he would be laughing. He had not realized how easy it was to play this game.

"Go on," Dartmouth says with a fixed smile, his fingers touching lightly.

"We already have two lots, and Stephanie Schmidt, Davis's next-door neighbor, is willing to sell. The price is a bit inflated, but overall, a fair enough prospect, so the issue rests entirely with Mr. Davis. In theory, Lockhart now owns the house, but the events of the last few days make this a PR nightmare. More protests are being planned, the national media is onto the story, and now Hollywood liberals are jumping on the bandwagon. This morning, both of our state senators called for an investigation, and the Justice Department is looking into the matter. I suggest we take the approach of the benefactor, that our law firm acknowledges that we didn't fully appreciate the situation and are willing to work with Mr. Davis to help relocate him and get him happily settled."

Dartmouth taps his fingers. "That's exactly the sort of thing I was thinking," he says. "And exactly why I knew you were the man for the job."

Alonzo considers whether to get a Buddha statue for his new office.

"It won't be cheap," he says. "Mr. Davis is no doubt aware of the advantage he now holds. If he isn't, interested parties will quickly educate him. How about I feel out this situation a bit more and put some figures together and run them by you?"

"Fine, fine," Dartmouth says. "Just keep me informed. You'll be reporting directly to me on this one."

"Good."

Dartmouth seems to like this response. He quits tapping and stands. "Katie at the front desk has been instructed to help you with whatever you need to get your office set up."

Alonzo jumps to his feet. Dartmouth shuffles to the Buddha and lights a stick of incense. He places his hands together and bows before the statue. Alonzo lets himself out and heads to his new office. He'll call Isabel as soon as he gets there. This is bound to make her happy.

Myron

Myron knows what he has to do. He's just not sure how he'll do it. After he scurried away from the security guards, he zipped across the street and stood in a small alcove just uphill from the hospital entrance. He had planned to head home, but quickly decided otherwise.

The four security guards still surround Bellamy, tower above her, scowl, hiss. One holds her by the collar. She sobs, tries to pull away. The more she struggles, the more they sneer and the tighter he pulls. Myron needs to rescue her. He knows that. And he knows he needs to do it quickly, before the real cops arrive.

He crosses the street and creeps down the other side, working his way toward the entrance. Steady showers fall, dim what little light remains, wet slate for sidewalks, gum-stained and cracked and riddled with slime. Fat drops slide off the building and splatter on the concrete like tiny cymbals.

Myron creeps around the security guards toward the front door. He stops, turns. The guards huddle closer toward Bellamy, joke, laugh, ignore her tears. He moves quickly, as through rushing out of the building, and leaps toward the guards.

"Quick," he shouts. "Quick." He pretends to be out of breath. *Huff. Puff. Huff. Puff.* "Inside. One of those protesters." *Huff. Puff.* "Near the elevator. He's crazy, I tell you. Crazy. Says he's gonna blow the place up." He grows nearer to the guards, glances up to the sky, catches the streak of blue. *Huff. Puff. Huff. Puff.* "It's in his pack. The blue one. Quick. Quick. He's crazy."

One of the guards yells, "Wait here!" And runs into the building. Two of the others glance at each other and run in after him. The one who holds Bellamy tries to see into the building, past the unsuspecting crowds, his muscles tense, body cocked.

Myron says, "I'll watch her."

The guard hesitates, shakes his head.

"Hurry!" Myron shouts. The guard lets go and runs inside.

Myron says, "We better leave, Bellamy."

She stares at him like a broken doll.

He takes her hand and leads her away from the entrance and toward the sidewalk. She glances back. Freezes. Casey dashes out of the hospital, laughing and waving his skateboard. She calls his name. He hesitates, then runs for the street and jumps on his skateboard and sails down the hill. The four security guards explode out of the hospital and chase after him. Myron urges Bellamy along the sidewalk and up the hill. She keeps looking back, but Casey is long gone.

They cross Boren and continue up past the rows of pricey apartment buildings, tall and stately and grim against the misty streets.

When they reach Broadway, Myron says, "Are you hungry?"

Bellamy stares at him with dazed uncertainty.

"Let's stop here." He gestures toward a burrito and taco dive, bright, fluorescent, filled with red and blue.

They stand before the counter. Myron orders two chicken tacos. He pulls a wad of bills out of his pocket and pays the woman behind the counter, then shoves the rest of the cash back in.

They sit at a Formica table, white, smooth, the booths red and plastic and cold.

"Eat this," he says.

She grabs a taco and nibbles off the edge.

Myron grabs his. One, two, three, it's gone. He waits for Bellamy to finish.

She picks at the crispy shell. A piece breaks and tiny slivers drop to the table.

"Eat," he says.

She obeys.

Outside the skies darken, clouds thicken, rain pours, streets glimmer with the haloed lights of storefronts and traffic.

R. H. Sheldon

Myron says, "We can go to Parker's house. You can rest and then decide what you want to do."

She finishes her taco.

They leave the restaurant and cross Broadway. The rain eases, but leaves behind lake-sized puddles.

Soon they stand in Cal Anderson Park, amid trash and fallen protest signs and broken bottles. Seagulls swoop over the reflecting pool. Ducks huddle at its concrete edges. Pigeons scurry for crumbs.

"Fucking birds."

"The birds are not fucking, Bellamy. They are looking for food."

They head toward the fountain.

Police outnumber civilians, but no one tries to stop them. Bellamy says nothing more, but stays close to his side. They wind around the fountain and then around the hill and cross Boxer Way. He leads her along the side of the house, into the backyard, and up the back stairs. When he opens the door, Sonuvabitch sticks out his head, sniffs the air, and squeaks.

Myron says, "Sonuvabitch, this is Bellamy. Bellamy, this is Sonuvabitch."

Bellamy's eyes flutter and her head eases to one side. She leans down and scratches Sonuvabitch on the head. Sonuvabitch squeaks again.

"Such a cute kitty," she says.

Myron says, "He likes you, Bellamy."

They enter the house and move through the kitchen and into the living room. Myron directs Bellamy to the couch.

"You can lay down," he says. "If you're tired."

She glances at Myron. "You better not try anything."

"Try anything?"

Bellamy looks around the room, studies the piano, the stacks of porn, the broken ceramic lamp.

"So this is the Parker Davis house. This is what all the fuss is about."

Myron steps away from the couch. "Your mother rested here, too. Last night."

"My mother."

"She'll be fine, Bellamy."

Bellamy plops down on the couch, squeezed toward one end. "My mother is always fine."

Sonuvabitch jumps up on the couch and climbs onto Bellamy's lap.

"Sonuvabitch *really* likes you, Bellamy."

She pets the cat absently. He curls into a ball and purrs, filling the room with a tiny rumble.

"What do we do now?" Bellamy asks.

"Now?"

"What do we do?"

"There's nothing to do, Bellamy. Everything is already done."

Myron slips around the coffee table and drops down into Parker's chair. He never sat in the chair before. He can smell Parker here, the tobacco-stained whiskey smell, the old and forgotten smell, the sick and getting sicker smell.

Myron leans back and stretches out his legs. He pushes aside the pink blanket and places his hands on the armrests, touching the smooth oily surface of the worn fabric. He lets himself move into Parker, feels his stiff joints and aching muscles, feels his anger and hopelessness, feels the depth of his fear and abiding loneliness.

Myron sighs.

Bellamy has fallen asleep. So has Sonuvabitch. If not for the knock on the front door, they would still be sleeping. But Myron is expecting the knock, so he pushes himself out of the chair just like Parker would and tells Bellamy and Sonuvabitch that everything is okay and saunters into the front hallway. When he opens the door, he finds an exceptionally short Alonzo, standing on a small pile of rotten boards.

Myron misses the porch. He liked standing on it and sitting on it and walking up and down its stairs. He will also miss the way Parker used to come out in his bathrobe and scratch himself and cough and spit out into the weeds and announce what a miserable day it is.

"Hi, Alonzo," Myron says. "You should be careful standing on those boards."

Alonzo looks down at his precarious footing.

"Climb on in," Myron says and reaches down and grasps Alonzo's hand and pulls him up and into the house. Alonzo flies through the door and lands face first on the muddy hallway floor. He grunts and pushes himself to his feet.

Myron returns to the living room. "Look who's here, Bellamy. Alonzo from the park."

When Alonzo steps into the room, he stops and pulls back.

Bellamy pets Sonuvabitch and stares at the floor.

Myron says, "You sit there, Alonzo." He points to the far end of the couch, opposite Bellamy, who still pretends she's alone.

Alonzo sits down, holds his spine straight like a lamppost, avoids looking to the left where Bellamy sits. He says, "I've come to see Parker. Is he around?"

Myron says, "Parker has been at the hospital visiting Olympia. She was shot last night. Did you know that, Alonzo?"

Alonzo nods. "I heard it on the news." Then he says out of the left side of his mouth, "I'm sorry to hear about your mother."

Bellamy shrugs. Sonuvabitch repositions himself and reaches out a paw to remind Bellamy to keep petting.

"When do you expect him back?" Alonzo asks.

Myron says, "Parker will be back soon. He has finished visiting with Olympia and he has no place else to go."

Alonzo turns his head, stares for a moment into nothing, then he says, "I'm sorry to hear that."

Just then, the back door bangs and feet stomp and Parker shouts, "Goddamn rip-off cab drivers."

Parker enters the living room, scans the room, and says, "What the fuck?"

Myron says, "Hi, Parker. How was your visit with Olympia?"

Stephanie

S tephanie steps back and examines their work. "Good enough."

Rocky gives her a light punch on the shoulder. "Good enough? What do you mean? This is art."

Stephanie shrugs, not wanting to commit one way or the other. "I'll defer to your aesthetic sensibilities. At least we've managed to keep the weather out."

"Just in time, judging by those clouds."

Stephanie glances up. A giant raindrop nails her right eye.

Just then, Georgia appears from around the side of the house, looking tired, distracted.

Stephanie says, "Everything okay?"

"Took more out of me than I expected." She notices Rocky, a wedge of brightness. "Here to arrest somebody?"

"You been bad?"

"Not yet."

Stephanie turns to Rocky. "I better get cleaned up. I have errands of my own to run." She reaches out a hand. "Thank you for all your help." They shake.

Rocky looks as though she's about to say something, but instead picks up a hammer off the ground and hands it to Stephanie.

Stephanie glances at Georgia, says she'll be inside, and heads into the house without waiting for a reply.

R. H. Sheldon

Inside the room is dark, lifeless, cold from the broken window. She cranks up the heat and pushes the furniture back into place. She heads into the bedroom, strips, and climbs into the shower. The water sprays, hot and steamy, pounding her head, her neck, her chest. She lathers, scrubs, rinses, stands as long as she can, until she feels the water begin to cool. In moments, it will be ice.

She shuts off the faucets and steps out of the shower, onto a mat still soaked from Georgia, cold and rough beneath her feet. She dries herself quickly, feels the warmth of the house take hold. She grabs a pair of jeans and pulls on a sweater and heads into the main room.

Georgia sits in the big chair, near the boarded up window, thumbing through a magazine. "Hope you saved some water."

"I thought you already showered. Otherwise, I just cleaned up someone else's mess."

"Figured I'd try another. Might help revive me.

"You'll have to wait then."

Georgia looks up from the magazine. "How long were you in there?"

"Long enough, okay? If you need a shower that bad, you can ask your friend Rocky."

"Rocky? What does she have to do with anything?"

"Just forget it."

"No, let's not forget it. That's what you used to always say. Every time something bugged you, that's what you said."

"You want to drag up the past? Is that what you want?"

"I just want us to talk, that's all."

"It's a little too late for that."

"It's not too late. At least not yet."

"I only meant...I can't. I just can't." She grabs her jacket and car keys and races out of the house. Georgia yells out, but the rain garbles her words.

Stephanie reaches the Beretta and climbs in, but doesn't start the car. She has no idea where to go. Despite what she told Rocky, she has no errands to run. She feels all twisted and turned inside out, like her yard, her garden, her house, a house that suddenly feels too small, too constrained, too much in the past. She's got to go somewhere.

She starts the car, backs out of her parking spot, barely missing Georgia's bumper. She stops and gazes into the garden, at the battered plants, the broken statues, the scattered pieces of trellis.

She imagines Rocky and Georgia standing amid the ruins, the rain falling, the wind picking up. They giggle, touch, make plans to rendezvous. The engine clanks and sputters and stalls. She slams her palm against the steering column, sending a wave of pain up to her elbow.

She starts the car and pulls back into her parking spot, as far away from Georgia's truck as possible. Through the camper shell she sees boxes and plastic crates and yard waste bags stuffed with clothes. The last of her Seattle roots.

Stephanie climbs out of the car, closes the doors amid squeaking hinges and bending metal. She returns to the yard and wanders along the side next to Parker's house, a massive black hole covered in mold and rotted wood. The place should be condemned as a health hazard, along with its owner, or used-to-be owner.

Stephanie looks around her own yard, the comparison no longer as stark. In some ways, her place looks worse, with the charred fence and infusion of trash and plants trampled into compost. It will take years to get the place back to the way it was. And money. Hell, she can't even afford to replace the front window. And with all the insanity surrounding Parker and his house, Stephanie will likely be stuck here the rest of her life.

The sound of a slamming car door echoes into the yard, a taxi, letting off a passenger. Across the street, a small group of protesters stand, waving to the cab. That must be the vigil mentioned on the radio.

Stephanie quickly recognizes the sturdy body and shock of salt-and-pepper hair. The Reverend Olympia Culpepper, the dunce who started this craziness, who fueled Parker's neuroses and self-destructive imagination.

At this point, though, blame hardly seems worth the effort. Everything has gotten so crazy she feels as though she's been dropped in the middle of the ocean, hanging on to a deflating raft amid a dozen circling sharks. Seems pointless now to blame the ship that dropped her here.

Olympia carries a backpack in her left hand, her right arm in a sling. She waves slowly to the protesters and moves cautiously through the debris and toward the side of Parker's house. Stephanie is tempted to run, but it's too late. She opts instead to remain still, hoping Olympia won't notice her.

Olympia is quick to spot her. She hesitates and proceeds slowly.

R. H. Sheldon

Stephanie nods. Olympia nods. An unspoken truce, perhaps, a recognition that there's no turning back, just like Stephanie's yard and her house and her career and her relationship with Georgia.

When Olympia passes, she gives a weak smile. Stephanie nods again, praying the minister will keep moving. And it appears she will. But Stephanie's fate again intercedes and Olympia stops and turns slightly.

"I want to thank you for your help last night," Olympia says. "Your professionalism and skills were a godsend that made the whole ordeal much easier to bear."

Stephanie hates this. She doesn't want to be thanked and especially doesn't want to have to act gracious. The truth is, she was more than happy to help. It didn't matter who it was. For the first time since retiring, she felt alive and more fully herself.

She says, "It was nothing."

"Perhaps, but thank you anyway." With that, Olympia continues to Parker's backyard and disappears behind his house, her obligation fulfilled, her need for pleasantries behind her.

Stephanie turns toward the front. A spiral of barbed wire snakes through the debris, attached to chunks of charred wood. She grabs a loose end and pulls the wire toward the center of the yard, mindful of the razor sharp barbs that twist around her ankles. She piles what she can near the space where the trellis used to stand, next to the pieces of broken statue. Later, she'll detach the rest from the part of the fence still upright.

She uses her foot to push the wire into a small pile. A single coil wraps around her ankle. She tries to kick it off, but it snags on her laces. She reaches down and tugs at the wire, feeling a slight tear in the lace. She pulls harder. The coil springs up and buries a barb into her palm. She grabs her hand and curses the wire. Warm blood seeps across her skin.

Olympia

Olympia knocks on the back door with her left hand. It feels odd, trying to do everything with only that hand, but any wrong move sends a knifing pain through her right shoulder. The surgeon said she could expect that for a few days, but then the flesh would start knitting together and the pain start to ease, as long as she doesn't do anything stupid.

Olympia knocks again. A wave of nausea surges through her guts and she feels suddenly woozy. She should have gone home and gone to bed, let the painkillers do their job. Food, too, would have been good. At the hospital, she did little more than nibble at the slop they called breakfast. How anyone can heal in such an environment is the greatest mystery of all.

She grabs the doorframe to steady herself, let the sour feeling pass. She needs to make the meeting a quick one, then head home to bed. She hates to waste time lying around, not with all that's going on, but even *she* has to admit she needs a rest, something impossible to get at the hospital.

She's about to knock yet again when the door creeps open and Myron sticks out his big furry head.

"Olympia," he says. "You're here sooner than I expected."

She assumes Parker told him she would be arriving.

"I'm here to see Parker," she says.

Myron glances upward and gives a sly smile, then opens the door the rest of the way. His look makes her feel as though she's about to preach to the crowds stark naked.

Myron says, "How is your shoulder, Olympia?" He closes the door slowly. The rusty creeks echo through the kitchen. Then that foul cat appears, a gnarly shadow slithering along the floor. It meows, rubs up against Myron. "In a minute," he says.

The kitchen smells of rotten food and backed-up sewers.

Olympia hurries into the living room. Stops. Gasps. Not only is Parker stretched out in that rancid overstuffed chair, but Bellamy sits open-mouthed at one end of the couch and at the other end is that reprehensible attorney from Bellevue.

Bellamy springs to her feet. "Mom! You won't believe what happened. I almost got arrested again."

Olympia pulls out the piano bench and sits down, feeling a lifetime of weariness. "I'm fine. Thank you for asking."

Bellamy stares as though she has never met Olympia.

"That's exactly what you said to Parker," Myron says. "At the hospital."

His sudden appearance makes her skin crawl.

Parker says, "Bring any smokes?" He searches the floor surrounding his chair, brushes aside broken bits of ceramic near the window. A man without hope.

Myron plops down on a small cushion on the floor next to the couch. The cat climbs onto his lap, lets out a huff.

Bellamy says, "Myron rescued me. Saved me from those awful police."

Alonzo stands and says, "I best be going." He turns toward Parker. "Mr. Davis, it appears we're in agreement. I'll be in touch about the paperwork."

Pain pinches Olympia's shoulder. She grabs it with her free hand and forces herself up off the bench. "Agreement about what?"

Alonzo offers a handshake to Parker. Parker does not seem to understand the gesture, his eyes focused mostly on the floor. Alonzo waits. Parker cocks his heads. He squints and returns a flaccid shake.

Myron places the cat off to the side and stands, then sails around the coffee table. Alonzo cowers. Myron offers his hand. "Goodbye, Alonzo." Alonzo looks as confused as Parker, but finally returns the shake. Myron simmers with glee.

Bellamy flits her head around like a chicken, pointing in every direction except toward Alonzo. When he exits the room, she's staring in the opposite direction. Myron picks up the cat and strokes his head.

Olympia lets go her shoulder. A throbbing ache radiates down her arm and up her neck. She needs a shower, but with this shoulder, that's not going to happen. At least she can look forward to a good night's sleep. She drops back onto the piano bench.

"What's this about?" she asks. "I thought we had decided to consult each other going forward. I thought *we* were in agreement."

Now Parker is the one to look at her as though she's the stranger. And maybe she is. Maybe she's dropped into another dimension, is lying in a coma, or already dead, sitting here like a shadow.

Myron twists his head around and stares into Olympia's eyes. She shivers and looks away.

Parker sighs, eases back into his chair. A small cloud of dust puffs out and shines in the light of the window.

"It's like this," he says, "Lockhart is willing to pay for my move, help me resettle someplace nice. And give me plenty of time to make it happen."

A sour taste rises to her throat.

"We discussed this. We knew they'd want to negotiate. But if we stand firm, we can accomplish much more."

"Like what?"

"Like maybe raising funds for others, like maybe getting better laws, like maybe increasing awareness."

Parker smacks his cracked lips. "That's all fine and good, but I'm the one who might soon be homeless."

Exactly the type of behavior she would expect from him, thinking only of himself. As long as he's okay, no other problems exist. The rest of the world could be drowning and he wouldn't move.

She draws in a deep breath. Her chest expands, tugs on the sling and sends a sharp pain through her shoulder. She grimaces, waits, then says, "We both know they're not going to evict you now, not with all the press. You've got the whole country behind you."

"That's what they said about Gandhi."

"I hardly think—"

Bellamy looks up from her phone. "I read about him in school. Wasn't he like a preacher or something?"

Myron turns his head, listens. A serious look crosses his face, the sun disappearing behind a cloud. He pulls the cat in closer. "Sonuvabitch and I are going for a walk. You should come with us, Bellamy."

Bellamy returns her attention to the phone.

Myron's voice grows quieter, at the same time fiercer. "I think you should come for a walk, Bellamy."

She glances at him and a sudden look of worry crosses her face. "Sure." She pushes herself up and knocks into the coffee table and nearly falls back down. She steadies herself, digs through her pack, and pulls out the phone charger. She plugs it into an outlet near the piano. She connects the phone. She says to Parker, "I'll let this charge till I get back, so it's ready to go." Parker shrugs.

Olympia says, "Go where?"

Now Bellamy shrugs, turns to her mother. "You going to be okay?"

This might be the first time Bellamy has ever asked about her welfare. "I'll be fine," Olympia says. "My car is right outside."

"You sure you should be driving?"

"I'll be fine."

Myron slips out of the room. Bellamy follows. She hears them move through the kitchen, the back door squeak. They clomp down the stairs.

Olympia holds her shoulder and breathes. She watches Parker out of the corner of her eyes. He stares at the floor. She waits. He leans over and pushes around more ceramic. She waits some more. He looks up at the ceiling. She says, "Now what's this about?"

He lets out a slow hissing sigh.

A loud crash resounds through the house. Voices shout. Glass shatters. Wood splinters and cracks. The front door busts open and drops off its hinges. More crashing in the kitchen. Several large men in black paramilitary uniforms leap into the front hallway, armed for a coup. More appear at the kitchen door. Guns drawn. Stances taken. Faces ready for carnage.

One shouts, "Homeland Security. Nobody move!"

Olympia falls back into the piano and bangs the keys. A loud, sour, discordant chord blasts across the room. She bounces off the piano, slides to the floor, and rolls onto her injured shoulder. She screams. An agent fires into the ceiling. Plaster explodes across the room.

Parker tries to move, but a gun pins him to the chair.

Olympia rolls onto her left side, her shoulder on fire. The same agent yells, "I told you not to move."

The room grows eerily still. She can hear his breathing, the tinny sound of muffled voices from his headset.

"Where are they," he says.

Olympia says nothing. She has no idea what he's talking about. She only wants the pain to stop.

Parker says, "They who?"

"Don't get smart with me."

Two of the agents run up the stairs. They stomp from one end of the house to the other. They bang. They crash. They slam. They race down the stairs and head into the basement, the noise muffled, but more of the same. They return with looks angrier still, edged in disappointment. "Nothing," one says.

Voices from outside carry into the house. They yell about cops and brutality and justice. They grow louder, more intense. Heads appear in the front door, in the broken window. More voices in back. They keep arriving. They hold up phones and snap pictures and shoot videos. The agents try to stop them, but there are too few of them and too many of the protesters. And they have seen enough and will share it with the world. Thank God for technology. Thank God for the Internet. Thank God for the world of mass communication.

Bellamy

Bellamy knows Myron's like totally weird, but there's something sort of cool about him too, like he doesn't judge and is safe and sort of a big brother, only really old. Maybe more a father, like they talk about in that book, the way people who get bitten start caring about the vampire.

But she can't really say what it's like having a father, since she's never met hers, and her mom refuses to say anything on the subject, which is really fucked up because she's always talking about the good old days, the traveling, the volunteer work, the protests, the communities.

Myron reaches over the fence and sets Sonuvabitch in the yard next door and whispers to him. The cat scurries off and Myron heads toward the alley. Bellamy follows.

He keeps glancing back over his shoulder, telling her not to speak, almost creeping out of the yard. And the air too feels different, still, quiet, almost tense, a heavy muffled feeling. Their steps scrape the gravel like injured coyotes.

They pass out of the alley and head toward John. Neither speaks. She hears a snap behind them, but is afraid to look. A chill passes up her spine and spreads into her shoulders and she huddles even closer to Myron.

They cross John and continue on to Harrison, then turn right and head straight up the hill, past a hodgepodge of apartment buildings that span the last hundred years. Bellamy struggles to keep up, until they reach Fourteenth, where the hill plateaus. From there, they stroll easily to Fifteenth.

Myron says, "You need more food," and heads up the stairs of a battered two-story building, battleship paint, stained and peeling. A curdled off-white trim covers the corners and frames the windows.

Bellamy creeps up the steps and follows him into a Vietnamese restaurant with tattered dark carpet and yellow-green walls dulled by the low light. A mix of red and gold décor fills the shelves and counters. Pseudo-Asian cutouts and prints pepper the walls.

Myron drops into a seat by the window, overlooking Fifteenth. Bellamy sits across from him and leans her elbows on the table. The jacket sticks to the surface.

"Good pho," he says.

Bellamy doesn't know what he's talking about.

"Noodle soup," he adds.

"Okay," she replies.

In the opposite corner, a rotund, middle-aged Asian man sits at a small counter before a blasting TV, watching the weather and eating a bowl of noodles. The weatherman smiles and jokes and dances around in an endless perkiness that makes Bellamy want to puke, despite a forecast of more clouds, more rain, more everything the same.

The man at the counter drops his chopsticks and pushes himself upright and carries two menus over to their table. Myron says they don't need them and orders two bowls of chicken pho. The waiter returns to the other side of the room, drops the menus onto the counter, and yells into the kitchen in what must be Vietnamese. Myron smiles and leans back in his chair.

Within a couple minutes, the waiter returns with two large bowls brimming with soup, along with a plate full of bean sprouts and basil leaves and wedges of lime and several slices of jalapeño peppers.

Myron drops a couple pepper slices into the soup and squeezes in the lime. Then he shreds a handful of basil leaves, drops them in, and sprinkles in a fistful of sprouts. Next he grabs a bottle of something called hoisin sauce and squeezes it on top of everything else. He picks up his chopsticks and pokes the food until everything is mixed in. Soon he's shoveling gobs of dripping noodles into his mouth.

R. H. Sheldon

Bellamy picks up one of the weird plastic spoons and sips the broth. She stops, drops in a basil leaf and a few sprouts, sips again.

Myron reaches the slurping stage and devours what remains. Bellamy is still unsure of the flavor.

The waiter, having returned to his seat and his noodles, turns up the TV. The words *Breaking News!* flash across the screen. A frumpy old white guy says, "We go now to Anita Franklin, live at the scene."

The camera switches to some goofy-looking black chick, acting all serious and important, like she's a famous model, only her clothes look like something out of Sears.

"Pete, I'm standing in front of Parker Davis's home, where Homeland Security agents have just stormed the house and arrested Mr. Parker Davis and Reverend Olympia Culpepper. The reverend, as you recall, had just been released from Elliott Bay Medical Center, where she had been treated for a gunshot wound she received last night on this very spot.

Bellamy drops her spoon into the bowl. Pho flies. "Mom!" She leaps to her feet.

The waiter glances over, quickly returns to his soup.

Myron wipes his beard with a shredded paper napkin and eases up from the table.

A swelling of off-camera shouting surges through the TV. The reporter holds a finger against her earpiece. The noise from the crowd grows.

"Pete, we know very little at this point." Her voice grows louder. "But we do have a witness who saw the raid." She signals to someone off-camera. A man in a blue flannel shirt and blue stocking cap appears.

"Pete, we have Garfield Singley from Occupy Seattle here on the scene. Garfield, can you tell us what you saw." She holds out the mike.

"Yeah, man. It was like all these cops dressed in black start swarming Parker's house and shout out orders and break down the doors and leap inside."

Anita pulls the mike back. "Leap?"

"No porch, man. That happened a couple days ago, when the cops herded everybody up there. Like it collapsed and about killed a bunch of people, some really old ones too."

She pulls the mike back again. "And then what happened, today...What happened after the agents leapt inside?" She returns the mike.

Garfield delivers. "Well, like a bunch of Occupy dudes and those churchgoers—we're here holding our vigil—crossed the street and looked through the front door and window. And these cops had their guns out and were holding Parker and the reverend prisoners. Jesus, like here's this old sick guy and this holy woman who got shot last night by another cop, looking into the face of an assault rifle. It was fuckin' nuts!"

Anita jerks back the mike. "Yes, thank you. And did the agents say what they wanted?" She reaches the mike out tentatively.

"The cops asked where *they* were."

"They?"

Garfield shrugs. "Never said. Based on all the tweets, it has something to do with that Casey dude and Bellamy chick, you know, the rev's daughter."

Anita retrieves the mike and the camera closes in, dismissing the witness. "That's all we know right now. Meanwhile, the crowds are growing and the squad cars are arriving one after the other. We'll be updating you throughout the afternoon. Pete, back to you."

Bellamy drops into her seat. She grabs a sprout and twists it into mush.

Pete the newscaster says, "So far, all we know is that Casey McDonald, if that's his real name, is allegedly part of Occupy Seattle and has been camped out at Seattle Central. The other suspect, Bellamy Burns-Culpepper has also been seen on numerous occasions at the camp, usually in the company of Mr. McDonald.

Bellamy grabs another bean sprout and squeezes. The TV camera zooms in on a picture of Casey. "This is a photo taken of Mr. McDonald at yesterday's rally near the Davis home." The camera pans to a second picture, this one of Bellamy, standing outside the hospital. Myron hovers nearby, his face obscured by shadow, looking mostly like a bystander. But her face is crystal clear, the tears, the smeared make-up, the puffy and half-closed eyes, looking like a goddamn clown.

The newscaster says, "This photo was taken of Ms. Burns-Culpepper earlier today by a security camera at the Elliott Bay Medical Center, after she allegedly threw a rock through the front window. Security guards claim she broke it to distract them while

Mr. McDonald was trying to plant a bomb. The police confirm that they've discovered suspicious materials on scene, but have provided no further details."

Pete scrunches his brow and puts on a sincere, apologetic look. "One of the guards is quoted as saying, 'They're terrorists, both of them, and should be treated as terrorists.' We have no confirmation yet from the Office of Homeland Security whether the two are suspected of terrorist activity, but a spokesperson warns that the fugitives could be dangerous and that no one should approach them but should instead call their offices." A phone number flashes on screen.

Myron reaches out a hand and helps Bellamy to her feet. He again pulls a wad of bills out of his pocket, drops two twenties on the table, and shoves the rest back in. "I think we better go," he says.

Bellamy follows him toward the door. The waiter eyes her suspiciously. She rushes outside, with Myron close behind.

They hurry down the stairs and walk quickly down Harrison toward Fourteenth, where they turn and head north to Volunteer Park, following the same path she took yesterday, only now her life more muddled and frightening than ever. When they near the corner of Republican, Myron steps out into the street and up to the window of a black sedan parked along the curb and knocks on the door.

She is ready to run, convinced Myron is about to turn her over to the cops, but then he says, "Hello, Alonzo. Bellamy and I are out for a walk." Bellamy moves in closer.

Alonzo cracks his window, grunts a greeting, but mostly stares at the apartment building across the street.

Myron says, "Who are you waiting for, Alonzo?"

Alonzo shakes his head. Bellamy struts past the car, making sure Alonzo notices how much she doesn't notice him.

Myron calls out, "Good-bye, Alonzo. We're going to finish our walk."

They continue up Fourteenth. Bellamy does not look back. When they reach Mercer, the wind gusts out of the north, sending an icy chill through her jacket. She moves closer to Myron.

He says, "Let's go back to the tower."

"Why there?"

He walks faster.

They scurry past the primped and pampered lawns of million-dollar homes with their shiny cars and tall, sturdy fences. They reach Aloha and cross. A giant black SUV with dark tinted windows races around the curve and nearly nails them. Myron flashes a peace sign. The driver glares at Bellamy. She races for the sidewalk.

They pass more primped and pampered yards and shiny new cars and tall sturdy fences and million-dollar homes.

Myron says, "It's not that big a deal, having money."

Bellamy glances at him, his mind impenetrable, hers a shattered window.

They reach the park and climb the concrete steps up to the base of the tower. The clouds thicken quickly. The air grows darker. A fine mist falls and dampens her cheeks.

They enter and turn toward the staircase. It looms before them, spiraling up into the blackness.

"Careful of the echoes," Myron says and steps softly onto the first stair.

Bellamy grips the icy railing and pulls herself up. She tries to walk as quietly as Myron, but can't muffle her wooden heels. Soon the clamoring echoes bounce against the water tank and fill the tower with a mournful, pulsating hum that haunts the air.

"Myron!"

He stops. She stops. Her steps continue. She doesn't know why she yelled his name, perhaps to reassure herself he was real. That she should seek solace in him distresses her all the more.

They continue. The echoes grow into confused sputters. Bellamy no longer tries to soften her steps, instead finding reassurance in the physical sensation of wood against metal.

When they reach the top, Myron says, "Yes." He stands in the middle of the round room. Bellamy stands next to him, waiting for the echoes to die down. She has no idea what he waits for.

The sounds ease into a gentle brushing and then nothing. She shuffles over to the bench, stirring up more echoes. Myron steps toward the window that looks in the direction of Parker's house. The breeze pushes through the bars and rustles his hair, his face a pale glow, almost demonic.

And that's when she sees him, lying on the next bench, as pale as the light brushing through the windows.

"Casey!"

The echoes sing out.

He opens his eyes, looks groggily in her direction. Myron glances toward him, says nothing.

She stands, creeps toward him, and whispers, "Have you heard the news? You know what they're saying?"

He grins uneasily. "Kind of freaky, huh?"

"What are we going to do, Casey? What?" Her whispers grow louder, more frantic. "Maybe there's someone we can call, someone who can help us? You got your phone? I left mine behind. Maybe we can tweet a message for help. Post something to Facebook." She reaches toward his pack.

He grabs her hand, squeezes hard. "Stop. They can track us with that thing. Leave it alone. I turned it off as soon as I heard what was happening. They almost got me in Belltown. That's when I flew up here. I remembered what you said about this place, about it being a good hideout."

Bellamy rubs her wrist. "You hurt me."

"This isn't a game."

"I hope you haven't harmed my baby."

Myron steps out from the shadows. "Hello, Casey. I'm Myron."

Casey jumps. "Where did you come from?"

"I'm with Bellamy, Casey. We came to find you."

"But no one knew..."

"I'm glad you're here, Casey."

Casey regains his cool, lets his shoulders slouch, his eyes wander. He leans back against the fence. "Wa's up, bro?"

"What's up?" Myron considers the question. "You and Bellamy are in trouble. You need to be careful."

"Yeah, bro. The hood ain't safe. Nowhere to roll up but here." He talks with both hands fluttering in practiced hip-hop gestures, like something gooey is smeared all over his fingers.

Bellamy stops rubbing her wrist and studies Casey, trying to make sense of his speech. "Get serious, Casey. We need to figure out what to do."

He flashes an annoyed look and drops to the bench and sighs. Finally, he says, "So how did you know I was here? I mean, I can't even figure out how this all started, why they went after me in the first place."

Bellamy hesitates, stutters, then points to Myron. "It's his fault. It's all his fault. He did this to us."

Alonzo

Alonzo closes his window against the cold and gazes across the street at the small courtyard that marks the entrance of Lita's building, her apartment still dark and quiet.

The building reminds him of a giant crack house, covered in dingy white stucco, with large chunks missing. Rotted boards edge the windows, filthy brown, long swaths of paint peeled off.

At one point, he calls his mother-in-law, but Isabel still isn't there and isn't expected. "Helping Lita," she announces. "Gone all week." So he sits here waiting, certain they'll show at any moment. But all he really knows is that Isabel's not at her mother's.

Alonzo has no idea how Isabel had convinced her mother to take the girls all week. She isn't really the grandmother type, at least not anymore. Even Isabel concedes this point. After her husband died a few years back, Isabel's mother became a new woman, playing bingo, joining tour groups, spending night after night with her girlfriends. Before he died, she always seemed so complacent and subdued, but she has since reinvented herself, and being a granny has little place in her social life.

Alonzo calls Isabel once more. Still no answer. He places the phone on the passenger seat and turns up the music, Mussorgsky, *Pictures at an Exhibition,* with its brassy entrance and bold onset of strings and the ongoing interplay between them, defining and uniting each complex movement.

He reclines the seat and closes his eyes, feeling the sometimes whimsical, sometimes threatening, often humbling mix of rhythms and harmonies and sounds, always pushing, always reaching, lifting him up, letting him down, a soulful essence that defies logic or understanding, setting him adrift and reeling him back home.

If only he had someone in his life who shared his passion.

A knock on the window jars him out of his reverie. He opens his eyes and finds Isabel standing next to the car, her face a patchwork of fury.

He opens the window.

"Don't think I didn't see her!"

Lita stands in front of her building, Lucas at her side.

Alonzo opens the car door. Isabel snarls. Lita leads her son into the courtyard and they disappear into the shadows. Alonzo climbs out of the car.

"I can't believe you would meet that skank here."

"Skank?"

Isabel flicks her head to her left, up Fourteenth.

"What are you talking about?"

Her eyes narrow, nostrils flare. "Don't play games. I saw her leaving."

Alonzo is about to protest, then remembers. Bellamy. Of course.

"You've been standing out here that long?"

"What difference does it make?"

"No difference. Because I didn't bring her here. I was waiting for you and they walked by."

"How convenient."

"It's not what you think."

"What is it, then?"

"What is it? It's nothing. She's Reverend Culpepper's daughter, that crazy woman who started all this mess."

Isabel gazes up the street. "Bellamy? That's the minister's daughter?"

"A bunch of fruitcakes."

"I hadn't put it together—her and Casey. It all makes sense." She looks almost amused.

"Casey?"

"So now you're hanging around with felons."

The wind gusts through the trees and sprays them with icy pellets. His flesh erupts into goose bumps.

"Isabel, I don't know what—"

She frowns and reluctantly provides an explanation about the raid on Parker's house and how Parker and the minister were arrested and the hunt for Casey and Bellamy in connection with an attempted hospital bombing.

"But I was just there, meeting with Parker. Nobody was plotting anything or talking about bombs. Parker and I discussed a settlement. We came up with a tentative agreement. That's what I came to tell you. That and what happened at the office."

None of this makes sense. It must be a mistake. It has to be. But what if it's true? Anything's possible with those whackos. And if it is, it might turn out the perfect opportunity. With Parker in jail and out of the way, they won't have to pay him a cent to move out.

"Alonzo?"

"They really arrested him? And the minister?"

She nods.

"Maybe that's not such a bad thing."

The anger returns. "You never see things for what they are."

He starts to protest, but has no idea where to begin—or even what to say.

"You mean us?"

"I mean something."

"But what? I need more."

"I don't have it to give."

"That's it?"

She turns away, hesitates, then crosses the street and heads toward the courtyard.

"I don't know either." He climbs into the car, starts it, and pulls away. He turns right on Republican and continues onto Fifteenth. He switches on the music, landing at the final movement of *Pictures at an Exhibition,* "The Great Gate of Kiev," where the entire suite comes together and mixes and amplifies the previous fourteen movements into a stunning crescendo of trumpets and violins and timpani and cymbals that send chills up his spine and bring tears to his eyes and fill his heart with an ache that nothing in this world can ease.

R. H. Sheldon

Stephanie

Stephanie clutches a charred piece of fencepost and stares across the street at the growing crowd. She feels like a perverted Statue of Liberty, her torch all but extinguished. It's hard to say how many are protesters and how many are looking for a party, plenty of both, she'd say. No doubt some even looking for a fight, especially that dark-hooded gang hanging off to the side. They say little, though. The rest shout, scream, curse. They wave signs. They shake fists. A mob in the making, if ever there were one.

A string of cops stands along Boxer Way, blocking the street in order to ensure it remains clear. More police arrive, a dozen of their cars within earshot.

Most of the Homeland Security agents left with Parker and Olympia, two separate vehicles, massive black SUVs, dark tinted windows, like tanks. A third one remains parked on the weeds in front of Parker's. Two agents linger nearby, watching Parker's house. They glance her way on occasion, sometimes long glaring stares, their faces stern, frozen, each in black flack pants, black bulletproof vests, black boots. One looks Native American. The other, a Dick Tracy look-alike. All he needs is his two-way wrist radio.

Stephanie turns away and drops the charred post into the pile at the center of her destroyed garden. She weaves through the debris with slow, cautious movements, feeling the heat of their eyes, the sense of paranoia that follows.

She hates this, the way they make her feel, their suspicions, judgments, presumptions of guilt. And to take Parker and Olympia away like that, with her injured shoulder, with his failing health, like criminals, like terrorists. A total outrage. She might not like either of them, but what just happened was beyond all human decency.

The crowd grows louder, demanding justice, accountability, freedom. Stephanie's right there with them, wants to scream out herself. But crowds frighten her, that mob mentality, on the verge of violence, as much as armed agents standing at her gates—well, what's left of her gates.

More protesters pour into the park, their ranks swelling across the sidewalks, out to the curb, bulging into the streets, men, women, young, old, a surprising cross-section of Seattle, not just the Occupy types or the New Age liberal types, but the full complement of races and classes and beliefs, as though the switch they've all been waiting for has finally been flicked on, the line at long last crossed, like the types of crowds she saw on TV as a girl, the civil rights marches and the anti-war marches, the marches she thought she would one day join. But the era ended as quickly as it began, eroding in a collective shift from human rights to human greed.

Stephanie picks up more pieces of fence, tossing them into the burn pile, separate from the pile for chunks of statue and the pile for fallen trees. She digs into a mound of debris near the house and pulls out the uprooted laceleaf maple, its bark shredded, the branches trampled into a pulp. She planted the tree several years earlier—an anniversary gift from her to Georgia. She realized almost immediately that such a gift was wasted on Georgia. She could never understand what the garden meant to Stephanie, what it felt like to plant and nurture, to feel a part of the process of growth and regeneration, even on this tiny plot of land. Georgia didn't mind the pleasure the garden afforded, but she never felt the urge to participate in the process.

The sound of a clearing throat pulls Stephanie out of her head. She turns. The Bellevue attorney, Alonzo Garcia, stands before her, looking somewhat less shimmering than she remembers.

She says, "I thought I would never see you again."

He waves his hand to indicate the crowd. "Now what's going on?"

"I wish I could tell you."

"Is it true they arrested Parker?"

Stephanie nods. "And the minister."

"The crazy one?"

"That's her."

"But why Parker? I had just spoken with him. We had come to an agreement."

She drops the ravaged tree into the burn pile. One more sacrifice.

"It gets crazier by the minute," she says.

He reflects on the crowd. "The whole world has lost its mind."

"You just figure that out?"

Alonzo turns slowly back to Stephanie. "You know where they took him?"

"You're the lawyer. Where do feds usually take their prey?"

He kicks a piece of plaster into the woodpile. "King County jail?"

"You asking me?"

"So crazy," he says, and kicks another piece of plaster. He speaks again, only this time to himself. "Around here they often take detainees to the King County jail, unless they went to the federal detention center, SeaTac."

A low rumble filters into her awareness, something felt rather than heard, but soon there's no mistaking the belching racket of loud diesel engines, and a glance toward Eleventh quickly confirms her suspicions, that matters had just gone from bad to worse. Six trucks come up Eleventh, headed toward her house. They crawl along the edge of the park, a parade of military vehicles filled with military soldiers covered in camouflage canvas. The National Guard has arrived.

When the first truck reaches Boxer Way, the parade stops and a dozen soldiers jump out of each one. They line up along Eleventh, creating an impenetrable wall. Trucks and soldiers also move up Tenth, nudging the crowds back into the park.

Another truck comes down Eleventh from John, stops at the intersection by Stephanie's house, and belches out a sooty black cloud. More soldiers hang off the side, dressed in battle gear—helmets, face masks, ferocious looking clubs—their faces deadened leather. Protesters stand at the corner of the park, jeer at the truck, the soldiers. A rock arches out of the crowd, like an ember snapping out of a fire, and clips the bumper. The soldiers jump off the truck and race into formation, booted, vested, clubs drawn. More protesters gather at the corner and push into the street. They wave fists, raise fingers. Stephanie feels the fear, the anger, a gathering of tides.

"I'm getting out of here," Alonzo says. "I'd advise you to do the same."

"And leave my place unguarded? You can see where that leads."

"The alternative could be a lot worse."

"Is that your professional opinion?"

He shakes his head, shrinks into a vague weariness. "It's only a house, Ms. Schmidt."

Yeah, a house, that's all it's ever been.

Parker

Parker sits on one side of the table, two men on the other side. A small room, cramped, like the inside of a lung.

The agents wear dark suits, one charcoal gray, the other black. The light-suited man is forty tops, skin as dark as the suit of the other man. The skin of the other agent is polished bronze and glistens like dew, also pushing forty.

They ask questions, voices low, calm, controlled, almost gentle, in a confessional sort of way, their tones nearly identical. If Parker were to close his eyes, he would not be able to tell them apart. Even their aftershave is the same—cheap and thick and stained with adolescence.

"Why did you go to the hospital?"

"To visit the reverend."

"Why did you visit her?"

"A cop shot her in front of my house. It seemed the courteous thing to do."

"Are you normally so courteous?"

"People don't usually get shot in front of my house."

"Have you known Reverend Culpepper long?"

"Only a few days."

"How did you meet?"

"I chased her and her daughter down the street naked."

Neither react. Neither seems to care. Perhaps if Parker were to expire in the fit of coughs, they would notice.

"Is her daughter Bellamy Burns-Culpepper?"

"The *Bellamy* part sounds right. Not sure about the rest. That really her name?"

"Why were they at the house?"

"We never got that far. That's when your goons busted in."

Not a blink.

"Why did Bellamy leave when she did?"

"She said she was going for a walk."

"Alone?"

"No, they—" Parker stares into the giant mirror on the wall behind the two agents, no doubt one of those see-through types with more of these guys listening in on the other side. It has a cheap Hollywood feel about it, the same mirror in a thousand spy movies. Just like his reflection, worn, tired, ready to be put to bed.

He feels a hell of a lot worse than he looks.

"Who is they, Mr. Davis?"

"Did I say they?"

"Yes, sir, you did."

"I meant she."

"You said they."

"Perhaps she said something about meeting a friend. I'm not sure. I felt pretty crappy by the time I got back from the hospital and wasn't paying much attention."

"Anyone else there?"

"The attorney."

"Would that be a Mr. Alonzo Garcia?"

Parker shrugs. Even that hurts. "Sounds familiar."

"And why was he there?"

"He was there to discuss the house."

"Your house?"

Parker nods toward the mirror. The deathly image nods back.

A knock at the door. A third suit pokes in another tanned face, asks Mr. Charcoal Suit to step out. He does. Mr. Black Suit watches Parker with a studied patience. Parker grows suddenly aware of how his underwear has bunched up around his crotch and pulls up his crack. Is adjusting himself a federal offense?

Mr. Charcoal Suit returns and announces that Parker's attorney is here to see him.

"My attorney?"

"Mr. Garcia."

Alonzo steps in. The door closes behind him. Magic in the King County jail.

Mr. Black Suit stands. "We'll let you two talk."

Parker gestures toward the wall. "These mirrors have ears."

"It's the best we can do," Mr. Charcoal Suit says.

They leave.

Alonzo sits down. He looks tired, uncertain.

Parker says, "When did you become my attorney?"

"Your attorney?"

"That's how they announced you. My attorney."

"No wonder they let me in so easily."

"Then why are you here?"

Alonzo looks down at his hands, sitting on the table in loose fists, the flesh smooth, free from wrinkles and spots and the swollen signs of arthritis.

"I heard what happened and hoped to learn what was going on. I didn't expect to be meeting with you."

"They just let you in?"

"Something like that."

"And now what?"

"I thought we had a deal."

"You're here because of our deal?" Parker wants to laugh. One look in the mirror stops him. "Man, your boss must really have you by the nuts."

Alonzo shakes his head slowly. Stops. Looks up. Nods.

This time, Parker does laugh. "That's how it is in life. Always someone ready to squeeze the life out of you."

"Yeah," Alonzo says, "no escape."

"The American way."

Alonzo sighs, causing his shoulders to droop. "Why are you in here, Mr. Davis?"

"They haven't told me."

"They just showed up and hauled you to jail?"

"They raided my house first."

"Did they find anything?"

"An old cock ring."

Alonzo tightens his fists. "But no formal changes? No reason for the arrest?"

"All they said is they're holding me for a bit."

"And what about that minister woman?"

"No idea," Parker says. "I imagine she's here somewhere." An army goose-steps through his guts and he feels suddenly lightheaded.

Alonzo leans in. "You okay?"

Parker closes his eyes, draws in a deep breath. His lungs erupt into a fit of coughing. He pulls a wad of toilet paper out of his pocket. Hacks and spits.

Alonzo stares at his hands.

Slowly the coughing subsides.

Alonzo mumbles, "I'll see what I can find out."

Parker gulps air, squeezes out his words. "You representing me?"

"I can't," Alonzo says. "Conflict of interest."

"Yours or mine?"

"Those are the rules." A look of relief spreads across his face. "But I'll try to find out why you're in here, how long they plan to keep you."

The door creaks open and Mr. Charcoal Suit steps in, a monk sneaking into a temple.

"Mr. Davis," he says, his voice as soft and gentle as a fishing pond, "you're free to go."

The knot in Parker's chest loosens. He coughs, pushes himself out of the chair, his knees and hips stapled with pain. He stares at the gaunt gray figure in the mirror.

He's been free to go for some time now.

Myron

Myron slinks into Stephanie's yard, hugs walls, shadows. Engines rumble and moan. Crowds jeer. The air on fire.

He sneaks along the cedar siding, the hefty scent of cut timber, even after years of hanging. He squeezes behind the rhododendron near the front door. Branches snag his beard and hair and pieces of flesh.

He knocks. The font door creeps open, only a slit. Stephanie. Sad. Uncertain. He slips out from behind the bush.

"Hi, Stephanie. Can I wait for Sonuvabitch here?"

She opens the door wider. He steps in, off to the side, out of view.

"I haven't seen Sonuvabitch."

"It's not safe out there."

She nods. The crowd roars. Voices blast out of bullhorns. Sirens scream. Protesters shout and call for help.

"Sonuvabitch will be by soon."

"A cup of tea?"

"Yes, Stephanie. That would be nice." He moves toward the counter. Georgia sits at the corner, her back toward the desk. Sad too. Scared.

"Hello, Georgia. How are you feeling?"

She shrugs, gives a weak smile, her mouth too tight, lines like cement, odor not quite right, Sonuvabitch's food dish.

Stephanie says, "You sure Sonuvabitch will show up?"

"He said he would."

Georgia's smile grows real. "Jesus, Myron, if it were anyone else, I'd say you're from another planet."

Stephanie glances at her, a hungry, confused look.

"I am, Georgia." His mouth muscles stretch wide and full, the joy of speaking truth.

More shouting outside, then a collective chant. "Occupy Parker's. Occupy Parker's. Occupy. Occupy. Occupy."

Myron says, "Occupy. Occupy."

Stephanie cracks open the front door, stares across the street. Engines moan, the smell of diesel seeping in. She slams the door.

"Wait," Myron says.

"For what?"

"Sonuvabitch."

He steps around her and cracks open the door. Sonuvabitch squeezes in, squeaks out a greeting.

Myron says, "Hello, Sonuvabitch."

The cat squeaks again, then rubs up against Stephanie's leg. She bends over, pats his head, the tension in her face easing. "Poor, kitty," she says and heads to the kitchen counter. Sonuvabitch prances after her. She pulls a small bowl out of the cupboard, fills it from the spigot, and sets it on the floor near Georgia's feet. Sonuvabitch laps up the water.

Stephanie always treats Sonuvabitch with kindness and consideration, as though this is his home too. When she gardens, Sonuvabitch follows her, flicking his tail while she pulls weeds and trims bushes and plants flowers. Sonuvabitch is lucky to have such a good friend.

The cat stops drinking, sits next to the bowl, and stares up at Stephanie.

She says, "What makes you think I have anything?"

Sonuvabitch meows.

Stephanie lets out an exaggerated sigh, reaches into the cupboard, and pulls out a bag of kibble. Sonuvabitch responds with another meow. Stephanie pours a handful into another bowl and sets it next to the water. The cat pounces.

Stephanie says, "I feel so used."

"You've always been an easy touch," Georgia says.

"Tell me about it."

Stephanie shoves the kibble back into the cupboard.

Myron says, "Sonuvabitch loves you, Stephanie."

"He loves my food, Myron."

"That too."

Loud popping sounds erupt outside. The crowd cheers and hollers and calls for more.

"Now what?" Stephanie heads back to the door.

"Firecrackers," Myron says. "Like the Fourth of July."

Stephanie opens the door. Myron steps up behind her. Troops have replaced the police on Boxer Way, their ranks closed in, strength in numbers. The crowd bulges out from the curb. Protesters wave signs, jeer, shout for the soldiers to leave, call them "Nazis" and "fascist pigs." Not just the usual crowd, the young Occupiers from the school, the ones that all look alike, but people of all sizes and shapes and ages and colors and sexes—a city awakened, pulled from their cell phones and computers and cable TVs, angry, frustrated, confused, the spark ignited, at least for today, maybe into tomorrow.

"A mob," Stephanie says.

"Yes," Myron replies.

She closes the door, wears a look of defeat. "I hope the lines hold."

"They can't forever," he says.

Georgia calls from the corner of the room. "What do you think, Steph? Should we head somewhere else?" Her voice sits on the edge.

"Maybe you should," Stephanie says. "Find someplace safer." She crosses the room and sits at the counter.

"What about you?"

"I'm staying."

"Then I am too."

"Me too." Myron drops into the armchair. Sonuvabitch jumps onto his lap and purrs.

"There's no reason for either of you to stay," Stephanie says. "This is my home."

Myron pets Sonuvabitch and asks, "Where's my tea, Stephanie? You said you would make tea."

"Yeah, I'd like a little too, Steph."

Stephanie pushes herself to her feet. She fills the kettle and sets it on the stove and turns on the burner. The flame flickers and hisses and soon rocks the teapot. Sonuvabitch stretches his legs and falls asleep.

Bellamy

S he follows Casey down the steps of the water tower, her pack weighing heavy, pulling her forward, into the shadows. The echoes spin through her head and send shivers down her spine.

"Where are we going?" Her whispers bounce off the hulking tank and twist up the tower.

"I know someone who might help."

"From the camp?"

"Not exactly."

They emerge into the gray afternoon, the air cool. A fine mist obscures distant trees and houses. The streets disappear into oblivion.

"We need to be on our guard," he says. "They'll be looking for us."

She draws closer to him. A chill passes through her, not all cold and fear. She still fells that draw, the pull of a magnet, the sense of home he brings. Doesn't matter, though. Once they get through all this—if they get through—she'll forget about Casey and his crazy causes and everything connected. She'll go back to being just plain and simple Bellamy and soon-to-be mom. She'll live like a nun, all that celebrate stuff. Until then, she must face life as a fugitive.

Casey ushers her through back alleys and small side streets. If a car comes along, they jump between buildings or behind fences or wherever they can find shadows.

They work their way east to Eighteenth, cross Aloha, past St. Joe's Church. Shortly before they reach Mercer, a cop car races around the corner. They dive into a holly tree, just before the car passes. The leaves scratch her face and hands and tear at her hair. The cop slows. She struggles not to scream. The blue-and-white metal passes within feet of the tree. Her heart thumps like it's inside the water tower. The car speeds up and disappears around the corner. She lets out her breath, along with a whimper.

Casey crawls out of the branches, then helps Bellamy. Leaves rip at her scalp. Her pack struggles against her. Her skin burns from the scratches.

She can't take much more. She wants to just curl up in some dark corner and die.

When the last razor leaf relinquishes its hold, she tumbles forward, a clownish summersault, her face landing in a muddy patch.

"Good," Casey says and pulls her to her feet. "Harder to recognize."

Just die. That's all she wants. Or maybe just a hole to fall into, like Alice, but less of this Wonderland.

She eases up to her knees. "Let's go to my house. I need to shower. I need to change. I want my own bed."

"They'll be watching." He looks as though he wants to slap her.

"How far does your friend live?"

"Not far."

She stands. Twinges of pain shoot through her ankle. Casey marches. She limps after him.

They continue their guarded trek down Eighteenth, toward Madison Avenue. Her skin crawls with the drying mud, stretching and searing the scratches.

They cross Howell and stop before a three-story apartment building, reddish-gray brick with touches of mud-brown stucco. They stand before two wooden doors with large glass windows, the wood chipped and scratched and beaten. Above the door a stone mantle with odd letters running across, like Greek or Latin or Roman or something. A sign is taped in one of the door windows, right above the kick plate. *Posted. Keep Out.*

Casey buzzes one of the apartments, last name Wang. No answer. He buzzes again. A deep, sleepy, crackly voice breaks through the static. "Yeah, what is it?"

"It's me, Casey."

A pause. More static. "Jesus…" The speaker goes dead.

"Let's go," Bellamy says. "My house isn't far."

"Don't be a fool."

Fool? Who's he calling a fool? He's the one who has them standing out next to the street, waiting for some freak named Wang. She'll show him. She'll take off on her own, turn herself in. She has nothing to be afraid of. Why the hell is she running anyway?"

A shadow passes on the other side of the glass. The door cracks open, a figure to the side. She moves closer and peeks inside. The cop from Casey's tent, black sweat pants, white T-shirt, tight against the lean frame, black hair scattered, waves of anger.

"What the hell you doing here?"

"We need your help."

"Help? Do you realize what kind of trouble you're in?"

"Come on, David, you know I didn't do anything. Just some crazy screw-up."

"Then turn yourself in."

Bellamy wants to punch that miserable face. "Let's get out of here. You can't trust a cop." She thinks she hears sirens, surrounding them in every direction.

"You've got to help us, man. We've like nowhere else to go. At least just until dark, until we can get all this figured out."

"You're crazy."

"Don't be like that. Didn't our time together mean anything to you?"

Bellamy wants to vomit. "I'm leaving."

David flashes her a look of part contempt and part relief. The sirens grow louder.

Casey's face fills with panic. "You didn't call the cops, did you? You wouldn't do that to me, would you?"

David sticks his head out the door and glances up and down the street. The traffic on Madison grows louder, as though it hadn't been there before. All she wants to do is run.

"Get in here." David pulls the door open. Casey smiles weakly and steps inside. Bellamy hesitates. The sirens grow louder. She looks up Eighteenth. A cop car races toward them. She leaps in after them, holds her chest, pants, her eyes brimming with tears. The car streams by, siren still blaring. David and Casey huddle together, to the side of the hallway. Bellamy stands as still as a

R. H. Sheldon

statue. The siren fades, replaced by the tower's echo, still circling inside her head.

Olympia

H er release from the King County jail came with a handful of clichés about not leaving town and staying out of trouble and not talking to the press and calling if she hears from her daughter. At least she's getting out. Nothing else matters. The arrest was a dose of reality she hadn't bargained for, making the protests and riots and police action—on top of being shot!—all the more poignant. She has never felt so ready to give in. She needs to step back and regroup and wait until everyone calms down, herself included. She's always been one to charge forward, never retreating, never backing down. But not this time, and if it weren't for their threats and ridiculous charges against Bellamy, she would head home right now. But she refuses to rest until she finds her daughter and gets this all straightened out.

Olympia steps out into the dull afternoon light. A throng of protesters block Fifth Avenue, the sidewalks on either side. A police line keeps the crowd from swelling up James Street along the side of the jail. The protesters carry signs that call for occupying Seattle and occupying Parker's house and occupying the jail. They carry signs that read *Bellamy* and *Casey* and *Parker* and *Olympia*. They carry signs that call for justice and fairness and liberty and freedom. And they shout and they chant and they sing and they scream, from concrete sidewalk to concrete curb to concrete wall to concrete pillar, a sea of protesters, agitated, frustrated, fed up, angry—with the world, with life, with everything.

R. H. Sheldon

A dozen reporters huddle near the blue and green mosaic to her right, a tiny courtyard covered in a nondescript splash of color, cold and dismal like the jail itself, the reporters no doubt waiting for the crowds to erupt, for *something* to happen to make their jobs more interesting. They spot her coming out of the door and rush in like vultures. Cameras aim, shutters release, phones wave in the air. *Click, click, whirl, whirl, click, click.*

She closes her eyes and gathers strength and reserves, plugging into her own frustration and anger, the same anger as those before her, aimed at the feds, the cops, the politicians. Just like those in the street. But not anything like them.

The crowd sees that something is happening and push in toward her. The reporters usher her to the top of the short set of stairs, before a sickly maple, brittle with yellow and brown leaves. Parker stands before her. Next to him, that attorney, Alonzo Garcia, looking as though he's risen from the grave.

She wants to question Parker, challenge Garcia, go home. Protesters shout her name. Shout Parker's over and over. He says nothing, shows no emotion. Half asleep. Half dead.

A reporter sticks a mike in her face, tries to ask a question, a camera at her back. Olympia recognizes her from one of the local news stations, Anita Franklin, competent enough, but usually relegated to store openings and the fashion beat.

The crowd squeezes in, yelling Olympia's name, then Parker's, then hers. Back and forth, until moving to Bellamy and Casey. Anita tries to ask her question again, but Olympia can hear nothing. The camera never wavers.

Olympia decides she should say something but is caught by the hoarseness in her throat, like molten lead, her head pounding, her shoulder on fire. Sleep is what she needs. Sleep, rest, a retreat.

Anita yells, "Have you been charged with anything?" Yelling seems foreign to the reporter, but she waves the mike without mercy.

Olympia clears her throat. *Ahem. Ahem.* A second mike appears, this one attached to a makeshift PA. Olympia tries to rally.

"The question," she says, "is whether I've been charged with any crime." Her words echo across the crowd. The silence grows. She gives them another *ahem* and continues. "If I was charged with anything, or even suspected of anything, they forgot to tell me what it was."

The nearest in the crowd boo and curse the jailhouse.

Anita Franklin tries to ask another question, but Olympia hasn't finished. "In fact, all they told me was that I shouldn't talk to any of you, that I shouldn't talk to anyone."

More jeers. More boos. More shouts for retribution.

This time Anita gets through. "Then why did they arrest you?"

Olympia stares out into the crowd, making eye contact with as many as possible. "Why did they arrest me? They forgot to tell me that as well. But I suspect it has something to do with my dear daughter, Bellamy, and those ridiculous accusations against her."

The crowd breaks into a discordant chant. "Bellamy. Bellamy. Bellamy." Her name echoes up and down Fifth Avenue. A name, but no sign of her daughter.

Anita shoves the mike into Garcia's face. His eyes grow wide and he inches back. Anita wastes no time. "Aren't you Alonzo Garcia, one of the attorneys representing Lockhart Investments?"

A brief hush descends upon those nearby, a spasm of hope that retribution will be theirs.

The attorney's eyes dart across the crowd, land on the police. Olympia never really looked at him before, such a pretty face, a fine carving, porcelain the color of teak. Too bad it's attached to a Bellevue attorney.

Finally, he says, "I've, ah, spoken with Mr. Davis and, ah, both of us agree that the best way to move forward is to work together."

Anita aims the mike at Parker. He merely nods in agreement.

Olympia glances toward James Street. A limo drives down the empty road toward Fifth Avenue, painfully sleek, stretched into long lines of glimmering black and polished chrome. It makes a wide U-turn and parks along the curb, near the corner of the jailhouse, facing up the steep hill. An accommodating police officer waves to the driver, signals that this is the place. Several other officers gather near the car. The chauffeur climbs out, crisp in his black uniform, and steps past the cops with indifference. He walks around the limo, onto the sidewalk, and hovers near the back door, where smoky dark windows hide the inside world.

Anita takes notice, her radar on fire. A low murmur spreads through the crowd. Heads turn. Bodies push and squeeze and bend. Forgetting Parker. Forgetting Olympia. Forgetting Casey and Bellamy.

Another limo, a twin of the first, stretches down the hill, turns wide and pulls behind the first. A chauffeur dressed identically to the other climbs out and saunters around to the curb and stands by the glistening black door and dark tinted windows and waits. The crowd grows mad with anticipation, pressing, pushing, squeezing, but the cops grow in number, out of the ethers, and push back the crowd.

A third limo inches down the hill, a clone, repeating their performances. An eerie silence swallows Fifth Avenue, faces pointed toward the cars, eyes wide, sparkling curious, the protesters in the road, the press on the sidewalk, the cops standing on James Street, surrounding the limos with dedication and determination. Then, as though responding to an unseen cue, the Stepford chauffeurs reach toward their respective handles, squeeze with firm grips, and inch open the black shimmering doors. The crowd draws in a collective breath, still as the night, and the cops step forward and puff up with self-importance.

Olympia feels the bile rise and leave a putrid taste in the back of her mouth. Everything about this scene—the crowd's awe, the reporters' obsession, the police's deference, the garish display of wealth—all of it, conspiring to turn any hope of change into nothing but a headline, a celebrity shootout. Whether they're politicians or movie stars or talk-show morons makes no difference. Nothing good can come out of this. Nothing.

Parker lifts his chin off his frail chest, directs his bloodshot eyes toward the limos, a glint of interest perhaps, or maybe indigestion. The lawyer only stares, his teeth clenched, a twitch in his left eyebrow.

Legs stretch out from the dark cavernous depths of the first limo, long paper-straw limbs, alabaster twigs atop four-inch stilettos, creamy white to match the skin. The chauffeur reaches out a strong grainy hand, takes the extended arm, white-gloved to the elbows. A body follows, mid-twenties, maybe thirty, clad in a puffy-white gown, an X-rated prom dress, plunging through breasts no more than nubs, the lean white flesh melded to her sternum. She stands, wobbles. The chauffeur steadies her while she adjusts the wide-brimmed hat, blood red to match her lipstick. Pale cheeks, angular and deep, poke out from beneath the shadows. She attempts a smile, a painful expression of disappointment, wobbles again, leans into the chauffeur's husky torso and straightens her sunglasses.

Someone in the crowd shouts, "Fondue," and Olympia envisions creamy white cheese dripping off a sour apple. More shouts. Applause. Screams for recognition. "Fondue" again and again. Olympia's stomach growls.

A man calls out from the crowd, "I love fondue." Olympia loves fondue too. But then she realizes what this is about. Not *fondue,* but *Fondeaux.* The infamous Fondeaux. One name. All that's needed for the reigning female superstar. Solid-gold hits and Grammys and MTV honors and sex toys on stage. Fans across the globe shout her name, cry for her music, would give their lives for her. And Bellamy is her biggest fan. She lip-syncs to Fondeaux's songs and shakes her bulky body in time with Fondeaux's anorexic gyrations.

Fondeaux eyes the second limo, wavers. A large round head pokes out, shaven, shiny, the color of charred wood. Chauffeur number two reaches out a hand. Passenger number two knocks it away, struggles to pull himself out of the limo, and stands next to the driver, an amused air, a short, rotund body, dressed in a black dinner jacket and slick black pants and a ruffled white shirt with a chartreuse bowtie. He reaches back toward the limo. An arm stretches out, matching sleeves, hands him a black bowler, like that of an English butler.

Parker leans toward Olympia, his breath the smell of vomit. "Christ, it's that fruitcake Jukes."

Olympia pulls back. "Jukes?"

"One of the biggest pop-star disco divas ever."

"But I thought a diva..."

A passenger leaps out of the third limo, a tall, gangly, over-aged punk, wearing a gray-and-black checkered jacket, pants drooping low, held up by one hand. He has reddish tangled hair, a brush of ginger on his chin, a pasty white face staring haphazardly into the crowd. The shouting starts, over and over, "Delaney. Delaney. Delaney."

"Jesus," Parker says, "more parlor games."

Alonzo seems to fold in on himself.

Olympia asks, "Who's Delaney?"

"The white man's answer to hip-hop."

"And that means?"

"A white guy who raps about the environment and social injustice. Right up your alley."

Olympia shakes her head. The crowd grows more frenzied.

"What's wrong with that?"

"Nothing wrong. At a million dollars a pop, he can afford to be concerned."

A long white fur coat appears from the first limo. The driver holds it while Fondeaux slips into the lush sleeves and disappears into a sea of fluff.

The three one-name celebrities gather in the blue-green courtyard, their smiles cautious as they move in mock affection. The crowd shouts and sings and hollers and calls their names. They wave their arms and jump up and down. They hold up phones and take photos and videos. Anita squeezes into the crowd of reporters, pulling her cameraman along. She waves her mike before her like a sword. The other reporters try to elbow her out, giving into their primal paparazzi urges.

Parker says, "I'm getting out of here."

"For once we're in agreement." She scans the wall of fans. "But how?"

A man appears out of nowhere and talks to the three celebrities. He is tall and trim and dressed in trendy power clothes, of the casual Polo variety. He wears a red baseball cap with a label that reads *Dive Rock Studios*. He speaks to the reporters, zeroes in on Anita. She points toward Parker. He herds the superstars into Parker's direction. Alonzo shrinks back and Parker holds his stomach and turns a ghostly gray. Olympia's shoulder feels as though she has just been shot.

The celebrity brood inches its way toward the makeshift stage, Anita and cameraman close behind. The chauffeurs remain with the limos. The police maintain a respectful distance. A fine mist falls. Olympia's face feels heavy and cold.

Mr. Red Hat whispers to Anita. She smiles and nods toward Parker. Jukes blows kisses to his fans, then raises his arms over his head, grasps his meaty knuckles, and shakes his arms in victory, like a boxer having just won the title fight. The crowd applauds and whistles and hollers his name. Jukes lowers his arms and flashes a smile that glistens like Christmas morning.

Fondeaux grabs one of those arms in mock solidarity. She stands a foot taller than him, weighs less than half. The breeze catches the brim of her hat, causing it to undulate in an unnatural rhythm that makes it look possessed.

The two scurry up to Parker, separate, and stand on either side. They each take an arm and turn him toward the cameras. Fondeaux gazes at Parker in what Olympia thinks is supposed to be a maternal look, although it could just as easily be one of contempt. Jukes definitely wears a look of contempt, thinly veiled beneath a plastered show of teeth, his body as far from Parker's as it can get without being across the street.

Parker glances at his arms, at his escorts, breaks into a fit of coughing, doubles over, hacks, spits, gasps for air. Jukes and Fondeaux jump back in full-frontal horror. Pictures snap, cameras roll, helicopters appear overhead. Anita tries to squeeze in closer, but Mr. Red Hat intercepts her and leads her off to the side.

Delaney sidles up to Parker, crouches down and looks at him sideways, while keeping an eye on the crowd. "We've come to help," he says. "Help you, Parker Davis. Help your cause." Delaney stands, turns halfway toward the press and halfway toward his fans. "You all hear that? We're fuckin' here to help Parker Davis. We're fuckin' here to help all the Parkers out there. The time has come!"

The crowd cheers. He waves.

Parker retreats into the background, his hacking slow to subside. Garcia is nowhere to be seen. Delaney squeezes in between Fondeaux and Jukes and grabs their hands. In unison, they step toward the crowd, knocking into Olympia and her injured shoulder. The fans pound their feet and throw up their arms and shout over and over, "Jukes. Delaney. Fondeaux. We love you. We love you. We love you." The cops can barely hold back the crowd. The reporters dutifully record the show. Mr. Red Hat smiles like a demon and nudges Anita. She grins. The audience screams and applauds and waves their arms high in the air. Parker coughs and disappears into the thick of the crowd.

Part VIII

If music be the food of love, play on,
Give me excess of it; that surfeiting,
The appetite may sicken, and so die.
—William Shakespeare, Twelfth Night

Parker

Mornings are the worst. All the aches and congestion and general malaise that are going to torture him that day usually get their start first thing in the morning, morning being relative to the hour when he actually crawls out of bed.

Today is no different. His lungs explode into a fit of hacking the moment his feet touch the wooden floor. He teeters on swollen ankles. Ice picks dig into his hips. He feels weak, achy, ready to drop. The room for a moment spins, as though he's coming off a three-day drunk, yet last night he dropped into bed sober, a few aspirin, a glass of water. And he still feels like shit.

At least he slept, a good thing, though it will take several hours to wake. His clock radio says eight-thirty, but it has held to that time since yesterday, when he knocked into the nightstand and sent the blasted thing to the floor.

He moves into the hallway and clutches the banister. He eases down the stairs. Something creaks. The steps. His joints. Something.

He shuffles through the front hallway and into the living room and drops into his chair. The usual cloud of dust puffs up from the cushions and is sucked into his lungs. He hacks, wheezes, spits into toilet paper. Myron lies on the couch, his big floppy feet pointing toward the chair, Sonuvabitch on his stomach.

Parker says, "Welcome home."

"Good morning, Parker. I'm glad you slept. I slept well. Very well indeed. I have a very nice bed."

Parker shrugs. The cat flicks his tail.

"The park is quiet," Myron says. "The protest party has moved downtown to Westlake Plaza."

"Good. I need coffee."

"I thought you liked the protests. I thought you wanted to keep your house."

"I want to crawl into a hole. What time is it?"

Myron looks over Parker's shoulder, out the window that faces the street and park, the window where the ballerina lamp once stood, the window that overlooks the missing front porch.

"It is nine-thirty," Myron says.

"Too fucking early."

Myron lifts Sonuvabitch off his stomach and places him on the couch. The cat lets out a short squeak and licks his balls.

Myron says to the cat, "I'll be right back." He pushes himself off the couch and onto his feet, his legs as steady as tree trunks. "I'll make you coffee, Parker." He disappears into the kitchen. Sonuvabitch jumps off the couch and follows Myron through the door.

Parker studies the piano. A layer of plaster dust covers the wood and keys, remnants of the shoot-out with the ceiling. Perhaps one day he'll have it tuned, maybe even replace all those old strings. One day.

Myron makes short pattering sounds in the kitchen. Cupboards open, water runs, a pot is set onto the stove. He mumbles to Sonuvabitch. The cat squawks. Myron opens the back door.

A wave of nausea spreads though Parker's guts, settles in his chest. His heart flutters. The room bends.

Myron soon returns with a cup of steaming coffee and hands it to Parker. "Two teaspoons of sugar," he says, "just the way you like it."

"Sweets for the sweet."

Myron chuckles, lets out a *hee hee*. "That's very good, Parker. Sweets for the sweet."

Parker squeezes the mug, feels the heat in his fingers, a slow thaw, temporary at best. He raises the coffee to his mouth. Steam lifts up his face. His eyes fill with tears. He sips, savors the sweet bitter mud, the burn sliding down his throat and into a stomach that churns and grinds and simmers with pain.

R. H. Sheldon

Myron drops back on the couch and sprawls out and says, "Sonuvabitch left to go on a walk and then visit Stephanie."

"Lucky cat."

"Sonuvabitch loves Stephanie. He would be happy living with her."

"That's one."

Myron reaches his arms over his head and stretches his legs and feet so they're pointing directly at Parker's face. He twists to his left, to his right, then settles into a relaxed prone position that looks more restful than anything Parker has felt in years.

Myron says, "I think I'll go down to the protest party this morning."

"Good, you do that."

"You going to the protest party today, Parker?"

"I'm done with protests and with parties."

Parker spewed out his comment with little thought, as he would any of his arsenal of flippant responses, but he realizes the truth of what he said, how finished he feels with all that, with so much of his life. All that interests him is trying to survive.

"Parker is tired," Myron says, speaking mostly to the air.

"Yes, Parker is tired. Tired of being sick and feeling like crap and trying to live in a body that's deteriorating so fast I can't walk across the room without feeling older than when I started. Parker is tired of being a has-been songwriter and a has-been piano player and a has-been human being. Parker is tired of being broke all the time and miserable all the time and lonely all the time and scared all the time. Yeah, Parker is just fucking tired."

He struggles for air, feels more life escape with each breath. Is there anything worse than the goddamn morning?

Myron cocks his head and studies Parker's face, but not his face exactly, the air around his face. "Play the piano," he says. "Play the piano for me, Parker Davis."

"Play the piano? Have you finally gone off the deep end?"

Parker drops his eyes to the floor, chipped and cracked and stained with beer. He wishes he hadn't said that. Myron might be ready to flip out altogether. He's gone off the deep end before, disappearing for days, coming back confused, disoriented, never saying where he's been, what he's been doing, probably not remembering any of it.

Myron pulls his knees up and crosses his arms over his chest. "I think you should play the piano, Parker. I want to hear you play. Please, Parker Davis."

Parker feels his resistance seep out, like the oxygen that struggles to infiltrate his lungs. Maybe he owes it to Myron, owes him something. But play the piano?

Myron watches Parker with hopeful puppy-dog eyes. "You should play. Playing is food for your soul."

"I have no soul."

He struggles to his feet, struggles to cross the room, struggles to sit on the piano bench, struggles to breathe.

He brushes some of the dust off the keys, cracked and brown with age, and sets his fingers down. The arthritis pokes at his joints, pulls at the swollen tendons. He closes his eyes and plays, a slow bluesy melody he wrote ten years earlier, the last piece he composed. He doesn't sing, though. He can barely remember the words. But he plays and, despite the sour tuning and deadened strings and hollow echoes of rotten wood, he is soon immersed in the music, focused only on a melody that rolls around in his head, his heart, the real melody, haunting, vicious, redemptive, the place where Parker resides, the place where Parker becomes Parker, a cavernous well swollen with memories and pain, for all he was and all he hoped to be. The Parker that needs not pretend or fight or struggle to survive. The Parker that needs not mourn lost ideals or lost hopes. The place where Parker becomes the music and the music becomes Parker.

Parker does not know how long he plays nor how he transitions from one tune to the next. It all just happens, a slip into the space between fifths and sixths, majors and minors.

He might have remained playing all morning if not for the pounding at the back door. The room snaps back into focus. The aches in his fingers, knees, hips, return with gleeful insistence. He lets the last chord linger, a pop-chart fade-into-black. He eases off the keys and raises his hands and turns toward the couch. He is about to tell Myron to send whoever is at the door packing. Parker is not accepting visitors. But Myron is gone, in his place, the dent in the cushions that conform to his husky body.

More knocking.

Parker pushes away from the piano, hoping the feds aren't once more at his door. The bench screeches against the floor like a banshee's cry. He leans against the keyboard for support, sending

R. H. Sheldon

a discordant plunk against the warped soundboard. He heads into the kitchen, caught off-guard by the clean counters, the lack of beer cans, food containers, empty whiskey bottles. He had forgotten the counters were green.

The back door is open. No telling where Myron has gone. Standing on the steps is a tall, skinny adolescent, no more than twenty, dressed like a model from Abercrombie & Fitch, the same guy that showed up at the jail yesterday, with those celebrity yo-yos.

"My. Davis?" He flashes a perfect set of bleached teeth. Parker shields his eyes.

"Who's asking?"

"Garth Kilroy. I'm an executive producer with Dire Rock Studios. I'd to talk to you about your music, about your future, about your career. We'd like to sign you to an exclusive record contract as soon as it's possible."

Stephanie

The newscaster speaks through the TV's cracked speakers, once again Pete Sizemore, once again focusing on the protests, the riots, the celebrity appearances, mostly the appearances, performers with names like Delaney and Jukes and Fondeaux, as if they're supposed to mean anything. The celebrity connection sickens her, makes the whole circus even more absurd—and makes her more grateful for having stayed out of the whole thing, unless she counts her yard and window.

The TV switches scenes. Anita Franklin stands amid an ocean of bobbing and waving and shouting heads. "Pete, I'm here in front of Westlake Plaza. Protesters have been pouring in from all over the region; more are expected from other parts of the country. The celebrity guest list continues to grow. A few sympathetic politicians are also on hand, as are a number of community leaders. Just look at all these people." The camera scans the crowds.

Pete Sizemore says, "I understand there are similar protests in other parts of the country."

"That's right, Pete. San Francisco. Chicago. New York. But the biggest crowds are expected here, ground zero."

The camera continues to pan the crowd, a dense throbbing mass of humanity, wedged between walls of concrete and steel and glass. They wave signs, wave arms, jump up and down. The camera zooms in on a line of soldiers, clad in full riot gear, stern faces half hidden, rifles at the ready. Groups of police hover nearby, clubs in

R. H. Sheldon

hand, their own version of riot regalia. The camera returns to Anita Franklin.

"Pete, the mayor has shut down ten city blocks in the area and may shut down other areas. We understand that more National Guard troops are on their way. Every city and county police officer is on duty today. Officers from nearby counties are also on hand. Pete, the city has never seen anything like this. Even the WTO seems a garden party by comparison."

Pete speaks from the studio. "And what are all these protesters demanding? What is it they want?"

"Pete—" The camera slips sideways, spins, shoots video of the sky. Voices shout, scream. The screen goes blank.

Pete Sizemore quickly appears. "Apparently we're having technical difficulties, but as soon as we're up and running, we'll get back to Anita.

"In a related story, the ACLU has filed a complaint against the Seattle Police Department for allegedly arresting a disproportionate number of young black men during the riots."

Stephanie flips off the TV.

"Hey!" Georgia flashes an annoyed look, drops her spoon next to her cup of tea on the counter. "I was watching that."

"I can't stand anymore."

"What?"

"I can't stand anymore."

"I thought you said I can't stand alone."

"I was talking about the news. The protests."

"At least they're not outside your door."

"But the damage is done." Stephanie drops into the armchair, longs for the house to herself, a moment's privacy. She never realized how small this place is. "Any doctor's appointment's today?"

A meow at the front door, made audible because of the missing window, the silent waiting that follows.

Georgia says, "Sonuvabitch is here."

Stephanie wants to tell her to get off her ass and get the door herself. But she doesn't. She never will. She rises from the chair and lets the cat in.

Sonuvabitch saunters over the threshold and sits near the front of the chair and licks his fur, his tail twitching in a slow methodical rhythm. Stephanie sits down and leans over and pats his head. His body erupts into a coarse, harsh purr.

Georgia laughs. "That cat."

Stephanie pulls back. "He's my rock."

"Some rock."

"I've had worse."

Georgia pushes back from the counter and lets out a sigh. She seems paler today, frailer, a sail losing its wind.

She says, "I thought I'd head over to Kitsap today, maybe spend the weekend with Jen and Claudia."

"They'll put you to work."

"Might do me good."

"I never pictured you a farmer."

"What did you picture?"

Stephanie catches a flash of defiance in Georgia's eyes, her tone tinged with a bitter edge.

Stephanie says, "You taking the ferry over?"

Georgia nods. "Easier that way. Fun too."

"Be careful downtown. Sounds like things are getting crazy there."

"I'll take the long way around. I do want to stop at the Market, but that should be far enough away."

"Just watch yourself."

"Yes, Mom."

Georgia eases off the stool and stands, leaving her spoon and tea on the counter, the honey too, lid off, jar covered in goo. She grabs her backpack from a pile in the corner and shoves in a handful of wrinkled clothes. She retrieves a small bag from the bathroom, sticks it in her pack, and heads for the front door. She offers a weak smile and a soft goodbye, then she's gone. Soon her truck is pulling out of the driveway and the house grows quiet.

Already Stephanie feels the emptiness close in, like an infection slowly spreading. She stands and heads out into the yard. Sonuvabitch follows.

The clouds hang low, the air heavy and thick, even for November. The street is quiet, unnaturally so, the park empty, at least at this end. Everyone must be downtown or out of town. The place feels like a large bay that's emptied before an approaching hurricane, the winds and tide conspiring to suck out all life, only to return and ravage the survivors.

Evidence of the protesters is everywhere—broken glass, overturned garbage bins, torn down fences, and an endless field of strewn newspapers and flyers and food wrappers and coffee cups.

Several signs lie on the ground, along with a half-dozen park lamps. Those that still stand have busted-out globes, just like most of the streetlights. Parker's yard has finally taken over the neighborhood.

But she can't be concerned about his yard or the park. She needs to be focused on getting her own place in order. She has no idea at this point if the house will even sell, but she knows it will take months just to clean the place up, and years to replace all the trees and shrubs, but at least she can get a start. She only hopes the protesters stay downtown and the police don't pull the same stunt they have in the past, drive everyone up to Capitol Hill, no doubt to protect the businesses at the expense of those who live up here.

She begins by picking up the bigger branches and adding them to the pile she started yesterday. Sonuvabitch perches himself near the front of the house and watches her carry debris from one end to the other. At one point, she passes him and says, "At least you could help." He lets out a timid meow.

She heads to the front corner of her lot, the side that abuts Parker's yard, to rescue an errant azalea. She kneels next to the plant to examine the extent of damage. The bush has been uprooted in its entirety. Clumps of dirt still cling to the roots, the branches broken and twisted, denuded of their leaves. She had planted the azalea in a large barrel next to the house, near the now-missing front window, right after she had met Georgia. They worked in the yard together that day, Georgia a willing assistant at the time, swearing a lifelong dedication to trees and bushes and flowers and anything that grew. The plant was just starting to flower, deep throated blossoms of blistering red.

A wave of sadness washes over her, emotions too pungent to speak, too brittle to let out.

She brushes off the loose dirt and pinches off the branches with no hope of survival. She stops. Music flows out of Parker's house. He must be plucking away on that rickety piano. Stephanie has never heard him play. The last time she heard the piano was before his mom died.

Despite the instrument's condition, his playing carries a fine soothing quality, like a deep flowing river, sad and gentle and full of longing. She always wished she had some way to express herself like that, some way to let out all the years and memories that lie so heavy. For the first time since knowing Parker, she feels a tinge of envy.

Sonuvabitch appears near her bended knees, rubs against the denim, offers silent comfort. She scratches his head, behind his ears, feels the warmth beneath his fur.

She goes back to work. Before long, the music stops. She hears voices, but can't make out what is being said.

She carries branches and trash from one spot to another, not quite sure what her overall plan might be. She spots a piece of broken statue. She crouches down to retrieve it.

A voice breaks over the piles of debris and burnt-out fence, filled with a smug arrogance reserved for young males, mostly straight, mostly white. Stephanie signals Sonuvabitch to be quiet—challenging her own logic only briefly—and peers through a pile of garbage. A tall lanky young man, no more than a kid, stands in front of Parker's house. He wears stylish and well-fitted clothes, perfectly matched shades of blue, the type of clothes she'd expect to see in LA. Not far from where he stands, a black limo sits double-parked, a chauffeur standing next to the car, bored, indifferent, looking at nothing.

The kid talks on the phone. "Yeah," he says, "I'm here." He glances at Parker's house with a look of derision. "You should see this dump." He pauses. "Of course, he'll sign. What choice does the loser have?" He frowns, picks at his teeth. "At least his stuff will sell. Those freaks are eating up whatever '60s crap comes along. Look at the shit Fondeaux is peddling." Another pause. "I just got out of there. We're heading downtown as soon as he puts on his Depends or whatever the hell he needs to do." He laughs. Waits. "Yeah, I've got the perfect agent for him. Believe me, Parker Davis will do exactly what we want."

Alonzo

Alonzo would like nothing more than to be feeding his kids a healthy, home-cooked breakfast, but given that Isabel did not come home last night and he needs to get the girls to school and himself to the office—soon—the only options are cornflakes and apple juice and toaster waffles, none of which he, nor they, find particularly appealing. Even Roscoe remains voluntarily glued to the kitchen corner, where he's often consigned during meals.

The girls weren't even supposed to be here. Their grandmother showed up at eight last night and announced that she had a date, but promised to take them after school today.

Teresa, the oldest, is the one most impatient with the prospect of another night over there.

"I can't study at her place," she says. "Granny always plays the TV too loud."

"I don't like the way she smells," Elena adds.

Teresa pushes her food away. "I can't eat all these high glycemic foods. It's not healthy."

Alonzo has no idea what she's talking about.

"I could end up with diabetes or heart disease or Alzheimer's. Is that what you want?"

"Teresa, honey, let's just try to make the best of it, at least for today."

Julia pushes away her plate of waffles. "I don't want this glaucoma stuff either."

Teresa raises her nose. "It's glycemic, not glaucoma."

"Whatever. I don't want to get old timer's disease."

Teresa rolls her eyes.

Elena wiggles off her chair. "Me too. Me too." She rushes out of the kitchen and returns with her beheaded Barbie and tosses it across the floor. Roscoe leaps up and chases after the doll. Alonzo picks up Elena and dumps her back in the chair. "Please, finish your breakfast."

Teresa nibbles at a cornflake. "Making us eat this could be construed as child abuse."

Construed? Where the hell does she get this stuff?

Julia pours half of the jar of syrup onto her waffle. Alonzo snatches the bottle and spills the rest all over his hand and the table. Elena starts to climb off her chair. He grabs her in mid-leap, but she wiggles out of his sticky grip.

Teresa points a fork at Alonzo and says, "What's up with Mom? Why isn't she here?"

"She's helping your Aunt Lita."

"Still?"

Julia says, "I thought she might be getting another one of her headaches. She gets them a lot lately. Why has she been getting so many headaches, Daddy?" She twirls a piece of the waffle in a pool of syrup.

Elena says, "I got a headache at school when I ate a Popsicle too fast."

Julia waves a finger at her younger sister. "You shouldn't eat that type of food. You'll get glaucoma."

Elena screams. "I don't want glaucoma. Daddy, tell Julia to stop giving me glaucoma."

Alonzo's cell phone rings. He wipes syrup off his hand and reaches into his pocket. He checks the caller ID. Someone from the office. He answers.

"Mr. Garcia?"

"Yes."

"This is Trevor, Mr. Dartmouth's personal assistant. He would like to see you in his office as soon as possible."

"This morning?"

"As soon as possible."

Elena squirms out of her chair and goes after her doll. Roscoe runs off with the doll in tow, ready to be chased.

"Okay, as soon as I get the kids to school."

He hangs up. In the past, he would have felt sick to his stomach, his chest tight, his head on fire. But this morning he feels almost numb. No, not almost. Completely. Indifferent to Mr. Dartmouth's demands and Isabel's disappearance and everything else that's been going on.

He finishes with breakfast, acting mostly as a referee, and manages to get the kids dressed and ready for school. He loads them and Roscoe into the Taurus and sets off for the middle school and elementary school.

Teresa sits in the passenger seat next to him, staring out the window with her arms crossed. He has no idea why she's upset. Julia and Elena sit in the back seat. They argue, scream, cry, and yell. Roscoe stands with his back end between them and his head between the two front seats. He barks at squirrels and pedestrians and traffic lights.

Alonzo pulls up to the middle school to drop off Teresa. She asks him to park off to the side of the building, where no one will see her. "My friends will be out front."

He pulls around to the side.

"Go right to your grandmother's after school."

"Why?"

"Because your mother is still helping your Aunt Lita."

"But why do I need to go there? I'm not a child."

"To help watch your sisters."

"What's in it for me?"

"What?"

"What if I miss the bus?"

"Don't."

She grabs her pack, jumps out of the car, and slams the door. She stomps off and disappears around the front of the building.

Alonzo drives to the elementary school. Julia opens the door. Roscoe jumps out. Julia jumps out after Roscoe. Elena follows. Then Alonzo.

He rounds up Roscoe and herds him back into the car and tells the girls what he told Teresa, to go right to their grandmother's after school.

"What about Mom?" Julia asks.

Elena says, "Will she still have a headache?"

Yes, what about their mom and her headaches? He wishes he had a good answer for them—and for himself.

He ushers them along and watches as they meet up with their schoolmates. Everyone immediately bursts into giggles. They climb the stairs and disappear into the school. He returns to his car, slides in behind the wheel, and pulls away from the curb. Roscoe sticks his wet nose into Alonzo's ear, sending a shiver through his body.

When he arrives at work, he brings Roscoe upstairs. Katie, the receptionist, sees the dog and quickly reverts to childhood. She giggles and puckers her lips and buries her face in Roscoe's fur. He wags his tail so hard he's about to take flight.

"Come, Roscoe."

The dog disentangles himself. A stricken look falls across Katie's face.

Alonzo puts Roscoe into his shiny new office, complete with windows and a chair that works. He heads to Mr. Dartmouth's office and knocks. The soft genteel voice welcomes him in. Inside the air is warm and moist and thick with frankincense. He notices something new, though, the tinkling of water. In the far corner, between the windows and the Buddha, a fountain made of black slate and copper tubing, a gentle stream trickling over a bed of shiny pebbles. Several miniature spotlights give the water a shimmering fluorescence.

"Beautiful," Alonzo says.

A pleased smile crosses Dartmouth's face. "You like it? It came in yesterday." He waves toward the chair. "Please, sit down."

Alonzo does. He feels as though he's off on a retreat in the middle of the forest, like those he's attended with the men's group at his church.

Dartmouth flashes a benevolent smile, a guru about to bestow a blessing. "Alonzo, I saw you on the news last night, standing next to Mr. Davis, in front of the county jail."

"Mr. Dartmouth..."

"Harold."

"Yes, Harold, I can explain."

"Nothing to explain. That was brilliant. Just the touch we needed to show the world we're not the adversaries. We're here only to make things easier for everyone. I knew you were the right man for this job. I knew you had the intelligence and sensibility this situation needed when we needed it." He nods to the Buddha.

Alonzo is afraid to say anything. He has no idea how Dartmouth's mind works.

Dartmouth continues. "I've heard from several directors on the Lockhart board. They're very impressed, calling it a stroke of genius. Alonzo, my boy, you're going to go far, very far indeed. With this one small gesture, you defused our critics, removed us from the spotlight, and painted us as goodwill ambassadors. The only bad guys in all this are the feds, and they can handle themselves. So tell me. What did you do to warm up to Mr. Davis?"

Alonzo describes the discussion he had with Parker and the offer he had made on Lockhart's behalf. "He was all set to go along. But then he was arrested."

Dartmouth claps his hands. Once. "Perfect. We try to make this work and the government makes it all worse. The media will be all over this. We'll make sure of that. This could be the best thing to happen to Lockhart and, subsequently, us. Here's what we're going to do. We'll play up the angle of how government regulations and interference are making it nearly impossible for honest people to do business, how they've once again thwarted the honorable dealings between the two parties. We'll also play up how the press has overreacted, without having all the facts."

"The press will agree to that?"

He gives a conspiratorial nod. "They love to rip their own kind apart. Makes them feel absolved."

Alonzo isn't sure what to do with this information. All he did is stand next to Parker and say a few words to the press. It was all chance. All circumstance.

He says, "How would you like to proceed?"

A sly look shines from Dartmouth's narrowed eyes. "You seem to have good instinct about this, Alonzo, and I don't want to force your hand. But if I were you, I'd buddy up to Parker even more. Show him—and everyone—we're on his side. Sweeten the pot, if necessary. We're not out of the woods yet, but with your finesse, we'll get there. Just don't let him out of your sight."

Alonzo realizes that a suggestion from Dartmouth is tantamount to an order. As soon as Alonzo leaves here, he'll be heading to Parker's house. He clears his throat and leans slightly toward the desk. "These protests could get out of hand. You think I should stick with him even down there?"

"Yes, even there. You don't need to be in the limelight—that's his job—but you need to keep an eye on him. We want the world to see that Lockhart Investments and the law offices of Higgins, Whitaker & Nye are all about justice and fair play. Even if you don't succeed, your presence will be noted.

"Lockhart has too many projects in mind to let a little one like this sidetrack him. Massive projects that will require careful PR. These protests won't last. Everyone will forget Parker Davis and the Seattle riots and this whole ridiculous turn of events. But they'll remember Lockhart Investments. And we want to make sure they remember them in the right way."

Olympia

Olympia never knows quite what to do with Crystal. At least with Bellamy, Olympia has a glimmer of hope that there's a brain in there, although lately, even that assumption has been severely challenged. Yet compared to Crystal, Bellamy comes off as a neuroscientist. Unfortunately, Olympia has nowhere else to turn but Crystal. Bellamy is still missing and the police are the last people Olympia wants to talk to. That's why she called Crystal and asked her to come over. That's why Crystal is sitting in Olympia's office, across the desk from her, acting like a schoolgirl caught eating a jar of paste.

"Think, Crystal. Did Bellamy do or say anything that might help us find her?"

Crystal squirms, wraps her fingers through her short gray-streaked hair, like straw caught in a fan. "Honest, Reverend, not a word. I saw her at the hospital with you. After that, I searched for her in the lobby and outside the front entrance, but never found her. It was sort of like she totally disappeared into the void, like she got abducted by those space alien people."

Olympia assumes that Crystal is telling the truth, not that she's all that trustworthy, but because she's not smart enough to be a good liar. From day one, she's been intimidated by Olympia and her *Reverend* title, a carry-over from her Methodist upbringing, always on edge when she's around Olympia, as though plugged into a low-voltage outlet, just enough surge to keep her tapping her feet or twisting in her chair or pulling at her hair, all of which she's doing now.

"And you've heard nothing from her since?"

Crystal shakes her head, a balloon wiggling on that skeletal frame, her hair bouncing like a ragdoll.

"Not a thing. It's like I said. She got abducted or something. You think that's what happened? You think those aliens got her?" She searches the ceiling for a moment, then focuses on Olympia, her eyes wide in fear. "Maybe it was terrorists. Maybe some of those bombers got her. Maybe they'll come after me." She shivers in an overly dramatic fashion.

"Those awful agents came looking for me yesterday. It was like the worst thing that ever happened. But I told them I didn't know anything, had no idea where Bellamy went. Showed them my phone, how I tried to call but no answer." She pulls her legs up on the chair and wraps her arms around her knees. "It's kind of like they thought I was already guilty, like I knew those dudes trying to bomb the hospital."

Olympia rubs her shoulder, feels the pain radiate into her head. She wonders if the agents who talked to Crystal experienced any of the same frustration. Crystal would have been on the verge of hysteria. Even when she's at her best, there's not much there. She's the type to spend all day on Twitter and Facebook, pouring over inane celebrity quotes and superstar images, and come off with nothing to talk about but the latest Fondeaux video.

Olympia pushes forward. "Crystal, if you were going to look for Bellamy right now, where would *you* start?"

Crystal unfolds her legs and sets her feet on the floor. She sits up straight and holds herself proudly. "Me? Where would I start?"

Olympia nods.

Crystal places her hands on the desk and stares into a ponderous void. After a moment, she speaks. "I would try to call her on my phone."

Olympia takes a deep breath and speaks in an even, calm voice. "Crystal, as I've told you several times, Bellamy left her phone behind and the agents now have it. Calling is not an option, unless you know where she might be."

Crystal scrunches her face in concentration, as though trying it out for the first time. Finally, she says, "The Occupy camp."

"At Seattle Central?"

R. H. Sheldon

"Yes, Reverend. That's like where all this started, where she met that Casey dude. Maybe they headed back there."

As surprising as this is, Crystal actually makes sense. Bellamy might wander back there because she might think it safe. Certainly, the feds are watching the place, but Bellamy might not realize that. Besides, Olympia has little to lose by checking it out. Bellamy has done some foolish things in her time, but never disappeared without a word. Something is wrong.

Crystal starts to speak, then stops. She folds back into her chair, places her hands on her lap, and acts as though she said nothing, which gives her more of that absurd schoolgirl look.

"Yes, Crystal, what is it?"

Her eyes drop to the floor. She purses her lips, makes slight gurgling sounds. "It's just that...you don't think...I mean, it's so like she couldn't, but still..."

"Crystal."

"I mean, Bellamy...you don't think she really did this...or tried to, you know, the bombing thing. Bellamy's not like a terrorist or something...I mean...she couldn't be, could she?" Her face turns bright red, and sweat beads on her forehead.

Olympia laughs. "No, Crystal, I don't believe that Bellamy is a terrorist. I think she's just stupid."

"But Reverend..."

"In the meantime, I want you to take me to the Occupy camp and show me around. Perhaps we can at least find a clue as to her whereabouts."

They'll have to walk to the college, not all that far, but an inconvenience. Her car is still by Parker's house. When she went to pick it up yesterday, after being released from jail, she discovered it had a flat tire—and she has no spare. By then, her shoulder and exhaustion made dealing with it way too much to handle.

What had surprised her the most, though, was the sudden evacuation of the crowd. While Olympia was surveying her tire and searching for a jack, the mass of protesters began a slow and methodical migration out of the park. Perhaps they heard about the celebrity appearances and were making their way to the jail. Perhaps they just got bored.

Now all the protesters are at Westlake Plaza downtown, foregoing Cal Anderson Park and the King County jail and the community college, where the Occupy forces have made their home. All eyes are now on Westlake and the superstar entertainers and the growing crowds, with people still pouring in from around the region and around the world.

"Reverend Culpepper?"

Olympia looks up. Crystal stares at her with a look of admiration.

"Yes, Crystal?"

"You really want me to take you to the Occupy camp? Me?"

"Of course, Crystal, and the sooner the better."

Crystal squirms with delight. Olympia can think only about the long, long mile in which she'll have to endure her walk with this dedicated flagpole.

Bellamy

She slept on the couch, alone, Casey and that David Wang creep in the bedroom, going at it all night long, like a couple of dogs in heat.

What bullshit. She would have left last night if she had any idea where to go. But Casey said the church was probably being watched and so was Crystal's house and everywhere else Bellamy used to go. But what the fuck does he know? Maybe he's wrong about all of it.

And now David says he has a plan, says neither of them will like it, especially Casey, but it's the only way. He opens the door to the hallway, says he'll be right back. Casey whistles. Bellamy looks around the apartment. Wood floors. Subtle pastel walls. Artwork hanging like they're in a museum. All too neat, too color coordinated, too gay.

She considers sneaking Casey's phone out of his pack and calling her mom. Instead, she drops onto the couch next to Casey. He acts all chummy, patting her knee, taking her hand, not like lovers, like brother and sister, high school friends, her the fag hag, him the fag. He says that David is awesome, helping them out like this. What would be awesome is if David dropped dead in front of them, going down in a fit of pain, suffocating in his own spit, like a fish out of water sucking in air.

She's about to pull her hand out of Casey's, but realizes how good it feels, even now, even after all that has happened, a low current running between them, a magnetic force pulling them together. Maybe this is what love is.

David returns, an older woman in tow, maybe her mom's age, streaks of gray, a small paunch, body a bit odd, face too, deep pockets for eyes, posture like a reigning queen, her lipstick a bucket of sour cherries. She carries a large plastic tackle box, navy blue with black handles. Bellamy feels her muscles tighten and her stomach twist into a knot. Casey leaps up from the couch.

"What the hell?"

"Easy, boy." David grabs Casey's arm and pats him on the shoulder. "This is Freda. She's here to help."

Casey pulls back and stares at the intruder, his look part interest, part disdain. "What's in the case?"

Freda winks. "Magic." She takes Casey's hands, raises his arm, and appraises his body. "Yes," she says, "he'll do nicely." She beams with pride.

"And her?" David points to Bellamy, but never looks at her.

Freda giggles. "Yes, indeed. She will be perfect. She will be my masterpiece." Freda claps her hands like a child at a circus.

Bellamy is convinced that however bad things were, they've just gotten worse.

David says, "Freda is a professional make-up artist."

"That's me. My fans know me as Freda Love. I'm an international sensation. Renowned far and wide as the master of rouge. But you can call me Freda." She curtsies and tosses a kiss toward Casey.

Casey puts on this shy, all-American boy act that makes Bellamy want to puke. She steps between him and Freda.

Casey says, "What kind of name is that, anyway? Freda Love."

"Oh, my dear. That used to be my drag name. I just couldn't let it go."

"Drag name? That makes no sense."

"It does if you used to be a man. You haven't considered a little MTF yourself, have you, my dear?"

Casey pulls back, stumbles on the Persian rug. "Hey that's cool man." Looks everywhere except at Freda.

Freda grins. "Relax, stud. I promise not to bite—much."

Bellamy feels her ship sinking.

David steps between them. "Freda is going to fix you two up, so you're less, ah, recognizable—at least until we can get all this straightened out."

Casey eyes Freda, then her case, then David, then back to Freda. "You don't mean…"

David nods, his eyes bright, almost amused.

Bellamy has landed on another planet. A stranger in a strange land, stranded on distant shores. Maybe now would be a good time to get out of here, cops or no cops.

Freda turns to her. "And you, my angelic palette, are so perfect the world will be groveling at my feet."

Bellamy grabs her pack and races across the apartment and reaches for the door.

Casey bolts after her and grabs her arm. "What are you doing?"

"What I should have done last night. Getting the hell out of here."

These guys are crazy, all three of them. Maybe that's what it's always like with these types, talking in riddles—or in secret code. Whatever's going on, she's had enough.

Casey pushes his body against the door. "If they arrest you now, you may never be free. They can hold you without a trial or let you see a lawyer or even talk to your mother. You will disappear, maybe end up in Guantanamo."

"Guantana-where?" She tries to push him aside.

"You can't leave."

"Then someone tell me what's going on."

David shakes his head and moves in closer. "What I'm proposing is that we disguise you two, give you costumes so outrageous no one will suspect it's you."

Freda raises her tackle box. "Yes," she says, "exactly. In here, I have everything I need to turn you two into something you never thought possible. It will be magnificent."

David says, "And while Freda is working on you two, I'll be out getting you clothes."

Freda points at Bellamy's feet. "Take note of the size of those honkers."

David looks down. His eyes grow wide. "I'll need your measurements before I leave."

He writes down their shoe sizes and waist sizes and bust sizes. David and Freda discuss Casey's perfect proportions, saying nothing about Bellamy.

David shoves the paper into his pockets and plants a kiss on Casey. "Well, I'm off."

Casey grabs his crotch and grins. "Not yet."

Freda separates them. "No time for that. Value Village awaits."

David leaves. Freda directs them to the two stylish stools near the kitchen counter. She sets her tackle box next to them and rolls up her sleeves. She grabs a handful of towels from the hallway closet, drapes one over each of their shoulders, and drops the rest on the floor. She stands back and appraises them one at a time.

"Now, my darlings, it's time to go to work. I'm going to turn each of you into an *objet d'art*. Perfect bookends to complement this dreary world of sordid tomes."

Tomes? This chick is like so damn lame, or is she doing more of that kink-talk stuff?

Casey groans. "I'm not going to like this."

Bellamy feels her reality slip even more. "Like this? Like what? Quit talking in code."

Freda rolls her eyes and offers a smug grin. She leans in toward Bellamy. "My dear, I'm going to make you two the most beautiful drag queens this side of Manhattan."

Myron

The image comes to Myron out of the mists, jungle, birdcalls, streams of sunlight, buffeted against broad leaves of shimmering yellow and green. A voice through speakers, a song, Parker's song.

Myron opens his eyes, continues his walk. Cal Anderson Park. A smooth, bluish-gray wave rolls across the reflection pool. Seagulls squawk, dive for trash. Trash everywhere, remnants of yesterday's protests, the day before, yet few people remain, his homeless friends, stoned, deadened to the mists and cool breeze.

He walks past the sports fields and out to Pine, past brick and glass and pockets of weeds. He crosses Broadway and angles toward the college, winding through the dark space where those Occupy protesters play their camping game: green sagging tents and plastic blue tarps and dilapidated signs extolling the virtues of equality and peace and a planet worth saving. Only a few campers on hand, though, most probably down at the protest party.

Myron stands beneath one of the tarps and looks up at the field of blue plastic, glowing with the morning's dim light. Drops of water crawl on the other side, amoebae sliding across the slick surface, a dance subtle and slow, like the simmering heat of the jungle.

He spots Olympia and her young friend creeping around a nearby tent, peering inside, peering around, peering beneath the folds.

Two people approach, flitting about like flies, wearing silvery gowns and feathery boas and wigs tall and full and as pink as cotton candy. The gowns are covered in sequins and trimmed with lace, white boots with thick wooden platforms, the boas fat and fluffy, wrap-around rainbows. They wear thick false eyelashes and thick red lipstick and wide strips of eye shadow as blue as a summer sky. They must be going to a costume party, or maybe the protest party at Westlake Plaza.

The costumed duo approach Olympia and her friend. One of them says, "Mom."

Olympia starts, the sound of a ghost. She collects herself, says, "Now's not the time."

"It's me, Mom. Crystal, it's me," the voice nervous and afraid. "It's Bellamy. Bellamy and Casey."

A switch must turn on in Olympia's head because her face lights up and then Crystal's face lights up and they both bump up against the costumed Bellamy and Casey and they all hug and laugh and act as though the party is here and now and not at Westlake Plaza. But then Olympia whispers, "What were you planning to do?" And the costumed Bellamy replies, "Head to Westlake." And Olympia says, "Why not just turn yourself in? You haven't done anything." The costumed Casey says, "No way. They get ahold of us and we'll never get out." Then Bellamy says, "Yeah, Mom, think of Guantizmo," which causes Casey to say, "Guantanamo." Olympia says, "Don't be so melodramatic," at which point Olympia's young friend says, "I can't believe that's you, Bell. You look so like a friggin' drag queen," to which Bellamy responds, "That's what I'm supposed to look like." Then Crystal says, "Have you seen all the tweets about you? You're like a big time celebrity. Both of you. The whole world knows about Bellamy and Casey." Bellamy smiles wide through all her make-up, but Casey only frowns and says, "Look, man, we can't risk staying in one spot too long. We're looking for our friends. They can help us." Bellamy says, "Sorry, Mom, but we've got to get down there." Olympia replies, "Then I'm going too," though she looks mostly like she'd rather get shot again, and Olympia's friend says, "Me too."

The four head toward Pine Street and turn right toward downtown and Westlake Plaza, except that the costumed Bellamy and Casey can't walk very well and they trip often on their platform boots and wobble a lot and generally look like jokers.

R. H. Sheldon

Myron hangs out beneath the tarp a bit longer, considering those rare moments when a cool breeze might weave through the jungle branches and soothe the forest and comfort the trees. Then he walks, staying a discreet distance behind the four pilgrims.

The closer Myron gets to Westlake Plaza, the denser the throng of protesters, and by the time he gets to Seventh, he can barely penetrate the thicket of bodies that cover many city blocks in every direction. The streets have been barricaded to prevent traffic from passing, not that it could anyway, and businesses have closed and locked their doors. Troops stand in the ready with rifles and riot gear, the police there to back them up with their own protection.

Myron worms his way toward Westlake Plaza. He has long lost sight of Olympia and the others. He can no longer see anyone, really, just an ocean of blue North Face jackets, packed in so solid they move like the tide.

The panic rises, a jungle fever, filled with fear and mists and broken nights. A voice blasts out of a circle of speakers, moving in every direction and filling the deep urban canyon, where echoes shift and splinter and splatter against the walls. He moves in.

A stage is shoved up against the concrete columns that mark the fountain. His breathing eases, the heat lifting from the meadow. A tall goofy-looking man shouts into the microphone, voice a leaky balloon. He wears a red baseball cap and chews gum like a teenage junkie.

He says, "My name is Garth Kilroy. I'm an executive producer with Dive Rock Studios. And I'm here to tell you, we *will* change the world." His voice drills into the concrete and steel girders and buckles their foundations. The crowd applauds and yells his name. He grins, pleased with himself, pleased with all of them. Alonzo thinks of snakes and big jungle rats.

Garth Kilroy waves toward a small group of people on stage with him, all in costumes, just like Bellamy and Casey. They show pretend smiles and pretend interest, but show too an edge of impatience. Garth Kilroy says, "Not that any of them needs an introduction..." The crowd cheers. He points to a short stubby man with skin darker then Myron's. "Ladies and Gentlemen, we start with the incomparable maverick of solid gold fame, the sensational Jukes!" The man named Jukes tips his hat to the audience and they, in turn, clap their hands and shout his name over and over, like a script on a TV show. When the roar subsides, Garth Kilroy continues. "Next we have one of the most fearless and talented artists of our time, the one-of-a-kind Delaney!" A frumpy looking white guy dressed like a street punk raises his hands over his head in a sign of victory. The audience again explodes with applause, shouting his name again and again. Then Garth Kilroy points to a woman with pearly white skin and a body that could blow away. "And finally, ladies and gentlemen, we are fortunate to have with us a woman of style and beauty and talent unlike any in the industry, the sexy and sensational Fondeaux!" The audience is practically frothing at the mouth. She throws kisses and is greeted by whistling and clapping and shouts of joy.

"My friends," Garth Kilroy says, "we start recording 'Last Stand' in the morning, right here at a studio in Seattle. Jukes is donating his time to this worthwhile cause. Delaney is donating his time to this worthwhile cause. Fondeaux is donating her time to this worthwhile cause. And Dive Rock Studios will make it all happen, without thought of profit or sales or rocketing fame."

The people clap their hands and pound their feet and chant the names of the three superstars. They squeeze closer to the stage. They push and shove. They suck all the air. Myron wills himself to stand firm.

Garth Kilroy leans toward Jukes and holds his microphone before him. Jukes steps forward, on cue, adjusts his bow tie, tips his hat once again, and begins to speak in a dribbling voice about just causes and the power of action and uniting as one. Myron decides that Jukes sounds like a mouse, all squeaky and sour, but in the end saying nothing.

Garth Kilroy follows with Delaney, who steps forward, raises a tattooed arm, and speaks into the mike. He too says nothing.

Fondeaux is next. She adjusts her glimmering white fur coat and leans her head to one side. She speaks like Jukes and Delaney, only more wistfully, her words, sounds, noise into nothing.

Garth Kilroy takes back control of the mike, flashes a sincere smile at his celebrity buddies, acting the proud parent or child or brother, then adds more of his own noise. "My friends, artists from all over the country are flying into Seattle to join us for this momentous occasion. Together, they will selflessly perform 'Last Stand' like it has never been performed before. They will join hands and join voices and join hearts. They will not be thinking of stardom or record sales or popularity. They will be coming together as one voice with one message. 'Last Stand' will be the first stand to a new beginning!"

R. H. Sheldon

The audience claps and yells and dances around the stage. Myron glances toward the fountain and sees Olympia and her friend and the costumed Bellamy and Casey, looking as out of place as penguins in a court of law. Olympia stares at the celebrities with a look of contempt.

Garth Kilroy says, "And now, my friends, the moment we've all been waiting for—the remarkable and legendary Parker Davis!"

Parker limps up the stairs and crosses the small stage and stands next to Garth. He looks slight, feathery, almost not there. Myron thinks Parker should go home and rest. Myron thinks both of them should go home and forget all this protest business. What's the point of making more craziness? What's the point of making more crazy people?

Music erupts from the speakers. Parker's song plays. The original recording. The solid gold hit that launched Parker to fame. Parker looks as though he is about to be sick, but everyone else takes on an ecstatic glow, the people on stage, the people around the stage. Even the police for a moment seem in a trance.

A hollow feeling nudges at Myron's insides, an insistence that he move, flee, forget everything he sees.

A gang of young men shove up to the stage. They wear black jeans and black boots and black sweatshirts with their hoods pulled over their heads and over their eyes, smiles sly, tense, full of trouble. Myron remembers them from Cal Anderson Park, when the protest party was up there, before all the trouble started.

One nods, bigger than the others, pulls a fistful of something out of his black backpack. Another one flicks a lighter. They huddle together. The big one yells, "Hey, Jukes, you little faggot, how about a dance?" He lobs the object toward the performer in a high arc of tiny stars. Jukes freezes. The object lands on the stage and explodes in a dance of sparks. *Pop. Pop. Pop. Pop.*

Firecrackers. Dozens and dozens. Garth Kilroy shouts into the mike, "They're shooting at us!" "They're shooting at us!" Jukes screams. Fondeaux screams. Delaney screams. The crowd screams and tries to scatter.

Delaney leaps off the stage and knocks one of the hooded teens to the ground. They grab Delaney and punch him and kick him and laugh. Jukes and Fondeaux run in circles, banging into each other like bumper cars at a carnival. Garth Kilroy shoves Parker aside and jumps off the side of the stage, where his foot catches a tangle of wires. When he tries to free himself, he stumbles toward the fountain and into the small pool at the base of the falling curtain of water, taking with him the wires and several bystanders and signs calling for justice and an end to police brutality. For a moment, Garth's face holds a look of surprise, like he has just won the lottery, but it quickly twists into one of horror. Smoke puffs up around him. His hair burns. His flesh fries. His eyes bulge out. He drops through the falling wall of water and into the pool, his body writhing, then twitching, then falling still. The bystanders he brought with him suffer much the same fate, signs and all.

Olympia and Bellamy and Casey jump back from the fountain and follow the retreating crowd, but Bellamy falls off her platform boots face first into the concrete. She grabs her ankle and cries out. Olympia stops and returns to her daughter. Casey disappears into the crowd, his wig flopping around his head, his platform-encumbered escape not unlike a deranged cowgirl having straddled a saddle for far too long.

The crowds continue to retreat. They push and shove. They yell and kick. They squeeze through and climb over whatever stands in their way. The fallen lie in heaps upon the concrete. They scream and cry for help. Many fall unconscious beneath the trampling feet.

The hooded hoodlums stop kicking Delaney and punch through the crowd. Delaney does not move. Jukes and Fondeaux still run in circles and wave their arms. She trips and falls off the stage and knocks her skull against a concrete planter. She gasps and drops into stillness, the blood from her skull mixing with the blood from Delaney's body. Jukes falls to the stage and pulls off his hat and opens his arms toward heaven. Windows break. Rocks fly. Crowds scream. Guns fire.

Myron now stands alone in front of the stage. Parker is gone. Myron climbs up and scans the crowd. The smell of singed hair and burnt flesh waft up from the fountain, smells he has known before. The panicked protesters spew out in every direction. The kids with the firecrackers climb through a broken storefront window and return with armfuls of clothes. Others quickly follow. Small groups of soldiers stand helpless and confused. They retreat against walls, into cracks. A string of cops back into the alley and disappear altogether. In every direction, throngs of protesters try to escape the chaos. Yelling turns to pushing, pushing turns to punching, punching turns to kicking. The fallen are trampled and left as sacrifices to robbers and muggers and roving thugs. More windows break. More rocks fly. More piercing screams to drain Myron's blood. Suddenly, shots ring out, echoing up and down the streets like blasting cannons. A large swath of protesters drops to the ground and cling to the steps of the Westlake Center shopping center, across from the plaza.

Myron turns full circle, but Parker is still nowhere to be seen. Myron eases past Jukes's whimpering body and climbs down from the stage. He hesitates for a moment near the motionless Delaney and Fondeaux, and then steps gingerly over their mingled pool of blood. He sets his sights on Pine Street, toward Capitol Hill and Seattle Central Community College and Cal Anderson Park and the home of Parker Davis, back into the jungle from where he came.

Part IX

Whoever said the pen is mightier than the sword
obviously never encountered automatic weapons.

—Douglas MacArthur

Myron

Myron huddles near the Interstate, just below the dog park, a steep strip of grass and weeds and roadside trash. The highway is closed. Earlier, Myron watched the black-hooded gang drop rocks on cars passing beneath the bridge. Horns. Brakes. Screeching tires. A dozen cars piled into a twisted heap of glass and metal and screams. Those on the bridge laughed, ran, tossed more rocks, all seen from Myron's perch.

That was when the protesters first spread out from downtown, fleeing like ants, up First Hill, up Capitol Hill, up Queen Anne Hill. It is now past midnight, the city shut down.

Now they roam in gangs and take strength in numbers. They break car windows and shop windows and apartment windows. They lob bricks at streetlamps and storefronts. They overturn garbage cans and tear down signs and knock over fences and rip out trees. They loot and laugh and set fires in doorways and along alleys and up the sides of old wooden power poles. Lines drop and sparks fly and the night darkens further into the smoky mists.

Myron has seen this type of behavior before, when young men lose all sense of proportion, when young men lose all sense of themselves.

He crouches closer to the ground and covers his ears, but he still hears the gunshots and smells the smoke and feels the darkness, cold against the wet bristles of grass that brush his face.

The sound of an engine seeps up through the shadows, a low rumble, tight, hard, passing through him in a grumbling wave, grabbing his guts, pushing, squeezing, making its demands. Headlights appear through the molten air. He huddles lower. The lights point up Pine, a steel blade cutting through the darkness.

An armored vehicle appears out of the mists, like a dragon about to heave a lung full of flame. The running lights cast an eerie glow and give form to the metallic giant, one of its scales, a decal of the American flag. The truck sits high, the tires like giants, and inside, amid a soft haze of light, the vague outline of soldiers peering through caged windows.

A rock flies out from the shadows on the other side of Pine, where a matching strip of grass overlooks the Interstate. The rock clangs against the steel and falls to the ground with a heavy thud. Another rock follows. Then another. The vehicle stops next to the concrete urns. Myron feels the engine grind through the ground, tearing apart the earth. He crouches lower and places his hands over his heart.

Another truck comes up Pine. Myron grasps a clump of grass and waits. Headlights appear out of the mists and squeeze up behind the first vehicle, a second fortress of steel, iron clones at Minor and Pine.

A spotlight jumps to life from the top of the first one, searing the night with a laser edge, panning up Pine, along the sidewalks, digging into cracks and crevices and shadows. Soon it reaches across the dog park, tipping the ground's head, inches from where Myron lies. He holds his breath.

Another rock slams against the steel, but Myron can't tell which vehicle takes the blow. The spotlight swings in a wide arc and aims toward the patch of grass across Pine. An amplified voice erupts from the vehicle, a man's voice, deep and harsh, like the engine. "Come out with your hands up. Come out now. You have ten seconds."

No movement. The voice repeats its demands. More rocks fly out from the shadows. Myron raises his head and tries to see across the street, but can make out only the chain-link fence, flooded in a white glare.

The second vehicle fires over the fence, not with an explosive blast, but more a lob and a clunk. Something hits the ground, hisses, breaks into a cloud of smoke. Tear gas, moving with the breeze. Soon his eyes burn, nostrils sting. Several black-hooded kids stagger out from the shadows, one carrying a makeshift torch. They hack and cough and gasp for air. The torchbearer staggers. He lights a fuse and tosses it through the air, a sparkling arc that lands near the second vehicle, the one nearest to where they stand. More firecrackers. More popping sounds like earlier on the stage. Smoke and gas fill the air. The first vehicle opens fire. The kids fall backwards, down the slope. The torch lies near the side of the road, a dull flame twisting into the night.

Myron crawls along the fence, away from Pine. His heart pounds. His skin burns. His eyes drip with tears. He inches past clumps of weeds and broken beer bottles and scraggly wisps of trees, fighting the pull of the steep slope down to the silent highway.

He reaches the edge of the grass, where the dog park fence meets the Boren Avenue guardrail. The sound of an engine comes from the direction of Pike Street, but not the low rumble of an armored vehicle. He pulls himself up and peeks over a clump of bushes. Soldiers stand at the intersection, where a generator drives massive lights that flood the corner and magnify his tears.

Then he hears it, the *thump, thump, thump*, a helicopter approaching, its engine like thunder. It hovers close the ground, making a slow sweep with its spotlight. He pushes himself into the corner, against the cold concrete and icy fence, in the shadow of a lone bush. He covers his head with his arms. He squeezes his eyes shut and gulps for air. The chopper grows closer. The ground shakes and the air erupts in a violent current of wind.

"Not again. Please, please, not again."

Alonzo

I f he avoids the main streets, he won't run into all those
military trucks with their spotlights and bullhorns and
armed troops. But if he stays to the side streets and alleys,
he risks running into one of those roaming gangs, out breaking
windows and starting fires and terrorizing anyone who gets in their
way. All the safe and sane people are locked into their homes with
their shades drawn and lights turned low or shut off completely.

Alonzo watches Lita's apartment from where he hides, across
the street from her building, a few doors down, behind a clump of
azaleas with brownish leaves and prickly branches, the only cover
he could find.

Fourteenth Street is not a major artery, but it's no back alley, so
Alonzo must watch for soldiers *and* thugs. He has seen no signs of
life from inside Lita's apartment, and he had given up trying to
reach them by phone. He has no idea where they might be or
whether they were anywhere near the riots. What he does know is
that he won't rest until he's certain Isabel is safe.

He's been searching for her since early this afternoon, when he
went to find Parker, but instead found himself in a city suddenly
shut down, enveloped in a violent explosion of rioting and looting
and pillaging and attacking. The military action soon followed,
putting the central part of the city in lockdown. Businesses closed
and services came to a standstill. No cabs or buses or Quickie
Marts, vehicles banned within a two-mile radius of Westlake Plaza.

R. H. Sheldon

He sat in his car and listened to the radio to catch what news he could, but by mid-afternoon he had to abandon it altogether, and by the time nightfall came, the only ones on the streets, other than the military and police, were the roving hoodlums intent on bringing the city to its knees. For the last eight hours, he's had to listen to bullhorns calling for order and obedience, reinforced by the occasional gunfire and the agonizing chorus of sirens that have spread through the city like a plague.

Late in the afternoon, after hours of searching but before the state of emergency had been called, he telephoned Isabel's mother. She verged on the edge of hysteria, after failing to reach Isabel and Lita herself, convinced they had already met a fate too dreadful to speak.

"I'll find them," Alonzo swore. "I will not give up until I know they're safe." What he didn't say is that Lita could stay lost as far as he was concerned. In the meantime, he asked her to pick up the dog and keep him with her and the kids. For the first time since knowing her, she agreed without offering resistance or advice or snide remarks about his capabilities as a father or a husband.

Shortly after talking to her, he lost cell phone service and no longer felt safe returning to his car.

Since then, he has walked block after block trying to hunt them down, without being seen himself, returning often to Lita's building. He saw protesters throw rocks at storefronts, at cars, at churches, at apartment windows. He saw cops take armed suspects into custody and soldiers fire into darkened alleys. He saw thugs overturn police cars and break into businesses. He saw homeless women huddle in the shadows between buildings and homeless men cowering behind grocery store garbage bins. He saw two cops running from a group of men waving sticks and knives and what looked like swords. He saw a soldier save a street kid from a group of muggers. He watched a cop punch a young man and push him to the ground and kick him in the head. Throughout all this, he kept his distance, slinking along shadows, listening for voices. He hid in doorways and alleyways and gangways, and always, he returned to the apartment in case Isabel and Lita made it home.

He now crouches behind the azaleas, his back against the cedar siding of a small house, one of the few single-family dwellings to have survived. The ground is damp and musty, with a thick ancient feel. He hears the murmur of voices from inside, a low secretive rumble. A dank breeze sifts through the branches and fills him with a cold dread. He stands. Sucks in air, wet, heavy, laced with gunpowder and tear gas.

How could this all have happened so quickly, with such ease? A few days ago, there were a few protesters, perhaps some agitators, but generally the world seemed a sane place. Now everyone is an enemy, with the fabric that held society together ripped to shreds, within a matter of hours. Is that all it takes? Really? Can people so easily revert back to savagery and have nothing that makes them human survive?

The breeze softens and stillness envelops him. The hairs on his neck stand up and his legs feel suddenly weak. He creeps out from behind the shrubs. Most of the streetlamps have been shot out, except one on the next block. It mingles with the soft outline of lights around the closed window shades, a world evaporated into uneasy shadows and ill-defined lines.

Footsteps, almost imperceptible, move furtively toward him from down the street. He holds his breath and backs into the bushes. A figure appears, bulky, off-balance, darting between shadows, no more than a silhouette. His heart pounds, his skin raw and damp. The figure moves through a stray beam of light. Lita, holding Lucas so close they could be one.

He calls softly. "Lita."

She doesn't respond. He calls again, louder. She stops. Her head darts around. He steps out from the bushes. "It's me, Alonzo."

She whispers in frantic short syllables. "What the hell are you doing here?"

"Looking for Isabel. Making sure you're both alright."

Lita squeezes Lucas in closer. "Not here." She scurries across the street. He follows and waits while she unlocks the gate to the building's courtyard. It opens with a harsh squeak. They slip inside.

He whispers, "Where is she?"

"Home. She headed home." A dim entry light, covered with cardboard, casts long shadows across the courtyard and highlights her face. Her eyes shine with tears. "I told her not to go."

"But how? That doesn't make sense."

"On foot. She's heading toward the I-90 bridge. Plans to walk across." Lita sets Lucas down, clutches his tiny hand. He stares at Alonzo with wonder.

"But that's miles from here, and many more miles to our place."

"I know. I know. But I couldn't stop her. And I couldn't go with her, not with him." She nods toward Lucas.

"If you two had just stayed here, we could have avoided all this. I've been searching for you all night."

Her eyes flare and she speaks through gritted teeth. "Who the hell asked you to come find us? If it weren't for you, Isabel wouldn't have been here in the first place."

"Because of me?"

"Of course, because of you."

"You're the one trying to sabotage our marriage."

She leans into him, their noses almost touching. "I'm not your wife. I don't have to listen to your crap. Now get the hell out of here."

He jerks back. He's never felt such frustration. Or anger. "Just tell me which way she headed."

Lita pulls Lucas up next to her. "She walked down Twelfth. She was going to follow it to Jackson or something, then head toward the bridge."

"Twelfth?"

"She thought it would be safer."

"That's nuts. What were you two thinking?"

"Us? I told her not to go."

"You should have tried harder."

"Your wife has a mind of her own. Or haven't you noticed?"

What's that supposed to mean?"

"You figure it out."

Alonzo steps nearer, then pulls back and glares at her out of the corner of his eyes.

"How long ago?"

"I just left her at Thirteenth and John. Ten minutes tops."

He flings open the gate and races into the street, catching the sudden glint of headlights. A truck rumbles around the corner. He runs for the other side and dives into the bushes. The light spreads out behind him like a flooding river.

Stephanie

The phone rings, rattles the nightstand. Stephanie bolts upright and stares into the void, reaching out of a half-panic dream state. Something has happened to Georgia. She knows it.

She fumbles for the phone, knocks over her book—*The Poetics of Space*—splat against the floor. Eyes spin. Adrenaline spews. She reaches again and collides with the receiver, sends it tumbling over, down onto the book, a second splat, then flat against pine.

The phone lets out another ring, deadened against the wood.

She leans over the edge of the bed and gropes through the shadows. A third ring. Her fingers land on the antenna, cold plastic. She snatches it up and talks into the receiver, her voice breathless, shaky. "Yes, yes. I'm here. I'm here."

"Stephanie?"

"Yes, Stephanie. What's happened?"

"This is Roger, at the ER."

"Roger? What time is it? What's wrong?"

"Nothing's wrong, at least not in the way you're thinking. But we need your help."

"My help?" She shakes her head, takes a breath. "Roger, you do remember I don't work there anymore."

"You're still current, right?"

"I don't see—"

"We're desperate, Steph. We need you. The entire city has gone berserk, and they've all landed in the ER. Every hospital in the city is overflowing. We're calling in everyone we can."

"But I retired over a month ago. I've already forgotten more than I remember."

Her tone must have carried some sense of acquiescence because Roger says, "A police car will be by to pick you up. Be ready in fifteen minutes."

"A police car?"

"State of emergency, or some such nonsense. It's the only way to get you here."

"This is insane."

"Tell me about it." Screams erupt in the background. "I've got to go. See you in a few." He hangs up.

She stares at the receiver, then returns it to its base. She moans and switches on a light.

"Christ, fifteen minutes."

She jumps out of bed and digs an old pair of blue scrubs out of a box in the corner, one of several destined for Value Village. She pees, splashes water in her face, pulls on her uniform. She runs a brush through her hairs and downs a glass of orange juice. She brushes her teeth and shuts off the light and slips out of the house.

The night is unnaturally dark. Only a glimmer of light slips out from the closed shades surrounding the park. The streetlamps are dead, inside and out of the park, and almost no breeze. A fine mist fills the air. Droplets touch her cheeks, her neck, pinpricks of ice, concrete, real, everything else a dream, entwined with the distant sirens and popping noises that sound too much like gunshots.

She stands close to the charred remnants of her fence, ready to spring back to the house in the event of danger. An eerie stillness pervades the space around her, the shadows all twisted, their outlines vague and unnatural.

She hears movement, a brief rustling, a bend in the darkness, near the corner of her lot. She freezes, tries not to breathe. The sounds move toward her. Then the explosion of phlegm.

Parker.

She moves quickly up to the fence. She can barely make out his tall narrow frame, the dim outline of Sonuvabitch draped over his shoulder, the cat's eyes glowing green against a black void.

"Parker! What are you doing out here?" Her whisper is frantic, pitched high.

He starts, looks around, glances up toward the sky, finally zeroes in on her.

"You seen Myron?" His voice hisses like a leaking tire.

"He's missing?"

"No. This is a game show and you're one of the contestants. Of course, he's missing. Why else would I be asking?"

"I haven't seen him, but you should be inside."

"And you?"

"I'm heading to the ER. I just got called in."

"That bad?"

"That bad."

He hesitates. "If you should see Myron down there..."

"I'll let you know. In the meantime, a cop car's on its way to pick me up. You probably don't want to be out here."

"Probably not."

He disappears back into the shadows. She hears his rickety gate open and thump closed, his heavy steps shuffle along the side of the house.

She waits. More gunshots, this time closer. She stares up Boxer Way and down Eleventh. No car in sight. She should have told Roger she couldn't do it, but that wasn't her way. And he knew it. He probably even realized she'd want to be there. And he'd have been right. She'd forgotten what it's like to be needed, to have a part to play, an important part. Maybe she's not ready to be put out to pasture after all.

At least she doesn't have to worry about Georgia, not at the moment, anyway. Stephanie's not sure why she thought of Georgia when the phone rang. Caring must be a hard habit to break. But Georgia's over on the Kitsap Peninsula, visiting Jen and Claudia, tucked away on their nice little farm.

A car turns off Pine and onto Eleventh. The headlights drill a tunnel before them, the glare growing harsher by the second. It must be the cop car, but she can't be certain. She crouches down behind of clump of torn shrubs, her heart pounding, her breath growing short. The vehicle quickly reaches Boxer Way and races around the corner, coming to a screeching stop in front of her house, a plain sedan, dark. The interior lights pop on, a lone cop behind the wheel. Rocky.

Stephanie hops over the downed pieces of fences and rushes to the curb. Rocky climbs out and walks around. They meet in the left headlight.

R. H. Sheldon

"Back so soon."

She shrugs, turns away.

Stephanie climbs into the car. A loud popping sound echoes up the street, coming from several blocks over.

Rocky drives. They pass groups of soldiers, their trucks, jeeps, armored vehicles, grouped along intersections, patrolling the streets. A helicopter hovers low, its searchlight scanning the fronts of buildings, down sidewalks, and along roadways. The police radio squawks incessantly, call after call, lootings, fires, break-ins, beatings.

Stephanie glances toward Rocky, her face cast in an eerie glow, the dashboard's greenish light, her mouth locked in a grim frown, a glint of fear in her eyes.

"I've never seen anything like this," Stephanie says. "It's all so insane."

The helicopter closes in. The winds whip up around them, the cop car suddenly awash in spotlight.

Rocky says, "I've already been stopped three times. Even when they learn who I am, they treat me like shit. You'd think they'd at least give us a break."

"Us?"

"The police."

"Not one of us common folk?"

Rocky flashes a look of contempt, quickly collects herself. "We're just trying to do our jobs."

Stephanie turns away, stares out her window. Several soldiers corner a young black man. They shout at him, shove him against the wall. Rocky drives slowly past them, stares straight ahead.

They approach Broadway and Madison, where the soldiers have set up a barricade. A dozen of them huddle near a monstrous truck, bathed in floodlights, their helmets casting diamond-edged shadows across their faces.

One steps out, waves the car to slow down. Rocky eases off the gas. The car rolls to a stop. She opens her window and turns down the radio and flashes her badge. The helicopter hovers above, the wash sending dust and debris flying. The air carries a metallic smell, fused with machine oil and gunpowder.

Stephanie feels the fear twist through her, rising up to her throat in a putrid, sour taste.

The soldier wears a bulky gray-green camouflage uniform, black leather boots, a helmet locked down tight. He shines the flashlight in their faces, the beam a searing white laser.

"Didn't you just pass this way?" His voice is throaty, dark, full of threat.

Rocky bites down, speaks between gnashing teeth. "I need to get her to Elliott Bay Medical Center."

The solider aims the light directly at Stephanie. "Who's she?"

"An ER nurse. Stephanie Schmidt."

The soldier scans the car with his light. He leans toward the back and searches the floor behind the front seat, the beam moving in slow, lazy spirals. He waves them on with a flick of his light.

Rocky eases forward until she's past the soldiers. She mumbles, "Fucking assholes."

They arrive quickly at the front entrance of the ER. Rocky pulls up. Stephanie opens the door and climbs out. She thanks Rocky for the ride, but receives no reply. Rocky pulls away.

Stephanie stands before the doors and draws in a breath, cops on either side, six in all, watching, waiting, all men, with looks like that of the soldier, grim, angry, full of hate. She steps up to the doors. They slide open and she walks into the waiting room.

A wall of steamy air hits her face on, full of blood and vomit. People talk and moan, scream and sob. They stand, sit on chairs, sprawl out on the floor. They lean against walls, against tables, against each other. Cops surround them, stand guard over a few, carefully study the rest. Staff members scurry from patient to patient, from the front desk to the ER, from the ER to the waiting room, all of them harried, stressed, ready to break.

Stephanie winds her way toward the ER, suddenly weak, afraid. Several cops eye her. Say nothing. Then one steps toward her.

Roger erupts out of the ER, sees her, rushes through the mayhem. "Stephanie, thank God." He grabs her hand. "Come on back."

He leads her past the two cops guarding the door.

Inside is much like out there. Patients wait everywhere, in gurneys, on chairs, on the floor. They hold wounds, stare into space, cry into their shirts, struggle to breathe.

Roger leads her through the throng and toward the central desk. They stand next to a patient lying on a gurney, her head bandaged, her face ashen, swollen, her arms and neck bruised, her

R. H. Sheldon

clothes soaked in blood. A monitor measures rapid and irregular heartbeats. A liter of blood flows into her arm.

Stephanie glances at Roger.

"Word is, she got run over by a truck down by the Market. Military vehicle of some sort. No one's admitting anything."

"And she's just sitting here?"

"On her way to the OR. Soon as they can make room."

Stephanie shakes her head. It's worse than she imagined. She looks down at the patient again, past the ghostly skin and lifeless body. Then she sees it, the lines around the eyes, the strands of hair sticking out from the bandage.

Georgia, lying on the gurney, gasping for air like a fallen angel.

Olympia

Bellamy is more useless than ever. She refuses to stand, move. She lies in the shadows, huddled up against the shrubs, whimpering like an injured dog. What else can Olympia do but wait with her, hiding with her, amid the ruins that have become this city?

After the explosion on stage, after they ran, after Bellamy fell off her platform boots, they tried to make their way out of downtown, but first the crowds prevented them, then the violence, then Bellamy's refusal to hobble another step, even though Olympia supported much of her daughter's weight, despite her own injured shoulder, despite her own fear.

They made it only a few blocks before Bellamy collapsed, and here they've been hiding from the roving thugs—the criminals, the soldiers, the police—a small courtyard near Seventh and Pine, enclosed in a short brick wall, dwarfed by a concrete tower, an ugly pile of prefab slabs, like a bleached car radiator, ready to spill over.

That was hours ago. It's now the middle of the night, with no light nearby. The building looms like a giant black tombstone against the surrounding gloom.

A light breeze blows off the Sound, pushing out the lingering smells of gunpowder and pepper spray. Gunfire riddles the air, only a few blocks away, followed by screams, then silence.

Olympia whispers, "How's your ankle doing?"

R. H. Sheldon

"Throbbing like hell, Mom. Worse than ever." Bellamy sobs. "How long will we have to stay here?"

Bellamy has asked the same question at least a dozen times, and each time Olympia tells her she doesn't know. What she'd like to tell Bellamy is that they could have already been home, safe and warm, if Bellamy wasn't acting so Bellamy, but Olympia resists and instead says, "Let's just turn ourselves into the next soldiers we see so we can get you some help."

Bellamy's whispers become frantic. "I can't turn myself in. I can't. They'll put me in that Guatemala place." Her sobbing grows louder.

"Hush, now. No one's going to put you in Guantanamo."

"Where?"

"Guantanamo."

"There, either."

"You haven't done anything wrong."

"Doesn't matter." She moans.

Olympia should just let her cry and carry on and make all the noise she wants so the soldiers are sure to discover them.

The breeze picks up, chilling the night even more. A mist shrouds the city and washes out what little light works its way down from the surrounding neighborhoods. They huddle closer to the line of shrubbery, the branches prickly and full of water.

Olympia hears footsteps, coming up Seventh, soft and muffled at first, but slowly growing louder, a small group from the sound of it, their movements quick and furtive, slapping against the wet pavement.

The sounds grow louder. Bellamy whispers, "What now? Who is it? What do we do?"

Olympia covers her daughter's mouth. Bellamy bites her.

"Quiet, you fool!"

Bellamy whimpers.

The intruders grow closer. Each step echoes against the building. They move, stop, move, stop. Olympia catches a whiff of marijuana.

"This is fuckin' awesome." A young man's voice, a kid, that nasally stoner sleepy sound.

"Yeah, sick, man. We can like do fuckin' anything."

They grow closer. Other voices close in, maybe a half-dozen, a roving gang, dodging cops, soldiers, looking for trouble, hoping for trouble.

Olympia can feel Bellamy's body grow rigid, just like her own. The group moves into the courtyard and stands around a small tree. One of them rips off several of the lower branches.

They pass around a pipe. The lighter flickers with each hand-off. The sweet smoky smell of pot drifts into the bushes. They pass the pipe around several times. They laugh. They snicker. They call each other faggots. They joke about finding themselves some pussy. They smoke more.

They must have a bottle, too, passing it around.

One says, "Gimme that. Need it after what happened to Tank and the others."

"I told them not to throw rock. 'No rocks," I said. 'No rocks. 'No firecrackers.' I told them."

"Just shut up and give me the bottle."

"I told them."

"Quit being such a pussy. They knew what they were doing."

The others grumble.

"Just give me the bottle." He drinks, gasps, gags, complains about the cheap whiskey. Another one pats him on the back. The bottle flies out of the group and slams against the building. Glass splinters into a million nights. More laughter. More jokes about butt fucking. More calls for young and juicy snatch.

They find a beat-up overcoat lying on the ground. One says something about a car and gasoline, disappears. Minutes later he's back. They grab the broken branches and wrap strips of cloth around them. Makeshift torches. The flames burn orange, cast savage glows across their hooded faces.

Olympia dares not move, dares not breathe. The boys mean business, and all she can do is pray that she and Bellamy find their way out of here.

One calls out, "Next bitch I lay my hands on, I'm gonna drill her till she's nothing but a carcass."

The others laugh, clap their hands. Bellamy gasps.

Olympia is about to muffle her, but it is too late.

The group grows quiet. One steps forward, carrying the torch before him. "Now what do we have here?"

He crouches down and holds the flame closer. The flare burns into Olympia's eyes and blinds her to everything around her. "Boys, looks like we found ourselves some dessert after all."

Parker

P arker stands at the front corner of his house, near the heap of rotten timber that was once his porch. He holds Sonuvabitch on his shoulder, petting him absently on the back. The light on the piano glimmers dimly through the window and mixes with the muffled lights from nearby apartments, barely cutting through the endless intersection of shadows.

Fog pushes into the city off Puget Sound and quickly blankets Capitol Hill, moving so fast it seems unnatural, adding to the unnatural darkness that surrounds him. Smoke permeates the air, but he can't identify the source or its direction, as though fusing with the suffocating fog.

He sets Sonuvabitch on the ground. The cat meows. Parker huddles close to the house and reaches inside his robe and pulls a cigarette out of his shirt pocket. He lights it quickly, taking little pleasure in the assault on his lungs. But how can he stop now? What would be the point?

He draws in a long drag and soon erupts into a round of hacking. He leans against the house. He gasps. He coughs. He sucks in air. He spits out long streams of phlegm. He drops the cigarette and grinds it out with his foot, his father's slipper clinging by a thread.

An eruption of voices, west of the park, on the side opposite the fountain, then silence, then a drawn out *whoosh*. The fiery burst rocks the ground and sends shockwaves through his body. Sparks fly into the night, a massive Roman candle. More shouting. Much laughter. Then blackness. Malignant. Malicious. Complete.

A power transformer lays in that direction, just this side of Broadway. Parker has no idea how large an area has been affected, but it doesn't matter. He's stuck here in the dark, shaken, shaking, on his own. Isn't that what he's always wanted? No interfering neighbors? No irritating roommates? No intrusions of any kind? Maybe that's what death is all about—at long last to be left in peace.

He reaches to his shirt pocket for another cigarette, grabs the pack with trembling hands. He fumbles with the wrapper, cellophane crackling. His heart races. His fingers twitch. The pack flies out of his hands and spills out in the cold wet darkness.

"Shit. Shit. Double-shit."

Sonuvabitch squeaks and meows and squeezes in next to his leg. Parker bends over and pushes the cat away, his hips on fire, his back about to snap. He combs through the weeds and porch debris, but finds only a wayward whiskey bottle and a tin can slimy and sticky and smelling like a rotting carcass. He struggles to pull himself upright, using the wall for support. He rubs his hands on his pants. He fumbles in his shirt pocket for his lighter, locates it, pulls it out. His fingers twitch and flick it out into the void.

"Goddamn it!"

He leans against the house to think. He sighs. He spits. He picks his nose. He tries to think some more. But he's a train too weak for this pass.

Then he remembers. Myron keeps a headlamp near his bed, on top of a pine crate he calls his dresser.

Parker turns and feels for the corner of the house. He gropes his way along the side toward the back of the building. He hears the cat creep along behind him, taking comfort in this, though he cannot say why.

Just when he reaches the back corner, his hand catches a splinter, cutting like a knife. He feels his palm with his other hand, locates the protruding culprit and yanks it out. He pulls his palm to his mouth, the taste of blood, his wounds complete.

He works around the house toward the back steps. His knee knocks into the invisible railing. Pain shoots through his leg and he nearly crumples to the ground. He uses the railing to steady himself, then pulls himself around and up the few steps and through the open door. He creeps through the kitchen, the refrigerator and cabinets his guideposts. He slides into the living room.

He locates Myron's dresser and feels around for the headlamp. He finds it quickly, in the back corner where Myron always keeps it. He switches it on. A rush of emotions overwhelms him. Tears well up in his eyes. He reminds himself that's he's prone to allergies, blinks several times. Sonuvabitch squeaks and rubs up against his leg.

They go back outside. Light governs the ground before them. He locates his lighter, then his cigarettes, salvaging what he can from the encroaching moisture. The wetter ones he carefully harvests and places on a dry plank next to the house.

He heads to the maple and drops to the ground, indifferent to the cold and wet. The bark against his back is like a salve, the dirt his only reality. He lights a cigarette and turns off the headlamp. Sonuvabitch climbs onto his lap and purrs. Parker pats the cat on the head.

The cigarette's glow provides an odd calming warmth, brings him into focus, offers peace. Perhaps it's just the nicotine. This afternoon, he returned from downtown in a state of complete agitation, not even sure how he made it through the panicked mob. He just kept walking without looking or listening or thinking, ignoring gangs gathering, windows shattering, soldiers soldiering, survivors crying for help. He walked like a horse wearing blinders, aiming for one destination, his sane and safe sanctuary, his fortress against all the madness and violence and absurdity that had taken hold. And once he arrived, he stripped off his clothes and drank the last few swallows of Jack and dropped into bed and slept all afternoon and into the evening, waking with a throat raw and lungs burning and eyes stinging with tears, which he, like now, attributed to his allergies.

He climbed out of bed and headed downstairs to talk to Myron, but Myron was not there, so Parker sat and waited and listened to the haunting sounds of the night, believing this must all be a dream from which he was destined to wake.

Now he is awake and Myron is still nowhere to be seen. He had mentioned heading downtown to the protest party, but Parker has no idea whether he actually got there and, if so, whether he got out.

"I got out."

The voice explodes through the darkness like a detonated transformer. Parker squeezes up against the trees and shivers.

Sonuvabitch jumps off his lap and disappears into the darkness. Parker fumbles around for the headlamp, finds it, flicks it on.

Myron stands before him grinning like an adolescent at a carnival sideshow.

"Myron! Where the fuck have you been?"

"Where the fuck have I been? I've been everywhere, Parker Davis."

R. H. Sheldon

Bellamy

They grab her by her hair and drag her out of the bushes. They stand her up and parade her across the wet brick, like ice against her naked feet.

They shove her from one punk to the next, whooping and hollering and rejoicing in their conquest. They squeeze her breasts, grab her ass, her crotch. They wave the torches in her face. They poke and prod and pinch and pull. They land drunken kisses on her face and her neck and her nipples. Her ankle burns and throbs. Pain shoots up her leg. She screams for help. They laugh. She begs for mercy. They laugh. She cries. They laugh.

One draws near, inches from her face, and unbuttons his pants. Fear grips her like a fever, her body locked in panic.

Her mother struggles to free herself. She swings her arms. She grabs and kicks. They throw her down on the brick. They punch her and kick her. They laugh at her and spit on her. She struggles to escape. One holds her down with his boot, pressing her injured shoulder. She cries out. He kicks her in the head.

Something happens in Bellamy, something deep and dark, welling up like burning lava, ready to shoot out, another spirit, possessing, controlling. She lets out a scream, not of fear, but of war, a shrieking rebel, a warrior in pursuit.

Strength surges through her body. Power swells through her limbs. She plunges forward. She kicks and punches and scratches, all the time yelling and screaming in a high-pitched cry. She kicks one guy in the nuts so hard she thinks she has killed him. He keels over, writhes in pain, whimpers and cries for help. She picks up his torch and uses it as a sword. She bats another guy in the head with a loud thump. His hood catches fire. He screams and runs into the darkness, his head shooting off sparks. The others come at her. She hits another one. Her torch leaves a trail of fire and soon his sweatshirt is immersed in flames. The remaining three surround her and slowly circle. She turns with them, lunges out with her torch. They close in slowly. She twists round. Her foot catches an uneven brick, her bad ankle. It gives out. She falls, drops the torch.

They pounce on her, punch her in the face, her stomach. They tear off her clothes, pin her against the wet brick. They curse. They grin. They snicker with delight. Two hold her against the ground. A third pulls down his pants and climbs on top of her. He grabs her by her hair and rubs against her body. She struggles. She screams. He slaps her. She spits in his face. He punches her in the jaw so hard the world turns sideways. Pain shoots through her skull, knives into her brain. Then she sees it, a glowing white light, too bright to turn away, too bright to see. She hears men shouting, running, rapid popping sounds, a rush of motion around her. Then blackness, like an icy river, carrying her away.

R. H. Sheldon

Alonzo

Alonzo dives into the bushes, the truck's light just skirting him. He lands in the same spot where he waited for Isabel, only now he isn't crouching, but lying flat on his back. His pants soak up water from an errant puddle that smells of dog piss, turning his ass frigid and numb.

The truck crawls past, engine roaring, its headlights burning a hole into the night. He hears voices from inside the truck, a radio, blaring out updates and commands. Panel lights cast an orange glow on the driver, his face aimed straight ahead, stern, unwavering. The truck belches out a cloud of diesel. Alonzo chokes off his cough.

The truck reaches the corner and turns toward Fifteenth. Alonzo creeps out from behind the bushes. Lita is nowhere to be seen. He hesitates, looks up and down the street, then sets off in the direction of the truck. When he reaches Harrison, he drops down to Thirteenth and heads south, leaping from shadow to shadow, one form of darkness to the next.

Why would Isabel have set off on foot? Why would she have headed this way, toward the police station, toward the worst of the trouble? It's all so insane. All of it.

He reaches East John. Down the hill, to the west, a barricade blocks Broadway, the intersection flooded with lights and the grumble of a half dozen engines. Up the hill, in the opposite direction, a smaller barricade blocks Fifteenth. Between the two,

John is lifeless and for the most part without light, an avenue of darkness, stretching up the side of Capitol Hill.

He rushes across the street and stands in the blackest of the shadows, behind a small camellia bush, with a low skirt of leafy branches. He pants, strains to see around him, listen for clues. Nothing. No one.

He crawls out from behind the bush into a different shade of dark, then continues his trek south. Light seeps out from behind the blinds of a few apartments, just enough to direct him forward, but little more.

When he reaches Boxer Way, he stands at the corner and stares in the direction of Parker's house. He can make out only vague outlines, but he can sense the place, almost smell it. Yet it's not the house he smells. It's smoke, something burning, but he can't tell where. It's the smoke that gets him the most, that plunges through him the deepest sense of fear.

Maybe Parker's house is burning. How fitting. The man who started it all—the riots, the looting, the state of emergency—now faced with a house little more than ashes. The washed-up drunk with the crazy roommate and deranged cat, with a house in shambles and a life even worse, suddenly accountable at long last.

If only the universe worked that way. If only the world didn't seem so unbalanced, so insane.

He tries to shake off the sense of foreboding and decide which way to go—down to Twelfth or continue on Thirteenth. But then he hears a loud *whoosh,* followed by an explosion so fierce he can feel it in the ground. To the west, somewhere past Parker's house, the sky lights up briefly, glaring against the low-hanging clouds, followed by a fountain of sparks taller than the nearby apartments, a good four stories into the air, but the sparks die quickly and along with them any remaining light, leaving him in total darkness.

He twists around and looks up what should be Boxer Way and then up what should be Thirteenth Avenue. The only light comes from the glowing spots above the military blockades.

He hears sirens and radios and the rumble of trucks, close enough, but not so close to make him run. Another round of shouting. Then gunfire. Then a strange stillness that fills him with an even greater dread. He feels himself shiver, hoping it is only him, and not the world around him.

He might have remained that way for hours, frozen in fear and uncertainty, his pants wet, his legs like ice, the explosion still

R. H. Sheldon

ringing in his ears, but he spots the dim glimmer of lights, coming from a few windows along Thirteenth, candles, perhaps, flashlights, even oil lamps, providing at least some level of guidance.

He creeps forward, trying to make out hidden obstacles, fences and stairs, shrubs and trees, the occasional rock, the mislaid toy, the abandoned bike. There's no telling where Isabel might be or what might have happened to her. Maybe she headed in a different direction, or returned to Lita's apartment.

He makes steady and slow progress, until he finally reaches Pine Street. He stands beside a massive six-story apartment building, still under construction, the silhouette looming large. More Lockhart construction.

He hears noise from down the street, just around the corner. He creeps along the wall, beneath a tower of scaffolding, and peers around the building toward Twelfth and Pine. The police station sits on the southwest corner, flooded by light. Cops swarm like bees. Soldiers surround them, armed and ready. Radios squawk and two cops bark out orders, one man and one woman. No one appears to be listening.

Alonzo eyes the scaffolding above him, a web of crisscrossing struts that disappear into the low clouds. He moves toward the back of the building, away from the light. He feels for a foothold and pulls himself onto a low rung. He lifts his leg and wedges his foot into a crevice where two bars cross. He slowly climbs up the side, negotiating the invisible posts and struts, feeling the strain in his arms, his back, his legs, cursing himself for not staying in better shape.

He eases over a thick rail, its edges barely a glimmer, and gropes for the platform that he assumes wraps around the building, level with the second floor. His fingers land on what seem to be rough planks, the makeshift floorboards typical of a construction site. He only hopes he's right.

He eases onto one of the planks, still clutching the rail, and shifts more weight onto the board. He releases one hand and gropes for the rail on the other side. He locks his fingers around the cold steel. He walks, one cautious step after the next, loosening his grip only long enough to slide his hands forward.

The planks feel relatively stable, surprisingly so, but he can see nothing between him and the corner, where the glow of the floodlights catch the edge of the metal. He places each step before him with surgical precision, feeling for something solid before shifting his weight forward, his movements short, a gentle rocking back and forth.

By the time he reaches the corner, his heart races and sweat covers his forehead. He lets out his breath in a loud gasp. A surge of panic rushes through him and he bites down, catching his tongue, the blood oozing in his mouth. But no one heard him. How could they, with all that racket?

The scaffolding follows the front of the building all the way to the far corner, the one nearest to the police station. There's more light in front, certainly, but much of the platform remains in shadow, and given how the lights are arranged around the intersection, all pointed toward the center, it would be difficult for anyone to see much outside that circle. Even so, he plans to take no chances.

He makes his way to the opposite corner, the planks now vague outlines. He studies the scene before him. At the center of the intersection sits a large van-type vehicle—a modern, oversized paddy wagon—its warning lights spinning and flashing, the left side facing Alonzo. A policeman pulls open the back door. Several officers herd a group of people out of the station—about twenty, men, women, teenage boys and girls—and load them into the vehicle, all with looks of panic and confusion and fear. Then Alonzo spots her. Isabel. She hovers near the rear, her eyes pointed toward the ground, shuffling behind the others. A dozen cops now surround them, their clubs drawn. Behind them stand more cops with pistols. Behind them, the soldiers with their automatic rifles.

What should Alonzo do? Try to rescue her? How? If he did try anything, he'd certainly be arrested like the others, like Isabel. Or worse still, he might get shot. But what sort of husband would he be if he did nothing? What sort of man would that make him?

At least Isabel is safe. Better than walking the streets, facing gangs, criminals, rogue cops. And if he's out here, he can do something. If he's arrested, what then? Yet this is his wife. He's supposed to be protecting her. It's his duty. He can't just stand here and watch them take her away.

The police quickly load the rest of the prisoners, Isabel included, and slam the doors shut. The driver starts the engine. Black smoke billows out of the exhaust. The van eases forward, heading south on Twelfth. Soon it's out of sight.

Alonzo drops to the planks and buries his face in his hands. What sort of man, indeed.

Olympia

The only thing Olympia can say with certainty is that she hurts. Her shoulder hurts. Her ribs hurt. Her back hurts. Even her knees hurt.

Given the beating she received, she's lucky it's not worse. And lying on a gurney in an ER is a hell of a lot better than lying in the streets, though she so wasn't so sure when they arrived. The staff raced around like chickens about to lose their heads, while police roved the corridors and patrolled the entries. Patients spilled out of every crack and corner, calling for help and attention and relief. It seemed more like a cartoon circus than a top-notch medical facility.

Bellamy had been steered directly into the ER, with Olympia left sitting in the waiting room. That was almost eight hours ago. But her turn finally came and now she lies in one of those cubicles, the curtain left partially open. The worst of the chaos has subsided, though the staff still race from cubicle to cubicle, taking care of the leftovers.

The whole place smells like rubbing alcohol and blood and looks like it was ransacked by one of the roving gangs. Trash overflows. Wrappers are strewn across the floor. Equipment sits haphazardly in any available nook.

She feels exhausted from head to foot, and sore every inch of the way, ready to get out of here and get home. But she understands the pressure everyone is under, and if she has to wait, she has to wait. Her bigger concern is Bellamy. No one has been able to give her an answer. All she's gotten are vague remarks that Bellamy should be fine.

A nurse steps in, a petite young guy who appears fresh out of nursing school. His name tag reads *Frank,* and he looks as though he hasn't slept in a month, the sagging shoulders and drooping eyes, set in dark-circled pockets.

"A doctor will be in shortly," he says, "but it appears you've cracked a few ribs, nothing too serious, though, and despite how sore your shoulder might be feeling, you don't seem to have caused any more damage. You've been banged up some, no doubt about it, but if all goes well, we can get you out of here shortly."

Olympia tries to prop herself up. Every part of her body screams. Banged up *some?*

"Listen," she says, "what I'm most concerned about is my daughter. No one seems to be able to help me."

"I'm sorry, but I can't..."

"Please, I need to know what's going on."

He sighs, looks at his watch.

"We were admitted the same time, attacked by the same gang of hoodlums."

This seems to raise a reaction. "What's her name?"

"Bellamy Burns-*hyphen*-Culpepper."

"Hyphen what?"

"Culpepper."

"Okay, I'll be right back." He slips out of the cubicle.

Within a few minutes he returns and tells Olympia that Bellamy has been admitted in the hospital and is doing fine, but she has a broken jaw and might require surgery. "And that's about all I can tell you."

"What about the baby?"

"Baby?"

"Yes, Bellamy is pregnant. Not sure how far along, but I believe several months."

"You'll have to talk to her about that when you get out of here. Even if I had that information, I couldn't give it out."

"I'm her mother."

"That might be, but there are laws."

"I was the one to sign the papers to admit her."

"Even so, I'm not supposed to..."

"Can't somebody just go up and talk to her? Tell her I'm down here and ask her for an update."

"We don't have anyone to…"

"Please, show some compassion. Rules or not, I'm still her mother."

Frank is about to protest again—and really, she does feel sorry for the guy—but she has no choice. There's no telling how much longer she'll be stuck here. She cocks her head to one side and projects a sympathetic, concerned look, while forming a question with her eyes, a silent *Why won't you help me?* She learned this ploy from her days at the seminary. The director had a chocolate lab that proved the perfect teacher.

Frank relents. "Let me see what I can do."

Olympia eases back into her pillow and closes her eyes. Even her face hurts. But at least Bellamy is safe. That's all that matters. There are worse things than a broken jaw, although Bellamy is not likely to think so.

Thank God those soldiers showed up when they did. The two of them might not have made it out without their help. She needs to come up with a way to show her gratitude. Perhaps she'll preach a sermon about the brave men and women who protect them every day against the evils in this world.

She peers through the half-opened curtain, out into the ER—staff still running between patients, viewing charts, checking computers, rolling gurneys and wheelchairs and futuristic machinery that might have come out of a spaceship. She'll have to mention these people in her sermon as well.

Several nurses stand near the central station holding a heated discussion. Off to the side stand two others, a man and woman, absorbed in a serious discussion. Olympia recognizes her from somewhere, something about the way she holds herself or her mannerisms or something. Then she remembers. Parker's neighbor, the one who helped Olympia when she was shot. What is her name? Frances? Francine? No, that's not right. Stephanie. That's it.

The man says something, his face gentle and full of concern. She stands frozen for several seconds, a stunned look in her eyes, but then she is crying. The man puts his arm around her shoulders and speaks to her. She nods and he leads her out of the room.

Olympia adjusts her position. Pain shoots through her back. Tonight, she plans to drug herself into oblivion.

R. H. Sheldon

Frank returns. He carries a clipboard. "Your daughter is fine."

"You told me that. I was asking about the baby."

"There is no baby."

"No baby?"

"She's not pregnant."

"But she said..."

Frank shakes his head. "I ran up to the recovery room. It was easier than trying to track her down, and I needed a break anyway. She was still groggy and it was tough for her to talk, but she wanted me to tell you there is no baby. She thought it was funny, in fact, though that was probably the anesthesia."

"Could she have miscarried? Is that it?"

"Nope. No baby. No pregnancy."

"But she swore—"

Of course. Bellamy.

"Thank you," Olympia says. "I'm sorry to have wasted your time."

"Like I said, I needed the break. The doc should be right with you." He leaves.

Not pregnant. Ha! Olympia should have known. Next time she'll ask for proof.

She should be relieved, she knows, but she was starting to get used to the idea of having a baby around, her grandkid. Might not have been so bad. Even so, it's probably for the best. It would be hard to build a new church with a baby crawling around. As she often tells her congregation, "God works in mysterious and quite confusing ways."

Parker

It's all so normal, negotiating the stairs, his body a torture chamber, the bottom step wobbly, the railing slick from wear, his solid-gold record, Myron sitting on his bed, reading pamphlets, listening to the radio, Sonuvabitch on his lap. The only thing out of place is the front door, still off its hinges and leaning against the frame.

"Why do you listen to that crap?" He can say that. It's his song that plays.

Myron looks up from the brochure. "It's not crap, Parker. It's your famous song from 1969. 'Last Stand.' Don't you remember?"

Parker nears his chair, snarls, not that he cares one way or the other. The snarl is mostly habit. "Can't you play another station?"

"They're playing your song all day long. They're calling it the movement's anthem."

"What movement?"

"The Parker Davis movement. The movement you started."

"Started? I didn't start any goddamn movement."

Myron flashes his deceptively simple grin and returns to his brochure.

"This is insane. You know that, Myron, right?"

"You've always said the whole world is insane."

"That I did."

Parker drops into his chair, feels into his shirt pocket for a cigarette.

R. H. Sheldon

"Any smokes around?"

"I had not read this part of the church brochure before. It says that everything is an illusion, that we're all playing a game, pretending it's all real. We're like children, letting our imaginations run wild. Alonzo Garcia, the attorney from Bellevue, said the same thing. I wonder if Alonzo heard that from Olympia. Do you think it's a game, Parker?"

"No. I think it's all a nasty joke. A big fat nasty cosmic joke. Now where the hell are my smokes?" Parker wishes that for once an exchange with Myron could be something easy. Or fun. "Myron, my cigarettes."

"I don't smoke."

"I know that, you twit."

Myron is about to reply when a harsh buzz erupts from the kitchen, followed by loud snaps and a low hissing moan. The light on the piano flickers and the radio hisses and crackles and cuts off Parker's famous 1969 song in mid-chorus. The light goes out.

Myron says, "I think we have lost power again, Parker."

"Yes, Myron, that seems to be the case."

"It was out all night. It just came on before you woke up. That's how come I could listen to the radio. But I didn't care about the electricity. I read by the light from the window. If life is all pretend, Parker, why does hurt seem so real?"

Parker stares for a moment, shrugs, searches around the chair for a wayward cigarette, his nerves pricked with toothpicks.

Myron reads.

Sonuvabitch sits up, sniffs the air, and jumps off Myron's lap. He eyes the kitchen door and meows three times.

Myron says, "Yes, you should go outside." He stands and walks to the front hallway. Sonuvabitch follows. Myron pulls the door away from the opening and leans it against the wall, covering Parker's solid gold record. Sonuvabitch stands at the threshold and looks out.

Parker says, "Just go, for Christ's sake. It's freezing in here."

"We need air," Myron says, "especially now."

"Will I ever know what the hell you're talking about?"

Sonuvabitch leaps outside. Parker glances through the window. The cat picks his way through the porch debris and stands out in the weeds.

Myron says, "Go and wait for Stephanie. She'll be home soon."

Sonuvabitch scurries out of the yard.

Parker says, "Now shut the door."

"Better not," Myron replies. He returns to his bed and slips on his sandals and grabs a backpack and fills it with items from his dresser. Parker can see only the headlamp and a toothbrush and a couple books.

"Going somewhere, Myron?"

"Yes, we are."

Parker shakes his head.

Something crashes in the kitchen, followed by a loud, fierce, cracking sound.

Myron says, "We better get going." He slips his pack on his back and moves to the front door and waits.

"What the hell…"

Parker pushes himself out of his chair and shuffles across the living room to the kitchen door. He is about to grab the handle when a small explosion throws it open and tosses him onto the coffee table. The table gives way and crashes to the floor, with Parker on top. He groans and curses and shakes his fist at heaven.

Myron returns to the living room and helps Parker to his feet. "We better get going." He heads to the front door, with Parker right behind him.

Myron climbs out of the house and positions himself on the broken pieces of porch and reaches back to help Parker down.

Parker looks up the stairs. "But what about my stuff?"

"It's just stuff."

Parker glances into the living room, back to the second floor. He hesitates, then wrestles the door away from the wall and lets it drop into the living room. It tumbles over the broken ballerina lamp, bounces off the armchair, and lands with a thump on the coffee table. He grabs his solid gold record and hands it out to Myron. Then Parker crouches down and sits on the doorjamb and wiggles his way off the ledge to the pile of timber. In the back of the house, boards crash and wood crackles.

Parker and Myron walk out to the sidewalk. They stand and face the house. The loud whoosh of flames echoes out of the front door. Black smoke swirls up to the sky, twists below the yellowish clouds, and settles in Parker's lungs. He coughs.

Parker says, "Now what?"

"I'll find a place for you to stay, Parker. You'll be fine."

"And what about you?"

Myron grins the same obnoxious grin he always grins.

R. H. Sheldon

Parker says, "And what about Sonuvabitch?"

"Sonuvabitch will stay with Stephanie for a while. Sonuvabitch loves Stephanie. Stephanie loves Sonuvabitch, and she needs Sonuvabitch right now."

"You're sure?"

Myron studies Parker's eyes. Parker turns away. Myron says, "You love Sonuvabitch, too, don't you Parker Davis?"

Parker feels the flush in his face, which he attributes to the growing fire and growing plume of smoke. He coughs again.

Flames appear through the living room window, lap at the front door. The crackling grows louder. Glass breaks. Timbers fall. Flames consume the roof.

This is it, his last connection to his past. He feels as though being pushed into the earth, the thumb of God, ready to wipe him out. All for a joke.

Myron grabs Parker's arm, helps to support him. "Come, Parker. Let's go get you settled."

"I have no clothes," Parker says.

"We'll get you clothes."

"I have no underwear or socks."

"We'll get you underwear and socks."

"I have no money."

A loud snap breaks free from the house. Wood cracks, sizzles, drops to the ground. The fire relents for a moment, then returns in full force, the house now engulfed. A black cloud hovers over them. Sirens sound in the distance.

They walk.

The streets are quiet, but look almost normal, despite the broken windows and damaged yards and defaced buildings. The military presence is still in evidence—troops patrolling, vehicles waiting—but it seems little more than a precaution compared to yesterday's melee.

No one tries to stop them, or even look at them. No one seems to care. Others walk the streets as well, everyone quiet, cautious, a compromise reached, temporary ceasefire.

Myron leads Parker down to Broadway and up past John. Businesses open. People flitting in and out. A few broken windows and damaged street signs and scattered shards of glass, but most of the buildings intact. If he had not seen all the craziness for himself, he'd hardly know that Seattle had been a city under siege.

At this point, he doesn't give a shit one way or the other. He has no money, no home, no place to go. A few riots more or less hardly make a difference.

"Here we go," Myron says. "They're just about to open."

They stand in front of a bank, a small branch office. Several people hover near the front. A woman on the inside unlocks the door. She wears a navy blue power suit with a well-tailored jacket and skirt and smooth silken shirt as white as crystal snow.

"What are we doing here, Myron?"

"We need some money."

"You can't just walk in and..."

Myron goes inside. Parker shakes his head and follows. When the woman spots Parker, she steps back and nods to the guard, but then she sees Myron and breaks into a sweet angelic smile. "Myron," she says. "How nice to see." She shakes his hand.

He says, "Hello, Janette. This is Parker Davis. His house just burned down." Then he turns to Parker. "This is Janette Zelder. She manages the bank."

She reaches out a hand. "I'm sorry to hear about your house, Mr. Davis."

He returns the shake but says nothing. He feels like fossilized amber. All he can think about is the ugly painting on the other side of the lobby, a picture of the Space Needle, the tip reaching into the clouds, as though about to snag them and drag them down.

Myron says, "We need money so Parker can stay in a hotel for a while, until we find a place for him to live."

Parker says, "What?"

"A hotel. Place to live."

Parker feels suddenly embarrassed for Myron and is convinced that she's just humoring them. Any minute, she'll catch on that Myron has gone off his rocker.

"I'm sorry," Parker says. "My friend has been through a lot these past few days."

Janette the manager looks at Parker as if he's the crazy one. She says, "Sure, Myron. Why don't you both come into my office and I'll get you what you need."

Parker realizes what it is he hates about the painting. The sun is shining. Despite all the clouds and washed out horizons and layers of mystical fog, the sun aims its enormous beams at the Space Needle, lighting it up like a friggin' Christmas tree.

R. H. Sheldon

Alonzo

He wakes in the back seat of his car, his neck an accordion of stiffness and aches. He pushes his jacket aside, now a rumpled heap, climbs out of the car, and slides into the front seat. A cold shiver races through him like channels of ice. He starts the engine and turns on the heat.

People walk along Fifteenth, not many, their looks cautious, actions subdued, but there's a normalcy about the scene that brings comfort. A few broken windows and overturned trash bins, but life returns. Only one store window boarded up, most other places open for business.

He flicks on the radio. A male newscaster describes yesterday's scene—the rally, the riots, the looting, the soldiers and police. By the early morning hours, order was restored, the roving gangs dealt with, the state of emergency lifted, although an eight p.m. curfew remains in effect. No problem. As soon as Alonzo locates Isabel, he'll pick up the kids and head home, and there they'll stay.

The newscaster goes on to describe the reaction of several city council members, who claim the mayor over-reacted, blaming him for the shooting of those unarmed young men, gunned down because of a few firecrackers. Protesters plan to hold a rally at Westlake again, this time calling for the mayor's resignation. Community and church leaders from around the state will hold a vigil for the boys at Boren and Pine this afternoon. They also plan to ask the mayor to step down.

Alonzo grabs the cell phone off the floor. He stares at the blank screen, thinking that the battery has died, but then he remembers. He had shut it down when he lost service. He clicks it on.

While it boots up, he listens to the weather forecast—cool, cloudy, scattered showers—typical of November, typical of half the year.

The phone comes to life. He turns off the radio and checks his calls. Thirteen missed voicemail messages, mostly from his mother-in-law, one from an unknown number. He listens to that. Isabel, shaken, exhausted in the Bellevue jail, where she spent the night. "Don't tell the kids," she says. "Don't tell my mother. I'll wait here till you come get me."

That was eight-thirty. It's now a few minutes after ten. He pulls away from the curb and heads south on Fifteenth, toward the I-90 bridge. The drive is surprisingly uneventful, marked mainly by the patrolling police and soldiers, their presence relatively benign compared to last night, at least that's how it appears on the surface. Yet traffic is barely a trickle, and those who have ventured out creep slowly along the streets, leaving their usual aggression at home. By the time he reaches the interstate on-ramp, he's ready to leave the city for good.

He clicks the radio back on. Same newscaster, same story. Violence broke out in many cities across the country, but nowhere as severe as Seattle. At an earlier news conference, the mayor congratulated the police and the National Guard on their heroic efforts to bring order to the city. The mayor is no longer giving interviews.

Many businesses have reopened this morning and most services restored. The area around Westlake Center, what the mayor referred to as *Ground Zero,* was hit the hardest, along with the neighborhoods immediately surrounding downtown.

The newscaster goes on to say that a number of organizations are calling for an investigation into the behavior of both the police and National Guard. Several class action suits are already in the planning. One activist is quoted as saying, "What we've seen in Seattle is just the beginning. Today we honor our fallen comrades and commemorate the man instrumental in leading us forward, Parker Davis, whose struggle exemplifies the tyranny faced by many in this country."

The newscaster then says that activists from around the country have declared this day to be *National Parker Davis Day* and have claimed his song "Last Stand" as the anthem that will bring them together in the name of freedom and justice for all. "Here it is, ladies and gentlemen, 'Last Stand,' written and recorded by Parker Davis in 1969." The radio plays the same nondescript folksy tune he suffered through yesterday, the simple and familiar melody, the repetitive and adolescent lyrics. "One last stand, one last for man, our last hoorah, our lonely stand." Christ. How pathetic is that?

Alonzo clicks off the radio.

He drives across the miraculously empty floating bridge and continues on I-90 until he hits I-405, where he heads north. He exits at Northeast Fourth Street and travels west to Bellevue City Hall, a rather pointless silver and red building with modern lines and severe angles. He pulls into the driveway. Isabel stands outside the building, ready to have a meltdown. He stops. She climbs into the car.

Alonzo is not sure what to say or how to act. His last meeting with her left him feeling in a state of limbo, uncertain if they had a relationship left at all, even more uncertain whether that was a good thing or bad. And then last night—the search, the arrest. And here he is, picking her up from jail, a total stranger.

He says, "How are you doing?"

"Just get me home."

"Should we pick up the kids?"

"They still at my mother's?"

Alonzo nods.

"Give me a little time. Then I'll go get them."

They drive home in silence. When they arrive, they climb out of the car in silence and continue the silence inside. Isabel trudges up the stairway and disappears into their bedroom. Soon he can hear the shower.

Even with her here, the house feels empty and sterile. Throughout the night, all he could think about was being at home with everyone there and safe, an oasis from the ugly violent world outside, but now it feels more like a prison. The insane night, the crazy past few days, felt more authentic somehow, despite how miserable and confused he was most of the time—even fearful for his life on several occasions—yet there was something real about being out there that defied and mocked his suburban tomb. Perhaps that's what Isabel had been after.

He climbs the stairs and enters the bedroom. He strips off his clothes and slips on his robe, a lightweight black-and-white yukata two sizes too small.

When Isabel steps out of the bathroom, buried in her blue terrycloth robe, he says, "Feeling any better?"

She nods. "A little."

"I need to jump in the shower, too. Then maybe we could pick up the girls together."

"All right." She heads out of the bedroom and down the stairs, her steps feathery soft on the carpet.

He looks down at his palms, filthy and scratched from climbing scaffolding and falling into bushes and rolling around in dirt and crawling through alleys. He goes into the bathroom and turns on the shower, the same way he has a thousand times. He drops his robe and climbs in. The steam rises in a thick band of clouds, making it impossible to see how close he stands to the precipice.

R. H. Sheldon

Stephanie

S he doesn't need a report. As soon as she sees Georgia, she knows. Georgia is a ghost, a shell that once held the woman she loves. The respirator still pumps and a line sinks into her arm, slow drips to keep it running, that's all. The monitor, too, only a witness, the slow erratic heartbeats, almost too weak to detect.

Stephanie takes her hand, lifeless and cold, her skin paper-clay, almost soap. She is a shadow, her breath no longer real, the smell sour, sickly, masked in part by dried blood and anesthetic and hints of Betadine.

Georgia occupies a small cubicle in recovery, outside the ER, where there was little they could do, the injuries too complete, the right side of her face swollen, sallow, the left more emaciated than when she left the house yesterday.

Stephanie sweeps the hair off of Georgia's forehead, like she's done a hundred times, and touches the skin with the back of her fingers, down softly to the bony cheek.

Georgia gasps. Her eyes flutter. Her head turns, more a twitch, and she lets out a long heavy sigh. And then she is gone.

Stephanie stares at the monitor. Soon there is no blood pressure. No pulse. The respirator continues to pump air, expanding her lungs, letting them fall, but the rest of her body lies still.

Stephanie walks out of the room and through the hallway and down the stairs and out of the hospital. She reaches the sidewalk and heads up the hill toward home. The fatigue grinds at her legs and back, pulls her into the ground. She doesn't know what else to do but walk. She doesn't know where else to go but home.

The roads are quiet, with few cars, few people walking the streets. Pockets of soldiers pepper the landscape, but they seem indifferent to her presence, to anything happening around them. Done with their war games and ready to go home. Even the city has rebounded quickly. Most of the damage seems to have fallen on the street lamps, one after the next shot out. Seattle brought to its knees only to ensure darkness.

At Summit Avenue, she cuts over to Seneca and continues up the hill. A tree full of crows protest her arrival. They screech and flutter their wings and rattle the branches. They fly out and circle above her. Some spread to the power lines and rooftops, their cries ferocious and calculating.

She races up the hill and does not stop until she can no longer feel their gaze. She works her way toward Pine and Broadway. The stores are open and people move in and out, not many, but enough to suggest normalcy, despite the damage being more extensive this way, windows cracked, shattered, planters knocked over, garbage bins too, signs knocked down, trees torn to shreds, all so automatic, the destruction.

She walks past the community college. A few protesters remain, but their camp has been decimated, tarps shredded, tents trampled, signs torn to pieces. Several men and women with serious looks and neatly pressed clothes pick through the rubble, federal agents, no doubt. The police stand guard. A bevy of soldiers linger near the intersection.

Once past the camp, she crosses Broadway and cuts through Cal Anderson Park. When she is almost to Boxer Way, she sees a massive fire truck in front of Parker's house, blocking out his entire yard. Red lights flash, but more as a warning than to mark an emergency. With the fountain turned off, she can hear the radio squawk and the low rumble of the diesel engine.

She crosses Boxer Way, giving the truck plenty of room. Then she sees Parker's torn down fence and his trampled yard and the space where once stood his house.

She rushes to the corner of their lots and stands, caught in the wrong moment in a dream. She closes her eyes and opens them.

No house, only a pile of charred wood. The panic rises, as though she has woken up in a strange town in the middle of the night, not knowing where she is, what's she's seeing, the world shifting and molten.

She notices then the smell of burnt timber, the aftermath of a giant bonfire doused by a sudden cloudburst. Slowly the world comes into focus, the smoldering beams, the blackened heap, the clear view to the maple tree's charred remains on the other side. She draws nearer to Parker's yard. Heat radiates from the debris, thin plumes of smoke winding out from pockets of blackened remains.

The gangway between her fence and Parker's house—what used to be Parker's house—are filled with pieces of the fallen wall, two-by-fours cracked into giant splinters, poking through the white pickets like black lances. The rest of the building has imploded in on itself and folded into the basement. Nothing remains.

Parker! What about Parker? And Myron?

"Hey, what are you doing?"

She turns. A cop glares at her, his face full of fatigue, anger. She walks toward him.

"I live there. I just got home." She points to her house and her shredded garden.

He grunts.

Any excuse, his look says.

She repeats herself, points again, then risks a question. "Anyone inside?"

The cop assesses her, studies her scrubs, the blood, stains, tears. "We don't think so," he says. "Where have you been?" His question is not concern, but suspicion.

"Working. Elliott Bay ER. Long night."

He nods and walks away.

Stephanie climbs over her fallen fence and across her yard, all the time eying the next-door lot. She reaches her house and stops. She got everything she wanted. Parker gone. Georgia out of her hair. No more work except for today's odd regression. What else was there?

She feels suddenly shaken and drops to the ground. The air sighs out of her, and she thinks about yesterday's time with Georgia—the frustration, the relief when she left. How is it possible to care so much for someone and still be glad she leaves? How can Stephanie miss her so much, yet know they can never be together?

It's all too much, nothing in her world as it should be. The city has been turned inside out, but on the surface, business as usual.

By the time she left the ER, it had grown relatively quiet. Sure, there was still a lot of cleanup to do and supplies to replenish and equipment to locate, but some sanity at least had been restored. No thanks to her, though. When she received word that Georgia wasn't expected to make it, she broke down in the ER, the first time ever to have done that, as though Georgia were leaving all over again, only this time for real, forever, as though something had been dug out inside her, left hollow, like the air where Parker's house once stood. And here she sits, leaning against her home, in a garden destroyed, a window boarded, a house as empty as a dry well. How can she ever go back inside?

A tear drips down her cheek and falls onto her scrubs, spreading like an infection on the blue cloth. She closes her eyes. Georgia before her, sitting at the kitchen counter, that mischievous frown when they first met, hands touching, the taste of her breath.

Stephanie hears something scrape the ground and opens her eyes. Sonuvabitch. He meows and climbs onto her lap.

"Oh, kitty, I forgot all about you. I'm so glad you're okay."

She cuddles up against him, pets his fur gently. She thinks again of yesterday, her last visit with Georgia, skin pale, cheeks sunken. Only now is Stephanie willing to admit how sick she looked.

The radio from the fire truck crackles, emits voices in short bursts, all indistinguishable, without importance. Even the engine's rumble no longer seems real.

She says, "Come on, Sonuvabitch, let's get inside. I'm freezing my ass off."

She places the cat on the ground and stands, the night catching up, settling in her bones and joints, fueled by sitting in the wet dirt like some brainless fool who doesn't know when to come in out of the cold.

She shivers and enters the house. She stops. She can feel it in the air, the loneliness, a room without hope, without a future. She looks at the places Georgia has been, the empty corner where she piled her clothes, the counter where the tea pot goes, how she sat there, sipping her genmaicha, dripping honey onto the counter, leaving a trail of dishes and cups and dirty clothes. No more, though. Never again.

Sonuvabitch moves toward the counter and meows. Georgia fills a bowl with kibble, another with water, places them on the

R. H. Sheldon

floor without ceremony. The cat breaks the silence with his crunching.

She switches on the radio and drops into her chair. She hears the words "Parker Davis" spoken by a male announcer who sounds too young to be taken seriously, an edgy, nasally, squeaky voice she wants to stomp out. Georgia must have turned the radio to this station.

The DJ praises Parker Davis, the way he has awakened people, brought them together. He describes the protests planned in the next couple days, calls for peaceful gatherings, evokes everyone's constitutional rights. They will hold vigils too, for those lost, injured, arrested by the feds. A memorial service is planned for Fondeaux. Delaney will not be able to attend because he is still in the hospital recovering from his injuries. Jukes also will not be able to attend because he is still in the hospital after nearly choking on a piece of king salmon.

Stephanie considers switching off the radio, but somehow it's her only connection to Georgia. Her last connection. She no longer listens, though, but thinks about when she and Georgia camped in the San Juan Islands, hiked in the Cascades near Stevens Pass, rode the train to Vancouver and splurged on a five-star hotel. But mostly Stephanie thinks about the way she would crawl into bed after getting home late from work and cuddle up next to Georgia and the warm comfort she felt and the safety, no matter how long or exhausting or challenging her shift in the ER.

The announcer breaks through Stephanie's fog when he says, "Once again, 'Last Stand' by Parker Davis."

The song plays. She had forgotten how it sounded. She has not heard it since it came out, over forty years ago. She recalls what a big deal it was, how often she heard it play. She recalls too that she had liked the song, but never thought too much about it beyond that. Like so many songs of that era, it came and went, never to be considered again.

When she hears the song now, with lyrics like "One last stand, one last for man" and "Our last hoorah, our lonely stand," she can see why it would have appealed to all those adolescent brains back then and why it seems so absurd now. Georgia would have loved it.

An ache settles deep in her heart and all she wants to do is curl up in bed and never get out again.

Sonuvabitch saunters across the room and jumps into her lap and together they stare at the space where Georgia would sit at the counter and drink her genmaicha tea and listen to bad music on the radio all day.

R. H. Sheldon

Bellamy

Her mom helps to prop Bellamy up in the bed, hold the mirror before her, the hospital room a prison cell, blue-gray, green-gray, stainless steel and white. If her mouth didn't ache so much, she'd puke up all over this revolting cover, a powder-blue baby blanket as thin as paper.

Bellamy stares into the mirror, her face more hideous than ever. A fractured jaw, minor, they insist, evidenced by the elastic band that wraps around the top of her head and beneath her mouth, crisscrossing with another at her temples. They called it a modified jaw bra. Looks more like a deranged jock strap.

Even with the bandage, she can see how the left side of her face balloons out, the exposed skin tinged with blue and green and mottled yellow, just like her eye, worsening by the hour—the pain right along with it. Her ankle too, throbbing and swollen, a sprain, that's all, so they say.

The remnants of make-up have left streaks across her face, blackened her eye even further, her hair a snarling cascade of knots and twisted clumps. She pushes away the mirror.

"It hurts," she says, "like they're still punching." She speaks through a mouth that can barely open.

Her mom sets the mirror on the tray next to the bed. "I know, dear, but it could be worse."

Bellamy turns away, the pain its own terror.

Silence stretches between them like a vast desert, but then Crystal rushes into the room, an unforeseen cloudburst across the horizon.

"Bellamy. Oh my God. This is like so terrible."

She dives into Bellamy, enfolds her in a hug. The pain shoots through Bellamy's jaw. If she dared open her mouth, the scream would be deafening, but all she can let out is a moan, dark and sinister, as hollow as a crypt.

Crystal recoils. "Oh, shit, Bellamy. Bell. I'm so sorry."

Olympia points to a chair wedged into the corner. "Perhaps you should sit down." For once, Bellamy is glad to have her mom around.

Crystal sits, stares, gulps.

Olympia says, "I'm surprised they let you in."

Crystal looks off to the side, picks at her sleeve. "I told them I was like her sister." She turns toward Bellamy, a look imploring, slightly nauseous. "It's not so far from true, is it, Bell? It's like we really *are* sisters."

Bellamy mumbles, "Yes, Crystal," her voice grainy and rough through the constricting bra.

Olympia says, "We need to let Bellamy rest, Crystal. She's been through a lot."

Crystal's eyes grow wide. "Oh, I know. I've been so worried. Ever since yesterday." She doesn't move.

"Where did you go?" Bellamy mumbles. "Yesterday. Westlake."

"I felt like a mocha, but everywhere was packed, so I headed up Pine. And that's when all the riots started, so I went home. I tried calling, but—"

Bellamy shakes her head, her jaw about to explode. "I need more pain killers."

Olympia takes Bellamy's hand. "I know it hurts, but give the last dose more time to work. You took them only ten minutes ago."

Bellamy pulls back her hand, turns away.

Crystal says, "So how bad is it, Bell? I mean, I know it's bad. It looks real bad. Your face looks like a pound of sausage, you know, the ground up kind with all that fat and weird colors. I've been so worried about you, about your face. I mean, what if it doesn't heal, you know, like my Aunt Agnes? Remember her? I told you all about it—how she got her jaw broken in a car accident and how it wouldn't heal and got all puffy and full of puss and she had tons of surgery and ended up looking like a deformed mutant."

"Crystal, please."

"Sorry, Olympia."

Bellamy wants to punch Crystal, especially because she apologized to her mom, but not to her, even though Bellamy's the one with the friggin' cracked jaw.

Bellamy squeezes out a soft, "Broken jaw," and lifts the ice pack to the side of her face. Perhaps Crystal will take this as her cue to leave.

"A minor fracture," her mom announces, as if there's anything minor about it. "They want to keep her here until tomorrow to make sure the swelling is under control."

"What about her ankle?

"A bad sprain, but she'll live."

"No scars? On her face, I mean."

"No, Crystal."

Her eyes fold down in disappointment. "But what about all that bruising and way her face sticks out?"

"She'll be fine, Crystal."

Crystal fiddles with a string in her blouse, but then a look of horror flashes across her face. "And what about the baby? Is it okay? Is she like going to lose it?"

Just then, like a magician appearing through a secret panel, Myron sticks his head into the room, grins, waves. "Hi Bellamy. Hi Olympia. Hi Crystal. How are you feeling, Bellamy? Is your jaw still sore?"

Olympia stares with a confused look, part wonder, part hostility. Crystal just stares.

Bellamy speaks through her bandage-constricted lips. "It's like all too much, Myron."

Myron cocks his head, looks sideways at her toes. "You'll be better soon, Bellamy. You'll be Bellamy again."

"My jaw and my ankle," she mumbles.

"Good to be reminded of how we stand and move and give our word." He pulls out of the room and disappears.

Olympia steps over to the door, peers up and down the hallway. Crystal sits with her mouth open, looking like a friggin' baboon.

Bellamy closes her eyes, lets the cold pack rest against the pillow. She feels her body relax, the pain in her jaw soften. A sense of drifting washes over her, like floating on water, a warm, silky feeling. Images of the past week fade in and out, like a YouTube slide show, one picture easing into the next, the Occupy camp, inside Casey's tent, walking with Myron. She stands before the crowds. She stands at the police station. She stands in the bushes. In the water tower. At David's house. Standing. Standing. Standing. The air swirling around her, the sky a glaring tornado.

She opens her eyes. Two men stand at the foot of the bed, surrounded by an aura of fluorescent light. They wear blue nylon jackets with blue T-shirts beneath and loose-fitting blue jeans and blue baseball caps that read *FBI*. Around their necks, IDs dangle like cowbells.

Olympia says, "She's in no shape to talk right now."

One says, "We have only a few questions."

"Not now."

Bellamy tries to speak, but her tongue feels thick and raw, swollen like a wad of cotton, her head swimming out in the ozone.

"Mrumph, mrumph, mrumph," she says.

Crystal shrinks into shadow, only her Bambi eyes in focus.

The other man says, "We're just trying to locate her friend, Casey McDonald."

"She doesn't know where Casey is. The last we saw him was yesterday afternoon, when he took off through the crowd. I have been with Bellamy since."

"Mrumph, mrumph, mrumph."

The first man says, "Are you sure of this?"

"Of course, I'm sure. He abandoned us in the middle of Westlake, right when the rioting started. That's when Bellamy fell, twisted her ankle, and I've been with her ever since." Olympia points to her daughter's injured limb.

"One more question..."

"Mrumph, mrumph, mrumph."

"No more questions. Now get out."

A church-mouse squeak comes out of Crystal's mouth. "I saw Casey." Barely a whisper.

The agents turn toward her, their looks uncertain, as though they hadn't realized she was there.

More squeaking. "I was looking for Bell...Bellamy. I didn't know she was here yet. I stopped by the church—their home—hoping to find them. A group of people were gathered outside, holding a vigil or something."

Bellamy wants more painkillers.

Her mom says, "Crystal, please, get to the point."

She shifts, tugs at her collar. "Then I went to Cal Anderson Park, near the fountain." She speaks to the floor. "I'm sure that was him. Still in the same dress he was wearing yesterday."

Myron

Today is the busiest day Myron has had in a long time. First he got Parker settled in the Bigelow Hotel on Madison. Then he bought clothes for Parker at Value Village. Next he stopped at Walgreen's to buy Parker a razor and toothbrush and toothpaste. Then on to Elliott Bay Medical Center to check on Bellamy. And now he is on his way to visit Stephanie and say hello to Sonuvabitch.

Myron usually does not like to fill up his day with so much business, especially in the fall. He likes to make time to sit under the trees and study the long lumbering limbs and feel the snap of cold when the wind whips off the water and carries the fish to his nose.

But today is different. He does not have time to watch the soft layer of clouds and feel the puffs of color on the small maples and listen for the winter to dip down from the north. Today he has business to take care of.

He walks along the shallow reflecting pool in Cal Anderson Park, now mostly filled with garbage and signs and branches and broken glass. He worries about the ducks that usually swim here, whether they'll get hurt, whether they'll find a new home.

He passes the fountain, a dry volcano, now covered in graffiti, lots of gang tagging, but the white glaring phrase *Occupy Parker's* is the most prominent.

Hovering nearby, a half-dozen men and women wearing blue jackets and blue hats that read *FBI*, like a fraternity, only more serious. One of the women approaches him, tight mouth, cropped brown hair. She holds out a flyer and says, "Have you seen this man?"

Myron recognizes the picture of Casey, standing in the hospital lobby.

"I'm Myron." He looks at her ID, tries to find a name, but too much glare on the plastic.

She holds her body in, arms tense, brown-green eyes like eagles. "Have you seen this man?"

Myron looks at the poster again. "I saw him on the news."

"Yes, but have you seen him recently?" She shifts her weight, drills into him with her pupils.

"I saw him on the news. At the restaurant with the noodles."

She withdraws the flyer, moves on to her next target.

Myron climbs up and over the hill and crosses Boxer Way. He stands before Parker's burnt-down home. Yellow police tape cordons off the pile of charred timber and trampled weeds. Much of the tape hangs limply, some dragging on the ground. The smell of wet cinders oozes from the debris like a rotting corpse.

It was time for the house to be finished, to be at peace. That much he knows.

He walks over to Stephanie's yard and climbs over the broken fence. This must be hard for Stephanie, to have her garden destroyed in this way, her little sanctuary to protect her from change.

He crosses in front of her boarded-up window and stands at the entry. The whispering voices of the FBI agents push across the street and stand beside him. He knocks.

He can hear her steps, muffled in wood and rug. The door opens. Stephanie stands before him, her face crossed with fatigue, or something more, like promises broken.

"Myron." She pulls the door wider.

"Hi, Stephanie. Georgia has left us, hasn't she?"

Stephanie nods, steps aside.

Myron slides past her, the room warm, closed, a touch of cinnamon. Sonuvabitch squeaks and stretches and jumps off the chair and rubs against his leg.

"Hi, Sonuvabitch." He crouches down and scratches the cat on his head and behind his ears, just like he likes it. Sonuvabitch vibrates with gigantic purrs.

Stephanie shuffles toward the counter and drops on the stool. Georgia's stool. Her eyes point toward Sonuvabitch, but don't really see.

Myron stands. "I'm sorry that Georgia is gone, Stephanie. I know you are sad."

Her mouth quivers, her face tired, wrought, the lines around her eyes bending under the weight.

"I miss her, Myron. I miss her something fierce. How is that possible when she was already gone?"

He eases toward her and rests his elbows on the counter. "Even rocks seek other rocks."

She wipes a tear off her cheek and gives a weak smile. "Myron, I never know what the hell you're talking about."

"That's okay, Stephanie, neither do I."

Sonuvabitch meows in agreement.

Stephanie pushes away from the counter, stands, a spasm of resolution. "Tea?"

Myron nods. Her home is different now, not just because of Georgia, but because of Stephanie. A change, movement. She must feel Parker's missing house, a history dissolved into burnt timber and soaked-black ash. Maybe that's where her truth lies.

"I'm sorry," she says. "I didn't even ask you about the house. That must be sad for you as well."

"It was time, Stephanie."

She starts, glances in the direction of the house. "And Parker? Is he okay?"

"Parker is okay, He's living at the Bigelow Hotel until his new home is ready."

"The Bigelow? But how can he afford..." She shakes her head, turns toward the sink, and fills the kettle with water. "What about you, Myron? Where will you stay?"

"Parker is still Parker, and Myron is still Myron. I will be with him."

She sets the kettle on the stove and turns on the burner. "You're a good friend, Myron. Parker is lucky to have you."

"We're lucky to have each other, Stephanie. We're rocks too."

"Okay, Myron, you win."

"Win?"

"What happened over there, anyway? The news is suggesting foul play."

Myron shakes his head. "Not foul play. Foul house."

"Was Parker smoking in bed again?"

"It was time, Stephanie."

"Yes, I know, you said that, but..." She smiles, pulls two cups out of the cupboard. Sonuvabitch meows.

"I just fed you."

"Sonuvabitch likes to eat."

"Apparently."

"Can he stay with you until Parker goes home?"

She jerks around, a startled, concerned look. "Goes home?"

"Then we'll take Sonuvabitch."

She drops back onto the stool. "Yes, of course, as long as he needs to."

"Sonuvabitch loves you, Stephanie."

She studies the cat, her smile as pale as the light in the room. "He's a good cat."

"Like a rock."

Part X

If you can't handle me at my worst,
then you sure as hell don't deserve me at my best.

—Marilyn Monroe

Olympia

S he can scarcely comprehend all that has happened since the last time she stood before her congregation a week ago, and now, as she looks out at the sea of faces, she can't help but feel overwhelmed and in no small measure humbled by what's before her.

Never has the church held so many people—standing, sitting, squeezed into every crack and cubbyhole, their faces curious, bright, blossoming with hope and expectation. Several reporters lean against the back wall, ready to spring into action.

The bodies fill the church with their heat, their sweat, their warm moist breath. The bandage around her ribs is tight and sticky, heightening the sense of being closed in and suffocated. Yet to see all these people here is worth the discomfort. If this keeps up, she'll have her new church in no time.

She wipes the sweat from her forehead and clutches the lectern, making eye contact with as many of her congregation as possible. She starts.

"My friends, I come before you unprepared. Since last we met here, much has happened. We have come together in a way few would have thought possible. In one week, we have gone from complacent indifference to launching a movement that's being heard around the world."

She studies their faces to determine how to proceed. She finds smiles, nods, and a flutter of clapping hands—just what she has hoped.

"We have joined forces with other movements, our Occupy friends, our union friends, our activist friends. It hasn't been easy, and not everything that has occurred is what we would have wanted. But we will learn and we will persevere and our numbers will swell like nothing this country has ever seen!"

Several people jump to their feet and raise their arms above their heads as a sign of solidarity. Others applaud. A few call out Olympia's name.

She realizes this is supposed to be a church, but these are extraordinary times.

"My friends, we came together for a common cause, a higher purpose, but it has not been without pain and struggle and sacrifice. My dear daughter remains in the hospital, her prognosis uncertain." She takes a breath, lets out the barest of sighs, giving them time to wallow in empathy.

"Our comrades have suffered beatings, imprisonment, injury, even death." Another poignant pause. "With us today are three of the bravest souls I've ever had the honor of knowing." Olympia sweeps her arm before the front pew. "Ida. Bert. Louise. Please stand so everyone here can see what commitment and perseverance and courage really look like."

The three congregants struggle to their feet. They again wear their khaki pants and rainbow sweatshirts and blue stocking caps, each emblazoned with large gold *LLC*. Ida's arm hangs in a sling. Several bandages cover Bert's face. Louise props her short and squat self on a cane. They turn toward the congregation, flash nervous smiles. Ida waves with her free arm in queen-like fashion.

The congregation breaks out in applause. Some stomp their feet, call out their names. The three look to the floor, flushed with embarrassment, but proud and happy. Janice Ying, who sits in the row behind them, holds her hands over her heart and calls out, "We love you." Digger sits next to her, his fedora slung low, looking as bored as ever. Crystal wallows on the other side, quick to ape Janice's sentiments.

Olympia climbs down from the lectern and embraces Ida, then Louise, and finally Bert, making certain everyone sees how long she holds them, how close, the tear of gratitude she wipes from her eye.

R. H. Sheldon

When the crowd settles down, the three return to their pew and Olympia returns to her lectern, where she offers them a final Buddhist greeting, hands together, a slight, humble bow.

She gives the moment several more seconds, flashes a ponderous gaze, and again clutches the lectern.

"My friends, we have accomplished much, but still have much to do. Each step along the way will be greeted by success and challenges. The powers that be are averse to change, ready to subvert our every effort."

She takes a breath, holds her ribs, winces, but only slightly, just enough to be noticed. Concern wraps across the faces of those nearest to where she stands.

"My friends, as you've probably heard, Parker Davis, the man we've been trying to help, lost his home yesterday morning." Whispering, flashes of anger. "That's right, his house has mysteriously burnt to the ground. He lost everything he held dear."

Several *boos* erupt from the back. Olympia gestures that they should be patient, wait. "It's too soon to say what happened, and we may never know. All we can do is keep Parker Davis in our prayers and help in any way we can—and help those who have also fallen victim to a corrupt and indifferent system."

More *boos*, cries for action. Olympia again gestures for calm.

"My friends, I know you're here because you care, because you want to help, because you want to make a difference. Now is your chance to be that difference, to be the solution to a terrible and dire problem." She clasps her hands, offers a warm smile. "Immediately after the service, those who want a voice in planning our next course of action should stay. All are welcome. Everyone has a say in what we decide. We will not, I repeat, *not,* allow anyone's voice to be silenced!"

The room breaks into loud applause. Many jump to their feet, pledging their support. Olympia smiles out to them, as she would a room full of children, her look one of benevolence and pride, taking them into her heart and soul. A warm presence swells within her, a divine spark burning brightly through the eyes of those who surround her. And then, right on schedule, a young man and woman, squeaky-clean and dripping with sincerity, pop out their guitars and start to play Parker's 1969 solid-gold hit, "Last Stand," in a slow, mournful dirge, dripping with heartfelt sincerity. The crowd listens with rapturous faces, like angels looking up to heaven, the room brimming with light, until the dynamic duo

reach the last refrain, playing it over and over, letting it fade into a
haunting, distant echo.

> *A stand we must, a stand we can*
> *Our last, our only, lonely stand.*
> *One last stand, one last for man,*
> *Our last hoorah, our lonely stand.*

R. H. Sheldon

Alonzo

I sabel has said nothing about the past week—not about her time with Lita or her night in jail or what happened between the two of them. Whenever Alonzo asks her about it, she tells him to drop it and goes about as if nothing has happened. She is, in fact, obsessed with this pretense of normalcy, carefully playing the role of wife and stay-at-home mom, a role she no longer seems suited for, as though she's rehearsing for the part, waiting for her cue to deliver her lines.

Alonzo's not sure whether he prefers this Isabel or the one from the last few months, two extremes, neither desirable. Not that he has any say in the matter. The current Isabel is more pleasant to be around, but the last one at least felt real, burned with her own fire, even if it was a simmering rage. Now there seems to be nothing.

But she did agree to accompany him to meet with Dartmouth at the golf clubhouse in Newbourne, a plush Seattle suburb catering to the region's elite. From what Alonzo understands, his home has a view of the first fairway

In all the years Alonzo has lived here, he has never been out to Newbourne, has never had a reason to go there, nor has he ever met with Dartmouth on a Sunday—or anywhere outside the office. And Isabel has never accompanied him to any business-related functions.

So many firsts.

What makes it even stranger is that Alonzo is not even sure what Dartmouth wants, though if he has to guess, he'd say his boss is upset about Parker's house burning down. The fire itself wouldn't have been so bad, but the suspicion of arson could delay the groundbreaking by months. No doubt the Lockhart people have been breathing down Dartmouth's neck since it happened. Yet it's hard to believe Dartmouth would have called him here to fire him, especially given he specifically invited Isabel. On the other hand, maybe he prefers a public setting so he can humiliate Alonzo in front of his wife without disrupting his office's *feng shui*.

They drive up the tree-lined road through Newbourne as it curves gently along the golf course. A lush palette of greens and golds, highlighted by dapples of orange and red, providing a fairytale backdrop for this enclave of wealth and privilege. At the end of the golf course, Alonzo turns right and then circles back toward the top of the hill where the clubhouse overlooks a flourishing valley to the west. The air has a misty quality that softens the landscape and turns the bright greens iridescent.

"Beautiful," Isabel says in a breathless voice. "I never knew this world existed."

"Not quite like the Crossroads area."

She shoots him a warning look. "Nothing at all."

When they reach the parking lot, Alonzo drives through the rows of costly sedans and SUVs and sports cars—Mercedes, Lexus, Audi, Porsche, Jaguar, even a Tesla—searching for an empty spot.

Alonzo says, "Look at this place. Even in November it's packed."

"It's Sunday," she says with a wistful, sorrowful tone.

"Maybe I'll take up golf."

"Park in the back."

He shakes his head. "No need. I see a spot in the next row."

"Park in back."

"What? Afraid someone will see you in a Taurus?"

He glances toward her, her mouth drawn tight, eyes toward her lap. He drives to the back row and parks.

"The exercise will do us good," he says.

Isabel climbs out and distances herself quickly. He catches up with her and together they walk into the clubhouse, a sprawling British colonial building with pale green walls and bright green roof tiles. A wide covered porch circles around the first floor, the beams gleaming white and perfectly spaced around the circumference.

The entrance stands at the center of the building, each side in perfect proportion to the other, mirror images, like a fine estate overlooking its vast holdings.

Isabel clutches his arm and they walk up the wooden steps, painted forest green, and enter through the front door, as if they belonged. Dark polished wood covers the floors inside, surrounded by soaring white walls and tall graceful archways glimmering white against the dark beamed ceilings. Artwork adorns every wall, as simple and eloquent as the surroundings, paintings of fruit or pottery or the occasional mountain.

The restaurant looms before them—the Bombay Bistro—the ocean of floor uninterrupted from one room to the next. They walk into the entrance and stand at the front. Carefully spaced tables with bamboo-backed chairs are scattered discretely across the rooms, with plenty of low walls and arches to give each table its own sense of intimacy. The room lends itself easily to the plantation feel of the outside. Alonzo isn't sure whether he should seek out Dartmouth or start waiting tables.

They linger for a moment near the front, until a polished and poised young woman, with menus in hand, offers a cordial smile and her assistance. Alonzo asks whether Dartmouth has arrived. He has. She leads them to his table.

With each step, Alonzo feels the tension mount. He's reminded of those boiling frog stories he heard as a kid. Put a frog in cold water and slowly heat the water to a boil. The frog will never realize that danger is at hand and will be dead before knowing what happened.

When they arrive at the table, Dartmouth lifts his stately frame out of the chair and offers a hand to Isabel.

"Mrs. Garcia. It's so good to meet you at long last. Please, have a seat." He pulls out the chair next to his and holds it for her until she is seated. Alonzo sits across from him, already at a disadvantage.

Dartmouth says, "You must feel very proud of your husband, Mrs. Garcia. It's not every lawyer who could have handled such an untenable situation with such *savoir-faire*."

A surprised look passes quickly across her face, and she says, "Please, call me Isabel."

He takes her hand in his two. "And you must call me Harold. Had I known Alonzo had such a charming wife, I would have invited you both to lunch long ago."

Isabel lets out a shy giggle, practiced and sophisticated beyond what he would have expected, sitting there with a deft poise that complements Dartmouth's gentlemanly and Old World attentions. How perfectly she fits into these surroundings, as natural as the spring, not like Alonzo, who'd be much happier gardening, even if he doesn't know anything about it.

A college-aged ingratiating waiter arrives to take their drink orders. Harold requests hot green tea. Isabel follows his example. Alonzo can't recall her ever drinking green tea before.

What he'd like is a nice tall beer. He orders coffee.

Dartmouth releases Isabel's hand and turns his attention to the menu. "I recommend the Seafood Cobb Salad," he says, "but without the bacon, of course."

Isabel scans the menu quickly, then shuts it and sets it on the table. "That sounds perfect, Harold."

Dartmouth smiles.

A seafood salad is the last thing Alonzo wants. A burger sounds more like it, to go with his nonexistent beer.

Dartmouth says, "And what about you, my boy? Shall we make it three?"

Alonzo closes his menu. "Sounds great." The least they could do is let him have the bacon.

The waiter returns with their tea and coffee and sets it before them as though they're having high tea at the palace. Then he takes their orders, although it's Dartmouth who does all the talking.

After the waiter leaves, Dartmouth says, "First off, Alonzo, I want to congratulate you on how things turned out at the Davis house. Everyone is quite pleased with the results."

"You mean the fire?"

Harold nods.

"But I didn't...I mean, I would never—"

"Of course not, Alonzo, but you've managed to get results where no one else could, and now nothing is preventing us from moving forward."

"But the fire could delay things, with arson being suspected."

"Not our problem."

Alonzo looks to Isabel for help. She studies her hands, a serene smile lingering on her face.

Harold chuckles. "I know. It doesn't make sense. But here's the thing. The Lockhart people are so pleased with the goodwill you created by showing up at the sheriff's department the other day and pulling Lockhart's name out of the mud, they've decided to follow suit and donate the land. Goodwill and tax breaks—a great way to get all this behind them."

"Donate the land? Lockhart?"

"Hard to believe, isn't it? But I had a good heart-to-heart talk with the chief last night, and he agrees that this is the best way to proceed. He wants us to handle the details, of course, but he specifically asked that you take care of them. You've made quite an impression on our star client, Alonzo."

Alonzo fidgets with his napkin. He will never understand the world of business or law.

"Of course," he says, "I'll get right on it."

"I knew we could count on you. We all know who created these problems, but that's ancient history now. You came in and cleaned up his mess, and did so with a finesse I've seen few achieve." Harold turns to Isabel. "Now you see why we're so happy with your husband and why you should be so proud."

She nods and smiles and touches his arm in gratitude.

Alonzo says, "Who are they donating the land to?"

Dartmouth's eyes gleam and his lips twist upward ever so slightly. "Why, that lady minister, of course, the one who started all the trouble."

"Olympia Culpepper?"

"That's the one. Gets her off our back. Makes everyone look like saints. From what we understand, she wants to build herself a bigger and better church. She's quite ambitious, that one."

"I didn't know that."

"She was on the news last night. That's where I got the idea. She has the public ear right now, so let's keep her happy."

Alonzo feels like a cannonball.

"I'll get started on this first thing tomorrow."

"Good man."

"What about the press? When do you want to make this public?"

Dartmouth gives another of his looks, not quite a smile, something almost sinister.

"No need to worry about that. The news has already somehow been *leaked* to the press. A spokesman from Lockhart fleshed out the details this morning. I'm guessing it's already hit the social media outlets. You can be sure Lockhart's PR engine is at work.

"Good," Alonzo says. "That's good." If he never has to deal with the press again, that would still be too soon.

"There's one other item I'd like to discuss." He turns to Isabel. "And I promise, no more business after this, my dear."

Isabel pats his hand. "You two take your time. I'm in no hurry." She radiates patience.

"If only my ex-wives had shared your sentiments."

Alonzo thinks of frogs.

Dartmouth turns back to Alonzo and folds his hands on the table. "Alonzo, my boy, I cannot stress enough all the fine work you've done on the Davis situation. You're a credit to your people. You have a calm head and an insightful mind, just the type of man we want a permanent part of our family." He pauses, as though intentionally building the suspense. "For this reason, we are making you a full partner in our firm, with all the benefits that brings."

Isabel's face brightens into an angelic glow. She claps once and says, "Harold, that is so wonderful."

Alonzo isn't sure what surprises him more, the partnership or Isabel's reaction. Nor is Alonzo sure that this is what he wants for himself. But the look on Isabel's face is enchantment itself. And then there are the kids to think of, the bills.

Finally, he says, "Yes, Mr. Dartmouth...Harold, thank you. Thank you very much. I won't let you down."

Harold beams, thrilled with his ability to play Santa. "You've earned it, my boy. I've no doubt we're the ones who will benefit the most from having you on board."

He reaches across the table and shakes Alonzo's hand. Isabel flashes a warm smile in Alonzo's direction.

Alonzo notices for the first time that music plays in the background, perhaps turned up louder than before, an instrumental version of Parker's song, "Last Stand," a call to arms against the very people sitting in the restaurant.

Bellamy

What if Crystal is right? What if Bellamy's jaw doesn't heal and she becomes like this deformed mutant, always drooling and talking with a whistle and her whole face crooked for the rest of her life? People will think she's a total freak.

The nurse said they'd be releasing her today. So did the doctor. But what if they missed something? What if it's worse than they thought and she gets infected or cancer and her face swells up like an elephant's and she can't breathe or talk or call for help?

It's not like her mom cares what happens. Or Crystal, for that matter. All they care about is that fucked up church and their movements and causes and good deeds and saving the world. What about all that "charity starts at home" crap her mom's always preaching?

Bellamy raises the back of her bed and readjusts the ice pack next to her face. The jaw bra feels like it's choking her, making the pain worse, squeezing in on all the swollen parts. Maybe it will cause a blood clot and she'll die from one of those brain anachronisms that so like killed her Uncle Theodore.

Bellamy grabs the remote off the bed tray. She clicks on the TV and flips through channels until she lands on a station not showing a commercial, in this case, the local news.

Pete Sizemore is talking into the camera. He's been around since before Bellamy was born, and it shows. He sits at his news desk, wearing a dark brown jacket and yellow shirt, but no tie, dark sockets for eyes, a crusty edge to his voice. "We're continuing our special coverage of *Protests Seattle,* bringing you the news as it happens."

He adjusts his jacket and sits up straighter. "Another day of protests and vigils is planned throughout Seattle. This afternoon at Seattle's First Congregational Church, the mayor and other city officials will be conducting a memorial service to commemorate the three police officers who died in the line of duty. In the meantime, Reverend Olympia Culpepper from the Lighthouse Sanctification Church, along with leaders from several other organizations, will be conducting their own memorial service for Fondeaux and the others killed and injured during the riots."

Pete Sizemore lets out a long sigh. Perhaps even he sees how ridiculous all this is, as if Bellamy's mother gives two shits about Fondeaux. She probably doesn't even know who Fondeaux is.

"In related news. The FBI are still looking for Casey McDonald, last seen on Saturday morning at Cal Anderson Park, dressed in women's clothing." Casey's picture flashes on the screen, sending a flutter through Bellamy's heart. Even in that crappy photo, he still looks sexy. "If anyone has any information about his whereabouts, please contact the FBI or the Seattle Police Department as soon as possible."

His picture dissolves and is replaced by one of Bellamy's mother.

"In other news, Lockhart Investments, the company that bought the Parker Davis property and the two adjoining lots, plans to donate the land to the Lighthouse Sanctification Church as a gesture of good faith and commitment to the community, according to company spokesperson Arnold Fedelini. We will be interviewing Reverend Culpepper in our studios later this afternoon, after the memorial service. Now let's switch to Anita Franklin, who's been covering events in the field."

Bellamy clicks off the TV.

Holy shit. Her mom is getting the land. She must be ecstatic. Bellamy can hear her now, talking about divine providence and having the right intention and lining up the cosmic energy. She'll be more impossible to live with than ever. And where will that leave Bellamy? Probably out knocking on doors to raise building funds, with her deformed jaw and blood clot and limp from her permanently sprained ankle.

She pounds on the bed with her fists. She hisses and snarls and huffs like a dragon. She clicks the TV back on and switches channels until she lands on one playing a Fondeaux music video, the one that caused all the uproar because of the big black dildo. Bellamy keeps the sound turned low, focusing mostly on the woman, her talent, innovation, willingness to take a risk. Such a loss, one Bellamy feels personally, like losing a good friend, someone she's known all her life. A heaviness descends on her heart and fills her chest with a dull ache, the tears flowing freely down her cheeks. She closes her eyes and thinks about the time she saw Fondeaux in concert, last summer at the Key Arena, along with Crystal, both mesmerized by the lights, the music, the awesome power of the show.

"Why so glum?"

Her eyes pop open.

"Casey!"

"Miss me?"

"What are you doing here? The cops are searching all over the place for you."

He grins, sets his skateboard next to the bed. "They like think I'm on a ferry to Bremerton."

He's dressed normal again, but no beard or dreads, of course, cut off when he got dressed up like a girl on Friday. And now he looks so young, baby innocent, but still cool.

"You shouldn't be here."

"Aren't you glad to see me?"

"Of course, but I don't want you to get caught."

He closes the door to the room and returns to the bed. "Don't worry about me, Bell baby. Besides, how could I not come to see you after what happened? Just look at you." He leans in to kiss her on the forehead.

"Don't. I don't want you seeing me like this."

"I already have."

"I look hideous."

"Hideous? I think you look sexy. Like a wayward nun."

She turns away, feeling the heat on her face, even through the bandage.

"Okay, but like don't make fun of me."

"I'd never do that, darling. Even with the bandages, you're still one hot chick."

She wishes she could believe him, but she knows how he is, how all men are. Still, she likes hearing his voice, his words, especially when he talks like that."

"Oh, Casey."

"How long you in for?"

"Why?"

"So I know where to find you. Someone's got to keep an eye on you."

A flutter ripples through her chest and she feels suddenly dizzy.

"You can't be worrying about me, Casey. They're looking for you. They think you caused all this trouble."

"They don't know their heads from their assholes. Besides, it's you we need to be worrying about. We need to like get you up and around and feeling better."

He nears the bed and eases down next to her. She can smell the heady scents of his sweat and weed, feel the heat from his lean hard thigh. A chill passes up her spine, passes out the top of her head. She shivers.

His fingers touch the back of her hand and trace the line of flesh along her arm, up past her elbow, his touch charged, hot with fire. His fingers wind along her shoulder, onto the skin of her neck, then down the front of her gown, into the soft warm fold. He strokes her breasts gently, touches each nipple until they're full and hard. His other hand works up her gown, moving between her legs in an smooth rhythm, easing in deeper, more fully, the moist warmth flowing freely, inviting, pulsating. She arches her back slightly, careful not to move her jaw or knock her ankle, aware too of the pain, welcoming it, letting it pull into her excitement. His eyes sparkle, focus unblinking on her body, pupils full and black. She reaches for his crotch, feels him thick and hard. He leans in closer, moans, his breath hot on her lips. She shifts toward him, squeezes harder.

A knock. The door swings open.

"You two having fun?"

The nurse with the drugs, efficient and amused, pushing her cart before her.

Casey jumps to his feet, grins. "Making sure the patient's okay."

Bellamy straightens her gown and pulls the cover over her, pretending nothing has happened.

The nurse says to Casey, "You might want to give her a little more time to heal." Her face remains stern, her eyes full of smiles.

Casey says, "I better take off, Bell. I've got this like awesome meeting to go to. No sitting around for me."

"When will I see you again?"

A mischievous look plays in his eyes. "No telling what the future holds." He pecks her on the forehead, grabs his skateboard, salutes the nurse, and scurries out of the room.

The nurse checks Bellamy's pulse and blood pressure and temperature. "Everything normal," she says, "considering your recent visitor," and hands Bellamy a small cupful of pills. Bellamy swallows them down in a single gulp. The nurse leaves.

Bellamy turns up the TV. Music plays, some lame-ass old-time stuff, but there's no video, only a still picture of a young man dressed in '60s drag. The caption at the bottom reads *"Last Stand." Words and music by Parker Davis. 1969.*

No wonder it sounds like crap.

Myron

Myron lies on one of the two couches in Parker's suite at the Bigelow Hotel, his head resting on a golden cushion with long tassels around the edges. He likes the way the cushion feels against his head, like cotton candy without all the stickiness.

The other five cushions sit on the floor, near the fireplace's marble hearth, where a fresh fire crackles softly between the mantel's white columns. Parker sits at the baby grand in the corner, between the potted palm and the French doors to the balcony, his hands resting on the keyboard, as though about to play.

Both couches are covered in orange and green tweed and fringed with their own tassels, which sweep across the soft floral carpet with its reds and greens and golds. The air smells like a bouquet of gardenias.

Parker says, "Why didn't you tell me you had money?"

Parker's question sounds like it wants to be angry, but there's no anger there, not really. Parker is still in a daze from the fire and the house. Parker forgets that it was time for him to find a new home.

Myron says, "You never asked me if I had money."

Parker rolls his fingers along the piano keys as though he pretends he's playing.

R. H. Sheldon

"All this time, all I've been going through. Why didn't you offer to help out? Why didn't you do something to save the house?"

"You didn't ask, Parker. Why didn't you ask?"

Parker shakes his head. "I just don't get it. All this time."

"Don't you like your hotel room?"

"It's fucking paradise, but that's not the point."

"What is the point?"

The fire pops and crackles then simmers down.

Parker sucks in a deep breath. Coughs. Jingles a chord on the piano.

"Let's try this," he says. "How is it you have so much money? This suite costs a small fortune."

"It has to go somewhere, Parker."

"What has to go somewhere?"

"The money."

"Then why didn't you give it to me?"

"I got you this room."

"I, uh...okay, right. Let me ask this then. How long can we keep this room?"

"How long do you want to keep it?"

Parker bangs out another chord.

Myron says, "Sonuvabitch would like this suite. I wish he could see it, but he's happy with Stephanie."

"Poor cat."

"Don't worry, Parker. Stephanie loves Sonuvabitch, just like you."

A small puff of air falls into the flu. The smell of fire drifts toward Myron, filling his nose with happiness.

"Myron."

"What, Parker?"

"Where did you get the money?"

"Does it matter, Parker, where I got the money?"

"I'll sleep easier."

"Really?" Myron will have to think about this. Why would Parker's knowledge of the money make him sleep better?

"Myron, please, give me some sense of what's going on. Everything's gotten too crazy."

Myron grins. "That's right, Parker, but not just right now."

"The thing is, Myron. I would hate to think you might be getting into some sort of trouble, doing something you shouldn't. I'm not judging you, Myron, I'm just saying, that's all."

"Thank you, Parker. I'm glad you're concerned about me. But I'm not getting into any trouble."

"Myron, please."

"Sure, Parker." Myron scratches his beard. "What were you asking?"

"Your money. Where did you get it?"

"Oh, that. It's no big deal. My parents gave me the money. They had lots and lots of money, but they died and left it all to me."

"You parents? They were rich?"

Myron nods. "I think so, Parker. But they were not very happy people."

"How much money? How rich were they? Are you?"

"I don't know, Parker. I never counted it."

Parker stares at the fireplace. A log drops through the grate and sparks fly up the chimney.

"I suppose I should be grateful," he says, "that you do have money and can afford this room."

"Yes, Parker, that is a good thing. I'm grateful I could get this room for you. You're my friend, Parker, and I like to take care of my friends."

Parker studies the piano keys, plays a few bars from a tune Myron doesn't recognize.

"You going to play the piano, Parker?"

"I am not. Turn on the TV. Let's see what all your money is getting us."

Myron picks up the remote from the large black-lacquer coffee table and switches on the television. The reporter Anita Franklin stands in front of what used to be Parker's house, now a pile of charred rubble, surrounded by trampled weeds and a mile of police tape.

"Pete, I'm in front of the lot where the house once stood. As you can see, little remains of this legendary musician's home. The fire department has yet to determine the cause of the blaze, but foul play has not been ruled out. Some groups are claiming that the government is behind this. Government officials have suggested that political activists set the blaze to further their agenda."

The tired voice of Pete Sizemore interrupts the scene. Anita Franklin appears to be listening through her earpiece, straining to hear.

"Anita," he says, "any idea where Parker Davis has gone to?"

"We believe he's being put up at a local hotel, for now, until he gets resettled. We hope to learn more as the afternoon progresses."

"And what happens next with the investigation?"

"Pete, I believe you asked about the investigation. The authorities will continue to question witnesses. All we know is that Parker Davis was last seen stumbling away from the house just as it became engulfed in flames. According to those on the scene, he was lucky to be alive, though he lost everything he owned, including the piano that had belonged to his mother. Parker is reported to have said he heard a popping noise in the kitchen, something that sounded like a small explosion, and suddenly there were flames everywhere."

The camera returns to the studio, where Pete Sizemore sits at his news desk and stares into the camera. "Thank you, Anita." Pete puts on a solemn look. "Know that our prayers are with you, Parker Davis."

Parker stands. "Shut that thing off."

Myron does. Now only the fire speaks, which is fine with Myron. He doesn't like to watch TV, especially the news. He would rather watch movies, but the VCR was burned up with the house.

Myron says, "Play the piano, Parker. I want to hear you play."

Parker looks as though he's about to protest, but he instead sits back down on the piano bench and faces the piano. He places his fingers gently on the keys, as though he's about to caress them, and then he starts to play "Last Stand," but it's only the music. No words come out of his mouth.

"That's good," Myron says. "I like when you play piano. I like when you play that song. That's a good song, Parker, a very good song."

Myron closes his eyes and listens to the gentle waves of music and the snap of the fire and feels their warmth like the sun cutting through a forest full of tall and beautiful trees.

Stephanie

W hen Stephanie opens the front door and sees Rocky standing before her, she feels as though a character has stepped out of her dreams, that same feeling as before, but more pronounced, the pieces scrambling to fit together.

Rocky is dressed in street clothes—jeans, denim jacket, stocking cap—and looks at Stephanie with a shy embarrassed look.

"May I come in?"

Stephanie pulls open the door. "Of course, Rocky. Please."

Sonuvabitch races outside.

"Don't go far."

Sonuvabitch glances back, meows, then darts into a pile of branches.

Rocky steps inside, and Stephanie closes the door. The house feels smaller than ever.

"I was just about to make tea."

"Terrific."

Stephanie moves toward the sink. An off kilter sense hangs over her. Rocky follows, drops into Georgia's stool.

"I've come to apologize," she says.

"Apologize?"

"For the other night. I was being an ass, letting everything get to me. I shouldn't have."

"You're only human."

"Tell that to the mayor."

Stephanie fills the kettle, places it on the stove. She pulls out the genmaicha, the last of Georgia's tea, enough for one more pot. She retrieves two mugs from the dish rack. She grabs the jar of honey and wipes off the sticky remnants Georgia left behind.

"It's been an odd week," Stephanie offers.

"I know. I know. But there's another reason I'm here, other than to offer my humble apologies—assuming they're accepted."

"You've nothing to apologize for." Stephanie had completely forgotten her ride with Rocky. How does she forgive someone for something she didn't remember?

"For the sake of argument, assume I do."

"In that case, apology accepted."

Rocky's eyes drop to the counter. "I also wanted to tell you how sorry I am about Georgia. I heard about what happened at the ER."

"Yes, I imagine word is out."

"It wasn't like that."

"I didn't mean—" She places the honey jar on the counter and hangs the dishtowel next to the sink. "It's all been so strange. First Georgia's gone, then she's back, then she's gone, and all this in the middle of the other craziness. I just don't get it."

"You can't help caring, though. No matter what happens. That's how it works."

"I don't have to like it."

"No one does."

"And now she's gone for good."

"Which only makes the caring worse."

The kettle gives off a low hiss, rocks gently on the burner.

Stephanie says, "The last day she was here, Friday morning, all I could think about was her getting out of here, getting my space back. The usual frustrations, on both our parts."

"You're only human."

Stephanie feels her mouth edge into a slight smile. "Well put."

"I'm not just another pretty face."

The kettle rocks harder, like a train engine climbing a mountain.

Stephanie leans against the counter, staying close to the stove. She lets out a sigh, or rather the sigh pours out of its own volition. "The thing is," she says, "I just don't know where to put all these feelings, what to do with them, what it is I'm actually mourning."

Rocky reaches across the counter and lays her hand on Stephanie's. "Give it time," she says. "It's a tough situation on a lot of levels. Just let it all sit for a while. There's nothing you need to resolve today."

Stephanie had nearly forgotten what it's like to receive a nurturing touch, even if it's only her hand. With Georgia, the nurturing ended long before their relationship did.

"You're right, I know that, at least on some level."

"Of course, I'm right. That's my job." Rocky flashes a crooked smile.

"You talking about your job as a cop or as a philosopher?"

"I'm a philosophical cop."

The kettle rings out in a loud whistle.

Stephanie turns off the stove and pours hot water into the teapot. She inserts the filter, scoops in the last of the genmaicha, and places the lid on the pot. She sits at the counter next to Rocky.

Rocky glances toward Parker's lot and says, "I hear the property next door is going to that minister, the one my partner shot the other night...my ex-partner."

"I heard that too."

"And?"

"And what?"

"What do you think of having a church next door?"

"Over my dead body."

Rocky shakes her head. "Not a fan of religion?"

"Not a fan of Reverend Dingbat, especially since she's the one who started all the trouble next door and everywhere else."

"What about your move?"

"No move. No more offer. And who wants to buy a house with a church going in next door?"

"Religious folks?"

Stephanie rolls her eyes.

Rocky says, "Maybe the church lady will want your place."

"No way I'd sell to that moron."

"That bad?"

"That bad."

"Sounds like you've decided to stay then."

Stephanie shrugs. "At least for now."

"Good."

She catches Rocky staring at her and turns her attention to the teapot. She pulls out the strainer and sets it on a small dish, then pours tea in each cup.

"There's honey if you want." Stephanie pushes it toward her.

Rocky opens the jar and dips in her spoon, then expertly transports the honey to her cup, without dripping on the jar or the counter. She twists on the lid and pushes the jar toward Stephanie.

"It won't be easy," Rocky says, "getting this yard back in shape. You'll need help."

"Yeah, but help doesn't come cheap."

"I do."

Stephanie's face must have betrayed her confusion because Rocky quickly adds, "With the yard. I can help you with the work. I even have a pair of overhauls." She grins.

Before Stephanie realizes what's happening, her eyes swell with tears and all she can think of to say is, "Oh."

"It will be fun. Besides, you'll definitely need an extra pair of hands if you plan to return to work."

"But how..."

"I heard that at the ER too."

"I'm going to kill Roger."

"Go easy. I had to force it out of him." She gives Stephanie a conspiratorial look.

Stephanie tries to act nonchalant. "Nothing is definite anyway. I'm just considering it."

"Might be a good thing."

"Might be."

Sonuvabitch announces his presence at the front door with a short meow. Stephanie lets him in. He saunters through the doorway and rubs against her leg. She picks him up, returns to her stool, and sits with him on her lap.

Rocky says, "Who's this little fellow?" She scratches his head. The cat sniffs her fingers.

"Sonuvabitch."

"I mean..."

"That's his name. Sonuvabitch. He lived next door and has taken up temporary residence here."

"Kind of scraggly."

"Kind of?"

"But in a cute sort of way. Like you. The cute part, I mean."

Stephanie feels herself blush and fiddles with her cup.

"How's your tea?" she asks.

Rocky sips, makes a bitter face. "It's kind of...perhaps it needs more honey."

"Yeah, I can't stand the crap either."

Parker

P arker stands in the lobby of the Bigelow Hotel, a luxurious setting with oak-trimmed walls and rough-hewn beams and a car-size fireplace. Acres of carpet spread out before him, a giant tartan weave of muted blues and greens, Christmas without the decorations or tree.

Parker feels just like the room with the clothes Myron bought for him, black-and-white checkered pants and a billowy pink shirt. Luckily, with the musician label, he can pull off such an absurd ensemble, as long as he pretends that was what he meant to do.

Before him stands a couple dozen reporters, a handful of photographers, and several men aiming video cameras in his direction. It never occurred to him until now that he's never seen a woman operating one of those things.

At least there are women reporters, and one of his favorite stands before him, Anita Franklin, that luscious lady from the local news, holding her mike between them in a phallic embrace.

"Mr. Davis," she says, "can you tell us what you plan to do next?" She reaches the mike toward his lips.

He chuckles at his dirty-old-man thoughts, then says, "My dear, I don't even know what I did yesterday."

She smiles. The other reporters laugh.

"I understand," Anita says, "that Dive Rock Records plans to move forward with the record contract, despite Garth Kilroy's untimely death."

"Well, Anita..." He loves calling her by her first name, like lovers breaking from a bit of *coitus dilecti*. "I haven't had an official word," he says. "I suppose I'll have to get an agent or lawyer or whatever people do these days to take care of all that."

He definitely has to find someone. He doesn't have the heart to face this whole circus on his own. The more of the dirty work he can turn over, the happier he'll be. He's lucky he had enough energy to come down here, let alone negotiate a business deal. He feels so worn, in fact, that even if Anita were to rip off her clothes, all he could do is look, and even then, he might not be able to last.

Anita says, "So you're basically in a holding pattern, until the details get sorted out."

He nods. Another reporter shouts, "Mr. Davis. Have you received any other offers for record deals or concerts or other events?"

Anita seems as put out by the intrusion as Parker feels.

"I've had inquiries," he says, "but nothing official."

"Such as?"

Another voice, different face. "What about the house? Any more news on what happened?"

"The house is gone. What more needs to happen?"

"What I meant..."

Parker feels wearier by the minute. He thought he'd be able to handle the press, maybe even have some fun, but the last few days have taken their toll, and all he wants to do is go up to the room and lie down. He should have listened to Myron.

Another question erupts from the crowd. "What about coke?"

"Never touch the stuff." He manages a smile.

"No, the Coca-Cola people. We heard they want to use your song in an ad campaign?"

"That's news to me."

Anita edges in closer, much to his relief.

"Mr. Davis, I understand that someone on the Grammy committee has nominated you for the Lifetime Achievement Award. Can you tell us anything about that?"

"Really, Anita, you heard that? You sure it's not another Parker Davis?"

"No, I believe...oh, I see, you were joking."

Several nearby reporters chuckle and whisper among themselves.

Parker grins. "Sorry to throw you, darling, but honestly, that's the first I've heard about anything to do with the Grammys. I doubt there's any truth in that."

Another reporter calls out that he's heard the same thing. Parker's about to say something about how honored he would feel, but one of those nagging coughs starts rattling his chest, trying to push out, and before long, he's hacking so hard that he can barely make out anyone around him. All he can do is find his way to a nearby wall and lean against it and ride out the violent attack on his lungs. But this one takes longer to abate than ever, and before long he can barely catch his breath. His chest burns and his throat fills with salty, sour phlegm. He pulls a wad of tissue out of his pockets and spits out a load of the nasty bile. More blood than ever before, darker in color, drawing from deeper in his lungs.

Someone is speaking to him, but he can't focus and wants only to distance himself from the press and the public. He stumbles toward the elevator and presses the button. The door opens right up. He steps inside and selects his floor, barely able to hold himself upright. When the door begins to close, Anita jumps in and together they ride up to heaven.

On the top floor, she helps him out of the elevator and into his room. She asks him no questions, but supports him gently until he's sitting comfortably on the couch. By now, his cough has subsided, but he feels exhausted and wants only to sleep.

"You going to be okay?" she asks.

"I'll be fine. Just tired. Just old."

"You need a doctor?"

"I'll be fine, really. This isn't the first time. I just need to rest. But thank you."

She leaves the suite, closing the door softly behind her.

He waits until his breath has returned to its abnormal normal, then looks around the room for Myron, says his name, but Parker is alone.

His gold-plated 1969 record in the walnut frame sits on the giant coffee table. It wasn't there when he went downstairs. Myron must have set it there before he left. Where is Myron, anyway? How could he have gotten out of the hotel without Parker seeing him leave? Parker wishes Myron were here now, lying on the couch with those big feet of his sticking up in the air, saying one dumb thing after the next, driving Parker crazy like he always does.

Parker picks up the framed record and studies the label—his name, the name of the song, the words *Solid Gold*.

He rubs his fingers along the glass—a hard cold surface that protects the record from dust and damage, from smudging and groping fingers. He hugs the frame to his chest and lies back on the sofa and closes his eyes and remembers what it was like when his record first went gold and the world was fresh and alive and full of hope and endless possibilities, when he was young enough to think he mattered, when what he did mattered, when the people and places around him mattered. That is the Parker Davis he wants to take with him.